The Star Writers Trilogy

THE STAR WRITERS CLUB

MARY K. SAVARESE

Book 2

of the

Star Writers Trilogy

The StarWriters Club

Mary K. Savarese

ISBN 978-1-953278-36-4 Hard Back
ISBN 978-1-953278-37-1 Soft Back
ISBN 978-1-953278-38-8 E-Book

Published by

INDIGNOR HOUSE™
Chesapeake, Virginia
www.IndignorHouse.com

for it is written in the stars

Familiarity with the opening novel of the trilogy, *The Girl in the Toile Wallpaper*, will lend to a continuation of theme and understanding that plays out in these character's encounters. Young adults who appreciate romance and adventure blended with history intertwined in mystery and fantasy will find expanded ideas and experiences while entering this realm.

D. Donovan, Sr. Reviewer
Midwest Book Review

Savarese showcases an uncanny knack for worldbuilding and character development as she delivers a fantasy adventure.

Mihir Shah
The US Review of Books

The StarWriters Club

The StarWriters Club

Mary K. Savarese

dedicate The Star Writers Club to …

Rosie B. - *a cherub from beginning to end and my inspiration for Rosie.*

Meg I. - *a young leader and the inspiration for my protagonist Em.*

&

Laura K. - *if ever there was a born director, you are my Ja Crof.*

… for your destinies were written in the stars.

The StarWriters Club

The StarWriters Club

INTRODUCTION

Since the beginning, a StarWriter is *acquired* at death, taken on as an apprentice. As part of an exclusive club, the StarWriter's motto states:

For it is written in the stars.

A StarWriter's *training* includes duties such as delivering the Plans of Purpose, wishes, prayers, and hopes to a soul's star.

On an occasion, a StarWriter will encounter a *prophecy* …

Tucked between The StarWriters Trilogy's earthly bookends, *The Girl In The Toile Wallpaper* and *Return The Girl In The Toile Wallpaper* lies the ethereal beyond, *The StarWriters Club,* where destiny surrenders and true life begins.

For it is written in the stars …

The StarWriters Club

Mary K. Savarese

The Acquisition

1:13 a.m., November 13th

With her long, golden-blonde hair waving past her shoulders and standing a little over five-seven, Em Iverson, sixteen, hated her many freckles. For that matter, she also didn't like dresses or anything – frilly. Her thoughts concentrated only on sports or boys. The harder her heart pounded the better she felt. Usually, she could sense the beats from inside her head. But now, nothing. Em felt nothing, and a darkness, blacker than black, surrounded her. No sound, no vibration, no anything. She couldn't even remember what she was doing a few minutes ago. Now that she thought about it, she couldn't remember yesterday, or the day before that, or the day before that.

A sweet melody of laughter echoed, filling her with a yearning for home. She glanced around and –

Is that one of my younger sisters?

It sounded like Lizbeth, who just turned thirteen, or maybe it was Celia, who wouldn't be ten for another few weeks.

"Liz?" No name escaped her lips.

Em reached out. Her hands swiped through an emptiness that felt – odd – foreign – unnatural. Taking in a deep breath, she held back the urge to panic.

"Cee!" Again no sound, no pounding heart, no anything.

A speckle of light hovered somewhere along the horizon, although, there was no horizon – no sky – no ground – no walls. Her eyes tried to focus on the little dot that seemed to be growing.

Where am I?

No heat, no coldness, no wind, no stillness. Everything, including her, drifted effortless inside this complete blackness. The light was now expanding, seeming larger than her hands. For some odd reason, the urge to run into the light felt overpowering. Her legs refused to move, but the black void that surrounded her was shrinking – somehow. The light didn't glow, exactly. But the growing dot was now consuming the darkness.

"Mom!" Em yelled and again no sound passed her lips.

She watched as the light grew wider and taller and more vast than her snow-topped mountains back home. However, the light did not shine, remaining inside its ever-growing circle. When the light filled her vision, she tried to see behind her, but the blackness seemed to be rejecting her, pressing her ever deeper into the light.

When the whiteness finally consumed her view, she screamed again, "Mom!"

A new type of warmness surrounded her that felt somewhat different, possessing every ounce of her inner being, overfilling her with an indescribable joy. A sheer ecstasy that felt unworldly, but still reminding her of home. The blinding light wasn't painful, not exactly. Whatever was consuming her was a finality. How she knew that she had no idea, but it was forever. When an emotion of complete love exploded with a deep recognizable longing, Em released her soul and dissolved into the illumination. As she became one with her maker, Em's cardinal life was no more.

It was Wednesday morning, and just a typical day for school. Standing at the granite island of their recently updated kitchen, Celia, aka, *The Snoop*, made a few smooching sounds. "Oh, Bowdyn! Where are you? Sit back here with me on the plane." Keeping one eye on Em and the other on her sister, Liz, she waited.

"Shut up, Cee!" Em wanted to shoot herself for leaving her phone unlocked. The Snoop had read her text and now had ammunition to use against her. Bowdyn was a Ski team partner, and they were still in training. To stand on the Alps with no little sister would be a dream come true.

"Knock it off, Cee. We gotta make the bus," Liz said. "Mom'll ground us if she has to drive."

"Not hungry anyway," Cee replied.

"Have a great time, Em," Lizbeth said, hoisting her backpack over a shoulder before darting out the side door.

Em glanced up from the refrigerator and nodded.

Celia grabbed her backpack and smiled.

"Have fun at school, Cee." Em said, still rummaging through the fridge. "I'll miss you."

Celia rammed herself into Em, wrapping her arms around her.

Em chuckled. "Love you too."

The back door slammed shut as her mother placed her purse on the counter. "Can't believe the long lines at the gas station. Is your father down yet?"

"No." Em took a bite from her breakfast burrito. "Ouch, hot."

"Careful," her mother replied, "always hot when you put them in the microwave."

Em nodded.

Her mother grabbed the kitchen rag and wiped the counter. "At least they made the bus. Your passport packed? We have an hour's drive with traffic."

"Yes, Mom." Em stared at her breakfast and smiled as she thought about Bowdyn sitting next to her in her mom's car.

"Late for an appointment," her father said, stealing a kiss from Em's forehead. "Gotta go. You have a great time. And don't do anything stupid. God knows how much this trip is costing me. Love you."

"Love you too, Dad," Em smiled. "And thanks."

"You're welcome. Have a great time."

Tossing the rag into the sink, her mother sighed. "Brian, what time are you coming home?"

"Around six." He kissed her mother and darted out the door.

Em waved.

Em's roommate, Danni, yelled, "You get the bathroom first!"

Em didn't move.

"C'mon," Danni said, shaking her. "We said we'd take turns. Get your ass up." She threw her pillow at the back of Em's head.

Again, Em didn't move.

"Em!" Danni yelled. "Wake up."

Danni shook Em's shoulder. She pulled Em's hair from her eyes and screamed. Em's face was a light blue and felt cold to the touch. Danni screamed again and ran from the room. The hallway was filled with students. She pushed a girl out of the way and squeezed between two others.

"Hey," a girl yelled.

Danni tried to breathe but it felt as if her head was covered in plastic. She banged on the door, catching her breath. It cracked opened.

An older woman peered out. "What is it?"

"C...c...ome n...n...ow!"

"What is it?" the woman asked again, opening the door a little more.

"My roommate, Em, is dead!"

The floor with a bright, white light should have been blinding. Em looked down and frowned. It wasn't a light, not exactly, but more of a no-darkness. The purest of anything she'd ever seen. Brown leather sandals now decorated her feet, and a beige toga, belted with a brown, leather strap, hugged her body. Reaching down, she grabbed her robe and sighed.

What am I wearing? The material felt silk-like and smooth to the touch almost as if she were holding a liquid ribbon in her hand. Again she glanced down. *Where am I?*

A young man stepped forward. His dark, black skin was rather a stark contrast to his long, white braids. As he walked, the space between them seemed to shrink as if they were being pulled together by an unseen but powerful force. The man made her feel something, although she wasn't sure what. Em touched her chest and took in a deeper breath.

The young man was not much older than her. His long, white, braided hair was decorated with streaks of black bands that seemed to take on a life of their own. The closer he walked, the darker his skin shown in the bright light. His features reminded her of someone from the islands. His crystal, blue eyes were mesmerizing. Wearing khaki pants and a white buttoned-down shirt, he reminded her of a tour guide from New Hampshire College.

He's cuter though. More of a frat than a nerd. Maybe that explains my toga. Am I at college? How did I get here? Why can't I remember anything?

"Welcome, Em. My name is Michael." His voice sounded more like musical chimes than human words.

"Who's Em?"

"You are Emika Iverson. However, your friends call you, Em. I am Michael."

"You're talking but your lips aren't moving. How can I understand? How do you know my name? Are my lips moving?" She reached up and touched her mouth.

"To answer your questions, you're not in college and –"

"How do you know what I was thinking?" Em took a step back.

"I apologize." He nodded and reached out.

Em shrugged accepting his gesture of friendship. When their hands touched, a strong sensation of warmth flooded through her. She stiffened and stared into his piercing, blue eyes. She smiled for he was somewhat possessive and beguiling at the same time.

"Have we met?" Em asked.

"Walk with me," Michael said with a huge grin. He held out a tablet that had two words written in bold, black lettering – *The List* – but his list was blank.

CHAPTER 2

1:31 a.m., November 13th

Aleia Jones worried about everything. Her school books – her chores – her life. Something else was bothering her today, but she couldn't quite remember what it was. It was something she needed to do, and it was something important.

Dark skinned and only twelve, Aleia often thought about mundane things as if they were her next crises to fix. Slender in build, her crayon purple hair held a life of its own. After pulling it up and into a bun, several strands struggled to escape. Her head, covered with curly whisps, gave her the thought of sharpened scissors. Concentrating on one stubborn strand, she crossed her eyes and blew. The strand flew into the air before snapping back into place. She shrugged.

A darkness, blacker than black, now surrounded her. There were no sounds – no vibrations – no anything.

Where am I?

She couldn't remember what she was doing just a few minutes ago. Now that she thought about it, she couldn't remember waking up or falling asleep.

A baby's cry caught her attention. "Trevor!" she yelled. "Where are you!"

A speckle of light just visible, hovered somewhere along the horizon. Although, there was no horizon. No sky – no ground – no walls. Her gaze focused on the little dot that seemed to be growing.

What is that?

No heat, no coldness, no wind, no stillness. Everything, including her, drifted effortlessly inside this complete blackness. The light expanded and was now larger than her hand. For some odd reason, the urge to run toward the light felt overpowering.

I can't move! Her legs refused to obey her commands.

The black void that surrounded her was now shrinking – somehow. The light didn't glow, but the darkness was definitely fading.

"Trevor!" She screamed louder this time. "Where are you? Mom'll kill me if I lose you."

The light grew wider and taller and more vast than the stars in the sky. However, the light did not glow. The light stayed within its ever-growing circle, eating away at the darkness. The light filled her vision, and she turned to see what was behind her, but the blackness was pushing her closer to the light.

When the whiteness filled her world, she screamed out Trevor's name again. A warmness enveloped her but it felt different. It possessed every ounce of her being, cradling her as if she was a baby. An overfilling of indescribable joy exploded all around her. A sheer ecstasy that was friendly but also exciting. The blinding light wasn't painful, although it should have been. Whatever was surrounding her was endless. She couldn't understand what was happening to her. When an emotion of pure love hit, Aleia released her reality, dissolving into the illumination, and her soul became one with her maker. Aleia's previous life had just disappeared.

It was seven in the morning, and with only one eye open, Aleia acknowledged her mother's presence.

"Aleia, honey. I'm leaving for work. Trevor's still asleep. Don't forget that I'm meeting with Ms. Yanz after work. See you around seven?"

Her mother's voice drifted slightly into Aleia's dream before waking her. So much for a day off from middle school because of parent conferences. Not only was she taking care of her eighteen-month-old half-brother, but she was also responsible for having dinner on the table by seven. Her new stepdad would be of no use as he was out of town on business. Therefore, she'd cut him a little slack. Caleb was good to her mother and her but was nothing like her biological father, Vis Jones. Vis had been her mother's high school sweetheart, and they married young. He disappeared shortly after Aleia was born. His surname was all he left behind. *And yeah,* she told herself, *Vis Jones is dead and soon to be gone forever.* Caleb was adopting her.

Hearing a slight whimper, she tried to ignore it. She pulled the covers over her head and listened. All remained quiet. Maybe she could sleep a little more.

Being highly responsible, Aleia was a great kid and never a problem. Collecting straight A's meant that she would win an award this year. Something her mother would find out about this afternoon.

The warmth radiated from under her floral comforter. She snuggled in deeper and relaxed. She wanted to recapture the sandman. All Aleia wanted was another hour of sleep.

A whimper and Aleia sighed. She tossed off the covers, and a loud shriek hit her ears. Her feet slapped against the cold, hardwood floor, and she struggled to stand. Shivering, she ran into the light blue room. Trevor's room overflowed with stuffed animals and baby paraphernalia. Always the manipulator, the mocha skin cherub stood proud, grabbing onto the rail of his crib. Bouncing, he smiled and his few white teeth glittered in the morning light.

Wanting to scold him, she sighed instead. "Trev, you're too cute for words. Go back to sleep. Pleasss …"

Trevor laughed and reached out for her. She changed his diaper and found his yellow ducky and pacifier hidden under his blankets. Climbing back into her bed, she reinforced his side with several of her schoolbooks. Trevor sucked and slept. The aroma of his night's bath lingered, lulling her back to sleep.

She woke to a slap on the face. Trevor sat back and laughed. She sighed as she climbed out from under the warm covers. Making her way to the kitchen with her brother on her hip, she stole a few kisses.

Trevor sat happily moving his duck around on the highchair. With the Chicago skyline providing the morning scene from their kitchen window, Aleia busied herself making breakfast.

"Open," Aleia said, gently filling his mouth with warm oatmeal. "Good boy, now say A-lee-a."

Trevor smiled and his cereal oozed out, spoiling his bib. She repeated her name over and over again. Trevor would soon say his first word, and she was determined it would be her name. Boys usually took a little longer to talk, but that didn't stop her from trying.

She glanced out the window. Brown leaves swirled from the piles she still needed to bag. She would finish that chore when Trevor took his nap.

After pulling out his beige woolen hat, brown jacket, and Big Bird blanky, she grabbed her black jacket. Gently sitting him inside his stroller, Aleia smiled.

"We're sitting on the stoop today. Let's go watch the people. What'd yah say to that?"

Trevor giggled.

They claimed their spots on the front porch and settled down.

The neighbor lady across the street stopped sweeping and waved. "Good mornin', Aleia. Mornin', Trevor."

"Good morning, Mrs. Sanchez," Aleia yelled back.

A car backfired, speeding up the block. A bullet flew from the street and over her lawn. Aleia gasped once before tumbling down the steps.

Mrs. Sanchez dropped her broom and stared at the speeding car. She ran to Aleia and pressed down on the child's bleeding chest. "Help!" Mrs. Sanchez screamed. "Someone, help me!"

"A-lee-a," Trevor said, pointing to his half-sister.

Em walked along a shore with the bluest teal water she'd ever seen. "Where am I?"

"You're almost in Heaven," Michael replied, "in a circular band that surrounds it."

"Never heard of a circular band that runs around Heaven."

"It's not widely published. A stealth place only visited by a few."

His gaze felt as if it was piercing straight through her. A warm sensation of security engulfed her with a longing, but a longing for what? A warmth she never felt before filled her with a deep satisfaction. *Is this how true love feels?* "Am I dead?"

"You're very much alive to me." Michael smiled. "Technically, you are dead in your previous world, but not here. I need you on my team."

"Team?"

"Let's call it an apprenticeship program. I only choose a few, and I'm investing in you. You will train to become a StarWriter."

Em giggled. "What does a StarWriter do?"

"You will deliver the plan … *His Plan* to all the stars within *His* universe where they will be accepted by the new souls."

"I don't understand."

"You will. And you will have a partner, actually several. Twelve StarWriters in all. They'll be joining us shortly."

Em felt the cool water as it crossed over her toes. She glanced down and noticed that her leather sandals and toga had remained dry.

"However, I will need you to foster one of your partners," Michael said. "She can be a bit rambunctious. Keep her on a short leash. At times, she may act a little devilish, but in a good way."

"Are you assigning me a dog?"

"No, a baby."

"A baby?" Em laughed. "What am I to do with a baby?"

A slight breeze caressed Em's neck as the sound of fluttering wings echoed through the air.

Glancing up, Michael smiled. "I see that you found us."

A plump cherub with pink wings and wearing a pink toga floated above them. Her pink baby toes, begging for a tickle, hung bare. A head full of pink hair decorated her bright and chucky face.

"Em, this is Rosie. Rosie, Em," Michael said.

"Hi, Rosie. You're cute. You must love the color pink." Em giggled. *What do I say to a cherub?*

Rosie hovered over Em, giving her the once over.

"Rosie? A little shy today?" Michael chuckled. "Quite unbecoming even for you."

"Do I teach her how to talk?" Em asked.

Michael laughed so hard that he made Em laugh. "I'm afraid to say that once she starts talking, you won't be able to shut her up."

"But babies don't speak."

"They do here," Michael replied.

Em and Michael walked together as Rosie remained a few floats behind. The three approached a huge tree that seemed to reach beyond the heavens. The rainbow-colored trunk glowed with more colors than Em could recognize. Satiny clouds hid most of the top. Trillions of heart-shaped leaves covered the slender branches.

"This is the Wondrous Tree," Michael said. "You'll discover why soon enough."

A figure of a young girl walked toward them. Her purple hair shone brightly in the bright light. Michael held out his tablet with the title – *The List*.

"Don't mean to rush you, Em, but I must welcome Aleia. I do require your signature. Just use your finger … here."

His smile touched something deep inside her. She brushed her finger across the board and the name, Emika Siobhan Iverson, appeared. She whispered, "You said I go by Em?"

Rosie flew up and giggled. "Ha! You don't really know who you are, do you?"

Em frowned.

"Em it is." Michael pointed to his tablet and the letters dropped off before reprinting the name Em. "You two wait here. Get to know each other," Michael said and vanished.

Em glanced around and shrugged. "Kinda weird here. Do you want to play hide and seek, Rosie?"

Rosie flew into the tree and disappeared.

Em giggled. "I guess that's a yes. I'll count to ten and then look for you." She examined the exposed branches. Were they climbable while she was wearing this stupid outfit and slippery sandals? Em closed her eyes and counted aloud. "One, two, three … ten. Ready or not, here I come." Looking up, Em couldn't see Rosie anywhere. "You're a good hider, Rosie."

Grabbing hold of the lowest branch, Em pulled herself up. As she found her footing and reached for the next, water flooded down, drenching her from head to toe. Rosie giggled from somewhere above.

"I thought that water didn't get us wet here," Em stated, wiping her eyes.

"I willed it," replied a squeaky and giggly voice.

Why couldn't you have been a dog? Em frowned and shook her head.

"I heard that," Rosie said.

"You read minds too?"

CHAPTER 4

"Welcome, Aleia, I'm Michael." Taking her hand into his, he pulled her in close.

She furrowed her 'brows. "Aleia?"

"Yes, your name is Aleia Vis Jones."

"Aleia Vis Jones?" A radiating warmth surrounded her that seemed somewhat unworldly. Feeling as if she recognized this place, she took a step back.

"Yes, I knew you before you were born," he replied. "You have never let me or anyone down. There are incredible joyful times ahead for you."

"Where am I?"

"You're in the band that runs between Heaven and Earth, and I need you to join my StarWriters. Please, walk with me."

Standing on a bright light, Aleia blinked several time, but the brightness didn't burn her eyes. Why was she dressed in such a costume? To her, it resembled a sheet that was tied with a leather rope.

A huge and colorful tree that raised toward the heavens filled her view. She felt drawn to the thing. It was as if she was meant to be there. Walking next to the stranger, she asked several questions. However, the man didn't say anything. A girl dressed in a similar costume stood near the tree, staring up and into the branches. Water dripped from her long hair, her gown soaked.

"The leaves …" Aleia whispered, "are … heart shaped?"

"Our wonderous tree does wonderous things," Michael said.

"You can come out now, Rosie," the girl standing under the tree yelled. "I give up. I can't find you."

"Having fun with Rosie?" Michael asked.

The girl frowned.

"Please, don't take her too seriously." He chuckled. "She'll come down soon enough. She just loves to have a little fun."

A high-pitched giggle echoed around them.

I must be hearing things. Aleia stared into the tree and saw nothing. "What are we looking at?"

"Aleia," Michael said, "this is Em and Rosie's somewhere up there playing *hide and seek*. They will be your partners should you decide to accept my offer."

"Hi," Em said. "Nice to meet you, Aleia."

"Yeah, you too," Aleia replied. "Nice to meet you too, Rosie. Wherever you are."

Rosie floated down and hovered next to Em. "Hi! Will you play with us?"

Aleia scrunched up her nose. "You're a baby and can talk? A flying pink baby?"

"Babies talk here," Em replied. "Be careful. She reads minds."

Watching Rosie, Aleia added, "Sure. I'll play with you. Don't want to get wet though. I look goofy enough in this stupid outfit."

"I agree," Em said. "Michael, why *are* we wearing these beige robes, and why is Rosie wearing pink?"

"It's what StarWriters wear," Michael said, placing a tablet in front of Aleia. "I need a signature, please."

Aleia stared at the board. It was blank except for two words – *The List*. "Sign where?"

"Just touch here," he said.

With her hand shaking, she pointed to the tablet. When her finger touched the soft and white nothingness, her full name appeared – Aleia Vis Jones. She shrugged and frowned.

Rosie yelled from above, "When do I sign?"

Michael smiled. "I thought you'd never ask."

Rosie touched the board, and her name magically appeared. "What about Lyon?"

Michael laughed. "Sure, Lyon can sign too."

Em and Aleia looked at each other and frowned.

Rosie pulled out a pink rabbit from under her robe. When she placed the rabbit's ears to the board, an outline appeared.

"The pink coloring and rabbit are a bribe," Michael replied with a wink as he faded into a bright mist.

"Where'd he go?" Aleia asked.

"You'll get used to it," Em replied. "He comes and goes often."

"Time to go back to sleep," Rosie said and the rabbit yawned.

Aleia stepped up. "So cute. Can I pet him?"

Rosie's eyes sparkled. "Sure, he likes that."

Aleia stroked Lyon's fur. "He's so soft."

Rosie glanced at Em. "You want to pet Lyon?"

"Can I?" Em smiled, stretching out her hand.

"Sure," Rosie replied.

"How'd you choose the name Lyon?" Em asked. "He's pink, why name a pink bunny, Lyon?"

Aleia nodded.

Rosie looked up. "Umm … I … don't really know. Umm … maybe I do. Can't say. Just know that when I got here Lyon was already with me."

"Do *we* get pets? Aleia asked, looking at Em.

Em shrugged.

"That's enough," Rosie said, pulling Lyon away. "I want to play." She tucked the rabbit under her robe.

"What do you want to play?" Aleia asked.

"Apparently, babies can play whatever they want," Em said, grinning.

"You're silly," Rosie replied. "*Hide and seek.*" She flew into the leaves and disappeared.

Em giggled. "Start counting, this may take awhile."

"I heard that," Rosie yelled.

CHAPTER 5

2:13 a.m., November 13th

Owning a cocky attitude and wavy, red hair, Landon Orly, fifteen, twisted from side to side as he listened to the familiar roar of his coach's voice.

"Ugh!" he yelled as he tried to move his legs. "Help, I'm stuck!"

Landon was late. Today was the championship game, and Coach would strangle him for sure this time.

"Help! Where am I?"

A darkness, blacker than black, surrounded him. No sound, no vibration. He couldn't remember where he had been or what he was doing just a few minutes ago. Now that he thought about it, he couldn't remember much of anything.

Hearing his coach yell again, he reached out and felt nothing.

"I'm here, Coach. Put me back in the game. You said you would. Please …?"

Landon lived for the play. He was good – no, he was great at the game. Hearing his coach for a third time, his heart pounded as fear filled him with dread.

"Wait, Coach!" *It's the pep talk.* He punched at the air. "Wait for me! You need me to win the championship for you." He punched into the darkness again. "For the team."

A speckle of light hovered somewhere along the horizon. He could see it. Although, there was no horizon. No sky – no ground – no walls. His eyes focused on that little white dot that seemed to be growing.

Where am I?

No heat, no coldness, no wind, no stillness. Everything, including him, drifted effortless inside an absolute blackness. The light expanded and was now larger than his hand. For some odd reason, the urge to run to the light felt powerful. However, he couldn't move his legs.

I'm stuck?

He tried and tried, yet his legs remained locked in place. The black void that surrounded him was shrinking – somehow. The light didn't glow anymore. Instead, the growing spot lit the area that was slowly being consumed. Reaching out, he wanted his sister. The urge to find her felt strong.

"Sunny! Sunny, why'd you lock me in the basement?" Landon yelled. If his sister did it again, he was going to be very angry. "I've got to get to the game. Let me out!"

The light grew wider and taller and more vast than an endless playing field. But it did not shine like a sun or flashlight. Instead, it remained inside the ever-growing circle. When it grew large enough to fill his vision, he glanced over his shoulder, but the blackness seemed to be rejecting him, pushing him deeper into the light. He screamed.

"Stop fooling around, Sunny. Open the door, now!"

A sensation of warmness engulfed him. Everything felt oddly indifferent, consuming his memories – his thoughts. An emotion he couldn't control or explain exploded from somewhere deep inside. It was pure ecstasy, and the sensation was exciting and new. The blinding light wasn't actually painful. Whatever was taking control reminded him of a fantasy or a final calling. How he knew that *now* would become an eternity, he had no idea. But a deep passion somehow immersed him into a pool of love and desire. He released his soul and dissolved into the illumination. He had just become one with his maker. Landon's cardinal life disappeared and so did his pain.

Landon arrived at his private school in Winchester, England with his veins filled with adrenaline. Dropping his lacrosse equipment onto the locker room floor, he massaged his knee. *Swollen again?* He cringed. Limping, Landon lowered his head to hide a wince. Wanting to avoid the coach, he backed into the locker room only to bump into the man.

"Sorry," Landon said, lowering his gaze.

"Don't like what I'm seeing," Coach Worbell said. "You're my best player and that knee looks swollen again. Can't afford you sitting out during the championship." He released a sly smile. "Especially with scouts in the stands. You're our best candidate for a scholarship."

"I'm fine, Coach. I'm ready."

"Get that knee wrapped."

Landon scored the winning point, his parents and sister yelled from the bleachers. His swollen knee ached and his hip throbbed. He stretched and held back a scream. Now, his back ached too. He shrugged and decided it was stress. Besides, the pain always went away after a good night's sleep.

It was his mum who reacted on it and started the months and months of doctors probing and prodding and needles and x-rays. The diagnosis?

"The boy is only fifteen," the British doctor had said. "Growing pains."

However, the bone specialists at Boston Hospital in the United States said it was a rare and aggressive cancer. A malignancy that had already invaded every cell of his body. But it was the chemo that pulled his spirit from his life.

When Landon gripped the edge of unconsciousness, his mum slipped in next to him on the hospital bed. His father sat on the other side, and his little sister, Sunny, crawled onto his legs. They cuddled together for hours.

"It's okay to go, Landon," his mum had said, barely clinging to her sanity. "You're free now, sweetheart."

His father had cried.

"I'll see you in Heaven," Sunny had whispered as she wiped away a tear. "I'll love you forever, big brother."

A large tree loomed in the distance. A man wearing khaki's approached and waved. The boy felt an urge to run to the stranger, which seemed odd but comforting at the same time. Instead, he remained frozen in place and just waited.

"Welcome, Landon," the stranger said. "I've been waiting for you." The man, whose skin was darker than an evening sky, extended his hand. "I'm Michael." Michael was quite tall and his blonde almost white hair glowed, brighter than a morning star.

"Where am I?"

"Walk with me," Michael replied. "I need you, my friend."

The boy followed the man toward the large tree, where two girls stood, looking as if they too, were somewhat lost.

"I need you to sign your name, here." Michael held out a blank tablet and smiled.

"Sure," the boy replied. After reaching out his hand, he stopped. "I'm sorry, but I don't remember my name."

"Of course you do," Michael said. "Just touch here, please."

The boy reached out again, swiping his finger across the board. The name Landon John Griffin Orly appeared. "That's my name? It's so long."

Michael shrugged.

The boy turned to ask another question, but he was now standing alone. He walked up to the colorful tree and the two girls. "Hello?" Landon said. "What is this place?"

"Hi." Aleia replied, "I'm Aleia and this is Em."

Landon nodded. "I was told that I'm Landon."

Em stared up at the tree.

"What's up there?" Landon asked.

A childish giggle echoed around them.

"Who's that?" he asked.

"I'm Rosie," a pink cherub replied, holding out a small rabbit. "This is Lyon."

Landon took a step back and frowned. "A rabbit named Lyon, a pink, flying baby named Rosie, and two girls. Where am I?"

CHAPTER 6

2:31 a.m., November 13th

Yutu Woo was in love. Who cared if he was only fourteen, and his parents forbid him from becoming serious with a girl. His school work was always the center of their attention, and his college goals were discussed every night at dinner. He was tired of their arguing over his future. His future was his not theirs.

The sweet laughter of the girl he loved grabbed his attention. "Amelia? Where are you?"

Nothing. No reply. Only a never-ending darkness that surrounded him. No sounds, no vibrations.

"Amelia? Are you here?" He reached out and felt nothing.

He couldn't remember where he was or where he had been just a few minutes ago. Ignoring his new and strange reality, he concentrated on Amelia and her beautiful smile.

She loved the talking teddy bear he had given her. The bear replayed a recorded message. It took him days to get it just right. *Amelia, you're the greatest person I ever met. You're sweet and kind and smart ...* he left a pause for only a second ... *will you go out with me?*

A speckle of light hovered just beyond his grip. Where was the ground – or walls – or anything? His eyes focused on the little, white speckle that seemed to be growing.

It's a bad dream that's all. He held back the urge to panic. No heat, no cold, no wind, no stillness. He just drifted effortlessly inside an endless blackness.

How is this possible?

The light seemed to be expanding and was now larger than his hand. He held out his fingers and compared the size. The urge to run to the light felt intense. However, his legs just hung there, useless. The black void that surrounded him was now shrinking – or was it? The light wasn't actually glowing. It was just getting bigger. The growing bright dot was now consuming the darkness.

"Hey, what's going on?"

The light grew wider and taller and more vast than an endless ocean. However, the light did not shine. The light stayed within its ever-growing circle. When the speckle filled his view, he looked behind him – but the blackness seemed to be moving away.

When the whiteness completely filled his horizon, he screamed, "Amelia!"

A warmness surrounded him and he felt – different. Something had taken over, seeming to possess him. He liked the odd sensation, an overfilling of indescribable happiness and love. A sheer ecstasy that gave him a sense of longing and familiarity.

The blinding light wasn't painful, not really. Whatever was taking control was an ending or maybe a beginning. A strong emotion filled him, releasing his soul, dissolving into his love. He became one with his maker, and his previous life faded into a heavy mist.

Yutu begged his new girlfriend, Amelia, to join him in one of his favorite pastimes. After studying for their biology exam, they left the school hand in hand.

"How 'bout a quick run in my dad's boat? I take it out all the time. We can watch the sunset. It'll be fun. Whattada' say?"

"Uhh … not sure. I should be home for dinner."

"Can't you call and ask? We won't go far."

"I guess."

Her ponytail swung back and forth as they walked down the street toward his house. She spoke on her phone, and he enjoyed just being near her.

"I'm to be home by seven-thirty," she said, shoving her phone into her back pocket.

He nodded and swelled with pride, opening the gate to his backyard. She stood on his dock as he readied the boat. He maneuvered the small craft down the inlet, and after a few miles into the bay, he turned off the engine. They snuggled in for the afternoon. As they shared a few kisses, the yellow-orange sun slowly disappeared below the horizon, and the sky turned purple.

"I think we should get back," Amelia said. She pulled her jacket tighter around her neck. "It's getting cold."

Yutu nodded and gunned the motor, slowly turning the boat around in the large bay. Amelia rested her head on his shoulder and he smiled. A mile from his inlet, a strong wind blew in from the south, pulling in the darker clouds. The boat rocked with the increasing waves.

"Yutu, I'm scared." Amelia grabbed his arm.

The boat rolled, and he gunned the engine. Their world fell quiet.

"What happened?" Amelia stared out at the threatening sky as a streak of lightening lit the heavens.

He nodded and turned the key, nothing. "This reminds me of my dad."

"Your dad?"

"Yep, 'one minute the ocean is an angel, loving, guiding, and calm. Then in a split second it can corner you like the devil. It'll manipulate, lie, and make you think all is lost. Stay calm. Think logically, and you shall overcome.'"

"But we're not moving," she stated, pulling her jacket in tighter.

"The engine just stalled. Give it a second." He stood tall, wanting to show Amelia he had everything under control.

Amelia reached for her phone. "I'm calling for help."

"We're good," he said. "I got this." Yutu turned the key and the engine roared to life. "See, we'll be out of this in a sec." He looked at her and smiled.

A wall of water and rain splashed against the boat and again the engine stalled. He turned and stared as a dark wall aimed directly for them. The stern raised. The clouds darkened. A streak of lightening lit the sky and a boom echoed. Their backpacks flew into the water and the boat flipped. The coldness pulled Yutu under. He kicked and pulled himself to the surface.

"Yutu! Help!" Amelia screamed.

"Amelia! Where are you!" he yelled. "God, help me please."

Yutu climbed onto the capsized boat. He spotted Amelia floating only a few feet away. "Amelia! Climb onto the boat!"

A rolling wave pushed her closer, and he grabbed onto her arm. They intertwined their fingers as the boat carried them deeper into the darkness. Her fingers slipped from his grip, and Yutu watched as the swirling water swallowed her.

Yutu stood alone within the brightness as voices echoed around him. The voices were talking and laughing.

"We will contact you when we are ready," one of the voices said. "And remember … only *we* can save her."

"What? Save who?" Yutu took a step.

"Say nothing to no one …" The teasing whispers had faded.

"Ah, there you are, Yutu," said a voice from within the shadows.

He turned and a man wearing khaki's and a white shirt smiled. He held a tablet and was writing something on it with his finger. The man was as dark as a moonless night, and his braided, white hair intrigued Yutu. "Who's Yutu?"

"You are, my friend … Yutu Woo."

"Who are you?"

"I am Michael."

"What is this place?"

"You're in a circle that surrounds Heaven." He reached out and pulled Yutu closer to him.

"Am I dead?"

"Only in a worldly sense. Otherwise, you are very much alive. Just beginning a new journey."

Yutu remained silent.

"If you accept my offer, your apprenticeship will be amazing."

"Do you know me?"

Michael smiled. "Walk with me?"

Say nothing echoed through Yutu's mind as he paced beside the odd stranger.

"I need your signature," Michael said, holding out the blank tablet.

Yutu stared as two words appeared – *The List*. He frowned and replied, "I have no pen."

"Just touch here, please."

Yutu reached out with his finger, and when he touched the board, his name appeared. "Then my name is Yutu Woo. How odd."

Michael shrugged.

A large tree now filled Yutu's horizon. Several people were either standing or sitting next to it. "What is this place?"

"I believe we covered that already. Please, meet the other StarWriters."

"The star what?" Yutu looked back at the man and froze, however, Yutu was now alone. He walked up to the tree and smiled at the small group. "Hi, I'm Yutu."

"Hi, Yutu," they said at the same time.

Yutu waved.

"I'm Em and that's Aleia and Landon and Rosie." Em pointed to the pink baby with wings. "And don't turn your back on her."

Hovering in front of Yutu, Rosie handed him a cookie. "Hi, I'm Rosie. Want a cookie?"

Yutu smiled. "No, thank you."

"What … don't you trust me?" the flying, pink baby asked.

CHAPTER 7

8:31 a.m., November 13th

Shoupi Mem, thirteen, felt her thick, black ponytail sway behind her.

Am I running?

She glanced down and could see nothing. Although, she could sense that her legs were moving. She was, however, surrounded by a darkness that was just too dark.

A tunnel?

She felt no fear, no loneliness, no nothing. As she tried to see around her, she noticed that something hard was pressing against her chest. Her arms were cuddling some *thing* as if it was important she didn't lose it.

A box or a book?

She couldn't move her arms. It was as if they were glued in place. Her heart pounded against whatever she was clutching. Trying to figure out where she was, she heard no sound – felt no vibration – no anything. She couldn't remember what she was doing just a few minutes ago. Now that she thought about it, she couldn't grasp onto anything that held a meaning. Yet she felt no fear. Something wonderful was about to happen, although, she had no idea how she knew.

A narrow beam of light hovered somewhere along the horizon. Although, there was no horizon. No sky – no ground – no walls – her gaze focused on the little dot that seemed to be growing.

This is so wonderful. I am not afraid. She squeezed the *thing* in her arms a little tighter.

She seemed to be drifting effortless inside a blackness that was swallowing her cell by cell. The small light was expanding and growing. The urge to run toward the light felt overpowering. The black void that surrounded her was now shrinking, and the little light didn't glow as much. The light, however, was swallowing the darkness.

She clutched her small treasure tighter, knowing that everything depended upon her safeguarding the secret item.

The small light grew wider and taller and more vast than an endless desert. The light did not shine and remained bound by its ever-growing enchantment. When the light filled her vision, she tried to take a step back, but the blackness rejected her and pressed her only forward.

When the whiteness surrounded her, she screamed. "I'll never let you go!"

The passion touched her soul, and she suddenly felt different. The warmness was all consuming, engulfing her with an overfilling of unspeakable happiness and passion. A ribbon of rapture born from outside her world but comfortably consuming it. The blinding light didn't hurt, but it seemed to have a presence, a purpose.

Then she understood. Whatever was destroying her reality was only a beginning. A start of something with no end. She belonged here, always did. Happiness filled her, and as she released her soul into *His* internal love and bliss, her mortal life faded into the glowing brilliance. She had become one with her maker, for her mortal life had just ended.

Shoupi listened as her parents whispered. She strained to hear the words through a small crack in the door. Her heart pounded and her hands shook.

"You leave in two hours," the stranger said. "Here are your new identities. These documents will allow you to pass through Greece where a plane will take you to America. You are Christian refugees seeking asylum. Nothing more. A church in America will house you and help you find employment."

"God has answered our prayers," her mother said, slapping her hands together.

Her father replied, "Is Shoupi ready?"

"Take only the clothes on your back." A man's voice sounded dark and sinister. "Nothing more."

Footsteps echoed through Shoupi's ears as the door opened. "We must go, Shoupi," her mother whispered.

"Where?" Shoupi asked.

"Ask no questions," her father ordered.

Shoupi sat in the back of a large truck and cried. As they pulled away from the only home she knew, she waved into the darkness as if to say *goodbye* to her friends and community.

Shoupi's mom hugged her. "Don't cry, daughter. We will soon be free. Never again persecuted for our faith."

The small community outside of St. Louis, Missouri and the local church would soon celebrate their arrival.

It was a bright and cheery morning, and Shoupi was taking part in her favorite activity. She prepared the altar to celebrate Mass before her high school classes would start. Shoupi loved her new school. Home schooled since a young child, she now enjoyed the daily interactions with her friends and teachers.

Wearing a white robe over her sweater and jeans, she waited and smiled as the elderly Father rushed into the Sacristy at the last minute completely out of breath.

"Shoupi, my dear, what would I ever do without you? You never miss a beat." He reached for the vestments from the closet.

"Thank you, Father O'Brien. I love being an altar server." Her heart glowed from his praise.

"And we love you. Do you have great plans for today?"

"Oh, yes, Father. Today will be a great day," Shoupi replied, smiling.

The morning Mass passed quickly, and as she rode the school bus, she said a prayer with her friends.

"Gather us together in *Your* name as we praise *Your* most high," a boy who was in his senior year said, ending the prayer.

"Amen," Shoupi replied.

With her bible still in her arms, she ran from the bus and into the crowded hallway. It should only take a minute to pass the library and find her math class. She turned the corner and froze as a girl's scream filled her ears. Students ran and darted into various rooms. A loud boom and a boy fell to the ground, blood pooled around him, his eyes staring blankly into the shadows. She turned to run. Several students darting past bumped into her, and she fell. Her bible skidded across the shiny tile. She crawled toward it, and as she reached out, a hiking boot landed firmly onto her outstretched fingers.

"What's your name?" a deep male voice asked.

She strained to see who was talking, but it hurt to move. "Shoupi Mem."

The boy released her hand, taking several steps back. She glanced up and stared at him. He was dressed in black and wearing a scarf that was wrapped around his face, just his deep, blue eyes glared down at her.

He laughed. "Show … pee, rhymes with doe … pee." His eyes trailed to her bible. "Denounce your maker, bitch!"

Shoupi sat up and grabbed her bible. She held it tightly to her chest. As her eyes raised toward the heavens, the boy pulled the trigger.

"I said you were doe-pee … Shoupi."

His laughter echoed through her ears as the bullet entered her head before lodging into a locker covered in skateboard stickers.

Shoupi stood on the brightest white light she had ever seen. As a man approached, her heart raced. She glanced down and smiled. She was wearing sandals and a beige robe. She adjusted a leather belt that was now wrapped around her waist. Feeling wonderful both inside and out, she took in a deep breath.

"Shoupi, my angel," the stranger said, "I've been expecting you."

A warm sensation hit, and she wrapped her arms tighter around her secret treasure. It was as if God was hugging her, but how could he do that? "Do you know me? I can't remember who I am or how I got here."

"I've known you since forever. You are Shoupi Mem. I am Michael."

"Hi, Michael," Shoupi replied. "I do feel as if we've met before. But that can't be. Where am I?"

"In the circular band that surrounds Heaven."

Shoupi lowered her gaze. "I'm not in Heaven?" She touched her forehead, looking at her fingers and frowning as if expecting something.

Michael reached up and cupped her face. "My child. What *He* has planned for you is beyond anyone's imagination. Trust me?"

Shoupi nodded.

"I need you as my apprentice. As a StarWriter. Walk with me?" He held out his blank tablet.

CHAPTER 8

8:33 a.m., November 13th

Milos Devosky liked his nickname – Milos Devos. The shorter name just sounded cooler. At fourteen, he could easily pass for seventeen or eighteen, which allowed him entry into places no fourteen-year-old would ever go.

Girls fancied his layers of long, black curls that decorated his emerging, large nose that he wished would disappear. He wondered why he was thinking about his nose as he stared into the complete blackness.

Where am I? I must have passed out.

The eerie feeling of not being able to see pulled in a flashback of him puking in bed. His pounding heart took command of his thoughts and he paused.

Let the puking begin!

In the distance there was something. A speckle of light that was teasing him. With no horizon, or sky, or walls, perhaps he was experiencing a nightmare.

Wake up!

His gaze focused on the little dot that seemed to be growing and expanding into the blackness that allowed him to float effortlessly. Funny how he couldn't remember yesterday, or the day before that, or the day before that.

He froze, mesmerized as the small light grew wider and wider and more vast than an endless city street. The light was calling to him, wanting him. He tried to move but couldn't. He had a strange urge to fling his arms, and when he tried, nothing happened. A warmness surrounded him just like when he was a child and his mother would cradle him in her arms.

Mama are you holding me? I can't see you.

The warmness was slowly consuming him as the light continued to push away the darkness.

It's so bright.

The light should have hurt his eyes but he knew it wanted him, welcomed him.

Unspeakable happiness and passion overpowered his fears. The black quickly receded as he accepted the light. He was now a part of it, happiness and everlasting joy consuming him. As he released his soul to the light, he became one with his maker. His previous life now over.

His mother walked into his bedroom, and the aroma of her Greek perfume tickled the air. "I can't do this anymore, Milos." She bent over and kissed the back of his head. "I have to go. Get away from that monster … I'm sorry."

After partying and drinking all night, Milos could barely move. He rolled over and watched as his father pushed his mother out of his room.

"Get up!" his father yelled. "She cares nothing about you. You are just a mistake to her."

Milos grabbed at the hand that pulled him from his bed. He stared into his father's bloodshot eyes and frowned.

"Without her around, you will become a man."

Milos took in a deeper breath as has father slapped him across the face.

"She babies you too much! And it all stops now!" His father pushed him onto his bed.

Milos held his breath, holding a pillow. He leaned against the wall as the front door slammed shut. His tears fell.

"Men don't cry!" His father kicked the bed before leaving him in the room alone.

The house quieted. Milos stood and rubbed his face. He glanced into the disheveled living room, searching for any sign of his father. He found him on the couch asleep. Glancing into his parents' bedroom, his tears fell again. The closet was empty except for a few crooked hangers and a pair of old high heels that his mother hadn't worn in years. He stood at the bathroom sink and stared into the tear-soaked face that stared back at him. Taking in a deep breath, he closed his eyes and sighed.

As his hand wrapped around his mother's sleeping pills, he laughed. He would become a superhero, the kind that could fly. Swallowing the pills one at a time, he whispered, "Someday."

The following morning, Milos woke with a headache and his bed full of puke. Today he would skip school and avoid his father, which wouldn't be too difficult as the man usually worked a double shift.

Milos sat alone in the crowded Moscow Metro. He held out his comic book, flipping through the pages.

"Boring!"

Milos tossed the book in the trash. He had already read it several times.

"You want to fly?" an older boy asked. "I'm recruiting." The boy picked up the comic book and smiled.

"I'm too young to join the military," Milos said, studying the boy's military-style jacket.

The boy pointed to an arriving train. "On top."

"I don't see anything."

"We're called Russian Flyers," the boy said. "No one can see us. We look just like part of the mechanism. When the train moves into the tunnel, we stand."

"Stand?"

The boy nodded. "Bolt our boots to the roof of the train and we fly!"

"Fly?"

"You want to fly?"

Milos nodded.

Several weeks had passed, and Milos was soon flying with the older teens. With rain pelting the world around them, the boys climbed to the top. Milos slipped several times, keeping his eyes on the older boys who shook their heads and laughed.

"I *am* a Russian Flyer!" Milos screamed as the train entered the tunnel. He stood and stretched out his arms, feeling the cold air rush past.

His right boot slipped first. He felt his leg give, and he reached out to grab onto – then he remembered, there was nothing to grab. Milos screamed as his fingers searched through the darkness and his other foot gave way.

Milos stood on a branch that was covered with heart-shaped leaves. Glancing down, he shook his head. He was wearing a beige robe, a leather belt, and sandals.

"What is this crap?"

Laughter filled his ears.

"Who's down there?"

A small group had gathered at the base of the tree. Now he wondered if they had heard him.

"Milos," replied a man's voice from somewhere below. "Come down, please."

"Who's Milos?" He had just stepped onto a lower branch when something pink buzzed past.

Milos lost his footing and watched as the ground sped toward him. Before he landed face-first on the bright green grass, his robe curled itself around a branch. Now hanging upside down, Milos stared at the flying pink object.

"What are you?"

The pink object giggled.

"This is crazy. My shirt's caught on a branch," Milos said, trying to pull himself loose.

"The robe will do that from time to time," the man replied.

"Okay," Milos said. "Can someone help me down?"

"You look funny," the pink *thing* replied.

"Milos, my boy," the man said. "Please, come down and meet everyone."

The gown slowly released and lowered Milos to the soft grass. Milos stood and brushed off his robe. "What in the world?" He glanced up, trying to see between the thick leaves.

"It's okay," Em said, stepping forward. "Weird things happen here all the time. I'm Em."

Milos nodded. "How could that happen with my robe?"

"It just does," Em replied.

Michael laughed. "Your name is Milos Devos Devosky, and these pretty, young ladies are Em and Aleia and Shoupi."

Aleia and Shoupi gave a quick wave.

"How can this be?" Milos asked again.

"As Em said," Michael replied, "it just does." Michael laughed. "These young men are Landon and Yutu." Michael pointed to each who nodded. "I am Michael. And that …" – he pointed to the flying pink thing – "… is Rosie."

"Rosie," Milos repeated.

Michael nodded. "Walk with me, Milos?"

CHAPTER 9

2:13 p.m., November 13th

Said to be cursed with a high IQ, Jenni Ramirez had just turned sixteen. She celebrated by rewarding herself with the cutest platinum-colored, pixie haircut. Holding a perfect SAT score, she was guaranteed to receive scholarships to various Ivy League schools. However, her brother would probably be the one to drive her. When it came to operating machinery of any type, Jenni was a complete failure. As an example, she was scheduled to retake her on-the-road driver's test for the third time.

Jenni marveled at the darkness, feeling rather joyful when the blackness surrounded her. In some ways, it reminded her of a velvet smoothness like when oil floats across water.

Blinking several times, Jenni thought about yesterday. However, nothing came to mind. The more she thought about it, all of last week was vague or hazy or a complete blur. Instead, she focused on her senses.

Glancing down at her legs, she giggled. "I'm floating. So where is the water?" Looking up, she sighed. "No sky, either." Glancing back down, she shook her head. "No ground."

Stretching out her arms and wiggling her fingers, she paused. "No walls … no sound … just nothing?"

Was she alive or in some type of a vacuum? Was this what death was like? She could move her arms although it felt as if she was somehow locked in place at the same time.

Still have my toes. I can wiggle them.

A speckle of light appeared in the distance. But there was no horizon. The speck grew larger and reminded her of a bouncing ball that was evolving into an endless expanse that was devouring the darkness. Magic was somehow unfolding as the light sped toward her at an ever-increasing speed.

"Who's there?" she yelled into the widening beam.

Jenni glanced around and relented to the push from the darkness as if it was gently coaching her to move into the growing illumination that sparkled with a radiance that surpassed the brightness of the sun. However, that was impossible. She could run, then again, there was no need. She felt no heat or danger. Concentrating on the brilliance that was seeping into her very essence, Jenni accepted the warmth as if her mother had just wrapped her inside a warm blanket. She snuggled into the depths of the folds. The strength of the energy felt different as if it was possessing her, becoming her.

An indescribable sensation of joy and love filled an emptiness she never knew existed. An unworldly ecstasy that now blended her into an intensifying reality of … *something*. Whatever *it* was – Jenni understood – it was permanent.

Releasing her soul into this new and revealing clarity, Jenni became one with her maker, forever leaving her cardinal life behind.

"Third times a charm," Jenni's brother said. "Text me when you're done. I'll be waiting across the street in the park."

"I got this." She smiled. "I'll *pass* this time."

Jenni stood on the sidewalk and waved at her brother. She took in a deep breath, waiting for the DMV evaluator.

A heavyset man with a wide gait exited the door, holding a clipboard. "Ramirez, Jenni?"

"Here," she said.

"Paper?"

She handed him her authorization slip and smiled. He pointed to her vehicle, and she slipped into the driver's seat. Inhaling and exhaling softly, she sighed. *I've got this.* Jenni adjusted the seat and her mirrors and checked behind her. "All clear."

"Then, pull out," the instructor said.

Jenni glanced at the dashboard and shifted the car into gear. Moving her foot from the brake to the gas, the car lurched in reverse and rammed into a car behind her. She froze and stared at the instructor. Tears ran down her cheeks. "I thought I was in drive! This is different than my dad's car. I only tapped it. Does that mean I failed?"

"You got that right," the instructor replied, writing FAILED across the test sheet.

"What's wrong with you?" her brother asked on the drive home. "That was your *third* try. You can work a thousand-piece puzzle with your eye's closed, memorize a book from cover to cover, but you can't drive a car? What gives in that brain of yours?"

She stared out the window and remained silent. *I'll show you. I'll show everyone. Who needs a license anyway!*

He parked in their circular drive and tapped lightly on her knee. "Next time. Coming?"

"Be there in a sec."

Jenni watched as he walked into the garage. She scooted into the driver's seat and pulled out her mother's spare key from her jean pocket. She stared at it.

"I should have passed!"

Jenni glanced at her phone and sighed. Her friends had already texted several times. If she didn't pick them up as planned, they'd know she had failed again.

"I'll just take the back roads."

Backing out of the driveway, she glanced at the garage. No sign of her brother or mother. All was clear. The traffic was light when she pulled onto the highway. Only a few minutes, and she'd be at her friend's house.

The highway running through the mountains always reminded her of a snake searching for a meal. After rounding a sharp bend, an eighteen wheeler had slowed and was now blocking the road. Jenni twisted her lips and beeped the horn several times.

"Move to the right. You're hogging the road!" she yelled.

The truck maintained its slow speed.

"Fine, if you won't move, I'll go around you!"

She glanced to her left and the lane was full of motorists heading for home. The lane on the right looked clear. She thought about her father's words of never passing on the right and shrugged. After pulling into the right-hand lane, she pushed on the gas pedal.

Moving half-way past the large truck, a red blinker flashed. Jenni glanced into her mirror and held her breath. She honked several times, but the driver of the semi could not see or hear the small car that was now perfectly stuck inside his blind spot.

Jenni's car skidded into the mountain's safety railing. Sparks filled her passenger's side windows. She screamed, and instead of hitting the brakes, Jenni slammed onto the gas. Her car crashed through the slender railing and flew off the rocky cliff.

Jenni knelt and dragged her fingers through the bluest teal water she could ever imagine. The coolness felt brisk and not painful. Rubbing her fingers together, she sighed.

"What is this?" Jenni stood and glanced around. "Where am I? My fingers are dry?" She stepped into the water, allowing the coolness to cover her knees. "Why am I not wet?"

Feeling no cold or warmth, she sat and allowed the water to touch her chin. She smiled as she rested back, the water covering her face. She opened her mouth and took in a deep breath. She exhaled and the water turned into tiny bubbles that floated into nothingness. Breathing in and blowing out bubbles, she started as a smiling face stared down at her. She sat up and smiled back.

"Welcome, Jenni," the stranger said.

"What did you say?"

"I said, welcome, Jenni," he repeated, extending out his hand. After pulling her out of the water, he smiled again. "You are Jenni Simone Ramirez, and you are in the circular band that surrounds Heaven. I am Michael."

"Then, I'm dead?"

"Your world is now here with us, and I need you on our team."

"Us?" Jenni glanced around. "Team?"

Michael chuckled. "The StarWriters team."

"What will I do on this team?"

"Perform *His Plan* for all souls," Michael replied, waving his arms through the air.

"Cool. What do I have to do?"

"Come and walk with me. I wish to introduce you to the others."

"May I ask a question?"

"Of course."

"How can I breathe under water and why am I not wet?"

Michael chuckled again. "Your robe and sandals are your friends. Never take them off."

Jenni glanced down at her feet. "Awesome. But I feel goofy."

"Please sign here. Just use your finger."

Jenni reached out and the name Jennifer Simone Ramirez appeared on the blank slate.

"Thank you," Michael said as he vanished.

Jenni stepped up to the Wondrous Tree and smiled.

3:13 p.m., November 13th

Her long black ponytail, streaked with blue, swung back and forth like that of a child playing. Keekee Nara, thirteen, was proud of her Japanese heritage and her deceased parents. She missed them greatly. She hated her aunt and uncle and referred to them as *The Custodians*.

Keekee sensed something – a presence? But, no – only a silent emptiness surrounded her.

"Okasan, Otosan is that you?" She waited before yelling out again. "Okasan, Otosan?"

The presence intensified.

"I feel that you're near. Where are you?"

The stillness grew thicker, stronger.

"Answer me … please. I'm scared."

She thought about what she was doing just a little while ago. Nothing tickled her memory. Not even yesterday gave a hint as to who she was or how she had arrived. Her tears wanted to fall but she held them back. The sound of her mother's laughter filled her with a silent yearning.

"Okasan? It is you?"

Her mother's laughter grew louder and more stern. She reached out for her warm embrace, praying that her arms were near.

A speckle of light hovered somewhere along a distant shore. Her gaze remained focused on the little dot that seemed to be growing and expanding.

Okasan? Otosan yes …

She reached out for the light that expanded and was now larger than her hands. The urge to run into the light felt overpowering. Her legs refused to work, however, she was still moving toward the light. The black void was leaving her behind as if pushing her away from the darkening shadows.

When only whiteness filled her view, she screamed. "I am here!"

A tenderness, that felt familiar and strange, enveloped her. It seeped deeply into every ounce of her being. An emotion of sheer joy with a longing to be with her parents.

Keekee exhaled and her soul released into the growing illumination. As she became one with her maker, her old world faded into the darkness.

Keekee could not remember the accident that took her parents' lives. She was tossed from the family car and had survived. Her parents, however, were not so lucky. It was her childless aunt and uncle who took her in. They raised and treated her as their own. Since they managed a large apartment building, Keekee referred to them as *The Custodians* and not her legal guardians.

Wanting so desperately to fit in at her private, middle school, Keekee had a plan to win the other girls' confidence. Stealing *The Custodians'* spare keys, the girls rummaged freely from apartment to apartment. With the tenants at work, their spree was free and clear.

"Hurry. What are you doing?" Keekee yelled. "My uncle will be making his rounds soon."

The girls walked out of a bedroom with jewelry stuffed in their pockets. They laughed.

"We will get good money for these," one of the girls said.

"And then we can buy more designer clothes," another replied.

"You're okay, Keekee," the leader said. "You're one of us now. Chill."

The lock on the front door clicked. The girls stared at each other.

"Oh no!" Keekee whispered.

"Quick, hide!" the leader said with only her lips.

Keekee ran into the bedroom. She glanced around and dropped to the floor. The bed was too low for her to crawl under. She stood and listened as the front door creaked. The bedroom window was open. Without a thought, Keekee crawled onto the slender ridge. Glancing down at the traffic far below, her heart skipped a beat. She took in a deep breath and stood. With her back tight against the glass, she turned to see the bedroom door swing open.

Keekee screamed as she locked eyes on *The Custodian* and her foot slipped. His arms reached out as his eyes grew wide, and the world darkened around her.

Standing on a white light, she bent down and touched the cloudy swirls, but the mist dissolved within her fingertips. She stared at a young, black man who stood solemn and quiet as if in contemplation.

She glanced down at her robe and her sandaled feet. Designer clothing filled her mind and she sighed. Her outfit itched and she was not comfortable.

"I am sorry you are uncomfortable," the man said. "However, the outfit will suit you soon enough."

"I look like an idiot." She furrowed her 'brows. "How did you know what I was thinking?"

"A logical conclusion," he replied with a smile. "Miss Keekee."

"Keekee?"

He took her hand and caressed it gently. "Keekee Nara. I've been expecting you."

White mist surrounded her. She could barely see anything. "Who are you?"

"Walk with me, Keekee."

"Who are you?"

"I am Michael."

"Michael? And where am I?"

"We are on the band that surrounds Heaven."

They walked slowly through the thinning clouds. At the end of the path, a tree, larger than the horizon, filled the sky. Several individuals stood under its glowing branches.

"What's that?"

"What is what?" Michael asked.

"That pink thing."

Michael laughed. "Her name is Rosie."

"A flying angel?"

Michael nodded. "That is correct."

"Impossible!"

"I would like you to meet, Keekee," Michael said as they walked up to the small group. "Another StarWriter."

"Hi, Keekee," Em said, stepping forward.

"Welcome. I'm Aleia." Aleia waved for the others to join them.

"Want a cookie?" Rosie asked, holding out a small morsal.

Keekee frowned and took a step back.

"I'm Shoupi."

Keekee stared at the small group.

The others took turns introducing themselves.

"Yutu, hi."

"I'm Landon."

"Just Jenni."

"I'm Milos."

Keekee smiled. She turned and searched for Michael, however, he was no longer standing beside her.

CHAPTER 11

5:13 p.m., November 13th

At six feet, nine inches, and dark skinned, Colton McMighty towered above the rest of his high school peers. At fourteen and just a freshman, he stood tall alongside the juniors and seniors. On his first day of varsity practice, the coach said that he would become the greatest basketball player at his high school.

"Where's the net?" Colton said, trying to perform a dunking move with his right hand. "I just had the ball. What happened to the lights?" *Gotta beat Stanton today.*

Colton hovered in the darkness as it seeped eerily around him. He thought about yesterday and today. Nothing came to mind. He didn't like this all-encompassing void. It frightened him. He wanted to run and jump but his feet refused to move. He could raise his arms up and down but not the rest of him.

"Where the hell am I?" Colton glanced around. "I get it. I'm being punked by the seniors. This is my initiation. Just throw me the ball. I'll get you the first win against Stanton. I promise."

No reply, just the darkness that was slowly consuming him.

"I'm really that good. Feet, start working!"

A tiny ball of light bounced somewhere along a distant horizon.

"There you guys are." He gazed at the little dot that seemed to be growing and expanding into a large basketball. "Come to me little ball," he yelled. "I know what to do with you. Toss you into the basket."

Colton glanced up and frowned. No basket for the ball. In fact, no anything. The urge to run into the light suddenly felt overpowering but his legs refused to move. He squealed when something pushed against his back. He turned and saw no one.

"Hey! Stop it!"

Again something pushed, and he felt himself moving toward the light. The black void receded until he was standing in the rays of sheer brilliance.

"Dad? Are you … here?"

A warmth that felt oddly familiar enveloped him. It seeped deeply into every ounce of his being. Somehow, he knew there was no turning back and only moving forward.

But forward to what?

Colton surrendered and felt the joy and ecstasy of the light. His soul merged into the brightness and his last thought was of his mother.

Up at five in the mornings, Colton practiced shots from every direction in his driveway. *Have to beat Stanton today. Everyone is relying on me. The coach … the seniors …*

"Last chance to beat 'em." He had heard a senior say. A few students liked him but others were mostly jealous.

As a freshman and approaching seven feet, Colton had more to come. His pediatrician often mused at how quickly he was growing. In fact, his doctor asked if his mother was feeding him *giant* pills or something. Colton worked long hours to coordinate and set his muscles to memory.

"I got this," he said, throwing the ball through the hoop from near his back door.

"Colton." His mother yelled and laughed. "Enough already. Come in here. It's cold. I made breakfast."

His stomach churned and his breathing felt labored. Nauseous and dizzy, he rested against the garage.

"Not cold. Not hungry. Gotta practice."

"You need food for energy," she replied. "I'm not asking."

Dropping the ball, Colton entered the kitchen. She hugged him as he sat.

"Your dad would be proud."

Colton glanced at the photo of his father wearing an Army uniform. He never knew his father since the man died in Iraq before Colton was born.

"Gotta beat Stanton today."

His mother smiled. "You will."

"Everyone's relying on *me*."

"Just do the best you can. That's what your dad would say. And I'm saying it for him." She slid a plate that was overflowing with scrambled eggs and bacon in front of him. "Getting calls from colleges about you already. Exciting stuff. Keep this up and you'll be offered a full scholarship."

Colton frowned.

"I'll see you after work." She hugged him again. "I'll meet you on the court."

"Gonna beat them today," his teammate said, pointing at Colton. "First time in our school's history."

With a slight smile, Colton nodded. His heart pounded in his chest as he lined up for the National Anthem. His mother arrived and threw him a kiss, rubbing her heart.

I have to do great today. He waved at her and his stomach churned. Never before had he felt this bad before a game. *Jitters, has to be. Beat 'em, first time in school's history.* His team and coach expected only the best from him, and he would play his best.

At times, the team was losing. A few of the seniors refused to pass the ball to him. With only two seconds left, his opportunity arrived. Slicing a three-pointer, *a buzzer beater,* they won. His school just beat Stanton for the first time by one point.

Staring at the 54-53 score, Colton's heart raced as a sharp pain fizzled into his throat. He grabbed his chest.

Students jumped onto the court from the stands, screaming. His teammates lifted him on their shoulders. As his mind tried to grasp the excitement, Colton fell silent.

"Sorry about the outfit, Colton," a man with braided, white hair said, staring at Colton's feet. "Yours should be a little longer. Perhaps a lot longer."

Colton gasped as the garment lengthened. It piled on the ground around him.

The man chuckled. "Perhaps a tad shorter?" The stranger moved his hand only slightly, and the garment adjusted to fit Colton's height. "That's it. I am Michael by the way." He nodded and smiled.

"Colton? My name's Colton? Have we met?"

"Colton James McMighty," Michael said. "And I've known you since forever."

"This outfit … it grew by itself? How'd it do that?"

"It'll listen to you too. Walk with me?"

The Wondrous Tree glowed, and the various leaves of green, purple, and orange flickered as Colton and Michael walked up. The sounds of laughter filled the air, somewhat calming Colton's nerves.

"This tree?"

"It's wondrous," Michael replied. "Everyone, please welcome Colton."

Michael glanced at his board and nodded. Only a few more signatures required.

CHAPTER 12

7:31 p.m., November 13th

If there was ever anyone whose smile drew a person in like a moth to a light, it was Smillie Sanjeev. Smillie was his actual birth name and he was fourteen. Smillie searched for something inside the darkness but he couldn't see a thing. Not even his hands. He tried to turn but couldn't move. He wasn't sure what he was searching for, but he had to find it.

Am I here for a reason?

He glanced down but again could see nothing.

I'm floating?

Trying to figure out where he was, he studied the silence. No heart beat – no vibration – no nothing.

"Help me?" he said, softly.

A tiny speck hovered somewhere in the distance. Although, there was nothing, no sky – no ground – no walls – no anything. He focused on the little speck that felt mesmerizing and was expanding into the vastness.

"Help must be on the way."

The urge to run toward the light was overpowering but he didn't know how to move. It seemed that the blackness was being swallowed piece by piece. It was as if the light was more powerful or something. When the speck completely enveloped him, he felt a warmth encompass his very essence. An indescribable sensation of joy and love became an unworldly existence of ecstasy. The brightness should have been blinding. Instead, he stared straight into it without pain. Whatever this speck was, Smillie understood it was permanent, and he would never return home. His mortal life had just ended and his soul had rebirthed.

Smillie never tired of his morning ritual. Having roti and dosas for breakfast with his parents and brother at his side, he would slather on the chutney. Then, he'd bike to school carrying the errand for his mother's home business in his basket.

"Smillie." Mummy sighed. "No more than two cookies for you. Remember, I save the crumbles, and you can have them after school."

"But –"

"No buts. You are eating my profits. I've heard from the manager of the hotel twice now. My six dozen, and he counts every last one, are always short by four to six. How you stay so slim is beyond me."

"Yes, Mummy."

Smillie biked through Mumbai's capital toward the Arabian Sea as if trying to win a race. Finishing off two cardamon spice and dried apricot cookies, he fumbled inside the box that was strapped to his bike. His mother's frown flashed before him. *Only one more.*

As the sunlight crest the top of the Charlemagne Hotel & Resort, Smillie skidded to a stop at the side entrance. His morning seemed unusually quiet with just him entering the hotel. Normally, other employees were arriving at the same time.

Walking into the lobby, he searched for the manager who was usually at the front desk.

Where is he?

No guests were mulling about. Where was the concierge? He was always planted by the side desk. Not wanting to be late for school, he would just leave the cookies on the counter with a note. From the corner of his eye, he noticed something. Someone was lying on the floor by the concierge station.

"Smillie, run!" the manager yelled from behind the desk.

The sound of a gun firing made Smillie drop his mother's boxes. Cookies spread across the marbled floor. A man held up a rifle and smiled as he picked up a cookie. He took a bite and nodded.

Grabbing his side, Smillie frowned. His white, school shirt was now streaked with red. "Manager, manager, you okay?"

The man moved and groaned. "Smillie, I told you to run."

"They went for the cookies," Smillie said, gasping.

"Your mother's cookies are from Heaven. A place I don't wish to see just yet." He coughed. "Is the military outside?"

"Don't know. I entered through the side door."

As the manager closed his eyes, Smillie took in a deep breath and closed his.

The man sitting next to Smillie smiled. From the top branches of the large tree, he could see far out in every direction. Although, there was nothing but a light mist.

"Try this." The stranger handed him a round, shiny cookie. "You'll like it."

"If it's as delicious as the last dozen I just ate, I'll know I'm in Heaven."

"I was saving the best for last."

Smillie's mouth glowed from the bite. "Yum. I've never tasted anything like this."

"One of a kind. Just like you, Smillie."

"Is that my name?'

"Yes, Smillie Sanjeev. Now walk with me."

"On what?"

"The clouds. I am Michael."

CHAPTER 13

11:31 p.m., November 13th

Matéo Hayden went by the nickname of Té. At sixteen, he loved music – every beat – every note. Writing ballads since before he could remember, his thoughts always returned to the relaxing melody of his latest masterpiece.

Now was the time for comfort. After placing the earphones over his head, he smiled and whispered, "Hmmm … hmmm … that's it … sharp beat." His body swayed to the tune as he sang. "Who would have thought, we'd meet this way … me liking you, you giggling at me. I could have sworn, you were my destiny. Who would have thought it took eternity …"

Now the bridge

"Stir it up, I lay it down …" As he hummed to finish off the song, he opened his eyes. "Why is it so dark?"

He reached up to take off his ear phones but paused. Nothing was on his head.

"What in the world?"

Steadying himself, he held back his thoughts. He couldn't move. Drifting somewhere between the edge of reality and the fringe of sanity, he sighed. All around him was a hovering twinge of sparkling blackness in a lightless sea. Té closed his eyes before rubbing them a few times.

"Dreaming. I gotta get out of this dream."

Opening his eyes one at a time, the black darkened with a rolling silkiness that hovered somewhere between a touch and a thought. In many ways it reminded him of swimming beneath the rolling waves.

Riptide?

Had he been here before? If he panicked now —

Té pushed his thoughts toward the surface. Feeling himself rising in the direction of the light, he held deeply onto a final hope.

Out in a sec.

As the light brightened, the darkness receded with a violent force that sent chills all through him. He tried to slow down but couldn't. Something was pulling him into the illumination that looked only inches away. He was moving so fast that whatever was pulling him would definitely crush him to death.

I'll get the bends!

An intense warmth surrounded him and a passionate sensation of joy dissolved his fear. His thoughts, his longings, his desires also dissolved as he entered the light. He was somewhere he had never been before. The light, so bright and warm, seemed to draw him in. He reached out and his emotions grew deeper and stronger.

"I want this!"

As his soul merged with his maker, Té left his cardinal world and the darkness behind.

Té's sister was part of an all-girl band. In Puerto Rico, she was known as *Pinky* and so were her partners. Buzzing the sides of his head, she left the top long. With the tips now a bright pink, she laughed and stood back.

"You have a man bun, now." She laughed again. "Maybe, I should say, *boy bun*."

Another band member stepped up and shook her head. Her pink hair flowed past her shoulders, reminding Té of a basket of flowers.

"Looks like you're part of the band now. Do you like it?"

He nodded. "I'm more of a man than that loser boyfriend of yours, Pinky, who believes he's your manager."

Pinky frowned. "Nicky got us the gig we're playing tonight."

"If he shows," Té said, admiring his hair in the mirror.

"He'll show." Pinky smiled. "Have a surprise for you." She glanced at the other two members who were polishing their nails a hot, shade of pink.

"What?" Té looked at his sister.

"You'll have to wait. We gotta get going." She handed him the car keys and smiled.

They finally arrived at Old San Juan's shanty town, and Té had wondered if their rickety van would make it. The smoke from the tailpipe flew out faster than the wheels turned across the broken pavement.

Pinky stared at the buildings. "Nicky said Club La Perla should be just around this corner."

"Is he already there?" Té asked. "Need help setting up?"

"That's why I brought you, little brother."

The others giggled.

"Don't worry," Pinky said. "He'll be here."

Té frowned.

After helping the band set up, Té glanced at the makeshift stage and searched for Nicky, their *manager*.

Not here yet.

Té leaned against a wall and waited. As more people jammed into the club, the more he looked for the *manager*. He tapped his foot as he listened to their kickin' dance songs.

Pinky mouthed over to Té, "Here's your surprise."

He listened as the lead guitarist strummed a familiar melody.

"This next song is very special to me," Pinky said, standing straight and winking at him. "It was written by my brother, Matèo …"

The music rose and his sister danced around.

"Stir it up!" she yelled into the microphone. "I lay it down. You make my life upside down … baby, I love you. Baby, I need you. Baby, I breathe you …"

It was his song. As dancing couples cozied together on the crowded dance floor, Té filled with pride.

"Té!" Nicky yelled, approaching the stage through the crowd. "Give me a hand." Nicky stood a few feet away, holding out his arms. "Push 'em back. They're getting too close!"

"When my song's over," Té yelled back.

"No, now!" Nicky yelled louder, taking a step toward him.

Té's eyes widened when flames suddenly ran up the dirty and torn curtains. Several people screamed as smoke filled the room. The dancers ran for the only entrance. A waitress dropped her tray and beer slid across the floor. Té's heart pounded. He jumped onto the stage, reaching for Pinky's hand.

"Let's go!" Té screamed.

The other band members followed through the billows of smoke. Té smelled burning hair and pushed harder on the panicking crowd, pulling Pinky with him. As they moved closer to the only exit, they were shoved back by a bottle neck of arms and legs fighting to find a way out.

"Where's Nicky?" Pinky screamed.

"Not taking care of you," Té replied, coughing.

Smoke and flames raised up around them. Té shoved Pinky and her band members through the shuffling bodies toward the exit.

He sat cross-legged on the white light and sighed. His eyes searched along the golden beams and when he glanced at his legs, he chuckled. *What am I wearing?*

An incredible sound that seemed to create an unearthly melody filled his ears. "Not quite Heaven but close," a soft voice said. "Their hymns … a work in progress."

"Who's there?" Té asked.

A hand appeared through the golden beams. "Allow me to help you to your feet."

Té shook his head. "You can hear my thoughts?"

"Welcome, Té … walk with me?"

"I'm who?"

"You're Matéo Sebastian Hayden, but you prefer Té."

"Are you sure? I'd remember that name. Where am I? Who are you?"

"Michael. The name's Michael, and you are on the band that surrounds Heaven."

"I'm where?"

"As I said, please walk with me."

They strolled down the path, and Té's eyes scanned the golden hue that surrounded them. No plants or grass or sidewalks. Just a bright light that seemed to flow on forever. A large and colorful tree appeared in the distance, and Té kept his eyes focused on it.

"Please, may I have your signature?" Michael held out his tablet.

Té touched the blank board and blinked as his name appeared. He glanced at Michael. "I guess I really am this Matèo *Té* Sebastian person."

"Then it is complete," Michael whispered.

"What's complete?"

"Come." Michael glanced up and smiled. "Let's meet everyone."

As they approached, a flying cherub glowing a bright pink hovered under the radiant leaves.

"Is that an angel? Are we all angels?" Té asked, glancing behind him. "I don't see my wings."

"Everyone," Michael said, "this is Té."

"Nice to meet you, Té. I'm Em." She smiled, running her fingers through her hair.

Té nodded. "Hi."

Rosie hovered behind Em, glaring at Té.

"I'm Aleia." Aleia waved.

"Hi," Té said.

Colton stepped forward. "Colton."

Té replied, "Wow, you are tall."

Colton grinned. "Helps sometimes."

Michael continued the introductions and pointed to each StarWriter. "This is Yutu and Milos."

Yutu and Milos nodded.

"And Landon … Smillie."

They waved.

"And Shoupi, Keekee, and Jenni."

Leaning against the tree, Jenni waved. "Hi, Té."

Shoupi nodded and Keekee glanced down at her feet.

"Hey!" Rosie flew forward. "You forgot me."

"Not at all," Michael replied. "I saved the best for last. This is Rosie."

"Wings?" Té's eyes widened.

"Bet you wish you had 'em." Rosie snickered.

"I do," Milos replied.

"Rosie. Be nice," Em said, stepping closer to Té. "He just got here and is not used to you yet."

"Why is she all pink?" Té asked.

"It was a bribe," Em replied and shrugged.

Frowning, Rosie whispered loudly into Aleia's ear. "She likes 'im."

"You think?" Aleia replied.

Michael cleared his throat. "StarWriters … your apprenticeship begins. An eternal journey that starts with a visit to Director Ja Crof who is waiting for you." Michael pointed at an ancient-looking stone façade building that resembled a fortress that sat high on the top of a tall mountain. The clouds hugging the distant ridge gave off a metallic glow as if lit from within.

"Where did that mountain come from?" Rosie asked.

"Your training begins," a female voice whispered.

"Follow the water," Michael said.

Landon glanced around. "What water?"

"Don't keep her waiting. You don't want to fall on her bad side." Michael nodded before vanishing.

"Where'd he go?" Té asked.

Em scrunched her shoulders. "He does that all the time. You'll get used to it."

Landon raised his hand. "I think we should get going."

"Which way should we go?" Smillie asked. "Don't see any water. Everything looks the same. All I see are those clouds and this tree."

Still leaning against the trunk, Jenni frowned. "Landon, who died and left you boss? Wait! We're already dead." She laughed and stepped between Em and Té.

"I'm really dead?" Keekee's tears fell.

Landon shook his head. "She's just trying to get us moving. Michael said not to keep the director waiting."

"He also said to follow the water. I see no water," Jenni stated. "I see nothing but clouds. Lots of colors, but still just clouds. And those mountains way over there."

"What's up with her?" Aleia asked.

Em shrugged.

"I think she's mad." Rosie giggled as she darted between Aleia and Em. "I think the clouds are pretty."

"Sounds like she's mad," Té replied, looking confused. "I wonder what she's angry about?"

Jenni stopped walking and stared at her feet.

"What's up?" Landon asked, hurrying to catch up.

"There's water here," Jenni yelled back. "You gotta see this! Oh my, blue light everywhere!" A river of shimmering teal ran across her feet, flowing into a deep valley and toward a ridge of dark mountains. Above the golden peaks, blue rays of various hue lit the sky. The tall trees gave the place an eerie but protective feel.

Jenni shivered.

"It's beautiful," Aleia said, stepping up. "And there's the fortress."

"Wow," Keekee added, wiping her nose. "But how do we get up there?"

Yutu stopped next to Jenni. His eyes darted across the growing landscape of blues and greens and reds, and colors he had no names for. He knelt and grabbed a handful of sand. "It's purple?" He sniffed. "Smells like sand." He tossed it into the water. "And it sounds like sand."

"We should not keep the director waiting," Landon said again, walking into the dark forest.

Em looked at Keekee who kept her head down. "Keekee, you okay?"

"I hate this outfit!" Keekee whined. "It's itchy."

Shoupi grabbed her hand and led her to the others. "It's really a lovely robe, and Michael did say it was special."

"I hate it." Keekee walked, slapping her sandals against the water.

"Look how beautiful this river is, "Shoupi said, smiling. "I've never seen anything this colorful before. It's a perfect blue."

"I hate my robe," Keekee said again.

Rosie rolled her eyes. "Oh, brother." She hovered between Em and Aleia.

Té walked behind them, keeping silent.

Em paused and waited for him to catch up. "Hey," she whispered. "We all arrived at pretty much the same time."

Té sighed. "I'm confused."

Rosie giggled. "Té is funny."

Em giggled. "Confused? Now that is funny. After all, we're dead."

Aleia kept her gaze forward. "We're getting closer."

"Em?" Té asked. "When did you get here?"

"I was first and —"

"Excuse me?" Rosie yelled. "I was first."

"Rosie, I was trying to say that you and I arrived at the same time."

"Oh, no! I was first." She stomped her foot in the air.

Em whispered, "Michael said we got here at the same time. Rosie's sensitive about being first."

"I can *hear* you," Rosie whined.

"You're lucky," Té replied. "You have a good sense of things."

"I'll help you. I mean … with *me* being first and you last."

"Yuck," Rosie spit out a raspberry sound.

"I wonder what our training as StarWriters will be like?" Té asked.

"Look!" Aleia yelled and pointed.

The others stopped.

"We're at the fortress!" Aleia stated. "Look at this place."

"How did we get here so fast?" Té asked.

"Makes no sense," Keekee added. "We were hiking up that path, and then … pow, we're here!"

The fortress appeared to be nothing but crumbling stone with a banner tacked to the medieval-looking, oak doors.

StarWriters

For it Is Written In The Stars

Welcome forthcoming StarWriters

Elite Apprenticeship Program

StarWriter Director Ja Crof

The small group stepped up to the lit board and read off their names:

~ Emika 'Em' Siobhan Iverson ~

~ Aleia Vis Jones ~

~ Rosie & Lyon ~

~ Landon John Griffin Orly ~

~ Yutu Woo ~

~ Shoupi Mem ~

~ Milos 'Devos' Devosky ~

~ Jennifer 'Jenni' Simone Ramirez ~

~ Keekee Nara ~

~ Colton James McMighty ~

~ Smillie Sanjeev ~

~ Matèo 'Té' Sebastian Hayden ~

"Now what do we do?" Smillie asked.

Landon shrugged. "Maybe we need to enter by the order of our names?"

Em stepped forward, and the others followed in the order that their names appeared on the board. Standing in the crumbling fortress that was situated on the band that surrounded Heaven, their hearts pounded and their minds whirled. They were after all, the StarWriters or so they were told.

for it is written in the stars

The Training

CHAPTER 14

Director Crof's vision pierced through the stone walls. Studying each apprentices' gait as they marched, she mentally took note of their mindsets.

"Easy … easy … handful …" – Ja Crof chuckled. "Know-it-all … troubled … schemer …" – she sighed before continuing – "… a delight … a dreamer …" – she took in a deep breath and held it for a few moments – "… d-r-a-m-a q-u-e-e-n!" – she laughed – "… easy … easy … wishful thinker." She sighed. "This group is going to be a handful."

Ja Crof kept her gaze on the approaching StarWriters.

"They don't have a clue. I hate working with a fresh group of apprentices."

Would these few be harboring good or evil inside their hearts and mind? Always the cynic and feeling suspicious, she watched as they entered one at a time through the double oak doors. She closed her eyes and whispered, "You chose *me* as the StarWriters' director." She bowed her head and sighed. "Why?"

Releasing the grip on the dusty drapes, she stood back, allowing her mind to wander. Her reflection that hung on the far wall grabbed her attention. Walking over to the broken and tarnished mirror, she allowed her eyes to study her short, reddish hair. She reached up and smoothed out the pieces that refused to stay in place. Pulling on a slender bow that held the cream-colored linen shirt around her shoulders, she frowned. Her brown, baggy pants faded, and she scratched her now naked leg.

"This will never do."

Ja Crof thought about the graduating class she released only moments before and nodded. They had been with her for almost two hundred years, which meant, she must adjust for the passage of time.

Raising her hand and allowing it to flow gently through the air, she whispered, "Motherly, yet youthful. Yes, yes."

The red hair and boyish appearance melted and Ja Crof now gazed upon a perky, younger-looking woman with choppy, light-brown hair.

"Needs something."

Again, she waved her hand and blonde highlights glowed between her darker strands. The rugged nose faded and a fresh, perky one appeared.

"I need a little color …"

Dark brown eyes blended and swirled until they turned a sparkling green. She smiled and her lips lightened and puffed, just a little.

"I'll miss that red hair," she whispered.

Blinking a few times, the linen shirt dissolved into a black t-shirt. Black jeans appeared, fitting tightly to her stately hips. Motorcycle-type boots replaced the brown slippers.

"I look good," she said. "Should I replace my horse with a motorcycle?" She thought for a moment before shaking her head. "No … keep the horse."

The names and faces of the incoming apprentices filled her view. She smiled. Would they someday warm her heart as the last group had? Standing a little more rigid, she again studied her outfit. Feeling self-assured, she aimed for the lobby. Her stiff, new boots echoed as she walked. The darkened halls gave her comfort and strength, reminding her of her *human* existence. She thought again about the graduating class. They seemed to have taken longer to learn than the previous ones. Now she wondered if it was something she had failed to do. Standing at the top of the old, wooden stairs, she glanced down at the small and scattered group. Each seemed to be concentrating on something that only their minds could explain. Looking up at the ceiling, she allowed her gaze to penetrate through the roof. Searching the heavens, she paused when her eyes fixated upon *Him*.

His quick wink and nod filled her with hope and anticipation.

"I'll do my best," she whispered.

Taking in a deeper breath, she again studied the newcomers. Their fear and wonderment could be sensed from where she stood. Remembering how it felt to feel helpless, she nodded and said, "Welcome!" Ja Crof took the steps two at a time. Her boots making a thud as she landed in the lobby, missing the last step by only an inch.

The frightened group froze and stared at her.

"Something wrong?" Ja Crof asked, crossing her arms across her chest.

The group shook their heads.

"Good, then to the next room. Through that door." Ja Crof pointed. "Em, Rosie, Lyon, you three first."

"Nice to meet you," Em said, giving a little wave.

"Emika," Ja Crof replied, motioning to the timid girl who seemed to be loitering at the rear of the group. "It is such a lovely name."

Rosie flew up to Ja Crof. "How did you know about Lyon? I have him hidden."

"I know everything, Rosie," Ja Crof replied. "I have eyes everywhere."

Em grabbed Rosie by the foot. "C'mon. Director said to go this way." She dragged the flying baby through the air.

"Hey!" Rosie protested. "You'll wake Lyon."

Ja Crof chuckled. "Gonna be a handful."

Aleia stepped forward.

"Welcome, Aleia. Don't worry, you will not trip and embarrass yourself."

You're reading my thoughts? Aleia asked from inside her mind.

"Unless I turn it off," Ja Crof replied. "Please, join your partners."

"Thank you." Aleia nodded.

"Landon Orly," Ja Crof stated. "Like the wavy, red top."

"Thank you, Director Crof," Landon replied, brushing his hair back with his hand.

Yutu Woo stepped up next. "Good day."

Taking a step back, Ja Crof nodded. "Welcome, Yutu."

Shoupi Mem gawked at the decaying ceiling before whispering, "Hello …"

"It's a mess up there. I have it that way for a purpose. May I shake your hand?" Ja Crof asked.

Shoupi smiled and shook the woman's hand.

Maybe someday, I'll say I knew you when. Ja Crof gave Shoupi a little nudge. "Milos … welcome."

Milos glared at her. "Okay … thank you."

Ja Crof scratched her nose. "Is it crooked again?

Milos shook his head and entered the room.

"Hello, Jenni." Ja Crof laughed. "And welcome."

"Nice to meet yah."

"Just follow everyone else."

"Thanks," Jenni replied, walking through the door.

Ja Crof snickered. *We'll keep you away from moving vehicles.* "Keekee Nara," she said, holding out a tissue.

"I hate the way I look in this. And these sandals!" Keekee grabbed the tissue and blew. "Why can't I wear what you're wearing?"

"Because you can't," Ja Crof replied. "You'll learn to love it. The robe, the belt, and the sandals." She motioned her to the door.

Colton stepped up, towering over her. "Hi." His voice was gruff and low.

She pointed at his robe. "Glad Michael stretched that outfit a little."

"My sandals." Colton pointed to his feet.

"Of course." Ja Crof nodded and chuckled at how his toes hung over by several inches. "Grow!"

Colton's sandals stretched and soon encased his extra large feet.

"Better?" she asked.

"Thank you." He smiled.

Ja Crof nodded and waved for the next young man.

"Nice to meet you, Director Crof," Smillie replied.

"Nice to meet you too, Té Hayden," Ja Crof said, pointing at his head. "Like the do and pink tips."

"Thank you," he replied, looking up. "Wow!"

"Can you hear them?" Ja Crof asked, glancing up.

Several hundred feet above the small group of StarWriters, a choir of angels swirled – their operatic voices in full glory. The sound lingered as each apprentice passed. But none could place their eyes upon the glorious sight.

"Sounds unbelievable," Té said.

"Good to know that you can hear 'em. Not many can."

Em leaned over and whispered to Aleia. "Where are we?" Em stood in the middle of the room, allowing her eyes to explore the strangeness that surrounded her. "Four walls of glass with an …" She stepped up to a clear wall, trying to see through. "An ocean? There's water out there. And fish? Aleia, come see."

"I'm good," Aleia said, shaking her head, not moving from the center of the room.

Em sighed and walked back over to her. "Really?" She glanced up and searched for any lights or a ceiling but saw only puffy white clouds. "Ah, come on!" Taking a step, she paused as her sandals filled with sand. Reaching down, she grabbed a handful and allowed the grains to fall through her fingers. "Purple sand for a floor? What is this place?"

Aleia frowned. "Looks like an aquarium."

Rosie flew up panting. "Check out the cute fish." She darted over and pushed her nose against the glass and shrieked. "I love it! I want 'em. Oooh, look at that pretty pink one."

Landon stepped up and chuckled. "Hope this glass holds."

"I see orange and rainbow and look there's … oh, the rainbow one … it's staring back at me. Ahhh, it's so cute." Rosie squealed again. "Aleia, Em, Landon, look! I think they like me. Hey fishy, fishy." Rosie tapped the glass.

"Don't do that," Landon whined.

Rosie turned and sighed. "Why not? I like the fishies."

"If that glass breaks, we'll all drown," Landon replied. "I'd rather *not* drown. Is this where we're going to train?"

Em and Aleia shrugged and shook their heads.

"I've never seen a square fish before," Landon said, not leaving his spot next to Aleia. "Just the round kind. Hey, Rosie, I think they're *following* you."

Rosie giggled. "They're playing with me."

"Nah, they're hungry …" Landon laughed.

"Ugh!" Rosie darted across the room.

Yutu entered. His eyes locked onto the dark ocean walls. As he walked, his face remained blank as if he was in some kind of a trance. Pausing near Rosie, he stood silently.

"Is Yutu okay?" Em asked.

"I think he's as afraid as I am," Aleia replied.

"Why are you afraid?"

"Oh, I don't know. Maybe it's because I'm standing in the middle of an ocean inside a glass box, and I don't know if it'll hold or not. And I'm wondering how far I'll have to swim to survive. Cuz I can't swim!"

"We're in the castle, remember?" Em shook her head. "So, it can't be real."

Em searched the small group for Té. Not seeing him, she kept her eyes on the door. She sighed as Shoupi entered next, holding the door for Milos and Jenni.

"Wow!" Jenni glanced around. "This room is wild. How can this be?"

Milos stepped up to Yutu and patted him on the back. "You okay?"

Yutu didn't reply.

"What's with you?" Jenni stood next to Yutu and held her arms across her chest. "Did a rat just crawl up your butt or something?"

Yutu shrugged but didn't respond.

Keekee entered, blowing her nose.

"Where is he?" Em whispered.

"Who?" Aleia asked.

"Nothing," Em replied, keeping her gaze on the door.

"I tried waiting for you, Keekee." Shoupi smiled. "This place is kinda weird. Are you okay?"

"No, I'm not okay. Don't like this sheet I'm wearing, and I don't like this room." Keekee blew her nose again.

Shoupi hugged Keekee and sighed. "Everything'll be okay. You'll see." As she tried to comfort her new friend, her eyes remained fixed on the large fish swimming only a few feet away.

Jenni muttered, "Cry baby."

Colton and Smillie entered. Colton's tall stature next to Smillie's shortness gave Em a reason to giggle. She turned and covered her mouth.

"Are those fish?" Smillie stepped up to Rosie and tapped the glass.

"Landon said they're hungry, and I'm their next meal." Rosie squinted at Landon and frowned.

Smillie laughed. "Nah, they don't even look hungry."

"Rosie!" Landon yelled. "Check out that big one with the sharp, white teeth!" Landon laughed again. "Yum!"

Té entered with his eyes staring into the clouds.

Why is he smiling? Em waved at Té but his gaze remained on the total whiteness that hovered above them. *Is he humming?*

Ja Crof liked the soft clicking that her black boots made against the cracked marble floor. Running her arms down the sides of her pants, she laughed. In the room behind the door, she knew she would find the small group of mesmerized StarWriters. Some afraid and some excited. She laughed again.

"Next time, there'll be no glass," Ja Crof whispered to herself as she opened the door, stepping inside. "If everyone would find their seats. Except for you, Rosie. You may hover. Welcome new arrivals, to the invisible band that surrounds Heaven. You will be training as StarWriters –"

Keekee raised her hand.

Ja Crof glared at the girl who interrupted her memorized speech. "Yes?"

"There's no seats."

"Sit on the purple sand. It won't hurt you … *yet*." Ja Crof glanced around at the others. "Lesson number one. You must remember that everything is alive … as are you, as are they …" Ja Crof waved her arms through the air, smiling up at the white, puffy clouds.

The small group's eyes darted around, each holding a blank expression.

Keekee raised her hand again. "There –"

"Blankets? You need no blankets. Your uniform acts as proper covering." Ja Crof shook her head as she sat gracefully on the purple sand. "Now, you see. I'm perfectly fine."

The small group stood frozen in place with their mouths gaped open.

"Sit!" Ja Crof yelled.

The new recruits dropped to their knees as Rosie hovered next to Em and Aleia.

Ja Crof pointed at Rosie. "I will place you into groups. Rosie, you and Em and Aleia." She waved her hand at the three. "You'll champion together as one. Landon and Yutu and Keekee." She pointed again. "Shoupi, Smillie, and Té." Ja Crof nodded and smiled. "Is something wrong, Em? Something with your group?"

Em shook her head.

"Good, I want my newbies happy. So, that leaves Milos, Jenni, and Colton. Please sit with your groups and spread apart so I can tell who is in which group."

No one moved.

Ja Crof stood and dusted herself off. Shaking her head, she spoke slowly and methodically. "If I must give my orders twice, we will be here a very long time. If I must yell at you after every order, I will not be happy. It is not smart to not make me happy." Narrowing her eyes, she yelled, "Move!"

The sand swirled around their legs as they hurried to make it into their small groups.

Ja Crof nodded at her new crew. "That wasn't so difficult now was it?"

A tapping sound made the group turn and stare at an orange fish with tiger stripes. Using its fins, it again tapped against the glass.

Ja Crof swiped her finger back and forth and shook her head. "Not yet, my little friend. Patience."

The fish pushed itself through the glass and swam around the startled group. Em sighed and laughed. Keekee shrieked and covered her face with her tissue. Colton chuckled and patted Yutu on the back. Landon laughed, tapping on Smillie's shoulder. Té shook his head and smiled, and Milos sat higher up on his knees.

Ja Crof sighed and crossed her arms. "That's why I didn't want you in here yet, Misha. Now shoo!" She motioned for the fish to return to the water. "Later."

Misha gave a huffing sound before squeezing herself back through the glass. A loud squeak echoed as her tail splashed water on the sand.

"How did it do that? Milos asked.

"Lesson number two. *Things* evolve." Ja Crof raised her hands into the air.

Keekee raised her hand again.

"Take a mental note and you will never forget," Ja Crof said, sternly as she sat back down on the purple sand.

"But –" Keekee said.

"Oh my, must I explain everything? You will remember. When needed, it will appear before you."

"How?" Aleia whispered over to Em. "That makes no sense."

"Look," Em replied as words floated a few inches in front of her. "I just made a mental note that I can make mental notes."

Ja Crof glared at the group and sighed. "You are wasting my time."

"She hears everything," Rosie whispered as she hovered above the girls.

"StarWriters," Ja Crof stated, "you have much to learn. Take note of your questions, and I will answer them later."

"Do what?" Colton asked.

"Store them in your head," Em said, pointing at her words.

Colton shook his head, looking confused.

The rest of the group seemed to be writing with their fingers. Chuckling, Landon shook his hand as if refilling it with ink.

"You are the elites," Ja Crof said, holding back a laugh. "The chosen few. Which is why you are here." She sighed as more words appeared before their eyes. "Stop it!"

"You said –" Keekee stated.

Ja Crof raised her hand, taking a deeper breath and letting it out slowly. "You are here to deliver *His Plan*. Every living creature has a purpose. *His* purpose." Ja Crof stood. "Now, questions?"

Keekee coughed but remained silent.

Té raised his hand.

"Yes, Té."

"And where are we delivering this plan to? And how do we get there?"

"You deliver *The Plan* to the stars in the universe." Ja Crof huffed.

"How?" Jenni asked.

"Rhopalocera Machina. Now follow me."

"Ropamaha what?" Té said, trying to repeat the words but jumbling them up instead.

Jenni laughed as they hurried to walk behind her. "Butterfly machines."

"Butterflies?" Em whispered.

Several other hands darted up as Ja Crof stepped toward the back of the room. "The universe is at your disposal." Ja Crof stopped and turned so suddenly that Em and Jenni bumped into her. "One area is *forbidden*!" Ja Crof tapped the glass.

"Forbidden?" Em whispered.

Three pastel colored fish, one blue, one pink and one yellow, pushed their heads through the glass. Misha shoved past, swimming around the small group. The three smaller ones hovered near Ja Crof.

Smillie chuckled and reached out but Misha was too quick.

Rosie chased Misha around before giving up. "Flying isn't as easy as you think," she said, trying to catch her breath.

"I wish I could fly," Milos said. "You're so free."

A loud thud echoed and the sand vibrated. The group turned as a large, purple fish tried to squeeze through the glass before becoming stuck half-way into the room. Ja Crof grabbed the large creature by its gills and pulled. After several tugs, the fish fell to the sand and gazed up at the frightened students.

"I told you!" Ja Crof yelled. "You're too big to fly, Tomas. You'll hurt yourself."

Raising up on his fins, Tomas wobbled toward the apprentices as if wanting to be petted.

The students rushed over to touch and enjoy the attention of the odd creature.

Ja Crof stood back and shook her head. *Who will be the first to disobey my orders?* There was always one or two who would enter the forbidden area, and they were always the first to be devoured.

"Apprentices," Ja Crof said, pointing to the door by which they entered. "Your training for the moment shall end. Follow the water's edge. It will lead you to the Wondrous Tree. Michael will meet you there."

Landon stepped up. "Director Crof, where is this water? How do we find it?"

"Yeah," Jenni stated, smirking. "Last time, the water just appeared from out of nowhere. Then after a while, the forests and mountains just popped in. Before we were about to give up, this place was right in front of us."

Ja Crof opened the door and waved her hand through the air. "Then … *here* is your *out of nowhere* somewhere."

Landon and Em peeked out the door and gawked. The wavy water was tapping against the purple, sandy shore. In the distance, the mountains towered high above, surrounded by blue lights.

Em frowned. "But - t … where did the lobby go?"

"Lesson number three …," Ja Crof replied, "… or was that two?" Ja Crof laughed. "Never can remember those stupid numbers. Anyway, always remember that we are in the stealth and *things* evolve."

"*Things* evolve," Em repeated.

"Go!" Ja Crof motioned them forward. "Stick together."

"Number three," Jenni said. "It's rule number three."

"I wasn't asking you." Ja Crof waved for the small group to leave.

After the last apprentice walked outside, Ja Crof slammed the door and the windows rattled. Having Michael ordering her to send the apprentices to the Wondrous Tree was an interruption she didn't need right now. There was just too much work to do. She stepped onto the cracked marble and climbed the rotting stairs back to her office. She glanced up, searching for an answer though nothing came back to her.

"Have I not done everything you've asked?"

No response. The room remained quiet.

What can Michael say to her new group that she could not? Why was he always intervening in her affairs? Yes, a couple of trainings ago things went a little awry, although through no fault of her own. And yes, it was Michael who corrected the problem. But that was ages ago.

Michael had carefully nurtured and prepared her for the role of director. Would she ever walk where he walked? Would she ever experience all that he had experienced?

"When will you fully trust in me?"

No response from the maker. The wispy clouds remained wispy. Ja Crof slammed her office door and again the windows rattled.

Rosie kept her eyes on the groups in front of her. It seemed that Em and Aleia were increasing their pace to keep up. Fluttering at Em's side, she tried to hear what the small groups were whispering about.

"You're going to love it." Landon chuckled. "You'll see."

"My robe feels like a ball and chain." Keekee yanked her robe a few times. "Augh!"

Yutu glared at Keekee each time she tugged. "Keep doing that and you'll stretch the material."

Keekee shrugged.

"Boring …" Rosie whispered, before flying back to Em and Aleia.

"What's boring?" Aleia asked.

"Keekee and her, *I hate my clothes,* complaint. She's always whining about the same thing."

"At least I can't *hear* her," Aleia said.

Em remained quiet.

Rosie huffed. "Hello? Why aren't you paying attention to me. Hello? Em?"

"Did you say something, Rosie?" Em asked.

"What are you looking at?" Rosie flew in front of Em and followed her gaze. "Why don't you just go and talk to him? He's what you want isn't it?"

Em waved Rosie away. "What are you talking about?"

"You keep looking at Té like you want him or something."

Aleia laughed. "I think *someone's* jealous?" Aleia raised her 'brows at Em.

"I'm *not* jealous," Rosie replied. "Everyone's talking about *something* except for us. Em is just staring at Té as if he's going to do something *special.*"

"I'm just thinking, Rosie," Em said. "Can't I do that without offending you?"

Rosie shrugged and frowned. She flew to the last group and hovered above Milos. Jenni and Colton were talking about the sparkling, blue sky and was wondering what it was made of.

"Rosie!" Em shouted. "Please come back. I'm sorry. You're supposed to stay with our group."

Colton waved and laughed. "She won't go far."

"Let her go, "Aleia said, pulling on Em's arm. "She'll be back. All babies come back."

"You know about babies? I mean, is she *really* a baby or an adult in baby form?"

Aleia shrugged and giggled. "Don't really know. But she acts like a baby."

"A baby that can hear everything," Em stated. "A baby that can read thoughts. She's such a handful. Michael asked me to foster her. Thought he was talking about a dog. Nope, it was Rosie."

"We can foster her together. Two *are* stronger than one."

After Aleia's word, *together*, Rosie aimed for her group. As she swerved around Landon and Yutu, Landon reached up to grab her foot.

"I'll get you next time," Landon shouted.

Rosie turned and stuck out her tongue. She hovered next to Em and crossed her arms. "You think you're all that!" Again she stuck out her tongue. Not wanting to hear an excuse, she aimed for the last group. She hovered behind Milos believing it was as good a place as any for a good pout. "Am I invisible or something?" Rosie asked.

Jenni pointed. "Look. There's the tree. It just appeared out of thin air."

"Odd how things just come and go around here," Colton added.

"Should we run?" Milos asked.

"I am invisible," Rosie whispered.

The tree's branches were growing higher, piercing through the clouds as if making a ladder to the heavens. Rosie urged her wings to move as she flew back to her small group.

Em sighed. "Sorry, Rosie. What do you want to talk about?"

"Lyon," she said, pouting.

"What about Lyon?" Em asked. "Where is he anyway?" Em looked around. "Why don't you introduce him to the others? I bet they'd love to meet him."

Rosie smiled and pulled out the pink rabbit from under her robe. It looked as if he was sleeping. "Wake up, Lyon. Say, hello."

The others congregated under the tree and waited. Rosie flew down and held out the small rabbit.

"He's cute," Shoupi said, petting him.

"We've met," Landon said, finding a place to sit.

Rosie, happy being the center of attention, seemed to be glowing. "Lyon wants to give everyone a warm pretzel. It's his favorite food."

The rabbit's ears perked and his nose sniffed several times. Phasing in slowly on the lower branches, crisscrossed dough appeared. As they watched, the dough baked and turned a light golden brown.

"What in the world?" Jenni asked, stepping closer. "They smell fresh." She reached for one. "Ow! They're hot."

"No duh, dummy," Rosie said, smiling. "They were just baked!"

"Cooked on a tree branch?" Jenni asked, sucking on her burnt fingers. "Impossible."

"Impossible or not, I can see why these are Lyon's favorite." Landon squeezed the remaining piece into his mouth.

Licking his fingers, Milos sneered. "How come Rosie gets a pet and we don't?"

"A bribe," Michael stated. "Lyon was a bribe."

"Don't do that!" Jenni yelled. "You scared the crap out of me!"

"Sorry," Michael replied with a sly grin. "I can see that Rosie has put Lyon's ability to good use." He chose a pretzel from the branch and took a bite. "Nice treat. Thank you, Lyon."

The rabbit's eyes widened and his nose twitched.

"Yes. Thank you, Rosie," Shoupi said, grinning. "And Lyon." She nodded to the rabbit.

The others nodded too.

"You're quite welcome," Rosie replied, taking a bow.

"Well, that certainly cheered you up." Aleia said to Rosie, winking at Em.

Em shook her head.

"Now that you've had a little something to eat, I must introduce you to *His Plan* room." Michael clapped his hands.

With the sound just passing through their ears, the twelve apprentices found themselves standing in an endless room. Rows upon rows of desks ran out in all directions – forward, backward, to the left, to the right, and straight up and straight down. A young person, not much older than they were, sat at each desk. They all looked as if they were concentrating heavily on what looked like golden scrolls. Wearing similar outfits, but a white robe with a brown rope for a belt, they seemed content – almost happy.

Hanging clocks were blinking *good* or *evil*. A constant change for every event. The minute hand kept flipping from three to nine, almost as if on cue.

"We are invisible to them," Michael whispered. "We will not disturb their work."

"What're they doing?" Yutu asked.

"They have to wear the ugly robes too?" Keekee asked.

Michael chuckled. "They gather *His Plan*." He pointed to the chutes that seemed to reach straight into Heaven.

Scroll after scroll fell into glowing baskets that seemed to be floating on an invisible conveyer belt. Once filled, a worker carried the baskets to the other workers who tied a gold string around the scroll before dropping it into the air where it vanished.

"I thought this was a *happy* place," Jenni said. "They don't look happy." She pointed to a girl who seemed to be moving as if in a trance.

"This is their choice," Michael replied. "We do not question another's definition of happiness."

"Definition of happiness?" Aleia repeated.

Rosie's wings fluttered a little louder as she moved closer to Michael.

"So much to learn," Michael said. "To bilocate is to be in two places at the same time."

Smillie laughed. "Two places at once?"

"Bi- what?" Keekee asked.

"Bilocate," Em repeated. "That's cool. Can we bilocate?"

Landon stepped forward. "Can we do that too?"

"No you may not," Michael replied. He ignored their pouts and grunts of dissatisfaction. "You must commit to the mission. Mostly for your own good." He held out his hands. "You will deliver each scroll. An individual plan for every soul. Every star in Heaven. A soul and a star exist as one. You will deliver *His Plan* as assigned. A blueprint of the forevermore."

Straining to hear, Em asked, "Our stars are up there too?"

"Yes," Michael replied.

"And we'll be doing this on Rhopalocera Machina?" Jenni asked.

"That is correct. Your groups will each be assigned a transport," Michael replied. "Let us move on to the next."

Staring down the vast row upon row of desks and workers, Té motioned to the other members of his group – Shoupi and Smillie. "Where does this place end?" he asked.

"Lots of souls around here." Shoupi giggled. "We'll be delivering forever."

"On butterfly machines," Smillie added. "Whatever those are."

"Everything seems to be quite literal here," Shoupi said. "Maybe they'll look like butterflies?"

As he followed behind Michael, Té glanced at a girl with waist-length, beige hair and extra-large, blue eyes. He watched as she removed a basket, replacing it with an empty one. The girl looked up and winked at him. Té stepped back and bumped into Smillie. "Did you just see that?"

"See what?"

"That girl." Té pointed.

"What about her?" Smillie asked.

"She winked at me."

"Maybe you *wanted* her to wink at you. You heard Michael. They can't see us. Only *we* can see *them*."

"Yeah, maybe you're right. Just my imagination." Té glanced back and frowned.

He wasn't confused. The girl had smiled and waved. Just before his eternity dissolved around him, an uptick in the clock's handle grabbed his attention. Was it moving slightly to the left toward evil? Was the girl waving to him or at him?

CHAPTER 16

Michael stood amidst the apprentices inside a small but amazing valley. Plush gardens magically appeared with exotic flowers in all shapes and colors that seemed to intensify the longer they stared – the colors deepening and becoming richer. Even the black flowers seemed to be glowing.

"Huh …?" Smillie said, tripping over a large *thing*.

Té grabbed his arm. "Careful, that's a beautiful … uh, beautiful orange polka-dotted … bush."

"Thanks, man." Smillie laughed. "I'd hate to kill a polka-dot … bush." He laughed again.

Té nodded.

The flowers and bushes seemed to flow out to eternity. The blooms were wild and shaped in a dimension greater than 3-D. Most of the colors they had no names for.

"Rosie!" Em shouted. "I've never seen square flowers before."

"They're more than just square," Rosie replied. "Look from over here."

Em ran to Rosie's side and gasped. Hundred of corners decorated the flowers that seemed to be enfolding upon themselves. "Is this even possible? 4-D?"

Rosie shrugged. "Maybe 10-D?"

"What's that smell?" Shoupi sniffed at a patch of black flowers that were opening and closing. "Hey, over here. These things are dancing."

"Never saw a black flower before," Aleia said. "Don't think I'd get too close if I were you. Remember, *things* evolve."

"Might bite yah." Rosie giggled.

Michael clapped and the group turned to him. "Quickly now. They are coming. Stand together in your groups. They will choose you."

"I'm not sure about this," Landon said, reaching out to hold Yutu's and Keekee's hands.

Yutu yanked his arm away and stood behind Keekee. Keekee just smiled and gently squeezed Landon's hand.

"Em," Michael stated, "hold onto Rosie's feet."

"Why?"

"Safer that way," Michael replied and then whistled. "Stand ready."

"Rosie … stop kicking!" Em tried to hold her feet.

"Let me go!" Rosie screamed and yanked away.

A sound that resembled a tornado echoed through the small valley. The ground vibrated and the air stilled. The sky darkened as the sound grew louder.

Rosie shrieked and flew into Em's arms. "Hold me!"

"I gotcha," Em whispered.

Rosie nuzzled her face into Em's neck. "I don't wanna see."

The sky grew darker as the sound deafened their ears. A sweet wind whipped through the valley that seemed to mix their terror with a strange tickling of delight.

"What's that noise?" Té yelled.

"Watch!" Michael replied, holding his hands up to the darkening clouds.

As the blackness slowly enveloped them, the air thickened even more. One at a time, millions upon millions of butterflies gently fluttered down, landing on anything and everything.

"They're gonna eat me!" Rosie screamed as her hair and back filled with vibrating wings.

The small creatures circled around Michael before darting for the apprentices. It was almost as if he was personally greeting each one. A few he whispered to, others he winked at or nodded at, and a few he kissed or petted.

"They're beautiful," Shoupi whispered, holding out her arms. Before a second could be counted, she was covered with flickering colors.

Jenni pointed and several dozen landed on her fingers and hand. She blew and their wings fluttered with colors that seemed to be evaporating, mixing with her essence. "I can sense them!"

Smillie shook his head as thousands of butterflies took flight.

Milos laughed and pointed. "You look like you're wearing a huge —" Before he could finish his sentence, his hand filled with flickering little creatures. "Hey!"

The sky darkened again as the butterflies rose high into the air. The glittering cloud hovered for only a moment before soaring even higher, disappearing from view.

"Some are still here," Yutu said, studying one that was clinging to his hand.

"You have been chosen," Michael said. "Introduce yourselves to your butterfly."

"That was so cool!" Colton shouted, staring at one.

The red monarch bowed and lowered its antennae.

Colton glanced at Jenni and Milos. "Mine looks … trained?"

"I have a blue one." Jenni gasped when the insect winked at her.

"Got a black one on my shoulder," Milos bragged. "Looks like a toughie."

"You can open your eyes now, Rosie," Em said. "They won't hurt you."

Rosie peeked out from her hiding space. "A gold butterfly?" Rosie whispered, staring at the one on Em's arm. "Do I have one?"

"On your shoulder … look." Em pointed.

"Pink! Mine is pink … just like Lyon. It's pink!" Rosie squealed with delight.

Aleia shrugged. "Of course it's pink, what other color would it be? I bet you wished it to be pink. I have a green one."

Rosie frowned. "I didn't wish for anything. I was hiding."

"Place your palms out," Michael said, holding out his hand. "Like this."

Each one held out their hand. A few of the girls giggled. The boys rolled their eyes. As they waited, the little creatures landed on their hands one at a time.

"They're so colorful," Shoupi whispered. "I can almost see through mine. And look, the orange is flowing onto my hand!"

"Same here," Té said. "The blue is almost a liquid."

"You should be in your groups," Michael said.

"We are," Keekee replied.

"Good. Slowly and gently, place your hands together, like this." Michael held out both hands, palms up. "Good, good. Now, reach out and allow your fingers to touch. Make a small circle."

The four groups took a step and raised their hands. After touching their fingertips together, they waited. The three little creatures climbed to the edge of the StarWriters' fingers and shivered. Their wings fluttered, increasing in speed. They were vibrating so fast that they almost became invisible. As the

StarWriters watched, the butterflies combined into one about the size of a football – their colors blending, creating a new fluorescent color without a name.

The girls gasped and smiled. The boys stared and shook their heads. Once fully formed, the large butterflies spread their wings and flew like a bird to Michael. They landed one at a time on his shoulders.

Michael nodded to each butterfly. "Your butterflies matched their essence with your souls. There is now a connection between you. A bond that cannot be broken. A pledge that just might save your spirits from nothingness."

Colton frowned. "Nothingness? No one said anything about nothingness."

"You mean evil?" Aleia asked.

Michael raised his hands, and the butterflies dissolved into flowing beams of bright light.

"Where'd they go?" Aleia asked.

"Your butterflies must transform," Michael replied.

"Transform?" Jenni asked. "Transform into what?"

"We must give the butterflies space. We shall join them shortly. Until then, we shall walk and enjoy the gardens."

"Walk?" Jenni repeated. "And enjoy the gardens? Is he for real?"

"I thought we were gonna shrink and ride them," Aleia stated.

"You would think of something like that," Jenni replied.

As they strolled down the endless path, the bushes and flowers evolved into different colors and varieties.

Té stepped over to Michael's side, trying to match his gait. "Michael," he whispered. "I need to tell you something …you might need to know this."

"You mean about the girl?" Michael asked.

"You know?"

"She winked at you, then smiled and waved," Michael replied. "Her name is Isla."

"But how?" Té furrowed his 'brows. "You said we were invisible. Could the others see us?"

"*Things* evolve," Michael whispered. "*Things* evolve."

"Do we … evolve?"

"Maybe." Michael chuckled. "Something else on your mind?"

"The clocks … the ones marked good or evil …"

"Ah yes, the gauges."

"They moved …" – Té took in a deep breath – "… to the bad side."

Michael didn't respond.

Té frowned. "Was it because of Isla and that she waved at me?"

Michael chuckled. "You did nothing wrong nor did she. The clocks tick to left or right all the time."

"Phew," Té replied. "I was worried."

Michael clapped his hands. "Your winged vessels await. Quickly, now."

Jenni brushed up against Té. "That girl, Isla? She really liked you, yah know."

"You were listening to my *private* conversation with Michael?" Té shook his head.

"You were talking very loud," Jenni replied. "I just happened to hear. In fact, everyone heard. Talk softer next time. It's called whispering."

Té looked around. "Did you see the clocks flip to evil?"

"No …" – Jenni sighed – "… well … maybe."

"Good or evil?" Té asked.

"What about it?" Jenni frowned.

"Michael says they move all the time," Té replied.

"Good to know," Jenni whispered. "I think."

The clouds thickened and the ground softened. Each step felt heavier but then again lighter at the same time.

"What's going on? Em asked. "Where are we?"

"Where did the pretty flowers go?" Rosie asked.

"The ground is gone," Keekee added. "Everything is now white. Is this smoke?" Keekee waved her arms through the air.

"I don't like this," Yutu said.

"Your vessels await," Michael stated.

Rosie clung to Em. "I don't see no vessels. I see only clouds."

"Dissipate," Michael stated.

The clouds parted and a large space opened before them. Glancing up, a bright orange sky hovered above. Glancing down, a blanket of clouds greeted their feet. The air felt cool but not wet.

"Nice," Smillie said.

"Amazing," Yutu stated.

"I still see nothing," Rosie added.

"Appear," Michael said and four transports appeared.

"What are these?" Em asked.

"They don't look *alive*," Jenni said. "They look like machines. Are they made from metal?"

"They are as alive as all of us," Michael said, stepping forward.

"If you say so," Jenni replied.

Four transports that resembled extra-large butterflies sat in front of them. Each a perfect size to accommodate three or four people. They resembled butterflies, but then again, they resembled a small plane. Each had four wings that were the color and shape of their large butterflies that had disappeared into the light. Each plane had four legs, as well as a head, thorax, eyes, and antennae.

Shoupi stepped up to the rainbow one and reached out. The plane turned its head and nodded. "It is alive!" She screamed, taking a step back. "The color is so shimmery. It's beautiful!"

"I think this one is ours," Smillie said.

"You hear that?" Milos asked.

"Hear what?" Jenni replied. "Do you mean the clicking sound."

"I think they're communicating with each other," Milos said, looking to Michael for confirmation.

"Correct," Michael replied. "They communicate through clicks."

Keekee, Landon, and Yutu walked around their orange, red, and black transport.

"What do you mean?" Keekee asked. "Do you know what they're saying?"

Michael chuckled. "They are talking about you."

"Picking on you, Landon," Keekee added with a laugh.

"Probably on you." Landon snickered.

Keekee pounded her foot into soft clouds. "Making fun of the stupid bed sheet I'm wearing?"

Ja Crof suddenly appeared with her arms crossed. "Another breech in the wall, Eternity Present."

Michael nodded. "Speed up the training."

Ja Crof frowned.

Michael vanished but his words lingered. "Be safe."

Ja Crof nodded again and glared into the orange sky. It seemed richer and darker than usual. Almost fire-like and she didn't like what she was looking at. It was an omen.

CHAPTER 17

Standing across from the vessels, Ja Crof furrowed her 'brows and crossed her arms. She glared at the flare-like flames twirling in the orange sky. The sky was turning creepy and worrisome. Michael's words lingered, *'Speed up the training.'* She cringed at the thought of moving up her schedule. It would require time and a delicate touch, introducing her apprentices to the joys of StarWriting – and the hazards.

The twelve apprentices circled their transports, tapping on the mechanical wings and playfully joking on each other.

Certainly not ready … further breeches in Eternity Present. Ja Crof lamented at the thought. She compared these twelve to her previous recruits. *Those groups were StarWriters! Young warrior-type men and women from a different time and place. They were almost ready at the start to accept their duties and what was needed from them. This ragtag bunch …*

Ja Crof glanced up at the passing clouds and nodded. Michael's face appeared, which felt somewhat reassuring. "I know I have a job to do. I'll do my best," she whispered. *Speed up the training.*

She watched as the small group ran around and played. Her nerves were on edge, and their gallivanting wasn't helping.

How would she ever have them ready in time? There was so much to learn.

"Apprentices!" Ja Crof clapped her hands, and the apprentices stopped and stared. "Your fourth lesson is upon you. Enter your transports."

The four three-member teams stared at each other before landing their eyes back on her.

"Are we riding on their wings?" Jenni asked.

"I said, enter. Not sit on top." Ja Crof shook her head. "Inside."

"Are they going to eat us?" Keekee asked.

Ja Crof shook her head again and waved her arm through the air. "Open, si vous plait."

"They speak a different language?" Rosie asked.

Aleia scratched her head. "I think it means, please. Don't know how I know, I just do."

The wings fluttered and steam hissed from their undercarriage. A rectangle door slid open and mechanical stairs extended down from under their thoraxes. With the butterflies now as large as airplanes, the stairs seemed to run up forever.

The group stared at each other again and shrugged.

Ja Crof took in a deeper breath. "What are you waiting for? Climb inside."

"Who're you going to train first, Director?" Landon asked, placing a foot on the lower rung.

Yutu and Keekee stood behind him with looks of horror written all over their faces.

Ja Crof did not respond.

Landon stepped back and bowed. "Ladies first."

"I'll wait," Keekee replied.

"Afraid?" Landon asked.

"No," Keekee frowned. "But you first."

"Who cares who goes in first?" Yutu parted them with his arms and stepped up the stairs.

"Let's get into ours." Aleia waved for Em and Rosie to follow.

"I've got the perfect name for our monarch," Em said, stepping up behind Aleia.

Rosie hovered behind Em. "I want to name it Pinky."

Rolling her eyes, Em sighed. "How about Serene? Like in Your Serene Highness."

"Like it," Aleia replied, bouncing on the top step.

"I guess it's okay," Rosie said, lowering her voice.

Aleia entered. "Here we come … Serene … ready or not."

Rosie flew next to Em, shoving her aside.

"Hey, wait your turn," Em said, giggling. "I'm older. Age before beauty."

Rosie huffed. "So what? I got here before you."

"Don't think so," Em replied, trying to get a foothold and grabbing the handrails.

Aleia ducked her head back out and yelled, "This isn't possible!"

"What's not possible?" Rosie asked, flying past Em and entering. "Let me see."

The three entered and stood side by side inside an empty, white room with no corners. The place was oval and large. Em walked around, touching the walls that were smooth and glowing.

"This place is as big as my bedroom," Aleia said. "How high are these ceilings?"

"Not sure," Em replied. "Maybe twenty feet?"

"No windows and no seats. How will we ever steer this thing," Aleia asked, wandering around. "The place is empty."

Rosie flew in circles. As if playing hide and seek, she covered her eyes before moving her hands away.

"Rosie," Em said. "You're awfully quiet all of a sudden. And what *are* you doing?"

"Nothing," Rosie said, soaring through the air, covering her eyes and uncovering them.

"Then we're all in agreement?" Em asked. "There's nothing here but a big, white, oval room?"

Rosie and Aleia nodded.

"What do you think everyone else is looking at?" Em asked. "Nothing?"

Aleia stared at her and frowned. "Michael said that our butterflies took our essence and combined them. Maybe our essence wanted a big, white room." She looked away and sighed. "How *do* we fly this thing?"

"Just heard Em talk about naming their vessel," Shoupi said, glancing at Té. "Rosie wants Pinky but Em likes Serene."

Té tilted his head, "Did you say Pinky?"

"Yes, why? They said they were going with Serene." Shoupi shrugged. "How about naming ours Irid? That's short for Iridescence 'cuz of all the colors."

Té shrugged.

Smillie gave a thumbs up. "I like Irid."

Té chuckled. "But how do we …?"

"What're we supposed to do?" Smillie ran his hand along the white walls.

Shoupi smiled. "It's very quiet in here."

Té leaned over, sticking his head out the door. "Hey, Director?" He glanced around. "Where are you?"

"Looking a little raw?" Ja Crof touched two pink spots on the butterfly's thorax. "There, that should feel better now. By the way, I like your new name. Nice to meet you, Serene."

Serene bowed.

"I must go inside," Ja Crof said. "The teams should be introduced to your evolving compartments by now. I should …"

Another raw spot appeared.

Landon, Yutu, and Keekee ran their fingers through the air.

"I think we're looking at an illusion," Landon said.

Yutu shook his head. "This place is definitely weird."

Colton ducked and climbed the stairs. He counted and when he reached twelve, he stepped inside. "Now, this is more like it." He stretched his arms up. "My butterfly definitely knows me."

Milos sighed.

Colton grinned. "What? I can't be happy that my tallness fits into this thing?"

Milos shrugged.

"There's nothing in here," Jenni said, glancing back out the door. She watched as Té waved and shouted something. "Director Crof?" she yelled. "What're we supposed to do in here?"

Ja Crof sighed loudly. "What do you mean, what are you supposed to do?"

Em stepped onto the stairs and glanced down. "There's nothing in here."

"What do you mean there's nothing in there?" Ja Crof walked over to the stairs and looked up.

"There is *nothing* but a huge, white room," Em replied. "And it *is* empty."

"Empty?" Ja Crof stepped back and glanced up at Serene. "Empty? Really?"

Serene rubbed her antennae together.

Ja Crof turned and placed her hands on her hips. "Playtime over! Reality please, my friends."

"Hey, check this out!" Milos' words echoed around the cloudy tarmac.

Jenni stepped back inside and stood next to Colton who was now speechless. "This is more like it."

Two large viewing windows had appeared on each side of the door. The fiery-orange sky created an odd hue against the shiny metal walls. Three curved, white seats suddenly appeared in the middle of the room. The middle seat had a rather intimidating control panel. A control stick was to one side with a large touch screen. The other two seats were left open.

Jenni grabbed for the handle. "This is more like it. Here we go!"

"Don't touch that!" Ja Crof ordered.

Jenni pulled back her hand and shrugged.

"I will give instructions soon."

Landon chose the seat on the right. He swerved from side to side and glanced up at Ja Crof. He flinched. "I guess you like us best, huh, Director?"

"Actually …" Ja Crof replied, "I'm standing in front of all of you at the same time."

"You're bilocating?" Landon asked.

"No," Ja Crof replied. "Not bilocating. I'm quadding."

"Quadding?" Jenni repeated. "There is no such word!"

Ja Crof sighed. "Take your seats and we'll begin."

The teams settled down and their eyes widened.

"If you have questions, just ask. You'll be able to hear each other as if you were in the same room."

"How is that possible?" Aleia whispered to Em.

Rosie hovered behind and giggled.

"Many things are possible," Ja Crof replied.

Rosie flew into Aleia's arms. "She *hears* everything! I think she's possessed."

"Apprentices!" Ja Crof raised her arms. "It is time for you to carry out *His Plan*. Every living creature that breathes has their life written among the stars. You will carry their scroll and deliver them. Remain inside your assigned quadrants and you'll be just fine."

"Deliver what to where?" Landon asked.

"And how do we know what goes where?" Jenni asked.

Yutu raised his hand. "What's a quadrant?"

"How many scrolls are you talking about?" Milos asked.

Shoupi chimed in, "What do we do once we get the scrolls to the stars?"

Ja Crof took a step back and slapped her hand to her forehead. She sighed and stared at the floor.

"If the monarchs are taking us there …" Em said, raising her hand, "… why do you need us?"

"Stop!" Ja Crof yelled. She took a deep breath and let it out slowly. Raising her eyes to the heavens, she whispered a small prayer. "Lord, help me!" After walking back and forth a few times, she whispered, "*I can do this …*" She took a step forward and said, "these transports are a part of you. So easily you seem to forget. You *are* the StarWriters. You were chosen." She raised her hands and again stared into the heavens. "We are done … for now."

"But we have questions," Em stated.

"We shall return now." Ja Crof waved her arms through the air. "To your butterflyselves."

The butterfly transports dissolved around them as the milky clouds filled their view. Standing together under the wonderous tree, four large butterflies the size of footballs, hovered several feet above their heads. The wind from their wings made everyone's hair sweep around their faces.

"I'm starting to feel dizzy." Landon frowned. "One minute we're here, the next we're over there, then we're back here again."

Ja Crof held up her arms. "Wait for it!"

Serene landed on Aleia's shoulder. The other three chose Colton, Keekee, and Shoupi to rest upon.

"Hello, Irid." Shoupi grinned.

"We're supposed to name them?" Keekee asked.

"We named ours, Serene," Em said. "As in Your Serene Highness."

Rosie frowned. "I wanted Pinky."

Té leaned closer to Rosie and whispered, "Did you say Pinky?"

Rosie nodded.

Em stepped closer to Té and smiled. "Serene."

"You're too much into pink, Rosie." Landon chuckled. "Give it a rest."

Rosie flew closer to Landon and huffed. "I *like* pink, so what's it to yah?"

Em whispered to Té. "She's still angry that we didn't choose Pinky."

"I like the name, Pinky," Té said. "Don't know where I've heard it before."

Ja Crof shook her head. "Rosie! Landon! Enough! You may name your butterflies if you wish. The monarchs might enjoy that. They probably have names for all of you too."

"They do?" Shoupi asked.

The butterflies nodded and fluttered their wings.

Shoupi giggled. "You're tickling my chin, Irid."

Clicking and fluttering their wings, the butterflies sang as they flew into the heart-shaped leaves and disappeared.

"Hey … where're you goin'?" Colton asked. "I wanted to name you Giant."

"After yourself?" Jenni asked, scowling.

"A little selfish with that name?" Milos asked.

"Not really." Colton smiled at his partners. "I was thinking … hmm … Three Giants … you know, to match the three of us? I'm a giant in height, Jenni's a giant in brains, and Milos …"

"I'm giant in everything." Milos chuckled and pointed at himself.

Jenni tilted her head and smiled. "What do you think Milos?"

"I'm cool with it," he replied.

"Let's just call ours T.G.," Jenni said. "Short for Three Giants."

"Okay, T.G. it is," Colton replied. "I like that."

Landon frowned. "We should wait until we get to know its personality better. Then pick a name."

"They're made from our personalities, right?" Yutu asked, furrowing his brow and glaring at Keekee. "I think we should name it Crybaby."

"Hey," Keekee yelped. "Who're you calling –"

"Enough!" Ja Crof yelled. "Stay here and talk. Learn about each other. Enjoy the Wondrous Tree." She vanished, and her words lingered for only a moment – "As you all are."

"That was weird," Jenni said.

"Everything around here is weird," Landon replied.

"What do we do now?" Smillie asked.

"You heard the director," Té said. "We need to talk and learn about each other. Let's sit."

Em sat on the ground and ran her fingers through the tall grass. "This is soft."

Keekee sat next to Em and ran her fingers through the flowing waves. "Yes, it is."

Té sat on the other side of Em and nodded. "Comfy."

Rosie scowled as she hovered over the small group. "Oh brother."

Once everyone was settled down, Em clasped her hands and said, "Who wants to go first?" She looked around. "To talk about themselves."

No one spoke.

"This is definitely getting everyone acquainted!" Rosie said, laughing.

Aleia cleared her throat. "I don't know about anyone else. But … I can't remember anything about where I was before."

Landon wrinkled up his freckled nose.

Scratching her head, Jenni added, "Uh …"

Milos smiled. "I got something." His eyes searched upward. "Not really, never mind."

Rosie poked her toe into Em's shoulder.

"You want to sit on my lap or something?"

"No." Rosie flew into the center. "I remember something."

"What?" Em asked.

"A bright light," Rosie replied.

Em grinned. "We all remember that much."

Rosie frowned and crossed her arms.

"We're making new memories," Landon stated.

Aleia giggled. "I like it this way. No baggage."

"Director Crof did say that we're evolving and learning," Em added. "Let's share something about ourselves. Or something we've learned so far."

Colton stretched out his long legs. "Maybe we're supposed to learn from each other."

"We need to evolve." Shoupi sat up straighter.

Keekee eyed the small group. "Me, first." She frowned. "I hate wearing this thing –"

"Really?" Jenni sighed. "Are we going there again? I'm tired of all the crying."

"No … I just think that maybe because I hate this outfit so much that maybe I can evolve and change it." Keekee frowned. "C'mon! We *all* hate it."

"The director and Michael keep saying it'll be our best friend," Té replied.

"It was my best friend when I first arrived," Milos added. "Rosie knows." He pointed at her.

Rosie giggled. "It was funny."

"How was it your friend?" Té asked.

"I lost my balance and my garment curled itself around a branch and stopped me from falling. I met Rosie when I was upside down."

"Cool," Jenni said.

Staring up at the tree, Smillie added, "When I got here, I remember cookies. I picked them from this tree and Michael handed me one that made my mouth glow. It was really good. Never tasted anything that wonderful."

"How would you know that?" Jenni asked. "If you can't remember what you liked or didn't like before? How can you know now?"

Smillie shrugged. "I just know … maybe I can sense it?"

Keekee jumped up and stood in the center.

Rosie flew back and gasped.

"I'm going to sense it too." Keekee closed her eyes.

Milos rolled his, and Yutu chuckled.

"Shh," Keekee stated. "I need to concentrate. Give me a sec."

Rosie flew up next to her face and stared at her.

Keekee opened her eyes and fell backwards, landing on her butt. "Don't do that! You scared me."

"Sorry," Rosie replied. "Just wanted to tell yah something." Rosie flew down and whispered into Keekee's ear.

Em stood and offered Keekee her hand. "You okay?"

"I guess." She stared at Rosie.

"Since we're all sharing our hearts with each other, why don't you share with us what you just shared with Keekee?" Em glared at Rosie.

Rosie lowered her eyes and sighed. "Fine." She frowned. "I said, sorry and that nothing was going to happen."

"How do you know that?" Keekee asked, staring at her.

"Umm … because … I saw you fall backwards and your clothes didn't change."

Stepping up to Rosie, Em pointed her finger. "I knew it! I knew something was up with you back with Serene."

"What'd you mean?" Té asked. "What did Rosie do?"

"Go ahead, Rosie. Tell 'em." Em placed her hands on her hips.

Rosie flew behind Aleia and frowned. "No, you tell 'em."

Em sighed. "Rosie can see the future. You saw the inside of our butterfly evolve. Didn't you? That's why you kept covering your eyes."

Poking her head out from behind Aleia, Rosie nodded.

"The baby evolved!" Keekee screamed. "Why can't I?" Her lips twisted into a frown.

"I was here first," Rosie whispered.

Sitting down, Em nodded. "We arrived at the same time, and I haven't evolved yet."

"No." Rosie shook her head. "I was first."

"Whatever, Rosie." Em smirked.

"Sounds like you two need a time-out." Landon chuckled. "Let's climb up this tree and check it out."

"Good idea," Aleia replied. "Change of venue."

Rosie smiled. "I'll lead the way. I've been almost to the top."

"Right behind you," Colton yelled.

"Then, 'cuz you can see ahead and into the future …" Em mused, "… let us know if anything is going to fall on our heads."

Aleia grinned.

Standing behind Em, Té chuckled. "You heard Milos. Our robes will save us."

Gazing at Té, Em giggled like a school girl. "Do we really want to know? I'd rather not fall."

"Maybe. Let's go. Don't want to be last." Aleia searched upward, peering beyond the layers of heart-shaped leaves. Grabbing a hold of the bottom branch, Aleia pulled herself up. "This is gonna be fun."

Limbs, too many to count and overflowing with leaves, touched each other as if in prayer. Thick roots, as large as a train, reached out for miles, anchoring the exotic giant as it soared toward the heavens. Its arms stretched out and into the clouds as if trying to reach the feet of God. Seeing the top was impossible, and therefore, no one tried. A mixture of spruce and eucalyptus filled the air as the heart-shaped leaves glittered in the warm light.

"Let's go." Té said to Em. "After you."

Humming, Té watched as Em reached and pulled herself onto several limbs. "See you reachin' high-er, higher you go," he sang.

"You sound great." Em reached for the next branch.

"Really?" Té asked. "Want to hear more?" He smiled at her.

"You have a great voice," Em yelled back. "Wish I could sing."

Té braced his body against the trunk. He lunged for a branch, and his sandal slipped.

"Té. You really want to go there?" a British sounding voice echoed through his ears.

Losing his footing, Té fell. "Ugh …" He landed on his back, trying to catch his breath. He opened his eyes and stared into the blue eyes that were framed with the wispy, taffy colored hair.

She smiled at him and offered a hand. "You okay?"

Feeling flushed, he nodded and stared at his clothing. *Oh well robe, you certainly weren't my friend today. More like an enemy.*

"*Uhh* …" Té rested on his back and moaned. He blinked up at the wondrous tree.

"Here, take my hand." The British girl stared at him with a slight twinkle in her eyes.

Feeling flushed, he smiled and glanced around. *We're alone? I hope?*

"You okay?" she asked.

Touching the silky warmth of her hand, his heart raced following behind a million thoughts … some good, some bad. "It's you." His eyes widened. "The girl from *His Plan* room." Locking his eyes onto hers, so piercing blue, his hands shook. "Isla, what're you doing here?"

She stepped back and gasped. "How do you know my name?"

"How did you know mine?"

"I have ways." She smiled.

"Then … so do I." He straightened his robe and stared down at his feet. His thoughts raced and now he wasn't sure what he was feeling. He had wanted to meet her, but then again, not exactly in this way. "What're *you* doing *here*?"

She smiled. "I wanted to meet you. Remember, you smiled at me in *His Plan* room."

Té tilted his head and frowned. He thought back and distinctly remembered that she had smiled at him first. And he even asked if he was in trouble for it. "Wait a minute ... I believe *you* smiled at *me* first. Cuz, I asked about it."

"Asked about what?"

"If I was in trouble, cuz you smiled at me."

"Were you?"

Té shook his head.

"Didn't think so." Isla chuckled. "I smiled purely out of shock. When your group appeared from out of nowhere with Michael, I was startled." She sat on a large root.

Té joined her." You know Michael?"

"*Everybody* knows Michael." She waved her arms through the air.

"No one was supposed to see us. How could you?"

"Don't have a clue. Why was I the only one?" Her eyes widened. "Maybe us seeing each other was meant to be." She moved closer.

"Then, I'm glad to meet you, Isla."

"Really?"

"Yeah." He scrunched his 'brows. "How'd you find me?"

"I'm bilocating."

"Hey, yeah, I know about bilocating." He laughed. "But you didn't answer my question. How did you know where I was?"

"I saw you in *His Plan* room, remember? And ... voila' ..." Isla moved her hand through the air like a magician. "Here, I am."

"I know that you're here, and I remember seeing you in that room ... but ... how did *you* get *here*?"

"Just thought about you," she whispered.

"Thought about me?"

She nodded. "I heard you singing." She giggled. "Then I watched you miss a branch and —"

"And ...?"

"And ... I wished to be here ... with you."

Té grinned, edging his legs closer to hers. *I like you. I like the way you speak.* "Is that what bilocating is? Thinking of someone and then just being there?"

Isla pulled on some grass. "What do you mean?"

"How did you do it? How do all the others in *His Plan* room do it? Michael said that you either choose to bilocate or stay in the ecstatic mode?"

She giggled. "It's called ecstatic trance. We can choose to work with *His* scrolls fully engaged or bilocate to one of seven villages." She rolled her eyes. "Well, one of them you have to be invited. But at the others, if we choose bilocate, our other self remains behind ... in a trance."

He stared into her eyes, feeling bewildered. "What does it feel like to be in this ... trance?"

Isla smiled. "You feel an incredible sense of overwhelming joy. Like nothing you've ever felt before. It's so meditative. So peaceful."

"Then, why would you choose to go to a village?"

"They're fun." Isla grinned. "We praise *Him* with others. We sing together." Her eyes glanced upward. "Although, I can name some workers who enjoy being fully engaged —"

"Sing? You sing with others?"

"You like to sing, Té?"

"I think so." He frowned. "Wish I could bilocate like you just did."

"You mean you haven't tried yet?" Isla glared at him. "You … a big shot *StarWriter*. Inside this exclusive club and you haven't bilocated yet?" She laughed, slapping her thigh.

Té felt his cheeks redden. "You find this funny?"

"Hysterical. Don't you? Here you are, one of the elite and you –"

"What do you mean by *elite* or *club*? I'm just an apprentice."

"C'mon, don't tell me you haven't heard of … the *elite*. And it's only … what … a dozen of you or so at a time?" She rolled her eyes. "Sounds like a private club to me. One that nobody can *just* join. You are hand-picked out of trillions. You're in the StarWriters Club whether you like it or not."

He looked down at the grass. "Yeah, but … guess I never thought of it that way."

Isla placed her fingers under his chin, forcing him to gaze into her eyes. "I'm just your average *worker bee* collecting and collating scrolls … for *you*." She turned away and pulled up more grass.

"No, Isla, that's not what Michael said. He never called you a worker bee. He said that we all have a purpose here. That we are all important." Té shrugged. "How were you chosen?"

Isla tilted her head. "Chosen?"

"For *His Plan* room."

She looked up at the clouds and sighed. "I just … arrived. I wasn't given a choice. I was told that I had some issues to deal with. Must be my penance."

"Maybe that's why you can bilocate or choose ecstatic trance … and I can't."

"Well … not anywhere," she whispered. "Cuz, I shouldn't be here with you now …"

"This is so much fun," Aleia said as she pulled herself onto the next branch. "The leaves are changing the higher we go. Look!" She glanced at Em and pointed. "Tiger-shaped with orange stripes."

"Cool." Em caught up to her and glanced down. *Where is he?*

Aleia sighed. "We're really behind now cuz I don't see anyone above us anymore."

"Nor behind us."

"What'd you mean?"

"I was talking to Té but I can't see him anymore. Hope he's okay."

"I'm sure he's fine." Aleia grabbed at another branch.

Em sighed. "What if he can't climb? What if he fell?"

Aleia laughed. "*Somebody* has a crush." She sang out the words. "Rosie was right."

Em twisted her lips. "Sorry … but you're both wrong. I don't have a crush. Yes, I like him, but strictly from a StarWriters point of view."

Aleia frowned. "Yeah, right. Keep telling yourself that." She grabbed the next limb. "We gotta catch up to the others."

"You go ahead. I'm going back to look for Té."

"Suit yourself. I'll cover for you when I get to the *tippy top* as Rosie would say."

Em looked around for an opening. "This is weird, these leaves seem thicker."

"To slow you down," a whispering voice said.

Em raised her head. "Rosie! Is that you foolin' with me?" She yelled in the direction of the voice. "Cut it out, it's not funny."

When no one replied, Em decided that it was just her imagination. The leaves crinkled from somewhere below and she stopped climbing. "Té?" she yelled.

A hand reached up through the leaves and grabbed the branch she was standing on.

"Té? That you? Are you okay?"

"I'm fine." Té stepped onto the thick branch and smiled.

Em frowned. "What happened?"

"Just fell a little behind, thinking."

"Thinking? Thinking 'bout what?"

"Keep going," he said. "I'll be right behind you. Talk when we get to the top."

"Promise?" she asked.

"Promise."

Glancing up at the endless twinkling stars embodied in the darkness, Isla held onto an empty basket. Her robe swayed as she walked as if it was listening to music. Standing in line behind the other workers, she sighed at the massive, hollow chutes that reached high into the heavens. Ancient scrolls continuously dropped into the baskets rotating on a circling platform. Placing her empty basket on the platform, she grabbed a full one. She turned and aimed for the back of the room. It looked endless but moved toward her as if she was standing on a conveyor belt. Her eyes twinkled and her smile curled at the edges. Still in the ecstatic trance, Isla's body jolted forward when her spirit returned. Her smile intensified.

That little meeting was nice and right on schedule.

Placing the basket on a desk, she glanced up at the floating clocks. Isla ignored the handles as they shifted a few clicks to the left.

"Hey, Grayson." She winked at a handsome, blonde-haired teen sitting behind a desk.

His eyes met hers for only a moment before glancing away. "Oh, hi, Isla." He worked diligently on tying the sparkly, gold ribbon around a scroll. He dropped the scroll and it vanished just before hitting the expanding clouds that were billowing out below his feet.

After another worker passed, she whispered, "Got wonderful news, brother. Just met up with that guy I told you about."

"What guy?" Grayson whispered.

"Remember?" She frowned. "The one I told you about that just appeared from out of nowhere?"

He took in a deep breath. "Barely. You know it's not permitted." He whispered back with a similar British accent.

"What do you mean?" She pouted.

"You know what I mean," he whispered a little louder. "Once you've chosen to trance, you can't keep going in and out like that. You'll be reported."

"You wouldn't tattle on me? Would you?" She smiled.

"If you keep doing this, I may have to. I told you. I want to be promoted to shift leader."

Isla frowned again. "But this is our only opportunity with the new StarWriters. We couldn't get anywhere with the other ones."

"What makes you think these will be any different?"

She leaned in a little closer. "They're *just* apprentices. Very pliable like young stalk. They don't know much … not yet." Raising her 'brows, she added, "And get this, they can't bilocate yet."

"He told you that?"

"He told me a lot."

"Yeah? And I'm sure he'll go running to the director or Michael and tell them about you bilocating to the forbidden territory."

"Nah. He promised he'd keep it *our* secret."

"How can you trust 'im?"

Isla puckered her lips. "We kissed on it …"

Glancing at the floating clocks, Isla shrugged as the handles ticked a little farther to the left and a tad closer to *evil*.

CHAPTER 19

Em rested against a think branch. Hearing voices from above, she waited for Té.

Té watched her through the various-shaped leaves. "Why'd you stop? Keep moving."

"Almost there. I can hear 'em. You good?" she asked, trying to decipher his mood. He had promised they would talk.

Climbing onto her branch, his eyes searched upward. "Had a little height failure back there, that's all."

"Thought that maybe you stopped to look at the tiger-shaped leaves or something." Em giggled. "They're cute."

"Didn't see any. Just shiny suns."

"These leaves are changing shape. Glad you got your climbing legs back."

"Yeah, me too." Té pointed up. "After you."

She stepped onto a thicker branch. "Ouch! Where did this thing come from?"

"What's wrong?"

"Stubbed my toe." What she had thought was another limb was actually a wooden step. Several more appeared as the clouds swirled around them. "Careful, steps are forming from out of thin air."

"What's forming out of thin air?" Té asked.

"Steps! There're steps up here."

"Stairs … in a tree?" Té asked.

"Yeah," she said. "They're leading up. I guess we should use them."

Té looked up and smiled. "Easier than these branches."

Popping her head above the wispy clouds, she spotted Aleia. "Sorry we're –"

"You're late," Ja Crof stated with her hands resting on her hips, "'bout time you two showed up. Take a seat."

Wispy clouds were scattered above, below, and to their sides. A billowing mist gathered at their feet as they stepped toward the director. Twelve ordinary school desks were sitting front to back in rollercoaster-style. The chairs were attached to the desks and the others were already seated, waiting patiently.

A classroom on top of a tree? Em glanced around and shrugged. *What's next?*

"Hurry along," Ja Crof said. "Find a seat."

The last two seats to this strange arrangement were empty. In the front, Rosie's chair was also empty. She was held by Aleia who was sitting at the second desk.

"What took you so long?" Rosie asked as they walked by.

Raising her 'brows, Aleia's eyes first fell on Té and then on Em. She grinned.

Em hurried her pace to the back.

Ja Crof cleared her throat. "Quickly now."

Em tugged on her robe and sat. Té smiled as he took the seat behind her.

"Great, we're all here. Let's begin." Spreading out her arms, Ja Crof nodded. "No talking. I want *complete* silence. Stay in your seats. Be alert. And remember … I will be with you the entire time."

Em glanced at Té and frowned. "What does that mean?"

He shrugged.

The clouds thickened and a strong wind howled. A gush of air, feeling larger than a house, slammed under the desks before dying down.

Em grabbed onto her chair, holding back a scream.

Rosie flew out of Aleia's arms and into Em's.

"Rosie?" Em asked. "You okay?"

"Lyon's afraid," Rosie screamed.

"Quiet and observe!" Ja Crof ordered.

Heat billowed out from above. Em glanced up and orange and red flames danced and shimmered as grotesque faces with hollow, black eyes glared down. The creatures drooled and their tongues reached out searching for something to eat. Cries of pain and fear echoed from their rotting throats.

"Don't hold your breath," Ja Crof said in a calm and normal voice as she studied each one. "I said breathe! Breathe in deeply."

Landon took in a deep breath.

"Good, Landon," Ja Crof said. "Air, water, wind, fire, and now … embrace the shadows."

The clouds darkened and the air thickened. Many black shadows emerged from between the swallows of rolling mist. The ghost-like creatures darted between the desks and circled around the apprentices. The air cooled and ice formed on the chairs. The creatures moaned and cried out for help. Floating near the frightened group, they whispered their names.

Aleia …

Jenni …

Colton …

Smillie …

Em …

Té ...
Landon ...
Rosie ...
Yutu ...
Shoupi ...
Keekee ...
Milos ...

Landon rested his head on his desk. Yutu, Milos, and Té covered their eyes. Rosie grabbed onto Em's neck. Em's robe grew in length, forming a protective cover around the two.

"Rosie?" Em whispered. "What did you do?"

"Nothing," Rosie said, pulling tighter on Em's neck.

"Maybe it's happening to everyone," Em said. She pulled the robe apart and peeked out. "No ... it's just us."

"My eyes are closed," Rosie whispered.

Ja Crof stopped at Jenni's desk. "Why are you smiling?"

"You know why," she stated.

Ja Crof slapped her hands together. "Enough!"

The dark spirits vanished.

"No one was in danger," she said, looking directly at Jenni. "Go ahead. Tell them."

Jenni stood and smiled. "It was fake. Just an illusion."

"Lesson number five," Ja Crof said, motioning for Jenni to sit back down. "Don't believe everything you see."

"Rosie, help me get this fabric off us." Em said, struggling with the tightened robe.

Ja Crof's voice echoed. "Back to normal!"

Em's robe instantly re-shaped just around her. "What was that?"

"You are evolving," Ja Crof replied. "Behold, onward and upward!"

"Not again." Rosie flew into Aleia's arms and screamed.

A seat materialized at the front and Ja Crof sat. "Lock and load!"

The sound of metal gears engaging filled their ears. With a strong jerk, the desks bolted together before shooting straight up and into the clouds.

"Wha-t-t-t!" Landon screamed.

"I said to hold on," Ja Crof yelled. "Relax and enjoy the ride. You will not fall."

As the thread of school desks spiraled down, the clouds thickened around the StarWriters. Various villages and quaint houses and farms decorated the mountainside.

"Around us are the seven kingdoms … *Wis, U-ing, Cel, Fort, Knowl, Pi, and LOH.*"

The desk-train rushed across the open fields and flowing streams. Em tried to pull her hair from her eyes, but it kept whipping back across her face.

"Below is the village of *Wis.*" Ja Crof pointed at a countryside village that was tucked into a snowy hillside. "Over there is *U-ing.*" She pointed to a distant dark green area. "A wild jungle filled with every animal ever created by *Him.*"

"Wow," Milos sighed, "do bilocators play with the tigers and lions."

"Yes, they do." Ja Crof laughed. "There is only love here."

"Look over there," Keekee yelled. "What's that?"

Skyscrapers that rose up through the clouds decorated the horizon. Behind the large city, a long chain of colorful islands stretched out into the foreverness, giving Em the sensation of feeling very small and insignificant.

"That is *Cel* and *Fort,*" Ja Crof yelled.

"Is this what Heaven looks like?" Shoupi asked.

"Of course not," Ja Crof replied.

"Have you been to Heaven?" Aleia asked.

Ja Crof did not answer.

"Will you take us there?" Milos asked.

Again, Ja Crof did not answer.

A strong jolt and the desks hovered above one of the skyscrapers.

Keekee screamed and covered her eyes.

The ride lurched and Ja Crof pointed at the large ocean. "One village is down there and is named *Knowl*."

"Underwater?" Landon asked.

"And the last one is up there." Ja Crof pointed to a distance twinkling amongst the stars. "That is *Pi*."

"Wait, that is only six," Jenni stated. "Where is the seventh?"

"*LOH* is with *Him*," Ja Crof stated.

"*LOH?*" Jenni repeated.

"*Love of Him*," Ja Crof replied, staring into the distance. It was as if she was contemplating something. "An invisible village that never remains in one place."

Shoupi giggled. "I would love to visit *LOH*."

"StarWriters, there is still much to learn," Ja Crof stated.

Té raised his hand and asked, "Director Crof, why do you call us the StarWriters?"

"What else would I call you but what you are?"

"Why are we considered the elites?" Té asked.

Ja Crof sighed. "Discuss with Michael if you are looking for clarification."

Té glanced at Em and frowned.

"Milos!" Colton yelled. "No!"

Milos leaned over and released his grip.

Keekee screamed. "Help him, he's falling!"

Ja Crof sighed, and the desk coaster lurched aiming for Milos.

"Milos … what are you doing?" Landon yelled.

Milos reached out his arms and laughed. "I'm flying!"

"Help him!" Jenni ordered.

"He'll die!" Colton yelled.

"He is already dead." Ja Crof stated. "Milos! Control your robe."

Milos stretched out his arms and laughed again.

"Lesson number six," Ja Crof said. "Your robe is part of your essence. Learn to use it."

Milos floated into his seat and nodded to Colton.

Colton hit him in the arm.

"That was cool!" Milos yelled. "I evolved!"

"I think we willed Milos to safety," Té whispered.

Em frowned. "What?"

"I think the director wanted us to be afraid so we would use our minds to help him," Té replied.

"You are correct," Ja Crof's voice echoed around them.

"Are you nuts?" Em asked. "That scared me to death!"

"You will figure it out," Ja Crof replied.

"That woman has incredible hearing," Em whispered.

Té frowned. "I think I can hear things too. And that may not be a good thing"

"I can't see anything," Rosie yelled, hugging in closer to Aleia.

The coaster train dove into a blackness that swallowed up the light. Keekee screamed and Em covered her eyes.

"Embrace the void," Ja Crof stated.

"What are those whispers?" Yutu asked.

Landon shouted, "What's that disgusting smell?"

"Sulfur," Ja Crof replied. "The sounds and smells of pure evil."

"Why are we here?" Landon asked.

"So you will recognize and know how to avoid it." Ja Crof sighed.

The coaster soared out of the dark shadows and into the billowing clouds. Below, a small village with gingerbread-style cottages decorated the snow-covered hills.

"That place looks like fun," Rosie said. "Can we go there?"

Ja Crof raised her hand. "No! StarWriters are not allowed."

Rosie stuck out her tongue.

"Welcome to *Wis,*" Ja Crof said. "One of the places where bilocators spend their days of relaxation and enjoying each other's company. We can take a closer look since we are invisible to them."

They flew past a group that were mulling about. Té leaned over and Em grabbed his robe.

"Gotcha!" Em said, pulling him toward her. "You don't want to fall out like Milos, do you?"

"Uh, no," he replied. "Thanks."

"See something interesting?" she asked.

"Not really. Just wanted to get a look at … uh, looks like they're having fun."

"We'll take a spin-a-bout *Wis* before heading over to *U-ing,*" Ja Crof said. "The jungle beasts are marvelous to watch. Then we'll visit *Cel, Fort, Knowl,* and finally *Pi.*

"Where's *Pi?*" Jenni asked.

"Among the stars." Ja Crof replied.

Ja Crof studied the small group congregating below on the streets lined with gas lanterns. She recognized a few, two in particular caught her attention. One of the older girls twirled her wheat-colored hair around her finger before leaning against a tall, young man with jet, black hair. They laughed along with the others. Nothing seemed to be important to them at the moment.

Michael had pointed out the young man to Ja Crof as Beck and the girl as *Isla*.

CHAPTER 20

Charming gingerbread-style houses glistened under the unworldly light that seemed to be shining from out of nowhere. The rays streamed from the heavens as if mimicking a waterfall. Overly tall evergreens dotted the snowy hillsides that gently cradled the village. Inside the small town of *Wis*, each home was of a different color and trailed through the gas lamps that lined the streets. Signs displayed welcoming words such as *Come In – Enjoy a Relaxing Stimulant* seemed inviting. Various young bilocators were crossing the cobbled streets before entering the various structures to unwind or visit with friends.

"Anyone interested in ice gliding the hills?" a girl asked Beck and Isla.

Isla shook her head. "Sorry, we have plans." She grabbed his arm, pulling him away. "Beck …" she whispered, "… need to talk. Got some info."

"Fine." Beck sighed and shrugged at the girl with long, blonde hair who was slapping her hands on her hips and frowning.

Beck and Isla entered one of the shops and glanced around.

"What's on the menu in this place?" Isla asked.

"They have a great variety of sinctures," he replied.

"'Giving you the *sense* of a valuable experience,'" Isla stated. "Yes, I've heard the jingles too. Okay, I'm up for one. I need that *real* experience that I can't seem to get around here." Isla slipped into a booth decorated with what looked like picket fences.

As Beck scooted across from her, thunder rumbled and a light rain sprinkled down around them. The drops danced across the table tops, before vanishing on the second bounce. The tables, floor, and patrons however remained dry.

"Speaking of your valuable experience …" Beck whispered, pulling a small vial from his robe. "I was able to get something to help you with that."

"For real?" Isla glared at the powdery iridescence that gleamed between his fingers.

"How else are you going to get *that* experience. It's forbidden. Remember?"

Isla thought of her brother, Grayson, and how he had slapped her hand earlier. "Just tired of hearing how things are forbidden around here." She frowned. "It's getting old. It's as if *He* doesn't want us to be happy."

"I believe *He* does. Just that certain memories were taken from us."

"Such as," she tilted her head.

"Not sure … bad memories?"

She shrugged. "It feels like I'm walking in circles. I *want* to remember." Isla placed her hand on top of his. "But I do have some info we can use."

"Info from where?" Beck glanced around and sighed.

"That apprentice … one of the new StarWriters."

"Let me guess. You bilocated into the secured territory, *their* territory." His gaze swayed as if he were judging her. He leaned over and squeezed her hand and whispered, "What did I tell you about that? It'll put you … us on the radar."

She pulled her hand away and frowned. "You told me –"

A young woman materialized at the side of their table, carrying a tray of goblets filled with a variety of colorful liquids. She smiled. "What will *we* be enjoying today? Are you pleased with the hour's ambience?"

Isla laughed and glanced up. She blinked as the drops bounced against her face before vanishing. "It's cozy." Isla pointed to the goblets. "What do the colors mean again?"

The waitress smiled and nodded. "Blue for tranquility, red strength, green freshness, yellow creativity –"

Beck held up his hand and laughed. "We will both have tranquility, please."

The waitress smiled and placed a blue goblet in front of each. "If you require anything else, just let me know."

Isla watched as the young woman walked to the next booth. "Beck," she whispered, leaning a little closer. "They can't bilocate!"

"What? Everyone can," Beck replied.

Isla shook her head. "He said they had to remain intact!"

"Whatever that means. What's this StarWriter's name, and why is he so forthcoming with all this information?" Beck shrugged.

Isla shivered. "I do know he doesn't like being called an elite or being part of a private club."

"What's his name?"

"Té and he's very talkative. I think he'll serve us well."

"How'd you get him to talk?"

Isla caressed the back of Beck's hand. "Long story. I'll explain after the experience."

Beck glanced around and waited as two girls slid into a booth. He slowly poured half of the powdery mixture into Isla's goblet. The white glitter swirled through the blue sincture, turning the mixture to a sullen orange.

He smirked and nodded to her goblet as if egging her on. "Dream on …"

She glanced into the goblet and smiled. Snatching the vial from Beck's grip, she poured the remaining powder into her drink. Using her finger, she stirred until the liquid radiated.

"I don't think that's such a good idea." Beck scowled.

"I don't need a bad memory," she whispered, glancing around. "I need a *nightmare.*"

Beck held her hand and squeezed. "I can't help if you get into trouble. Understand?"

"I know," she whispered. "I'll be on my own."

Releasing his grip, Beck sat back and stared up at the falling rain.

Isla touched the goblet to her lips. She looked at him as she gulped down the shining brew. She wiped her mouth, placing the empty goblet on the table. Slipping deeper into the curve of the booth, she rested her head against the hard wood.

"Good luck," he whispered. "I'll be here waiting for you, sipping on my blue sincture and enjoying a few wonderful memories they pre-programmed for us."

"I'll be back," she whispered as she closed her eyes. The thunder boomed from above, and the gentle raindrops slowly lulled her to sleep.

Isla stared at the large Victorian home that was tucked amidst a sea of greenery deep inside an English countryside. Her heart felt warm as if she was finally returning home.

She closed her eyes and took in a deep breath. When she opened them, she was sitting alone on her bed inside the room she once shared with her ten-year-old sister, Melissa. A girl she had nick-named, Messy. Everyone, including Grayson, teased the child so much about her messes that the name simply stuck.

The other bed was a jumbled heap of covers, splattered with various clothing. Isla laughed. "Wonderful and messy."

Scattered papers and school books covered most of the wooden floor. Isla stood and picked up a colorful, orange tabby.

"I had forgotten all about you." She cooed and petted the animal that she cuddled in her arms. She kissed the tabby and smiled. "Whiskers … I'm so happy to see you."

Whiskers purred and pushed his nose close to hers.

She placed the cat on the bed and walked over to the window. Peeking out through the sheer curtains, she smiled.

Messy and Grayson were kicking a soccer ball back and forth across the green lawn that was speckled with brown leaves. Their light blonde hair waved in the breeze as they ran.

Grayson yelled, "Kick the ball with the *side* of your foot … kick it hard."

Messy ran toward the ball and slipped, landing on the ground. She threw her head back and laughed.

"I thought you were going to take this seriously. You'll never make the team if you don't."

"I'll try again," Messy yelled. "Don't give up on me so easy."

Offering her his hand, Messy jumped up, glancing at their bedroom window. "Isla!" she yelled. "Come join us."

Isla took a step back, stumbling over a doll's head. Startled, she fell and landed hard on the wooden floor. Her heart raced. *What's going on? How could she see me?* Her thoughts swirled. Nobody was supposed to be able to see her – not inside a memory. It was forbidden. *The powder!* Beck's powder must be doubling the affects.

Whiskers pried open the bedroom door and darted out. A wafting of vanilla and cinnamon filled her with a childhood yearning.

"Isla!" a voice yelled from the bottom of the stairs. "What is all that ruckus?"

"Mum?" she whispered. Isla's hands shook and her stomach cringed. "Nothing," she yelled back. "Just tripped over Messy's things."

"Will that child ever learn to pick up her clothes? I give up. You must work on her habits, Isla, and do come down. I baked your favorite biscuits."

Grabbing onto the top rail, Isla glanced down at her robe and sandals. "Oh no." She took a step back. "I can't be seen like this."

Wanting to search through her closet, she darted into her room. She reached to pull off a sandal and paused. Penny loafers were now on her feet. She wiped her hands on her hips and laughed.

"I'm wearing my favorite, plaid skirt."

She smiled at the familiar red and green lines. The reflection in the hallway mirror grabbed her attention and she admired the view – white-collared, button-down blouse and a green sweater.

"I've always hated this blouse." She shrugged.

"Isla!" her mother yelled again. "Who're you talking to? Come down for biscuits. I'm icing them now."

She always has the best hearing in the house!

Grayson attributed their mother's extraordinary hearing ability to the layout of the rooms. 'She can't have supersonic ears. Can she, Isla?' Grayson often asked when he was caught doing something he wasn't supposed to be doing.

Taking a step on the thick carpet, Isla paused. "Not talking to anybody, Mummy. I'll be right down."

Whiskers ran into the living room and dropped to the floor.

"After you, kitty," Isla said, chuckling.

Her heart pounded as she walked into the kitchen. She held her breath and glanced around. Reliving her memories was forbidden. Bilocating to the StarWriters' training grounds was one thing, but to return home?

She stepped into the kitchen and stared at the floor with the wide, wooden planks. The old appliances filled her with a longing of familiarity. She sniffed and glanced over her mother's shoulder.

"What are you making?"

"Gravy for the roast," her mother replied.

I'm home! She closed her eyes and hummed.

Her mother wore a blue gingham dress and white apron. She concentrated on the steaming liquid bubbling on the large gas stove. Isla glanced at the cuckoo clock. It was close to dinner time. The calendar had a big X on September sixth.

Mum's crossed off Friday already. Then today is Saturday. She always marked the calendar before she went to bed.

The year was 1940. Her dad would return from the military next week. She thought about how they always looked forward to his visits even if it was just a short time. Her childhood memories flowed through her as quickly as the blood pumped through her veins.

"Here you go. All iced." Mum said as she stood back wiping her forehead.

Whiskers jumped onto the table and meowed.

"Get down," her mother scolded.

Whiskers darted out of the kitchen and skirted around the corner.

Isla giggled just appreciating her mum's presence.

"Are you feeling ill? Why so shy? You normally lunge at these biscuits before they're completely iced."

"I'm fine, Mummy, just taking it all in."

Her mother stared at her. "Whatever do you mean by that?"

"Nothing … it's just —"

Grayson and Messy bolted through the kitchen door.

"Last one to eat the biscuit is a rotten egg!" Grayson yelled, grabbing two at once.

Messy reached for a couple before sitting at the table.

"Copycat." Grayson chuckled.

"Am not," Messy replied.

"Are too."

"That's enough." Her mother sighed as she pulled her hair from her eyes. "Leave some for your sister."

"Here, Isla, take one of mine." Messy extended her hand. "I for one know how to share."

"Hah." Grayson's mouth overflowed with sweet dough. He reached for another.

"You're only allowed one more," her mother said, pulling away the biscuits. "Don't want you spoiling your dinner."

"Oh, Mummy," Isla said, "you know they won't."

Her mother sighed. "Only one more."

Taking a bite of her favorite biscuit, Isla relished the flavor and sensation of the melting sugar and cinnamon on her tongue. As Grayson and Messy bantered back and forth, the feeling of *being home* was almost overwhelming. Not wanting to ever leave, she honed into every word.

Her mother pulled out the steaming roast and as she reached for a large spoon, she froze. "Did you hear that?"

"Hear what?" Isla asked.

Grayson and Messy glanced around as they finished their sweet biscuits.

"Told you," Grayson whispered, reaching for another. "She has supersonic hearing."

"There it is again …" Her mother tensed and glanced out the back door. As her eyes scanned across the skies, she screamed. "Children … to the bunker now!"

A high-pitched whistle screamed through the kitchen as the ground vibrated. The windows exploded and sprayed the room with tiny shards of glass. Isla felt as if she was being ripped apart. Her feet left the floor, and she was yanked backward. Her eyes widened, staring up at the large beam that grew larger as it aimed for her head. Something moved the kitchen table that was now crushing her legs. The pain radiated up to her hips, burning deeply into her back. She tried to scream, but nothing escaped her lips.

"Isla! Grayson … Messy … help me. We're coming, Isla," her mother's voice echoed through the dense haze.

Her ears rang and the room grew dark. Again the ground shook and more dirt and rock flew through the broken windows. A large tree fell and the cracking of wood sent fear all through her.

"Isla!" her mother yelled. "Grayson … Messy … she's pinned under this beam. Help me!"

Her mother crawled over the smoldering lumber of what was once their kitchen floor. She picked up the beam that pinned Isla to the ground and reached out her hand. Grayson and Messy stood behind their mother with wide eyes and broken smiles.

"Come, children!" her mother yelled. "We don't have much time."

Isla stood and stretched out her back. Her skirt was ripped and her blouse soiled. She glanced down and one of her shoes were missing.

Her mother pushed open the kitchen door that was hanging on by just the lower hinge. The wall to the living room was gone and flames shot up from the stairs.

"Mummy," Messy whispered. "We can go through the other room."

"No, children," her mother replied. "We *must* come this way. Messy, hold my hand. Isla, you take Grayson's."

Smoke rose from the floor. The heat pelted their arms and back. Isla squinted, trying to see through the darkening smoke.

Whiskers scampered across the pebbled path and stood at the stone wall.

"Mummy," Messy said. "It's Whiskers. Can I bring him with me?"

"No, my darling," her mother replied. "Whiskers has another life. We do not."

A strange woman, wearing a white suit, waved at them.

Am I the only one who can see her? "Mummy, who's that woman with blonde hair?" Isla asked.

"Our guardian," her mother replied. "We must follow her, and children … do *not* look back."

"Why not?" Messy asked.

"We no longer live in this world," her mother replied.

Isla tried to look behind her. The need to understand what had happened felt overpowering.

Grayson jerked on Isla's arm. "No!" he whispered loudly.

They followed their mother into the silence as the soft sound of pebbles crunched beneath their feet, filling their ears. The path led to a huge stone wall.

Grayson stopped and stared at the ground.

"I must know," Isla whispered.

"Mum said not to look!" He scowled.

"But I *have* to. I can't explain it. I must know what happened."

"What difference does it make?" he asked. "We're dead. We do not have to see any of it."

Isla sighed, allowing her hand to slip from her brother's grip. She turned slowly and stared into the powdery iridescence that was slowly consuming the world around her. She stared at their once beautiful home that was now nothing more than smoldering rubble. She spotted her mother's bloody apron that was stained with a dark brown. Isla shrugged and decided it was the gravy she'd been stirring. Her sister's hair was tangled inside the branches of the large tree that had crashed into the kitchen. She couldn't see what had become of her or Grayson. The family car was still burning, a large red glow now surrounded it.

Grayson grabbed her arm and turned her around. "Don't look," he ordered.

Isla nodded.

Grayson pointed to the woman in white and smiled.

A door with no walls, no floor, and no ceiling was waiting for them under a glowing tree. Isla understood what it was. The entrance to their new life, and the woman in white was their escort.

They passed the bunker their dad had built during his last visit. The metal structure was not far from the end of the stone wall. Her father knew that the Germans wanted to invade London. He honestly believed that his bunker would be close enough for them to hide in when the sirens sounded. Several times, she had crawled into the tight space followed by Messy or Grayson. Isla thought for a moment and frowned. *No siren had sounded.*

The pebbled driveway faded into a white light. Holding onto her brother's hand, her sense of self seemed to be growing stronger. She felt a strong essence of warmth and unending love. They followed the guardian through the door that seamlessly closed behind them. However, the stench of death now filled the air.

"What's that smell?" Isla asked.

"Sulphur," Grayson whispered.

A dark cloud folding onto itself now blocked their path. The woman opened her mouth and a high-pitched screech echoed, dropping the four to their knees.

Still holding on to her brother's hand, Isla shook as something dark ran close. Close enough that she could feel the heat. She reached out and screamed as the shadows darted past.

"Mummy!" she yelled. Her fingers searched for her mother through the darkening mist. She screamed again, staring at her empty hand. She was alone. Inside the fiery, hot darkness, she was alone.

"Isla? Isla, come back," Beck whispered. "Come back to me, Isla."

Isla rubbed her eyes and took in a deep breath. The strong aroma of stench was gone. The air felt cool and calm. She slowly opened her eyes and looked deeply into Beck's rugged face.

"You okay?"

"I have to go to Hell," she whispered.

Beck didn't reply.

"Did you hear me?" Isla asked. "I have to go to Hell."

"I think you drank too much powder," he said with a chuckle. "You're slightly overreacting."

Isla reached out, allowing the rain to touch her hand before evaporating. She glanced around and frowned. "I think I took just enough."

"What did you see?" he asked.

"I relived the day that ended my life. There's always something they can't erase. I have this feeling that's been haunting my soul. I understand now what it is –"

"Understand what?"

"That there was a reason for Grayson and me to come here. And there is something I must do."

Beck stretched out his legs. "Did you get what you needed?"

Isla nodded. "I saw what they had erased from me … tried to erase."

The young waitress picked up the empty goblets. "May I bring you something else? Did we enjoy our happy memories?"

"Tremendously," Beck replied, sighing.

Isla grinned. "We must be leaving."

The waitress nodded.

A clap of thunder broke and their booth rumbled.

"You were saying …" he whispered.

"I saw what was erased, and I need your help."

"Help for what?"

"I have to rescue my mum and sister," she said as she wiped away a tear. "They are being held in Hell."

CHAPTER 21

Ja Crof stepped onto the balcony, gazing past the mountain range. She watched as the orange glow slowly rose into a steamy vapor. Darting red flames seemed to add to the eeriness of the distant background. Michael had warned her about the flames.

It has begun.

Through the ancient and large gothic doors, her latest group of StarWriters would soon enter. The tall, oval arch, delicately carved with a flowing outline of a serpent entwined with various vines served as the only passage into the fortress. Grotesque animal faces guarded the door with four panels, creatures that were a mix of animal and human. The antique wood was worn and had aged with the millennials of time. Inside the huge hall, the rotting walls and decaying ceiling captured the imagination of the most astute visitor, unless of course, Michael or Ja Crof imagined something different.

Ja Crof sighed.

Her thoughts fell to Michael, and the role she played as director. Some things were meant to be and some things were hers to accomplish alone. Ja Crof stared at the flaming horizon and allowed her mind to search her deepest and most private fears for answers. Souls assigned to serve – *His Plan* room with the scrolls that fell from the ether that were distributed throughout the universes – the Wondrous Tree and it's everchanging leaves – and the seven bilocation areas created to give the spirits a place to grow and evolve. Everything was designed by *His* guidance – *His* approval. And it was up to this new batch of StarWriters to protect and preserve. How could she ever elevate them to the level of *His* desire in time?

Michael's mission was to safeguard Heaven by ensuring that no one discovered its true location. Her primary mission was to train a new batch of StarWriters every century or two. Her very existence was starting to wear on her nerves. How much longer would she last inside this ever-evolving circle of beginnings and endings? Was she condemned to exist somewhere between the darkness and the light while ensuring that her trainees grew in both spirit and mind?

Impossible, for this new group is missing something.

Ja Crof's eyes searched upward, looking for answers.

Will they be ready for what is about to come?

When no reply filled her thoughts, she concentrated on Heaven and the stealth band that surrounded it – protecting it.

We walk on your path … Eternity Past, Eternity Present, and Eternity Future.

Her eyes darted back to the dancing flames. They had ascended higher as if meeting the heavens before extinguishing.

"It is coming, Ja." Michael had warned about what was hovering just beyond the veil. "There is a breach in Eternity Present."

How many times had she experienced a breach? More than she wanted to count or remember. Life's very existence continued to rest on her shoulders, and at times, it felt as if it was too much to handle. She could still hear the pleas of the precious ones as they faded into the shadows – the eeriness of the time, the odor of death knocking on her door.

She wiped her eyes and held back a scream. Glancing down into the vast valley, she wondered if it would be beneficial if she simply jumped. Then again, what good would that do?

"Something heavy on your mind?" a deep voice asked from behind.

Ja Crof turned and frowned. "Michael ... sneaking around again?"

Michael chuckled. "Your soul reached out to us, and thus, I am here."

Ja Crof sighed again. "Yes, something is indeed weighing heavily upon me."

"Such a beholding sight." Michael stepped onto the balcony and gazed out at the burning flames. "Although beautiful, also quite deadly."

"This present group that *He* has sent me. They're the most rag-tag bunch I've ever had the displeasure to train." She shook her head, placing her hands against the cold stone of the railing.

"Perhaps you take things too literally?"

"What makes *them* so special? They're not at all like my previous graduates. Maybe under different circumstances ... perhaps *He* should recall the previous StarWriters?"

Michael smiled. "You know that is an impossible request."

Ja Crof nodded. "I probably shouldn't feel this way but I do."

"You're thoughts are easy to read," he said, shaking his head. "You must work harder for what is coming."

"Why this group?" She slapped the railing several times. "Why these ... kids?"

"They make *Him* laugh."

"They make *Him* laugh?" Ja Crof repeated the words. "Under these circumstances and *He* chooses the ones that make him laugh?"

"Humor is important to *Him*." Michael chuckled. "Maybe you should try it sometime."

"I laugh."

"Not enough, my friend, not enough. Perhaps you take your position too seriously. Add a little humor."

"Training the apprentices to *His* code is a serious job."

"It is. And you do your role perfectly."

"Have I?" She grunted and sighed. "I do have another assignment."

"*He* is aware of your responsibilities, and *He* appreciates that you volunteered, stepping into this position for me."

Ja Crof glanced down at his feet and frowned. "I can never fill your sandals." She grinned.

Michael smiled. "Now that's exactly what I'm talking about … humor."

She crossed her arms.

"They will rise to the occasion," Michael said as he took a step back and vanished.

Ja Crof breathed deeply, allowing her gaze to study the dancing flames. She glanced down at the winding river and sighed. Her apprentices were now following the water's edge. Today's training would prove to be critical, although sooner than she had planned. Ja Crof cringed. In her day, they *trained* as warriors – they *acted* as warriors – they *were* warriors. Her new recruits' playful voices echoed through the valley and sizzled down her spine.

"You're not even close to becoming warriors. You're acting more like …"

Milos ran in front of Landon. He reached down and grabbed a handful of purple sand. Throwing it at Landon, he laughed as he kicked the water. "Got yah!"

"Hey … stop fooling around." Landon splashed Milos and instead of hitting his intended target, Jenni and Keekee screamed.

"Agh!" Keekee yelled.

"Ignore 'em," Jenni hollered. "Just keep walking."

Smillie splashed Té. Té turned and kicked the water at Shoupi and Colton. Landon laughed and jumped onto Té pulling him into the water. Em, Aleia, and Rosie stopped walking and watched.

"The director is waiting for us!" Em frowned, slapping her hands on her hips. "Hope she punishes you for being wet."

Aleia laughed. "Think she'd do that?"

"Let's keep going," Rosie said, fluttering past. "I don't want to get on her bad side."

Landon grabbed ahold of Rosie's foot and pulled her down.

"Let go!" Rosie giggled.

"Don't get her wet," Aleia yelled, running to help Rosie.

"Ah, come on. Have a little fun." Landon let go of Rosie's foot but splashed water at her. "Nobody's getting wet. We're staying dry. Just having a little fun."

Rosie's face turned redder. "You're getting Lyon wet." She pulled a sleepy, pink, bunny out from under her robe.

"Hello, Lyon." Landon laughed, filling his hands with more water and splashing them both.

"Stop it!" Rosie yelled. "We don't like that."

Em stepped in between them. "Cut it out, Landon."

"Get out of my way!" Rosie held Lyon by the nape of his neck and rushed at Landon.

Lyon's jaw opened and four sharp teeth glowed.

Aleia giggled. "I guess she wasn't kidding."

Stumbling, Landon fell into the water, pulling Smillie down with him. They laughed as they tried to help each other up.

Stepping out of the water, Landon's sandals squeaked. His robe was now soaked. "Why am I the only one that's wet?"

"Don't know," Smillie said, shrugging.

"I willed it. "Rosie laughed and shoved Lyon back under her robe. "Go to sleep now." She oozed with sweetness.

Em glanced at Aleia. "I don't get it. Michael wants *us* to foster *her*."

"I think it should be *her* fostering *us*," Aleia replied.

Thunder boomed and the apprentices looked up at the gathering clouds. A descending layer of mist had darkened and was now swirling like a tornado. Shoupi and Aleia covered their ears. Keekee screamed.

"What's going on?" Landon asked. "I feel sick …" – he spat on the ground – "…metallic, sulfur taste in my mouth."

"Ugh, what's that noise?" Smillie grabbed his stomach and puked several worms into the tall grass.

Yutu stepped back, knocking into Té.

"You want to fight!" Té jumped up, curling his fist and kicking sand at Yutu, a little splashed onto Colton.

"Cut it out!" Colton yelled. "Or I'll smash you!"

"Stop it!" Em screamed, running over to them. "What's wrong with you guys?" She glared at Milos.

Keekee knelt and cried.

Jenni pointed up at the black swirling clouds and grinned.

Rosie's wings vibrated and she landed hard on the sand. She didn't move.

"Rosie!" Em shouted. She grabbed her stomach and yelled, "Help us!"

A blanket of warm air swept around them as if in a strong embrace. The black clouds fizzled and the sky cleared. The scent of lilacs filled the air. Michael hovered only briefly before vanishing into the clouds.

"You are not children!" Ja Crof's voice echoed through the dense trees. "This is training … not frolicking. Stop wasting my time!"

"Oh no!" Jenni snapped out of her trance. "She's mad." She waved at the others.

The small group ran for the fortress and up the wide, wooden stairs. They entered through the gothic doors and stood huddling together, shoulder to shoulder. Em on the left and Landon on the right.

Landon glanced at Té. "What happened to us out there?"

"I think we had our first taste of pure evil," Té whispered.

Ja Crof walked back and forth, glaring at each as she passed. She sighed and crossed her arms. The small group glanced at each other and shrugged. Their eyes darted from their partners to Ja Crof and back.

Ja Crof stopped in front of Landon and frowned. "You are here to *train* and not *play* as children." She shook her head and her eyes glanced up and down at his dripping robe. "Did you learn a lesson from any of this?"

Landon wrung out the lower part of his rope, and the water puddled on the floor. He sighed and whispered, "I wish to be dry." The water evaporated around him until his robe was now free of weight. He stared at her. "Director, did you grant my wish?"

"No, Landon." Ja Crof dropped her arms. "I did not."

"Oh, yesss …" He pumped his fist into the air. "I just evolved."

"Lucky you," Keekee said, pouting and kicking the floor with her sandal.

"Oooh," Jenni whispered. "So what?"

Ja Crof raised her hands, and the aged and crumbling wall lifted as if a stage curtain. The small group now stared into an empty field.

"Rhopalocera Machinas," Ja Crof stated. "Irid … Serene … T.G. … and one not named, show yourselves …"

The air cooled and a loud humming filled their ears. Colorful and fluttering wings magically swooped down from a distant cloud. The butterflies landed one at a time on top of the sandy platform. Their soft appendages materializing into shiny metal, each forming a transport the size of a small plane. Their wings spread out and the doors sloped open as steps descended.

"Wow," Jenni said. "Now *that's* amazing. Welcome back, T.G."

"Well?" Ja Crof asked. "What are you waiting for? Board your transports. We don't have all eternity waiting for us." Ja Crof snickered to herself thinking about what Michael had said – not owning a sense of humor. "Find your seats." She coughed a few times to hide her smile.

The teams didn't need to be asked twice. After darting to their transports, they hurried up the stairs and disappeared inside. Ja Crof stood back and smiled. In many ways, they seemed too young and then again, they seemed too old. If only they acted wiser.

Ja Crof appeared in front of the small groups, her arms again folded across her chest.

"Are you quadding, Director?" Jenni asked.

Ja Crof nodded.

"Wish I could bilocate somewhere." Jenni lowered her gaze as if checking to see whether her body was fazing out. "Not yet …"

"StarWriters are forbidden to bilocate." Ja Crof glared at Jenni. "You've been warned."

"Why not?" Jenni asked, crossing her arms.

"You are apprentices and are evolving. A soul must remain fully engaged at this time. Bilocating is therefore not possible nor advisable." Ja Crof lowered her voice. "Again, you have been warned."

"Are we your favorites, Director?" Milos asked with a chuckle.

"Whatever do you mean?" Ja Crof asked.

"How can you be quadding if you're talking to us and not the others," Jenni asked with a grin.

"Yeah, that must mean you're starting with us for a reason." Colton stretched out his legs.

"I'm standing in front of each of you. I am capable of having more than one conversation at a time."

The group stared at her but remained silent.

Ja Crof studied the seating of each apprentice. "The ones in the middle are in charge." She watched for reactions and when Landon frowned, she continued, "Is this how you choose?"

They nodded.

"Em … Yutu … Té … and Jenni … you have chosen the center seats. Therefore, you will be responsible for the ones sitting next to you."

"Anything wrong with our choices?" Jenni asked.

I would have thought Té, Jenni, Em, and Landon. Ja Crof allowed her eyes to study each one. They seemed agreeable on where they sat. Since it was not her choice as to who accepted the role, her concerns didn't seem valid. Ja Crof waved her arm through the air and the four groups were now sitting side by side. "You may see each other as I do."

"Too cool," Colton said, waving at Té who waved back.

"You are to carry out *His Plan*," Ja Crof stated.

"The scrolls," Em added.

Ja Crof nodded. "You will carry the scrolls to your assigned quadrants, adhering to the universal, consistent, eternal time clock."

"How do we know where our quadrants are?" Yutu asked.

"Each transport knows and accepts their destination," Ja Crof replied

"How many scrolls?" Milos asked.

"Your transports will house the number."

Shoupi sighed loudly. "What do *we* do once *we* get to the stars?"

"The transports will guide you," Ja Crof replied.

"If the transports are doing all the work," Em asked loudly, "why do you need us?"

Ja Crof glanced around and studied the young and innocent faces. For some strange reason, she felt more protective over this group. They seemed too carefree and what they were about to endure, they would never be ready for in such a short time. And the consequences of their reactions or non-actions would seal their souls' fate. Ja Crof allowed her thoughts to center on *His* mission, and her heart pounded. Whether or not these souls would evolve into the higher spiritual plane or if their frequencies lowered all depended on her ability to train them. And in her mind, this group would never be fully ready.

"StarWriters … your mission is to take the scrolls to the individual stars. This in and of itself is quite easy and safe … however –"

"However?" Jenni repeated. "This doesn't sound promising."

Ja Crof sighed. "You have another task … a personal and important undertaking."

Keekee raised her hand.

"Yes?"

"Do we have to evolve before we can do this *other* task?" Keekee asked.

"No, not necessarily."

Keekee grinned.

"Then what is this *other* task?" Jenni asked. "Our jobs just keep growing."

Ja Crof allowed her gaze to fall on each apprentice. "Prayers …"

"You want us to pray?" Milos asked."

Ja Crof shook her head. "Some call it a wish …"

"We have to wish on a star?" Smillie asked.

Ja Crof shook her head again. "Others may call it a plea for help or a hope or a second chance –"

Shoupi laughed. "There's no such thing as a second chance."

Ja Crof smiled. "Your journey includes requests from the living that only *He* can answer … all in accordance to *His Plan*."

Shoupi raised her hand.

"Yes, Shoupi."

"And how do those *requests* come here?"

Ja Crof nodded. "They come on a breath of air … it is *He* who hears all and it is *He* who transcribes them onto the scrolls. You will deliver all scrolls … unless …"

"Unless …" Té repeated.

"Unless they are redirected," Ja Crof replied.

"Redirected?" Shoupi furrowed her 'brows.

"Some are forwarded to a Saint," Ja Crof added.

"A Saint!" Jenni stated. "You expect us to go to a Saint? A real Saint?"

Ja Crof laughed "A Saint was once a person just as you were once alive. Now, they grant miracles in *His* name. Nothing to be concerned over."

"Nothing to be concerned over?" Jenni repeated.

"That's cool," Smillie said. "I've never met a Saint before."

Shoupi giggled. "Wish we could read the requests first."

Smillie laughed and a bright light shot out landing directly on Shoupi.

Té chuckled. "Hey, Smillie … I think you just evolved."

Smillie raised his hand in front of his face and stared at the light. "I just evolved?"

Ja Crof smiled. "You'll be putting that to good use. Light! Stop!"

Smillie's light diminished.

Ja Crof's thoughts drifted to Michael's request of speeding up the training. She always prided herself on having the apprentices ready before their first mission. There are dangers out there – pitfalls as well as temptations. They have not yet evolved and there just isn't enough time. She had to remain obedient to *Him* and *His Plan*. But she also felt responsible for these young souls.

Ja Crof took in a deep breath to redirect her thoughts. "Apprentices, let's get to work." Tilting her head, she added, "Monarch's … release your control."

Joy sticks appeared in front of the middle seats. The small groups started and sat back. Jenni reached out and touched the smooth surface. She smiled. Té laughed and glanced at Smillie. Yutu sat back as far as he could, folding his hands in his lap. Em leaned forward as if examining it.

Walking back and forth, Ja Crof sighed. "You will now practice."

Jenni giggled. "I'm driving!" She grabbed the stick with both hands.

"Careful with that," Milos stated, "you'll break it."

"Now we're talking." Yutu chuckled, jerking the stick from side to side.

Landon leaned into Yutu. "I can help if you want."

"I'm good," Yutu replied. He reached out and paused before pulling his hand back as if afraid.

"It won't bite!" Keekee laughed.

Rosie hovered behind Em and sighed. "Sure you can handle this thing?"

"Of course she can," Aleia replied, frowning. "Can you?" she whispered to Em.

Em sighed. "We'll be fine … I hope."

Té sat silently as if waiting for further instructions. Smillie nudged him with his shoulder and pointed to the stick. Té shook his head.

"To guide your transport, push the stick in any direction," Ja Crof stated. "Up … pull up. Down … push down. Forward … push forward. Got it?"

The apprentices nodded, but no one moved.

Ja Crof frowned. "Then go somewhere! I would recommend *up* to start."

Two of the groups slowly raised before lowering back down. Jenni and her group remained on the purple sand.

"Jenni, do something," Colton whined. "We're not moving."

Milos leaned over and whispered, "I can drive if you can't."

Jenni's cheeks turned a light pink. "I've got this!" she stated, jerking up the stick with both hands, then she pushed it forward.

Nothing happened. She shoved the stick toward Colton and then over to Milos. Again, nothing happened. "T.G.'s broken!"

Ja Crof chuckled. "Relax. You're trying too hard."

Jenni's hands wrapped tighter around the control.

"*Think* of where you want T.G. to go," Ja Crof said, "and use the stick to guide your vessel."

Jenni removed her hands from the mechanism. She shook them out as if just finishing an exercise.

"Director, if she can't do it, can I try?" Milos asked, grinning.

"C'mon, you can do this." Colton smiled. "Just relax."

Sighing, Jenni grabbed the stick again. Yanking on it a little harder, she completely pulled the mechanism out of the floor.

"You broke it!" Milos yelled. "Now we'll never go anywhere. Director!"

Turning even redder, Jenni screamed. "What's wrong with this stupid thing! Uhhh, I said to go *up*."

T.G. raised a few feet above the purple sand and hovered.

Milos looked at Ja Crof and sighed. "What just happened?"

Colton laughed. "I think Jenni just moved it with her mind."

Jenni held out the stick and shook her head. She stared at her hand and frowned. "This is oh so not happening."

Taking the stick from her, Colton leaned in and whispered, "See if it will move with just your thoughts."

Jenni closed her eyes. "T.G. … go to my right."

Milos and Colton cheered as the machine moved slightly to the right.

Opening up one eye before the other, Jenni grinned. "Now go left."

Ja Crof frowned. "Hmm …"

Four metal butterflies darted around on the landing pad. Ja Crof stood back with her hand on her forehead. The monarchs maneuvered with precision as the teams practiced while not running into each other. Although a machine, they were still sentient butterflies.

Em, Aleia, and Rosie cheered every time Serene moved in the direction they chose.

"You got this," Aleia said, clapping. "We'll be StarWriting before you know it."

Ja Crof took in a deep breath and counted to ten before appearing before the small groups.

"Rosie!" Ja Crof stated firmly. "When in flight, you *will* remain seated."

"But, Director," Rosie whined, "it's not easy for me to do that. My wings are too big. I can't sit down."

"You'll have to figure that out for yourself. Em can help you."

"But …" Em said and her eyes darted between Rosie and Ja Crof. "I don't know how to deal with wings!"

"You protected her earlier, didn't you?"

"You mean when I used my robe?" Em said, sliding her hand up and down the stick.

"Yes," Ja Crof replied.

Rosie scowled. "That was not fun. I do not wish to be cocooned with you again."

Sighing, Em laughed. "You always think that I —"

Rosie screamed. "Watch it!"

Serene lifted and jerked to the side. The small group flew from their seats and hit the wall. Aleia pushed herself up and darted to the back of the compartment. Rosie screamed as she tumbled through the air. Aleia reached out and grabbed onto Rosie's robe, pulling her to her chest.

"I gottcha!" Aleia yelled.

"Straight and forward, Serene," Ja Crof said, and the butterfly leveled out.

Em stood. "What just happened?"

Rosie flew up to Em and yelled, "You were careless and stupid and you almost got us killed! That's what happened."

"You mean … killed again?" Aleia asked.

Ja Crof appeared before their seats. She clapped her hands twice and coughed. "Now that I have your attention … can you tell me what happened?"

Rosie looked at Em. "I'm not really sure. I just knew that you were going to tip us over, and I wanted to stop you."

"Aleia?" Ja Crof said. "What did you see?"

"I saw what was going to happen if I didn't grab Rosie." She clasped her hands together. "Splat."

"Director," Rosie said, smirking. "I think Aleia should be in charge." She stuck her tongue out at Em.

Em sighed. "Glad you evolved, Aleia."

"Thanks," Aleia replied.

One moment ahead of the Next for Rosie, and two moments beyond for Aleia. *He* must have something up *His* sleeve. Ja Crof glanced up and frowned.

CHAPTER 22

Beck bilocated to *Pi*, the city of skyscrapers nestled amongst the stars. His other half was still in *His Plan* room. Dropping baskets of scroll after scroll just wasn't his thing. He always used his free will to venture about the kingdoms. Although, he still hadn't been invited to *LOH* to meet with *Him*.

He stood next to his peers on the white light. They laughed and told jokes under the open ballroom. He kept glancing up at the twinkling stars.

"Beck, come join us," a young man said. "I'm hoping to attract the attention of Heaven's angels during their overhead choir practice."

"Have you seen 'em?" a young woman asked.

"I don't think anyone has ever *seen* them," another replied, pointing to his eyes.

"Have you heard them?" a woman asked.

"I've heard *of* them," the same young man replied. "I'm hoping they'll hear us and report to *Him* of our praises."

The group gathered and sang out with a soprano chanting.

A perfect time to reflect. Beck glanced up as a star twinkled in the distance. He sighed for somewhere past that tiny light was the forbidden quadrant.

"Beck!" a young woman yelled. "Join us."

"Come with me," a voice whispered into Beck's ear. "Take the elevator to the top and come alone."

Beck glanced around and shrugged. "Maybe later." He smiled at the girl.

The area with the elevators was near the back of the building. As the doors opened, he nodded at several bilocators who walked out. Now standing alone, he pressed the SPIRE button. Soft music played as he waited. The doors opened and he stepped onto a powdery cloud. He had been here before.

He was now on top of the tallest skyscraper in *Pi*. He took in a deep breath, engulfing the sweet aroma. His pulse raced as he thought about the first time he walked this path. To be afforded such a privilege above other bilocators was an honor.

During his first visit, Beck had been asked a question by the howling whispers. "Do you know who you were before you walked in this realm?"

"I don't understand," Beck had said, not remembering anything except working within *His* glory.

The whispering voice hissed. "Had it not been hidden by *Him*."

"I cannot remember a thing. What are you talking about?"

"Your memories," the voice said. "Your memories were removed."

"Why?"

"Would you relish to know what you would have been had you remained alive?" the whispering voice hissed louder.

"What? I don't understand."

"A girl … Isla. She holds the key."

During his first visit, the clouds had dissipated, and he remained hovering above the buildings with the stars surrounding him. He had felt powerful. He had felt important.

"What do I have to do?"

"You shall be responsible for the ones who breech Eternity Present. Those who steal souls when they leave their earthly planes."

"And do what, exactly?"

"You will take these lost souls to Sheol," the whispering voice had hissed.

Was this going to be a similar meeting? Would they commend him on doing a good job with the recent breeches? His pulse raced anticipating the reunion with the shooting stars. He longed to hear the adulation.

Standing within the clouds, he gazed down at the other skyscrapers. The stars surrounded him, and he screamed as a force pulled his feet up, pushing down on his head.

"What's happening?" Beck yelled. "I've done everything you asked."

"Have you?" The hissing whispers grew louder, firmer. "And the girl?"

"Yes! Isla will comply." Beck struggled to free himself.

"I shall release you if you tell me *why* they are suspecting."

Beck's ankles were now chained together. His body felt stiff and out of control. He descended toward the city's street as if free falling.

"Help!" he screamed. "I'll do anything!"

He was suddenly standing inside the ballroom with the songs of the chanting echoing around him. He glared at the two he had recruited. Motioning them over to a secluded corner, he frowned.

"You idiots," Beck stated. "What just happened?"

"What?" one of the young men asked.

"What went wrong?" Beck growled.

"Nothing went wrong," the boy with the purple hair replied. "We intercepted, grabbed, and dropped off. No one's the wiser."

The choppy-blonde sighed, "Yeah man, when the elixir faded, we came here as instructed."

Beck smiled and relaxed. *Phew … then, I passed the test.*

CHAPTER 23

Isla vaporized into *His Plan* room, not intending on fully working. Following the others, she glanced around, trying not to make eye-contact with anyone. She grabbed a basket and held it under the chute, collecting several scrolls. Again, she glanced around. Most were looking straight ahead as they gathered the scrolls and headed for the various workers.

He always sits directly under a good/evil clock. So ... where is he?

Isla allowed her gaze to trail through the endless rows of desks after desks filled with workers tying the golden strings that were crafted from angel wings. It was obvious that many were bilocating since their faces wore nothing but a blank stare.

She laughed, understanding that her brother always worked in the whole. Now, she wondered why he never bilocated. She didn't know anyone who loved this place as much as Grayson. He always refused her offer to bilocate together.

Stepping up to her brother's desk, she sighed. It was empty. "Have you seen Grayson?" She asked a young man who was dropping a few scrolls onto Grayson's desk.

With his eyes glazed over, he slowly pointed.

"Where?" Isla asked.

The young man was bilocating and would only say a few words. If they were to dive into a full conversation, his other self would be pulled from the village, and she didn't want to bring attention to herself. Therefore, she had to be careful on how she phrased her questions.

"White room," he said, walking away.

Isla shook her head. *Where else would he be besides the break room!* She took in a deep breath and let it out slowly. Glancing up at the *good/evil* clocks, the hands clicked once to the left. Shrugging, she looked at the scrolls in her basket. She sighed. Taking the scrolls anywhere was forbidden, and she didn't need to be written up again. Looking around, everyone seemed either busy or out-of-touch. Sitting the basket on the closest chair, she closed her eyes. As she vaporized, a familiar voice echoed.

"Excuse me … you can't –"

Great! I'll be written up now for sure.

As she materialized, the light beamed from one side to the other. Grayson was sitting next to a copper-skinned girl with teal hair.

He never talks to anyone let alone a girl. He just wants to tie gold strings. Slowly, she walked over to her brother.

Grayson glanced up and motioned her closer.

"Grayson," Isla whispered. "Since when are you *not* tying strings?"

Grayson shook his head and shrugged. "This is Zee. And this …" – he raised his hand at Isla – "… is my sister."

"Hi." Zee smiled. "I'm new, and your brother's been just wonderful helping me to understand."

Raising her 'brows, Isla laughed. "Oh, really? Grayson?"

"Zee likes tying the gold as much as I do," he replied. "Just knowing that the string is made from the pure essence of angels gives me such energy." He chuckled.

Isla looked at Zee and nodded." Maybe you can persuade my brother into bilocating. He never leaves this place."

Zee smiled at Grayson. "I feel the same way. I *love* it here." She waved her arms through the air. "Gotta get back to work. Nice to have met you, Isla."

Isla smiled. "Yeah, ditto."

"I'll join you." Grayson stood. "Maybe we can have your seat changed. It would be nice if we sat together. I'll ask *His Plan* attendant."

Zee giggled. "That would be nice."

Isla placed her hand on her brother's shoulder. "Sit down. We need to talk. It's important."

"See you later," Zee said, dissolving into the white light.

Grayson frowned. "What's up?"

"What can you remember about Mum and Messy?"

Grayson rubbed his chin. "We came here … and Mum and Messy were taken to the gates."

"Your wrong," she said, placing her hands on her hips.

Grayson tilted his head. "They're not here. So … they must be there."

Glancing around again, Isla took a step closer to her brother and whispered, "I took a remembrance powder. I saw something."

Grayson's eyes widened. "That's forbidden! You'll lose *Him*. Maybe what you think you saw isn't true."

"The remembrance powder is guaranteed," she whispered a little louder.

Grayson grabbed her arm and pulled her to a chair. "What do you think you saw?"

Isla took in a deep breath and let it out slowly. She again glanced around the room. When she was sure no one was paying attention, she said in a low voice, "When we were following our guide, I saw something grab them. It was only a flash, but I know what I saw."

"That proves nothing."

Isla nodded. "When our guide brought us to the door, I looked around for Mum and Messy. They were not with us. Our guide answered me through my thoughts. *'The pathway to everlasting fire.'* That's what she said."

"Makes no sense." Grayson stared at her. "Whoever is making you do this is using you."

"No one is using me. He's *helping* me." Isla looked around and smiled at the couple at the next table. "I've always had these bad feelings about Mum and Messy. Something I can't shake. It's a feeling that I —"

"That you what?"

"That I have to find them." She wiped away a tear.

Grayson sat back and crossed his arms. He glanced up and sighed deeply. "Who's helping you? I want to know."

"I can't say."

"If this is real, why don't *I* have the same feelings?" He looked at her and frowned.

Isla reached out her hand. "Our bad memories were erased, remember? We can only remember the good."

Grayson hesitated but held his sister's hand. "I'm confused."

"Just trust me and don't tell anyone. Especially, not your new little friend."

Grayson squinted and smiled. "You must be careful. Don't do anything stupid." Again, he glanced up at the bright sky and sighed. "Or ... you'll lose *Him*."

Isla frowned. "I'm always careful."

After phasing back into *His Plan* room, Isla stood near the baskets and shook her head. She held out the demerit and frowned.

"Six …" she whispered. "Four more and I'm out. But out where?" Shrugging away the thought, she grabbed an empty basket and headed for the chutes.

As usual, she aimed for her brother's desk. He was talking with an attendant. No doubt in her mind what it was about. After dropping off several scrolls at various desks, she walked to a section she rarely visited.

A man reached up and patted her arm. Startled, she took a step back. The scroll box attached to his desk was empty. She nodded and refilled it. He didn't respond since he was bilocating.

Beck, two desks away looked somewhat busy, although he was not mentally there. Only knowing him in his bilocating state, Beck always appeared strange-looking, very robotic in his actions. She'd only recently met his awakened self in *Pi*.

When they first spoke he had said, "Hi. I'm Beck. I can feel about the past just as you can. Perhaps, we can help each other."

How he could know about such things seemed strange. She tried to ask more questions, but he'd simply answered with, "Not important, but I can definitely help you."

With her hands shaking, she stepped closer, tilting her basket until the remaining scrolls dropped onto Beck's desk. He reached up and held on firmly until the last scroll fell. She nodded and stepped back. Beck picked up two scrolls that had fallen onto his lap. He glanced up only briefly, and somehow smiled through his eyes.

As she walked back to the chutes, two liquid vials rolled across the basket. One red and the other green. Without looking back, she cautiously placed them inside her robe's pocket.

As she walked past, she looked up at the *good/evil* clocks. Hoping they had returned to normal, she frowned as the handles moved closer to evil – to the left. While dropping off the empty basket, Isla stared at the growing pile of scrolls.

A siren blared and a mechanical voice stated: "Bilocators … those who are currently bilocating must immediately return to their stations." The stern voice had echoed from between the clouds. "Apprenticing StarWriters are behind on delivering *His* scrolls. The holding bins have reached capacity, and we need assistance in filling the transports."

Isla followed the line of workers to the StarWriters' waiting butterflies, holding out a large basket filled with gold-stringed scrolls.

Ja Crof drew a large circle in the air in front of her. She divided the circle in half and then in quarters. Within the center she added a mini circle that intersected each quadrant, highlighting it in yellow. Beginning on her right, she moved clockwise. After the names Serene and T.G. appeared, she stood back and nodded. In the third quadrant she added a question mark. In the last square, she printed Irid. Pointing at Yutu, Landon, and Keekee, she smiled. "Have you given your butterfly a name yet?"

Yutu shook his head. "Any thoughts?" he asked, glancing at his partners.

"We don't have a name," Landon replied.

"Let's think of one," Yutu stated.

"How about Phantom?" Landon asked.

Shaking his head, Yutu frowned. "Sounds corny."

"I'm thinking, like … or LYK," Keekee said, with a focused gaze. "L for Landon, Y for Yutu, and K for me." She pointed at herself.

"I like it." Yutu chuckled.

"Me, too, "Landon replied.

"LYK it is. I approve." Ja Crof printed an L Y and K in the empty space.

The small group laughed.

"The forbidden place!" Ja Crof yelled. She punched her fist through the yellow highlighted area, and their names blew out followed by vibrant colors only to reassemble inside the circle. "Your souls will depend on it."

The apprentices grew quiet.

"Never enter the forbidden areas of your quadrants," Ja Crof said.

"Why not?" Té asked.

"Your souls would be devoured … shredded and spit into the universe. You would no longer exist."

Colton adjusted in his seat and stretched out his legs. "Why would we want to go there if we're just gonna be eaten and spit out?"

Ja Crof sighed. "Let me help you to fully understand."

Colton sat up straighter. "I don't *want* to fully understand." His words came out stronger than he intended. "What I meant was … why *would* we enter the forbidden area?"

Colton's seat grew to three times its size. Milos and Jenni watched as his head raised much higher than the others.

"What's going on?" Landon asked.

Staring up at him, Jenni laughed. "You're evolving!"

Milos clapped his hands.

"Not so high," Colton stated, and his seat adjusted, giving his legs more room to stretch out. He tried to high-five Milos, but his hand was now larger than his friend's head.

"All three of *us* have evolved." Jenni glanced at Ja Crof.

"Great question, Colton," Ja Crof stated loudly. "Why *would* you venture into the forbidden area?"

"Serene will keep us away," Em said.

"As co-pilots, we won't let you get close," Aleia stated.

"I'll yell at you!" Rosie flew closer to Em.

Em motioned for Rosie to sit on her lap. Instead, she fluttered above her seat.

Yutu extended his hand. "I'm in charge and I'm not going there under any circumstance."

Keekee and Landon said together, "We wouldn't let you."

Shoupi covered her eyes. "I'm afraid now."

"Don't be." Té glanced at her and then at Smillie. "You have *my* word. We'll never go there."

Smillie scrunched up his nose. "I'll take the controls if that happens."

Picking up Jenni's non-working stick, Milos added, "I'll take over if you do."

"Hey, I'm not planning on it!" Jenni stated. "Don't worry, I got everything under control."

Ja Crof furrowed her 'brows. "Listen and listen good … as StarWriters delivering *His Plan*, you will be tempted." She clasped her hands. "The promises sound good. The secrets are vast. The rewards are never ending. But if you succumb, you will be sucked into …"

Shoupi covered her eyes again.

Ja Crof punched her fist through the yellow, highlighted circle again and yelled, "The entrance to *Hell!*" She swirled her arm through the hovering colors and added, "Better yet, I'll show you!"

The StarWriters screamed as they soared into a dark abyss. Flames shot out, setting their arms and legs on fire. A pain so deep and vast as to fill them with an immortal dread shot straight through their souls. Evil creatures ripped into their blistering flesh, exposing muscles and bones. The entities smiled as they slurped up the dripping blood.

Keekee screamed. "I don't want to be eaten!"

"Make it stop!" Aleia cried out.

CHAPTER 24

"Godspeed," Ja Crof said. "Your scrolls with *His Plan* and the hopes and prayers of the living are loading now. She clasped her hands. "The butterflies will take you to your quadrants and guide you." Her eyes glanced up. "The fusion from the stars gives them energy, they yearn for these trips. You will leave as apprentices and return as StarWriters." As she fizzled into the mist, Ja Crof added, "Go with strength and boldness, return with knowledge and joy for it is written in the stars …"

The vessel, Serene, hissed steam from her undercarriage that fogged the viewing windows.

Rosie whined, "I think we're first but I can't see a thing."

"Take a seat," Em said. "It'll clear."

"I can't take a seat … remember?" Rosie fluttered in the air.

"I know what to do with your wings so you can sit." Em patted her knee.

"Really?" Rose hovered and frowned. "What can you do with 'em? They're mine not yours."

"I'd trust her," Aleia stated.

Rosie sighed. "I'm not too sure about this. Is *this* your plan? Sit on my lap?"

"Just sit." Em patted her knee again.

"Why can't you just tell me?" Rosie asked.

Aleia sighed. "Ugh … will you stop already, stop being so difficult. Em's not gonna hurt you. She just wants to help. Besides we're getting ready to take off." She raised her voice a little. "So sit already."

"Fine." Rosie landed on Em's leg.

Em held her wings, carefully pinching them together.

Rosie giggled. "That tickles."

"As long as it doesn't hurt. Now, raise your arms."

Rosie raised her arms.

Em covered Rosie's wings with the bottom of her robe. "Band together," she said.

"Tickles." Rosie giggled again.

A pink band materialized, binding Rosie's wings behind her back. "There. This will keep you safe and when you need it off just say … *remove*."

Rosie frowned. "I can't fly now."

"That's the point." Em grinned. "Director wants you seated, and I had to figure it out, which I did."

"I love it," Aleia stated. "It's pink and pinches your wings back so you can sit in your chair."

Em placed Rosie in her seat. "When you want it off, just say …"

Serene jerked forward and Aleia grabbed Em's arm.

"Gotcha," Aleia said.

"Thanks." Em smiled. "Did you see *me* splatter against a wall or something?"

"Didn't see anything. Just reflex." Em's thoughts ran through the possibilities. *Rosie and Aleia's ability to see a few moments into the future, first Next and Second Next, only happens when they're surprised.* Em shrugged. *Is this to avoid danger?* Em wrapped her fingers around the joy stick. She leaned forward and stared at it for a moment. *What do I do now?* The director's words echoed through her mind. "Serene will take control." Em took a deep breath and let it out slowly.

"Okay, Serene, we're ready whenever you are. I'll watch how you maneuver and try to follow along."

Serene's legs blasted them up as if a rocket had just shot through the white, billowy clouds. Within less than a moment's thought, the vessel was soaring toward the trillions of twinkling stars. The double windows expanded, merging into a single, curved viewing screen.

"This is unbelievable!" Aleia shouted.

Em gasped.

Rosie giggled.

"How're your wings doing?" Em asked.

"Okay … I guess," she replied. She squirmed in her seat. "Look … shooting stars." Rosie pointed and frowned. "I hate not being able to fly."

Em laughed. "You're flying in a whole new way."

Milos tapped Jenni's arm. "We're not moving. Are you using your brain waves?"

"Yup." Jenni squinted. "I'm concentrating. Hey, butterfly, let's go. Take off, move, do something, *dammit.*"

"Serene just took off," Colton said, pushing his back against his now larger seat.

"You want the stick back?" Milos asked.

Jenni glanced at him and smirked. "Nah, keep it. Don't think that's it. Director said the machines are in teaching mode. I'm thinking that T.G.'s blocking my thoughts."

"Maybe you have to talk to him," Colton said.

Jenni shrugged and sighed. "T.G., c'mon … let's get going. You're holding things up. Are you napping or something?"

Milos laughed.

"I'd ask him a little nicer, if I were you," Colton whispered.

"It's *just* a machine." Jenni huffed. "What am I supposed to say to it?"

"They may be just machines for delivery," Colton added, "but they still have feelings. Remember, they change from the living to the mechanical. How about, please and thank you."

Jenni crossed her arms and leaned back. "Please get –"

T.G. lifted a few feet off the ground and hovered.

"Told, yah." Colton grinned.

The vehicle shot straight up, and the apprentices grabbed onto their seats. Not one of the three spoke. Instead, they stared out at the twinkling and colorful sky. The windows merged into a single screen, and the small group almost drooled at the scenery.

Jenni allowed her mind to speak. *Great job, T.G. Take us to our first star.*

"Tell her to take us to our first star," Milos stated.

"Already did," Jenni replied.

"But did you say please?" Colton asked.

"Fine." Jenni huffed. *Please.*

T.G. glided into the twinkling and colorful star cluster.

The six mechanical legs leaped forward.

"We're next in queue," Landon said, sitting up straighter.

Yutu pulled up on the joystick. "Hmm, that didn't work." He jerked the stick to his right and then to his left. "Why isn't LYK moving? It did during practice."

"Try again," Keekee said. "Maybe you're not doing it right."

Landon placed his hand on top of Yutu's.

"What're you doing?" Yutu asked, trying to push his partner's hand away.

"Director said that our butterflies will show us the ropes," Landon stated. "They'll teach us. I don't think you have control yet."

"When will he have control?" Keekee asked.

"Don't know," Landon replied. "Just wish we could take off already —"

LYK shot up, blasting through the clouds.

"Landon? Did LYK just obey you?" Keekee asked.

"Nope," Yutu replied. "It's on cruise control, remember?" Landon grinned.

LYK exited the band circling Heaven and soared toward the sparking stars. Keekee, Landon, and Yutu jumped out of their seats and raced to the curved windows.

Yutu howled. "Wow. See this?"

Landon smiled. "I'm glad I'm a StarWriter."

"Wish I could see more," Keekee said.

The two windows merged, forming one large screen. The small group jumped back.

"Did I do that?" Keekee asked, laughing. "Did I just evolve?"

Smiling, Yutu replied, "Sorry, Keekee. Don't think so. It's just LYK teaching us."

Landon sat back in his seat and sighed. "Yup, teaching us."

"Whatever," Yutu said, slipping back into his seat.

Keekee plopped into hers and pouted. "I'll never evolve. Seems everyone is but me."

"If it makes you feel any better," Yutu said, "I haven't either. We're in this together."

"I guess," Keekee whispered. "Just wish it would happen soon."

"Don't worry," Landon added. "Seems to happen when you least expect it."

LYK lunged before blasting into the darkness.

Isla loaded her scrolls onto the remaining transport and pulled out a tiny red vial from her pocket.

"We're done," announced one of the workers, vaporizing along with the others.

Isla glanced around before raising the vial to her lips, allowing the slimy liquid to warm her tongue. Along with the last drop, the vial disappeared.

Isla's bilocating other self returned to *His Plan* room with a slight glow and fixed gaze. She picked up a basket and waited for the next scroll to drop. After filling her basket, she walked behind the others, heading to her brother's desk.

The stairs raised, folding upon themselves. Isla held back a scream, feeling a push and being tossed across the floor. She rolled several times before slamming into the back of the middle seat.

Té turned around and stared into the dark shadows. "What was that?"

"What was what?" Shoupi asked.

Isla pushed herself against the base of Té's seat, trying not to make a sound.

"Something just hit my chair."

Smillie chuckled. "We haven't even moved yet. They just finished loading the scrolls."

Té looked over his shoulder again. "I know that something banged into me. I felt it." The butterfly jerked again, and Té's knees bumped into the joystick.

"Looks like we're ready to go," Shoupi said. "I can't wait to fly into the heavens."

Smillie pointed to the control stick. "You're up, Té."

Sitting back, Té grabbed the controls. Pulling it up gently, he whispered, "Okay, Irid, ready whenever you are."

Isla slowly crawled to the back of the compartment. *If the potion wears off … gotta get outta here before –*

Irid shot straight up causing Isla to slide into the back wall. "Ugh!"

Té twisted around. "Did you hear that?"

"Hear what?" Smillie asked. He gasped along with Shoupi. "Té … what's wrong with you? The action's up here, not back there. Turn around. You're missing it."

"It's so incredible …" Shoupi cooed. "I'm finally in Heaven."

"It's just that –" Té stared at the viewing screen. "Wow. But don't tell me you didn't hear the thump and scream."

"What scream?" Shoupi asked.

"I didn't hear anything, "Smillie added, gazing into the vast universe.

Isla leaned against the curved wall, inching herself into the back compartment that housed the endless piles of scrolls. Hearing the gasps and wows, she took a chance and looked out the window. As the twinkling grew in size and color, she forced herself to look away. *I have a mission to do.* Isla tapped the wall. *Gotta be here somewhere. Just like Beck said, tap and a sliver of separation will appear leading into the back compartment.*

The wall released and Isla pulled the membrane apart. She glanced back at the StarWriters. It had to be timed perfectly. Opening the gap too wide would attract attention. If she didn't open it enough, she would become stuck and they would surely see her. Cautiously stepping through, she thought about Té. *I need to get him back here alone.*

Isla pulled the green vial from her robe. *Oh no!* She gasped as her hand appeared and disappeared multiple times. Knowing that she would be fully visible soon, she inched her way deeper into the back section. *Gotta get farther in.*

Remembering what Beck had explained, she searched for a spongy section that was between the stiffer membranes. As her hand felt along the cool surface, she sighed when she touched something warm. She opened the vial and dripped the oozing, green liquid into the softness of the butterfly's belly.

I'm coming mummy and Messy. I'm coming.

CHAPTER 25

Moving at light speed through the heavens, Irid jerked to the right – back to the left – stopped – jumped back – jerked to the right –

Shoupi and Smillie grabbed their seats and held on.

"What're you doing?" Smillie asked, struggling to remain in his seat.

Té sat back, pulling his hands to his chest. "It's not me. I swear."

Shoupi screamed and grabbed onto Té's arm. "Why is it doing this? Are we going to crash?"

"In space?" Smillie asked, laughing. "Kinda fun!"

"Fun? Are you nuts?" Shoupi screamed again. "Irid, stop!"

Irid stopped and hovered amidst the swirling stars.

"Guess we're here?" Té replied. He moved the stick forward and the vessel remained motionless. "Nothing's happening. Maybe we are here."

Shoupi ran to the window and stared out. "Here where?" She turned and shrugged. "There's nothing out there but stars. I mean … it's pretty and all … but something's not right."

"Maybe it's prepping the scrolls." Smillie jumped up and joined her at the window. Pressing his cheek against the glass, he stretched to see. "Doesn't look like anything's happening from the cargo section."

"Something's wrong, Té!" Shoupi placed her hands on her hips. "You're in charge, do something."

"Like what?" Té waved his arms through the air. "The thing won't move."

"Maybe we're broke?" Smillie added.

"Yes …" Shoupi nodded. "We must be broke."

Té sighed. "I thought I heard something. Check the back."

"Back what?" Shoupi asked, staring out the window.

"Maybe that's what you heard," Smillie said. "Something broke and now it's flapping around. Want me to check it out?"

"I'll go." Té sighed. "You two stay here. If Irid starts moving, let me know." Té stared at the slender gap in the back wall. "This section is loose. Maybe this is what's wrong. I'll make sure nothing else came apart."

Té squeezed through the small opening, allowing his eyes to scan across the towering piles of scrolls. Light from the main hull reflected, creating long shadows. He shrugged and shook his head.

"All looks good," he yelled.

The shadows were oddly shaped and didn't seem normal. He raised his hand and a long dark shadow followed. He laughed and turned to leave as a different shadow moved – but only slightly.

The shadow disappeared and the light again filled the room. He shrugged, taking a step toward the panel and the shadow reappeared.

"What in the world?"

"Anything wrong?" Smillie yelled from the other compartment.

"Not sure. Just looks weird in here."

"We are inside an insect that's filled with scrolls, yah know!" Shoupi yelled. "That's pretty weird if you ask me."

"It almost looks as if …" Té turned and raised his arm again and watched as his shadow followed. He counted to five, and again that strange shadow appeared before disappearing. "It's as if something is in here."

"Yes," Smillie yelled. "The scrolls."

Té walked toward the distorted shadow. All seemed normal except for the strange way the light was reflecting around it. It was as if something was blocking it, but only for a few seconds. He waited and nothing happened.

"Nothing," he said mostly to himself. "Just the outside light playing games with me."

That thump from when they took off echoed through his mind. Reliving the sudden jerk from something hitting his chair, he took a step toward the opening, but the membrane sealed shut.

"Just great," he stated.

The room darkened. Té blinked several times. Not able to see a thing, he swiped the air in front of him with his hands. His fingers touched the smooth surface of the wall. He banged on the side, but no sound.

"They won't hear that," he whispered. "Hey, Smillie! Shoupi! I'm stuck!"

The room remained quiet.

Té sighed and closed his eyes. "Okay, don't panic. What can I do?" He glanced around and laughed. "Can't see a thing and I'm looking around." He slapped his leg. When his hand touched his robe, he chuckled. "Duh! Robe … give me light!"

Nothing happened, the room remained dark.

"Darn!" Té said, taking a step back.

Michael's words echoed through his mind, *'Your robe is your best friend.'*

"Oh yeah," Té said.

Thinking about his robe and how much it was worth to him, he grabbed the garment and rubbed his hands as if heating it up. A light flickered and the sparks pricked his fingers.

"Please," he whispered.

Rubbing faster, his robe lit. He glanced around and could now see a little. Not as much as if the slit was open, but enough to find his way out.

Some *thing* whimpered.

Spinning around, Té stared at a dark figure that was pushed into one of the curves.

"Who's here?" His heart pounded as he stepped toward the shadow that seemed to appear and then disappear. "Answer me! I know you're in here. It was *you* that hit my chair."

The shadow moved and Té jumped back.

"Té?" a weak voice whispered.

Té's mind whirled. He knew that voice. "Isla?"

Isla coughed and sniffled.

"Isla, is that you? Answer me." His voice grew in authority.

"Yes. It's me." She sniffled again.

"What are you doing here?" he asked.

"Don't be mad, please," she begged. "I'm … I'm in trouble. I need your help."

Té watched as her body materialized. Now standing eye-to-eye with the girl he had shared a passionate kiss, his heart fluttered. He smiled before regaining his composure. "What're you doing here?"

Tears ran down her cheeks. "I need your help."

He held her hand and nodded.

"Remove my band!" Rosie yelled. "Remove my band!"

Serene came to a sudden stop.

"I want to see the stars!" Rosie screeched.

Aleia dashed to the window. "Look at the colors, blue …
orange … red."

"Get this thing off me! "Rosie struggled from side to side.

Em sighed. "Rosie … I told you the word to say …
remember? Say *remove* and it'll disappear."

"Remove!" The band dissolved, and Rosie flew next to
Aleia. She pressed her nose against the glass. "See any pink
stars?"

Aleia laughed. "Pink? Sorry, no pink ones."

"Drats," Rosie replied, pouting.

Em remained in her seat. "Okay, Serene. I guess we're here.
We're ready to learn."

The clear, rectangular panel that floated just above the
joystick seemed to be beckoning them. Letters popped in one
after the other.

"Hey, guys … Serene is trying to communicate with us."

Aleia step closer. "I can read it from over here."

"Wait for me. "Rosie clapped her hands together. "I want
to read it for us. Please … let me do it."

Aleia giggled. "Babies that can read, fly, and prank –"

"And with a pink rabbit that grows bigger on demand. We
better stay on her good side." Em laughed. "Go ahead, Rosie,
if it makes you happy. Enlighten us."

Rosie hovered above the panel and read. "*Hello … Em,
Aleia, and Ro'* … why is my name always last?"

"Because you're the youngest?" Em replied.

"Oh …" Rosie shrugged. *"Welcome. You are at the entrance to Quad One. Your eternal StarWriting begins here. Deliver His Plan and your prayers to each soul's star.'"* The message disappeared. "That it?" Rosie flew back a little and frowned. "That didn't help much. Stupid butterfly!"

"Serene … how?" Em asked.

THOUGHT CONTROL scrolled across the screen.

"She's answering you." Rosie pointed. "But thought? What kind of a stupid answer is that? Thought control? How many thoughts can a person have?"

Em held onto the joystick. "Maybe she means I write with this?"

A smiley face appeared on the screen.

Rosie giggled. "Great, now the dumb butterfly is drawing for us."

"Let's see if I can write with the stick," Em said, pushing it to the side.

The stick refused to move.

"It won't budge," Em said between grunts.

"Pull it up," Aleia added.

Em huffed and sat back. "Well … *this* is a nothing burger."

"Let me try it." Aleia stared at Rosie and frowned. "Forget it, I'm stronger than you."

Rosie flew behind them and sighed. "Pull harder."

Two antennae extended out from the front of the butterfly as the three watched from the viewing window.

Aleia sat back and pointed. "Something's happening."

The antennae jerked around as if searching before the two slammed into each other becoming one. Dashes of light shot into the darkened space with scrolls following behind.

Em's eyes widened. Aleia and Rosie laughed.

Em stood and took several steps toward the window. She gasped as she read off the words, "Well … this is a nothing burger."

"Oh no." Aleia sighed. "This is not good."

The words hit the closest star and it brightened as if absorbing the sentence.

"Uh-oh …" Rosie pointed to the screen.

"What?" Em asked, not taking her eyes off the bright light.

"It's asking for your next words." Rosie slapped her hands on her hips.

Aleia stared at the screen and shook her head. The screen read: NEXT.

"I don't think that was a good thing you just did," Rosie stated. "Don't think that's what you were supposed to StarWrite out there. Nothing burger? Really?"

Standing in front of Té, Isla wiped her eyes with the back of her hands.

"You shouldn't be here." Té glared at her. "We're in training. How did you get onboard?"

Isla blinked several times. "I know," she whispered. "I shouldn't be here. It's against all the rules for us workers."

Té felt sorry for her but understood the ramifications. He stepped back and glanced around. It was as if he half expected Ja Crof to appear at any moment.

"I desperately need your help," she said.

"What can I possibly help you with way out here? Why didn't you ask when we were on the band?"

"It's my family." Her voice cracked.

"How can you remember your family?" He sighed. "I don't remember anything except what's happening here and now."

"That's just it." She blinked again and wiped her face. "I've … I've had these memories. Memories I can't shake." Isla looked down at her feet. "I'm afraid that if I tell you, you won't believe me."

"Let me decide what I will or will not believe."

Isla leaned in closer and whispered, "I took a memory potion."

"A what?"

"Shh … 'it's the pathway to everlasting fire. It'll be you, Isla, to free them.'"

Té shook his head. "I don't understand. You're talking gibberish."

"The afternoon of the bombing … when I died … our guardian took the four of us … Mum, me, my brother, and sister on the path of Eternity Present. It was beautiful. I trusted her. The light was so bright and clean. And I felt love. It was incredible. I knew we were going somewhere wonderful, together, as a family. I knew not to worry about my dad. That he would be taken care of −"

"You heard all of that?" Té frowned.

"I felt it deep inside my thoughts. I knew that he would be fine, and I didn't have to feel sad. I was thinking about our new world, and how we'd be a family again, but that's when I smelled this …"

"This what?"

"Grayson said it was sulfur −"

"Okay, something stunk, but why are you on *my* StarWriting transport?" Té asked.

"Please … let me finish. A dark cloud hovered over us and everything turned black. It was hot. Oh, Té, it was so hot and smokey. The guardian screamed so loud. I never heard anything like it. It was horrible. I reached for Mum and Messy and then I saw it."

"Saw what?"

"Something moved."

"Something moved?"

Isla nodded. "They were grabbed and taken to Hell."

"How do you know that?"

"I just know." She gazed into his eyes. "The white path divided us. The guardian led Grayson and me to a silver gate. The thing must have been a hundred feet tall. I asked her in my thoughts, *'where was Mum and Messy?'* She said, *'The pathway to everlasting fire.'* Then I was in *His Plan* room and bilocating to our new life."

"Does Grayson remember any of this?"

"Nothing. And that's why I have to get to Hell. I have to save them."

Irid lunged and Isla fell into Té's arms.

He gazed at her and felt his heart race. He felt weak but remembered Director Crof's words to stay away from the forbidden area. He did not want to be sucked into the entrance of Hell and torn into a billion pieces.

"We're not allowed anywhere near the forbidden area."

"I don't want *you* to go there." Isla shook her head. "Just me. Your butterfly can take us there and communicate with the forbidden quadrant, so *I* can go there."

"Irid can't do that. It's not allowed." He sighed.

Isla cried. "I have to save Mummy and Messy. That *thing* stole their souls."

"What stole their souls?"

Isla shrugged. "I have to find out."

The membrane opened and light filled the room. Smillie poked his head inside.

"Té, you in here? I think we're ready to move again. Something's happening out there."

"I'm here," Té replied, releasing Isla.

Smillie squinted. "Where? Don't see you." Smillie stepped inside. "Wait, who's that?"

"Isla. A worker from *His Plan* room."

"The girl that smiled at you?"

"Guilty," Isla replied, sniffling. "I'm sorry to meet you like this."

Glaring at Té, Smillie shook his head. "You brought her here?"

Té frowned. "I didn't bring her here. She stowed away without us or Irid knowing."

"Why are you here?" Smillie asked.

"She's —" Té started to say.

"Let me." Isla held out her hand. "I need help."

"What for?" Smillie asked.

Isla whimpered. "To get into Hell."

Rosie glared at Em. "Hope nobody saw that one ..." She stomped her foot in the air. "Makes us look like idiots!"

"Funny," Em replied.

"Aleia ... you try it." Rosie raised her voice. "Em really messed it up ... nothing burger ... geesh!"

Em slapped her head and sighed. "Okay ... so what just happened? Did what I just say get StarWrited for all eternity to see?"

Aleia raised her 'brows. "Ah ... yes? The words flew out just in front of the scrolls."

Rosie fluttered between them and coughed. "Excuse me ... that is exactly what happened. You wrote something about food and ... boom ... out it went. Some *in charge* person you turned out to be."

"Serene ..." Em stated. "I need you to fix this." Em clapped her hands. "That soul cannot have *'Well, this is a nothing burger'* written all over it. Can you correct it?"

Letters appeared on the screen. YES, I CAN ... WHAT DO YOU WANT TO STARWRITE IN ITS PLACE ...

"Can you erase it?" Em asked.

NO

Em sighed. "What do you mean by *no?*"

"Maybe you have to be more specific," Aleia replied.

Rosie pointed at the screen. "Look … it's answering you. Will you two pay attention please?"

I CAN ONLY REWRITE … BUT … MUST USE THE SAME AMOUNT OF COLORS …

Rosie flew closer and frowned. "What in the world does that mean? You really broke the darn thing this time."

Aleia laughed. "Rosie, you're pink … you fly … you are a baby … you talk, unfortunately, so why can't you interpret for us? What is this butterfly trying to say?"

Rosie sat on Em's leg and stared at the screen. She touched the joystick and waited. Glancing out the window, she laughed. "I think I get it."

"Get what?" Aleia asked. "Can you explain it to us?"

"Well …" Rosie flew in front of them and hovered. "Butterflies don't talk. They flutter. And they fly from flower to flower. How do they know a flower from a tree? They don't. They go by colors. Therefore, those words you sputtered out, which you were not supposed to say, are colors to them. They're not words. Let's see, *well, this is a nothing burger,*" is six colors or eight if we're considering syllables. We just have to figure out what word is what color."

"What word is what color?" Em repeated. "That's crazy."

"No, it is not," Rosie stated. "It makes sense. I see *burger* as brown or green. *Nothing* is probably blue. Maybe the regular words, like *a* or *well* are black. See, it's not hard. Say something similar but different."

"Something similar but different," Em repeated.

"I didn't say repeat *my* words, I said –"

"I know what you said …" Em took in a deep breath. "Let me think."

"Well, think fast, cuz we're looking pretty stupid about now," Rosie stated, crossing her arms.

Em coughed and cleared her throat. "Serene … please replace my quote with … *May your life and beyond prosper.*"

"Oh brother, I hope this works!" Rosie flew to the window and watched as the colorful words flew into a distant star. A bright flash shot out in all directions. "Hey, I think it worked!"

"You know more than you're letting on, Rosie," Aleia said.

"What do you mean?" Rosie turned and frowned.

"She may look like a baby," Em said. "But a baby that's evolving. And she's changing even now."

Rosie laughed. "Of course, I feel smarter every second."

Aleia squinted. "Not the kind of babies I know."

"And how many babies do you know?" Rosie asked. "Or should I say … remember?"

"Serene," Em said, trying to defuse an argument before one started. "Teach us about what StarWriters should write on the stars. Please …"

The screen lit and several words flew across.

"She's writing a lot this time," Rosie said, hovering behind Em.

YOU SHALL HAVE IT WRITTEN IN THE STARS
YOU EACH WILL DELIVER *HIS PLAN*
THEIR WISHES
THEIR PRAYERS
THEIR HOPES, BUT …

"Okay …" Aleia sighed. "But what … what does that mean?"

ON THE SOUL'S STAR YOU WILL COLOR
FROM YOUR HEART … YOUR
STARWRITER'S MESSAGE

"Serene did replace my *nothing burger* message." Em smiled.

Rosie gazed out the window. "May your life and beyond prosper. Yup … that's five … six colorful words and makes no sense at all. Very good. Everything is matching."

"I'll go next," Aleia stated.

THOUGHT CONTROL, appeared.

"We can probably go at the same time," Aleia whispered. "Just use our thoughts."

A pink heart lasered off to a distant star followed by several scrolls. Rosie crossed her arms and tilted her head. "That was me."

"Rosie! That is not a word or wisdom," Em said.

ACCEPTABLE, appeared on the screen.

"See …" Rosie stuck out her tongue. "That's how *I'm* going to write … with my colorful and pink hearts."

Em frowned. "Why do I even bother."

MAY YOUR LIFE HAVE MEANING …

"I like that, Aleia." Em ran her hand across the screen. "Quite profound."

"Thank you." Aleia nodded. "This is fun."

"I think I want to sit down," Rosie said, landing on Em's knee. "Can you bind my wings again?"

Em glanced at Aleia and then Rosie. She smiled and nodded.

They remained busy sending out their messages and scrolls. Em inhaled deeply for she felt truly in charge for the first time.

"*We* are a StarWriting team." Em laughed. "Director Crof would be pleased."

"I wonder if the other StarWriters are having as much fun as we are," Aleia replied and Rosie nodded.

Smillie stood next to Isla with widened eyes as shadows flickered around the room. "Isla, even if we could get close to the forbidden quadrant, Irid would never allow us to actually enter."

"Yes, it will," Isla said, tapping her foot.

"No, it won't." Té shook his head.

Isla nodded. "Oh, yes it will, 'cause Irid's under a trance. A trance of *my* doing, and she will obey my commands."

"Impossible." Té glanced at Smillie and frowned.

"Yes, it *is* possible," a deeper voice echoed through the room. A whisper of swaying, black hair materialized with large, dark and glaring eyes.

Smillie took a step back as a tall and muscular body materialized.

Té glared at the imposing figure that was now towering over them.

"What are you doing here?" Isla yelled.

"Making sure your plans are where you need them to be," the figure replied.

"And why would you do that?" Isla asked. "You don't trust me?"

The stranger snickered. "Took a double dose of the red elixir and followed you here."

"I was invisible —" Isla said.

"You glow," replied the stranger.

"Others saw me too?"

"Just me. That was the plan."

"How did you get on the transport?" Isla asked.

"I was right behind you. As the stairs folded, I pushed you into the damn thing, otherwise the door would have shut on us both." He chuckled. "When you crawled under the seat, I snuck back here without anyone noticing."

Té cleared his throat. "Isla? Who is this?"

Smillie stepped closer, placing his hands on his hips.

"Té and Smillie," Isla said, tilting her head, "this is Beck. He's been assisting me. My plan is to find my mum and sister who were taken by the evil spirits."

"Yes," Beck added. "And bring them back with you on this mechanical butterfly." He grabbed Isla's arm and gave her a little shove. "I think we should get started. Don't you, Isla? As you're the one who's put this … *thing* into a trance." He walked to the membrane and yanked it apart. "You first, Isla." He stopped Té and Smillie from following her with his arm. "Don't think about doing anything stupid."

"This won't work," Té said.

"It already has." Beck chuckled.

"What took you guys so —" Shoupi turned and gasped. "Well, hello. Who are you? And why are you here?"

Beck pushed Té and Smillie. "Another StarWriter? Aren't *we* the cozy crew."

"Shoupi …" Té shook his head.

Isla glared at Beck. "Why do you have to sound so mean?"

Shoupi wrapped her arms across her chest and sighed.

"Don't worry Shoupi. We won't hurt you." Isla's voice oozed with sweetness. "I'm Isla and this is Beck. We just want to get into Hell." Her words rolled as if she were doing *them* a favor.

Shoupi's eyes widened and filled with tears.

"Don't cry," Isla whispered. "It's just for a little while. I have to find my mum and sister. Irid will hover, I'll run down and get 'em, and then we'll leave. We'll have you back to the band in no time." Isla sighed. "Please help us? It'll be okay. I promise."

"Irid cannot fly anywhere near the forbidden quadrant." Shoupi wiped her eyes.

"We already told them that," Smillie added.

Isla shook her head. "I gave Irid an elixir and she'll —"

"Enough, Isla." Beck pointed at the three StarWriters. "Against that wall … no talking … girl in the middle. I have this elixir that will dissolve your spirits, and I'm not afraid to use it!"

"Her name is Shoupi." Isla frowned.

"Whatever." Beck held out a vial of a dark liquid, waving it through the air. "Watch 'em." He walked over and sat in the middle seat.

"Beck's a good guy, usually," Isla whispered, glancing over her shoulder. "He's just trying to help me find my family."

"By dissolving us?" Té tensed as Beck grabbed the controls, and a red cloud moved slowly toward them. Té nodded at the window, and Shoupi and Smillie gasped. They looked at Té as if searching for reassurance. Té clenched his fist, the fear in his partners' eyes mimicking what he was feeling. The forbidden quadrant was a place no one wanted to go. He wondered what lay ahead. None of it could be good. He had to speak up. "What you're doing is wrong, Isla."

She tilted her head and shrugged.

"Irid," Beck said. "You will listen to my voice. Only my voice."

Irid bumped forward. The three stumbled toward Isla. Isla grabbed Shoupi's arm.

"Thank you," Shoupi said, moving back to the wall.

Té was refusing Isla's advances. When she looked at him, he looked away. He had liked her at first, but now his feelings were switching to dislike – distrust. *She used me.*

"I command you, Irid," Beck stated. "Go to the forbidden quadrant … if not, then your precious StarWriters will be nothing more than a vapor!" Beck's voice raised in authority.

The butterfly inched slowly closer to the glowing red horizon.

"Irid!" Beck stated. "Stop and hover." He stood and stepped over to the window. He placed his hands on the wall and stared out. It was as if he had just been hypnotized or something.

Isla clapped her hands. "Mummy!" she yelled. "Messy … I'm coming."

"When were they taken?" Shoupi asked.

"When our guide was escorting us through Eternity Present. Some *thing* grabbed 'em. Me and my brother were taken to *His Plan* room. My mum and sister disappeared."

"How do you know that?" Shoupi asked. "I don't remember anything before –"

"Isla, get ready," Beck ordered.

"Stay here." Isla held up her hands. "Beck promised it wouldn't take long." She turned and walked toward Beck.

Beck remained frozen, staring out the window. Irid jerked forward several times, and the red glow flickered as if calling to him … urging him forward.

"Beck?" Isla asked. "What's happening? It's as if the butterfly is fighting us."

"Not anymore," Beck replied. "Looks like we're all going along for the ride." He turned and smiled, but his face no longer resembled a kind and caring Beck.

Landon watched the dashes of light zoom out from the antennae. "LYK, you're unbelievably helpful. Thank you."

YOU ARE WELCOME

"Yeah, I don't remember the last time I had such fun," Yutu said.

Keekee clapped her hands. "Can't wait to do it again."

"Are all the scrolls delivered?" Landon asked.

YES

"Let's head back," Yutu said. "Maybe LYK'll let me take the controls now." Yutu shrugged.

YES

Landon chuckled. "Not very chatty are you LYK?"

GOODBYE

The rectangular screen grew dark and vanished.

"Okay then. Bye, LYK." Yutu sat up straighter. He concentrated on moving the joystick back and forth.

Landon pointed at the window. "A red glow ... what's that?"

"I don't know," Keekee replied, stepping closer. "It's not a star. It wasn't that bright before. Doesn't feel right. I don't like this."

"You were poetic with your StarWriting," Landon stated.

"Thank you, I didn't want to sound silly," Keekee replied, rubbing her arms. "Yours sounded ... thought provoking."

"Think so?"

"Yeah, I do." Keekee giggled, but her eyes remained focused on the growing red glow. "What we are doing is important."

"Agreed." Landon nodded and rubbed his arms. "Hey, that cloud's getting redder … and closer. I think we should go. I don't like this."

"Like what?" Yutu asked.

Yutu! Help … help me, please.

"Huh, what?" Yutu glanced at his partners. "What did you say?"

"I said, we need to go," Landon replied. "That cloud is coming right for us, and I don't like the looks of it."

Yutu pulled back on the control stick. "C'mon LYK. We're done here. Let's go."

Yutu! Help … help me, please.

"Help you with what, Landon?" Yutu looked at his partners and frowned. "Stop playing around."

Landon sighed. "Are we ready to leave?"

"Then we should sit down," Keekee said.

LYK swerved and soared away from the expanding red cloud.

Milos, Jenni, and Colton ran down the stairs and stood in front of T.G. They high fived each other and yelped.

"That was *so* cool," Jenni screamed. "Can't wait to go again."

Milos and Colton danced around.

"Wow …" Milos said. "That was —"

"I know …" Colton high-fived Milos again.

The wind whipped and the sound of fluttering wings filled the air.

"LYK's right behind us," Jenni said. "Let's head back to the tree. Everyone'll go there. Can't wait to share our stories. We *are* StarWriters now."

"You leaf the way, oh fearless leader." Milos laughed.

Colton shook his head. "Oh … I get it … leaf … tree. Ha, ha."

"I need some alone time," Yutu said. The door opened and the stairs glided to the ground. Yutu darted passed Keekee and Landon and ran down the stairs.

Landon furrowed his 'brows. "Is it something we said? He was quiet when we left the quad."

Keekee shrugged and pointed up. "Let's wait for Serene. It's Em, Aleia, and Rosie. I want to compare notes."

Landon pretended to guide in the butterfly by raising his arms. "Yeah … that's it … keep coming."

Keekee covered her mouth and laughed.

Yutu walked along the shore and sloshed through water, but his feet remained dry and warm. Staring at the ripples, he allowed his mind to wander.

Who was talking to me?

He shrugged as he walked. The soft voice kept repeating through his mind. *Yutu! Help … help me, please.* He had heard that voice before, but he couldn't remember where. He needed an explanation. He needed answers.

The air felt cool and the wind seemed to be picking up. A roll was forming at the top of the waves.

Yutu! Help … help me, please. The voice roared toward him only this time it was clear and concise.

He glanced up at the mountain peaks and something was moving along with the clouds. He concentrated and a small skiff formed, fading in and out. It was as if someone was playing with a shadow figure or maybe his mind was forming images inside the clouds.

Yutu bilocated and floated above the mist. Below him a scene was playing out, almost as if the actors were there just for him. A large wave rolled and aimed at the small boat. It raised higher into the air before falling back and capsizing. The backpacks and life jackets flew out and floated dead in the water.

A girl screamed. "Yutu! Help me! Help me!"

Through the spraying waves, Yutu watched. He felt helpless and afraid. A boy climbed onto the top of the capsized boat and tried to see through the blinding rain.

"Amelia! Grab my hand!" the boy yelled.

Their fingers touched, and the boy pulled her onto the boat.

"Hey, watch it!" Yutu screamed out as the girl's hand slipped through the boy's.

The boy searched for her in the darkness. He yelled over and over again, "Amelia! Amelia!"

Yutu yelled, "Take my hand, Amelia. I'm here." He reached out and grasped at the dark waters covered him. It was now he who was falling into the blackness and disappearing.

Yutu stood back on the shore, his heart pounding and his mind twirling. He was again standing in the calm water.

"What just happened?"

A voice whispered around him. *"A vision, Yutu. He shall call to you … Amelia is in Sheol and only you can save her … this time … you have been given another chance. Remain quiet, Yutu, or the offer will be rescinded …"*

"What? Amelia who?" Yutu glanced around but he was alone. "You mean the girl in the water?"

No reply.

He jumped as a hand slapped him from behind.

"Here you are!" Landon stated.

Keekee smiled. "We've been looking for you. Director Crof wants us under the tree."

"I … I think I … just evolved." Yutu felt weak and his hands refused to stop shaking.

"That's great!" Landon slapped him again on the shoulder. "You okay? You don't look so good."

"I'm fine." Yutu glanced up at the clouds and frowned.

"Tell me what happened," Keekee said, staring into the sky with him. "I'm now the only one who hasn't evolved."

Tell no one, the voice again whispered into Yutu's ear.

"Forget it." Yutu walked away.

Ja Crof stepped onto her balcony and gazed up at the sky. The clouds were a deeper red, reminding her of blood. She also thought about death. Her eyes widened. It had begun and there was no stopping it.

"Three of the four groups have returned as StarWriters," she stated to herself. "However …"

Michael visualized next to her. He too stared into the crimson sky. "*The Prophecy.* It has begun, my friend."

"Yes," Ja Crof replied. "It has begun."

"They will soon learn who she really is."

Ja Crof nodded. "We must prepare the returning StarWriters." She stared at the light and dark ribbons, allowing her mind to wander. *How can they be prepared for the horrors that await?*

"Show them who they are," Michael replied.

"Reading my thoughts again?" Ja Crof sighed.

"Not really," he replied. "I just know you like a book."

Mary K. Savarese

The Prophecy

214

CHAPTER 27

Irid jerked as an invisible force pulled them toward the growing red clouds. Its wings fluttered and tugged against the current. The metal creaked and groaned from the strain.

"Don't fight it, butterfly," Beck stated. "Just let it take you." Beck pushed on the joystick.

"This is not good," Smillie said, staring out the window.

Shoupi whimpered. "The red cloud will swallow us!"

Té nodded and grabbed Shoupi's hand. *What have I gotten us into?* His legs trembled and he felt weak.

"We'll be there shortly." Beck glanced at Isla and smiled.

She leaned over to Beck. "Get close like you said. We'll bilocate in and grab my mum and sister … they'll …" – she nodded to the back – "… stay here."

Beck smiled again, holding up the glowing vial, his eyes now glowing a dark red.

"Right?" Isla asked.

"Sure," Beck replied, not blinking.

Isla turned and smiled. "See, Té. Everything'll be just fine. Really."

Té tilted his head and frowned. His stomach felt funny and it hurt to swallow. What was ahead for the three of 'em? Did anyone know they were not StarWriting? They never had the chance to send even one scroll or one word. Would anyone come to rescue them?

Irid jerked again as the red mist crept closer, covering the viewing screen. It was as if the cloud was alive. The StarWriters could sense it, feel it. They knew – it wanted *them*.

Shoupi gasped, slapping her hands over her eyes.

The light faded into darkness. The kind of darkness that didn't just reflect the light but completely absorbed it. The strong aroma of sulfur and rotting flesh filled the air. Té blinked several times. He held out his hand and shook it. Nothing … it was too dark to see anything. He gagged.

"Beck!" Isla whined. "We're too close –"

"Just entering a different realm," Beck replied, "Relax, it's cool."

Té grabbed Shoupi's hand.

"I'm afraid," Shoupi whispered. "I can't see anything."

"I know." Té again gagged.

The blackness dissipated as a charcoal-haze filled the compartment. Smoldering ash covered the windows, again darkening the room.

"Coming in for a landing!" Beck yelled, yanking on the control with both hands. "Hold onto something. Gonna be a rough one."

Isla jumped from her seat. Her gait swayed as she aimed for Té.

"Order your robes to lock to the wall!" Té yelled.

Irid weaved and jerked radically.

"Stop fighting me and land already!" Beck screamed.

Isla lunged backward, stumbling into Té's arms. Té reached out and grabbed her.

"Thanks," she whispered. "It'll all be good."

Té refused to answer.

"Land, damnit …!" Beck screamed. "Stop fighting me."

Isla wobbled back to Beck and her chair. "What's going on? Tell Irid to just hover … not land!"

"Our butterfly's fighting back," Smillie whispered.

"You're right." Té replied.

"Hope it keeps fighting," Shoupi added.

"You think we can take Beck? "Smillie asked.

"He's bigger than both of us," Té whispered.

"Maybe the elixir is wearing off," Isla stated.

"No, not yet," Beck replied.

"How would you know?" she asked.

"Because I gave it a double dose after yours." He turned and smiled at her. "This *thing* is completely under my control."

Isla stared at him. "What do mean … *your* control?"

Irid landed with such force that it bounced before gliding to a standstill. Three red domes now rose high into the sky several feet in front of them. Large rod-iron gates with miss-matched weave stood open, welcoming the new arrivals.

Beck held up the vial, waving it through the air. "Welcome to Sheol! Ready to disembark?"

"We're here just to rescue Mummy and Messy," Isla said, turning to stare at the three who were still glued to the wall. "Why do we need them?"

"Butterfly, open and cargo release," Beck stated.

Isla sighed.

"Sorry 'bout this, Isla. Plans have changed a little." Beck laughed and pointed the vial directly at Té. "You three out first … then *you*, Isla. Go stand by those gates."

Glancing at his partners, Té shrugged.

Shoupi descended the steps followed by Smillie and Té. The heat felt smothering, glowing in shades of orange and red. She took a step and the ground crunched beneath her. "What is this stuff?"

Smillie grabbed her arm.

"I'm so sorry," Isla yelled from inside Irid.

"What are we walking on?" Smillie asked, trying to stand and not fall. "This ground's not stable."

Té sighed. "Bones."

"Bones?" Shoupi repeated.

Té nodded. "Bones … remember? *'You shall be sucked into the entrance of Hell and spit into a million pieces.'* That's what Director said."

"Is this what she meant?" Shoupi stared at the ground. Broken and chipped human bones littered the pathway. She screamed just missing a human skull. "A graveyard?"

"Apparently, yes." Té nodded.

They stepped up to the gates and stared. Three red domes, the first smaller than the other two, stood side by side. No doors or windows from what Té could tell.

"I think it's worse on the other side of these gates," Smillie stated.

"Remain strong and pray. *He* will help us." Shoupi gagged and slapped her hand over her mouth and nose.

"How could you know that?" Té asked.

Beck pushed Té, shoving him through the gates. "Shut up and keep walking."

Isla placed her hands on her hips. "This is *all* wrong, Beck."

"Isla … my dear …" – his voice oozed with sweetness – "… what's waiting for you is spectacular."

Isla smiled. "You found Mummy and Messy?"

"Even better." Beck grinned.

Isla ran over to Té. "Did you hear that?"

"Hear what?" he asked.

"Beck just told me something better is in there. I think he means that Mummy and Messy are waiting for me."

Té scowled. "I don't trust anything about him. He lies and uses people. Namely, you and now us … for whatever he or they have planned."

"I disagree." Isla smiled. "We'll just grab my family and leave."

Té felt somewhat sorry for her. He glanced at his partners and frowned. It was his fault for liking this girl, and now they were suffering along with him.

"Té," Isla said with a bounce in her step, "did you hear me? We'll just grab them and leave."

Té couldn't bring himself to look at her. He wanted to shake the smile right off her cheery face. Then he would convince her about how Beck had used her and was now using them. He stared down at the gritty surface and thought about the countless souls that had been spit into millions of pieces that were now forming the decaying path. The path to –

"Isla," Té said, grabbing her arm. "No one *ever* leaves Hell."

Sitting under the wondrous tree, Colton pretended to write in the air with his finger. "May you forever prosper." He chuckled. "That's the one I used the most while StarWriting."

"After a while I became redundant myself." Landon nudged Yutu. "What about you?"

"Huh?" Yutu stared out at nothing. "What'd you say?"

"What did you StarWrite?" Landon asked.

"Ahh …" Yutu continued to stare into nothing.

Landon shrugged and looked at the others.

"I don't know about you, but I had a blast," Jenni replied. "Can't wait to get out there again."

Hovering, Rosie giggled. "It was fun. I wrote in pink hearts."

"I need to think of something more thought provoking," Aleia replied.

Em nodded. "Ditto."

Keekee smiled. "Who are we waiting on?" She counted the members in the circle. "Milos …"

"Here," he said, raising his hand.

Giggling Keekee continued, "Jenni … Colton …"

"Here and here," they replied.

"Okay …" – Keekee nodded – "… Landon, Yutu, and me." She pointed at herself.

Rosie flew in closer. "We're all here except for Shoupi, Smillie, and Té."

"I wonder what's taking 'em so long?" Em scratched her head."

Rosie whispered loudly, "You worried about Té, Em?"

Em frowned. "We *all* are. They should have returned already. And … where is Director Crof? We were supposed to meet her here."

Ja Crof and Michael watched and listened to the StarWriters. Sitting on an upper branch, the two were hidden by the heart-shaped leaves.

"It's time," Michael stated. "They need to know what is about to come. Why *they* were chosen. Come into my thoughts to better understand."

Ja Crof sighed. "Must we enter Sheol?"

"You know *The Prophecy*." Michael frowned.

"And a child shall free them," she replied, nodding.

"It is *His* decision not ours."

"I know … tell me why again?"

"*He* loves children and weaves their souls. *He* watches as they grow and protects them. *He* loves them like no other and hopes that someday they will return to *Him*."

"Understood," she whispered, furrowing her brow. Ja Crof glanced down at the StarWriters.

"You have guided and taught them well."

"Reading my thoughts again?" She grinned. "Thank you for the vote of confidence."

"*He* does as well." Michael pointed up.

"Where do we go from here?"

"I'll start with Em and Aleia. We will bilocate to Eternity Past. They shall only see their portion of *His Plan*. Just that, which will sustain them for what is about to come."

"Why not take Rosie along with Em and Aleia?" she asked.

"Oh," Michael sighed. "Rosie already *knows* who she is. Behold, I shall show you." Michael placed his hand above Ja Crof's head. Rosie materialized and Ja Crof sighed and frowned.

Michael stood over a dark-haired baby sleeping in the bustling children's ICU. A small pink cap off to one side. He reached down and picked it up. After staring at it for a moment, he placed it on the child's head.

"To keep you warm," he whispered.

The baby blinked, staring up at him. Various IVs and electronic wires were attached to most of her frail, ten-month old body.

"Hello, Rosie." Michael rubbed her hand. "You shall soon understand."

Rosie yawned.

"Do you know how much *He* loves you?" Michael's eyes twinkled in the dim light. "*He* created you to demonstrate perfection to this world."

She blinked and closed her eyes. As her spirit floated up, hovering next to Michael, the alarms sounded. Several nurses ran to the incubator and played with the tubes and wires. Michael waved his hand through the air and everyone froze.

"What's going on?" Rosie asked, hovering over her body. "Is that me?"

"Yes," Michael replied.

"I don't understand."

"You will."

"What's wrong with me?"

"It's a genetic abnormality. It happens sometimes." Michael nodded.

"I'm abnormal?"

"In his eyes, *you* are perfect," Michael replied.

"Perfect? Does that look perfect?" Rosie flew a little closer to the still baby. "Look at me … it … me. Everyone is always crying when they see me." She huffed. "What did you do to me?"

"Nothing," Michael replied. "The roulette of DNA is always unknown."

Rosie flew up to Michael and placed her face close. "Who are you?"

"Oh, my dear little cherub." Michael chuckled. "You *are* going to be a handful." He smiled. "I am Michael. We need you. Your brother needs you."

Rosie glanced at the baby sleeping in the other incubator. He, too, was hooked up to various tubes and wires. The baby boy did not move

"Is he dying?" Rosie asked.

"Yes," Michael replied. "But you can save him."

"Save him?"

Michael nodded. "For your parents."

Rosie thought about her life and how warm it was inside her mother's womb, sleeping so close to her brother. She sighed. "How can I help?"

"Your strength and beyond." Michael nodded. "Your beating heart can save him. He will live long and prosper. He will never forget, and one day you will be reunited."

Rosie placed her hands on her hips. She glanced over her shoulder and smiled. "I have wings?"

Michael nodded.

"Let me get this straight … you want *me* to die so my twin can have *my* heart. What's wrong with his?"

"It is very week and too small," Michael replied.

"Okay, and if I do this, what's in it for me?"

"What do you want?" Michael asked.

Rosie glanced around the room. "See that toy lion over there." She pointed.

Michael turned and smiled.

"I want a real one."

"A real lion? Lions are finicky. Difficult to negotiate with." Michael sighed. "And they sleep most of the day."

Rosie frowned.

"What about a bunny?" he asked. "There's one sitting next to that lion."

Rosie's eyes widened. "I like pink."

"How about a real bunny. You can be a team."

"A team?" Rosie smiled. "Can I have pink hair?"

"Everything about you will be pink …"

Rosie closed her eyes, holding the pink bunny close to her heart. As the little nose twitched, Rosie whispered, "I'll name you Lyon."

Michael leaned over, listening to the child's labored breathing. "It is time, Rosie."

Rosie nodded and the two vanished.

Machines beeped and a nurse yelled, "Code blue, code blue!"

Ja Crof laughed. "I always knew Rosie was a firecracker." She grinned. "She's perfect."

"*He* created her to be perfect," Michael replied.

She nodded.

"Ja Crof … you shall see and hear all," Michael said, fading into the mist. "We will begin with Em and Aleia."

Ja Crof nodded again and closed her eyes.

Michael slowly walked up to the base of the large tree. He nodded at the small group. "Hello, Em and Aleia."

Em and Aleia smiled.

"Will you two come with me?" Michael asked.

"Are we bilocating?" Em asked.

Michael nodded.

"Ready," Aleia said.

Em and Aleia stepped away from their bodies that remained sitting near the large trunk. Rosie hovered next to the sitting Em and smiled.

"Can I sit in your lap?" Rosie asked the sitting Em.

Em tapped her knee.

Michael and Em hovered over a girl who looked to be in her mid-teens with long, blonde hair. The girl grabbed at her chest and gasped for air.

"Do you know where we are?" Michael asked.

Em nodded. "That's me. I'm in bed. We were in Switzerland. My high school team was with me." She took a deep breath and touched her chest. "My heart hurt. I couldn't breathe. I never felt anything like that and then … nothing, I must've blacked out."

"What do you remember after that?" Michael asked.

"A bright light and I heard someone say, *'do not be afraid, Em.'* It was you!" Em glanced at Michael. "It was *you* who came to me when I was dying?"

Michael nodded and waved his hand. His image appeared next to the bed.

"Am I dying?" the girl in the bed whispered.

He nodded to the girl. "If you live, your younger sister will not. A silent killer lurks within your bodies."

"What silent killer?" the girl asked.

"*He* created you in *His* image. However, from man's sins, the genetic defect was born. If not detected in you, then it will be too late for your sister. However, with your death, the silent killer will be uncovered and they will survive."

"They?"

"Your sister and mother."

"They will both live if I go with you now?" the girl asked. "Because of the defect we carry?"

"Yes."

Em nodded and watched as the girl's chest rose before falling silent.

Michael and Aleia hovered over the front steps of the Chicago brownstone.

"Hey," Aleia said. "That's Trevor, my little brother."

Michael nodded. "Then you know where we are?"

"Yes, that's me and I'm putting him in …" Aleia stared at Michael. "This is where I died?"

Michael shook his head. "Not yet."

"Okay, Trev," the young girl said, placing the little boy inside the stroller. "We're gonna sit here for a bit. Do some people watching."

Trevor giggled.

"Can you say A..lee..a"

Trevor giggled again.

The girl frowned. "We'll work on my name after your nap." She sat on the step next to him.

Mrs. Sanchez waved as she swept the sidewalk in front of her brownstone. "Mornin' Aleia. Mornin' Trevor." She waved from across the street.

"Good morning, Mrs. Sanchez," Aleia yelled, lifting Trevor's hand in a wave.

The young girl stood and threw herself onto the stroller as several loud bangs echoed through the street. Two cars sped away. The young girl tumbled down the stairs and remained still on the sidewalk. Blood pooled around her

Mrs. Sanchez screamed. "Help! Somebody! Help, call 911!"

Trevor giggled and said, "A..lee..a."

Aleia smiled at Michael. "His first word was my name?"

"Trevor will never forget you," Michael said.

Michael and Aleia hovered over the young girl now lying on an operating table.

"I remember this," Aleia whispered.

"What do you remember?" he asked.

"You came to me during the surgery. You said that I saved Trevor's life. That someday he'd be a great man. That he'd stop the killings."

"Yes. I gave you the choice …"

"And I chose to go with you so my brother would become great in my memory."

Michael nodded.

The doctors worked diligently to save the young girl's life. A man kept pumping on her chest while another tried to stop the bleeding. A nurse yelled into a phone for more blood. The line on the machine remained straight and a signal blared.

A young female doctor wiped away a tear. "These killings must stop. She was so young. Why?" The woman took a deep breath. "Turn off these damn machines!"

Landon and Keekee bilocated with Michael.

What about Yutu? Ja Crof whispered into Michael's mind. *He's part of their crew.*

He will know after The Prophecy is fulfilled. Michael replied.

Landon stood next to Michael and frowned. "Hey, we're in the Boston Hospital —"

"You remember?" Michael asked, placing his hand on Landon's shoulder.

"Yes," he replied. "That's me in that bed."

"Yes, it is." Michael nodded.

The boy on the bed reached out to touch his sister's hand. But his hand lowered and fell. The young girl stared at her parents. The three hugged the boy as his breathing labored.

"My dying was hard on them … why?" Landon sighed.

"Yes," Michael replied, squeezing Landon's shoulder.

Landon pointed to his father. "Dad's crying and Mum's just trying to hold it together."

"It's okay to go," the mother whispered. "You'll be free from pain if you leave."

Landon glanced at Michael. "You were there too, but I couldn't see you. You're over here now. But you talked to me from over there? I heard you."

Michael chuckled. "Yes. I wanted to give your family time."

"You said I could have a miracle … if I went with you …"

Michael nodded. "Do you remember anything else?"

Landon nodded. "That my dad would relive his pain over and over again, and because of his pain, his biogenic company would discover something … something that would help people with cancer like mine."

Michael nodded. "And?"

Landon closed his eyes. "Cure my sister, Sunny."

"Yes." Michael smiled. "I promised that Sunny would live. Due to human sin, your family's DNA carries the defective gene."

The boy exhaled and remained still. The machines beeped.

"I'll love you forever, brother," the girl said, resting her head on the now silent chest.

Landon stepped up to his family and reached out. His hand swiped through his father's back. He turned and smiled at Michael. "I think I understand now." Landon nodded. "Thank you."

As the howling wind rustled their robes, Michael and Keekee stood on a cloud that hovered just outside the apartments. Michael glanced down and shook his head. The fortieth floor was quite high, and the traffic below reminded him of nothing more than children's toys. He shivered at the thought.

"I know where we are," Keekee stated.

"And where is that?" Michael asked.

Keekee glanced around. "We're outside my uncle's apartment building. I know because we have those really big windows. They always used to scare me."

Michael nodded.

Keekee gasped as a living Keekee climbed out and stood just outside the window, pushing her back against the bricks. Her eyes were wide and her hands trembled. The wind whipped her hair across her face.

"Now I remember," the Keekee standing next to Michael whispered. "My friends and I were stealing from the tenants. I climbed out so my uncle wouldn't find me. I was scared and my hair kept covering my face."

"What else do you remember?" Michael asked.

Keekee wiped away a tear. "My uncle's dead because of me. I used to call him *The Custodian* because I hated him so much. You're making me watch this for my atonement, correct?"

"Do you remember anything else?" Michael asked.

The living Keekee standing on the ledge covered her eyes with her hands.

"Do not be afraid, Keekee," Michael said to the Keekee floating next to him. "Listen … observe …"

Her uncle's hand reached out. "Keekee!" he yelled. "I know what you have been doing. Come inside. I will fix this."

"No!" Keekee yelled. "I betrayed and shamed you … I have shamed my family's name."

"Keekee!" he yelled. "Please come inside. We will talk. Everything will be okay."

Keekee wiped her nose with the back of her hand. "You raised me and showed me love. Don't you get it … I *hate you* and I want to be with my parents." Keekee cried.

"My brother would never want that. Come inside," he ordered.

"No! I want to be dead like them."

"We will reckon this, Keekee. Please come inside." Her uncle climbed out the window and cautiously stood. He wobbled and grabbed onto the window frame. He stared inside before looking down. His eyes widened and he frowned.

The Keekee standing next to Michael gasped. She reached out to her uncle, *The Custodian*, but was too far away to touch him. "Michael, he will fall … it's all my fault! I must get closer. I have to stop him."

Michael shook his head. "No, Keekee. Please … just watch."

The uncle grabbed the living Keekee by the arm. He tugged on her but she tried to pull away.

"No! I want to die," she screamed.

Her uncle stumbled and his arms flailed through the air. The living Keekee screamed and took a step toward her uncle. She pushed as hard as she could, and he fell back through the window. The living Keekee screamed as her footing slipped on the ledge. She screamed again as she reached out, catching onto nothing.

"I remember now," Keekee whispered. "You were standing behind my uncle on the ledge. I know that now. Why didn't I know that then?"

"Yes, you can remember now," Michael replied.

"You said you could save one of us. That I had to make a choice."

The living Keekee hit the sidewalk and didn't move.

"Keekee!" the uncle screamed.

Michael glanced at Keekee and smiled. "You saved your uncle's life. You also changed your friends' future."

"Is my uncle okay?" she asked.

"Yes. Your uncle is fine and your friends returned everything they had stolen to atone your memory. Your uncle was exalted as a hero for trying to keep you from jumping."

"He risked *his* life for me ..." Keekee sighed.

Michael nodded. "Your uncle loved you as much as your parents did. He is now most honored by his family and friends, and your friends are a part of your family now."

Michael and Milos hovered together just outside the tunnel of the Trans-Siberian Railway. A train approached with several teens on the first car.

"Hey ... that's *me* ... standing on top." Milos laughed. "I don't remember what happened."

"We shall watch and see," Michael replied.

"Look at me!" the living Milos yelled "I'm a superhero. I'm flying!" His long hair flapped behind him as he waved his arms.

"Get down!" A boy screamed from behind. "You idiota ... we're not to be seen!"

As the commuter train exited the dark tunnel, a girl yelled. "I'll get 'im down." She tried to balance herself as she edged closer to Milos. She reached out and touched his leg. The train lurched, and the girl slipped, losing her balance. She screamed, grabbing a handful of air.

Milos aimed for her arm. "I gotcha."

Their hands clasped and he pulled. It was enough for her to reach the metal bar. He pulled again and she scooted onto the top.

"Get down!" screamed the boy. "The station's just ahead."

The train lurched again. Milos' foot slipped. He fell, skidding down the top of the car. He grabbed onto the slender bar. As his fingers lost their hold, he tumbled. First his head hit the side of the car, then his body was sucked under the moving train.

"Idiota," the boy yelled. "Got what he deserved."

A worker two cars back glanced out just as Milos slipped under the wheels. He pulled the emergency stop and the train slowed. "Stupid flyers," the man said to another worker. "Just lost another one."

"They think they're invincible," the other man said. "We're always cleaning up after 'em!"

Milos sighed. "They didn't care about me dying?"

"You saved that girl's life," Michael stated. "You could have allowed her to fall and saved yourself."

Milos stared at Michael. "I remember now. You were there when I took those pills. I prayed and you said, "'I will save you so you can save another.'"

Michael and Colton stood staring out at the basketball court. Colton glanced at the score board and sighed.

"We were losing …" he said to Michael, "… 51 to 53 with two seconds remaining. Look, a three-pointer I sliced through the air. And now the buzzer!" Colton jumped up and threw his fist.

The auditorium screamed as his teammates ran toward the living Colton who had just collapsed on the court.

"I remember now," Colton said. "I thought you were a doctor. You helped me up …"

"And?" Michael asked.

Colton's eyes widened. "You said, *'hi'* … and that you knew my name. You helped me stand-up …"

"And?" Michael repeated.

"I looked at my body. I was dead wasn't I? Everyone was screaming …"

"Anything else?"

"I asked what happened. You said that I'd save others."

"Yes."

"Did I? Save others?"

"Yes. You are saving lives right now." Michael smiled.

"Now?" Colton scratched his head. "How?"

"You have a rare genetic defect. Because of the autopsy, what causes many tall people to die once they pass puberty was discovered. A cure is being created as we speak."

"You said you'd take care of my mother."

Michael nodded.

Michael and Jenni stared down at an overgrown ravine. The car was crushed beyond recognition. Steam spewed from what remained of the hood.

"Am I dead in there?" Jenni asked.

"Do you remember when I came to you?" he replied.

"Yes." Tilting her head, she looked away. "There was water all around me. I slipped under and was still breathing. It was very blue. I remember now."

"What else do you remember?"

"Nothing."

He took her hand. "Close your eyes. We will watch."

Jenni closed her eyes and once again, she was sitting back in the car. Her anger grew as she thought about failing her driver's test. As she sped down the driveway, her brother walked out of the garage. He jumped into his car and followed.

The living Jenni's phone rang. "Damn." She pressed decline. It rang again. "What does he want?"

Shifting lanes around an eighteen-wheeler, Jenni's tires skidded. The car ran through the railing and flew over several large bushes. The side mirror broke as it slammed against a tree.

Jenni stood next to Michael and screamed. "Don't tell me that he died too?"

Jenni's brother clawed his way down and into the ravine. He was yelling into his phone. "Help!"

She watched as he banged on the back window and it cracked.

Jenni turned toward Michael and wiped away a tear. "Will he be okay?"

"We are watching over him."

Jenni bilocated back to the tree and into her trance-like body. Sitting cross-legged with the others, her eyes stared into the grass. She remained silent while the others shared their StarWriting stories. She fully remembered her first encounter as death approached, but it wasn't with Michael.

Michael and Ja Crof stared out at the red and glowing horizon.

"Looks like they're ready," Ja Crof stated.

Michael nodded.

CHAPTER 29

Ja Crof materialized at the base of the tree.

"Hello Direct —" Landon froze.

The director raised her hand. She didn't frown nor did she smile. Instead, her gaze was solemn and stern. "Welcome back StarWriters. I trust you learned something from your inaugural voyage."

"It was great." Colton grinned. "How come the stars twinkle so bright out there?"

"And so many colors," Jenni added. "How?"

"I would like to know more …" Ja Crof sighed. "However, I must tell you … *He* wants you to see it, experience it, so you can work for *His* glory." She glanced away as if searching for something. "Although, all that must wait. We're missing a few StarWriters."

The small group stepped closer, remaining silent.

Ja Crof watched and listened.

"Something's wrong," Em whispered to Aleia and Rosie. "Why haven't they come back yet?"

"She looks mad," Rosie whispered.

"Where could they be?" Aleia asked.

"Please, I need your attention," Ja Crof stated.

Aleia shrugged and whispered, "She has big ears."

Ja Crof clapped her hands.

Sorry. Em mouthed.

"Té, Shoupi, and Smillie are trapped in the forbidden quadrant," Ja Crof stated.

"But Director …" – Milos took a step – "… you told us never to go there."

"We'd be chewed up and spit into a million pieces …" Jenni added.

Ja Crof stared at her hands. "They were taken against their will –"

"How do they get back?" Jenni asked.

"You must rescue your fellow StarWriters …" Ja Crof stated before adding, "… from Hell."

The StarWriters' eyes widened as eerie whispers grew louder.

"Will you be leading us?" Em asked.

Ja Crof shook her head. "No … it is forbidden."

"Michael?" Em asked.

Ja Crof shook her head. "No … it is forbidden."

"Who will guide us?" Em asked.

"*She* will." Ja Crof pointed to Em but kept her eyes on her StarWriters.

Isla stepped up to Té and whispered, "What did you say?"

Té glanced over his shoulder at Beck and frowned. He leaned closer to Isla and replied, "I said … *nobody* ever leaves Hell."

"You two …" Beck yelled. "Stop talking!"

Isla shook her head and whispered, "Jerk."

"Just keep walking," Beck stated. "Almost there."

Té's mind raced. *Almost there?* Almost where … to Hell? And he couldn't save his team. And … it was *his* responsibility to protect and lead them.

The red domes appeared to be joined together at the base. Each were of a different height and were smoldering. Not smoldering, as if a chimney, but smoldering as if burning from the outside. Rounded at the top, they reminded Té of a kiln his grandmother used for baking. No windows from what he could see. The tallest seemed to be as high as a twenty-story building. The other two were shorter and varied in width and height.

He watched as the heat radiated from the – bricks? He couldn't tell what the buildings were made from exactly. The outside wasn't smooth, but rough, as if from a porous-type material.

Té tugged on his robe, squeezing the fabric between his fingers. *Give me a weapon. Something!*

It was obvious that his robe was useless here. While onboard Irid, he was able to request help. However, here, it ignored him. Requesting a weapon, any weapon to stop Beck would have been appreciated. But all he received was the touch of fabric.

He stepped closer to his companions and whispered, "We need a plan for when we get inside of that … place." Té again stared at the wavering heat and wondered how they would survive.

"The plan is to find my mum and sister. I need to get them out." Isla lowered her voice, speaking between clinched lips.

"I think *he* has something different in mind," Té replied, frowning.

Shoupi and Smillie stopped in front of the massive doors. Té and Isla stepped up behind them. Leaves larger than his hand were intricately carved into the wood or metal. Té couldn't tell what the doors were made from. Several cherubs were placed along the corners and seemed to be holding something. He wasn't sure what. He didn't want to get any closer. One door creaked slightly open as if inviting them inside.

Té grabbed Smillie's and Shoupi's arms, pulling them back.

Beck laughed from behind. "We are being welcomed my friends. A warm welcome made especially for me."

Isla turned around and placed her hands on her hips. "What do you mean by a *welcome* especially for you?"

He grinned. "Step inside and you'll find out."

Isla pulled Beck aside and they argued.

Té leaned in closer to his team. "Sorry … this is my fault. I fell for Isla's sweetness and look where we are. She really had me fooled with her mum and Messy speech."

"A little late now." Smillie glanced at Isla who was still arguing with Beck. "Am I the only one who's feeling this heat?"

Shoupi touched Té's arm. "You have my forgiveness. I believed Isla too. Beck is using her, and she has no clue."

"We need a plan," Smillie whispered. "A signal or something. We don't know what we're going to be walking into."

Shoupi turned to the door. "Nothing good, I'm sure."

"They may divide us," Té said. "And our robes won't work here. They're of no help."

Shoupi's eyes widened. "Sheol's a place of darkness. It's in the bible. It's where the dead go to be punished."

"Then how can Isla's mum and Messy be in there?" Té asked.

Shoupi shrugged. "Don't know."

"You mean like … purgatory?" Smillie asked.

"Exactly …" Shoupi replied, "… or limbo. Those red domes … there's something about 'em that gives me the creeps." She looked up, allowing her eyes to trail into the swirling red and black clouds. "They remind me of holding pens. A place to hide a soul before a final judgement or something. I think that Hell is just beyond the third dome."

"Maybe there's truth in what Isla said about when their guide was leading her family." Smillie shook his head. "Maybe something evil grabbed her mum and sister."

Shoupi nodded. "I think that this is something the devil does. The last time *He* opened the gates and released the souls was about two thousand years ago. And I believe that Satan's been collecting souls ever since. Isla and her brother were spared, but we don't know why."

"Maybe we can find them and leave?" Smillie suggested.

No one ever leaves Hell, echoed through Té's mind.

"Everything's going to be okay." Isla bounced away from Beck and stood next to Té. "Beck promised."

Té squinted and frowned. "What did Beck promise this time?"

"That we're exchanging my mum and Messy for the scrolls."

Shoupi took a step back. "What? You can't do that. Those scrolls are *His Plan* for the new souls. *His* answers to prayers and hopes for the living." She took another step back. "Saints' answers to *His* peoples' cries for help. You can't have them. I won't let you."

"Sorry, Shoupi," Isla said, almost singing out the words. "Too late. They took them already. They're inside."

"But … how? When?" Shoupi's eyes widened.

"Let's go." Beck said, stepping up. "They're waiting for us." He pulled open the doors.

"I'm ready to find my mum and Messy." Isla said, taking a step.

Shoupi's hands shook as she whispered to Té, "We *have* to get those scrolls back. They are under our protection."

"What do you mean by *I* will ..." Em glared at the director.

"Em, you evolved into a *Protector,*" Ja Crof stated.

"A Protector?" Em yelled. "What are you talking about?"

Ja Crof took in a deep breath and replied, "When you protected Rosie with your robe. Your actions sealed your fate and therefore, you will lead the StarWriters into Sheol."

Em's eyes widened. "You said the forbidden quadrant. What's Sheol?"

"Sheol is in the forbidden quadrant," Ja Crof replied.

"What will the rest of us be doing?" Jenni asked. "I mean ... to help Em?"

Rosie hovered above Aleia. "Oh, she's jealous."

Aleia tapped Rosie with her elbow and shook her head.

Ja Crof motioned for everyone to sit. "I will explain."

The group sat and stared at the director.

"I understand your confusion. You're still in training and now I'm sending you into the belly of the beast. And yes ... some call it Hell or Sheol."

Keekee and Milos gasped.

Ja Crof shook her head and sighed. "Perhaps I should explain *The Prophecy* ... breeches that are forming in Eternity Present."

"Breeches?" Yutu repeated.

"*The Prophecy*?" Landon shrugged.

"*The Prophecy* ..." – Ja Crof sat next to Keekee – "... and the child that shall lead them. One leading the others to free those gripped by the loss of *Him.*"

Em raised her hand. "What are you talking about?"

"The one and the others shall rescue those taken into the grips of Sheol," Ja Crof replied. "*He* had freed the righteous from Sheol and opened the gates to Heaven. This time … however … *you* will be freeing Sheol for *Him*."

"Director," Jenni stated. "You said we were just to save our StarWriters."

"But are not the stolen StarWriters a part of *The Prophecy*? Are they not the same as those poor souls who were taken from Eternity Present on their way to Heaven?" Ja Crof raised her hands.

Jenni nodded.

"Since the gates of Heaven were last opened by *Him*, breeches in Eternity Present have spread." Ja Crof studied the blank stares that had landed on her. How in *God's* name had *He* chosen this rag-tag group of neophyte StarWriters to rescue the lost souls that were ushered into the pre-gates of Hades? Those innocent souls stolen from their eternal life with *Him*. Let alone survive and return?

Now, now Ja … you know why. You know of their virtues. Michael's voice echoed through her mind.

She closed her eyes and sighed. *I'll proceed … but I don't agree with this.*

I am here if you need me, Michael replied.

Ja Crof glanced up. *Thank you.* She looked back at her frightened StarWriters. "Your journey so far has only been from the band around Heaven to your quadrants."

"Is this part of *His Plan* … for us?" Jenni asked.

Ja Crof nodded. "A plan that only *He* knows. We are simply players within *His* perfect divinity."

Rosie flew down and sat on Em's lap.

"The breeches opened soon after Heaven's gates opened." Ja Crof sighed. "Eternity Present is a journey the righteous take once their earthly life ends. The guides lead the souls to their final destination … to Eternity to be with *Him*. Just as *He* promised in *His* covenant. "A soul may vanish along their path. It happens so fast that the guides cannot stop it. The soul is simply gone within a blink of an eye."

"What do I need to do?" Em asked.

"Think of a plan," Ja Crof said, looking directly at her. "When you have one, I shall return." Ja Crof disappeared and reappeared on a higher branch of the tree. She glanced at Michael. "Now … we wait."

Michael nodded. "And … now we wait."

"Uh …" Em said.

Rosie hovered and winked at Em. "You've got some planning to do." She giggled.

"Uh …" Em's stared at the other StarWriters who were staring back. *Help.*

Milos smiled.

Landon grinned.

Jenni frowned.

Keekee played with her robe, basically ignoring the whole situation.

Aleia gave a thumb's up.

Rosie stared at Em.

Colton nodded.

Yutu pouted.

Em took a step back and sighed. She clapped her hands and shook her head. Taking in a deep breath, she whispered, "Okay …" She nodded. "Everyone … I need you. I mean … we're a team, and we can do this … but only if we work together."

Colton nodded. "I have an idea."

"Great." Em looked at Colton.

"How about us posing as guides and souls?" he said.

"What a brilliant idea!" Em's eyes widened. "What if we go to Eternity Present and act as if we're on our journey … maybe whoever or whatever is stealing the souls will take us?"

"I'll be a guide," Milos stated. "I'd be good at it." Milos puffed out his chest.

Em took a deeper breath. "We need one guide and two souls. Any volunteers? Other than Milos."

Colton nodded. "I'll be a soul."

"I'll be the other one." Jenni shrugged.

"That's very brave, Jenni," Em replied. "But we have no guarantee if anyone will be taken. We're just hoping."

"Yeah, but isn't that the plan?" Jenni smirked. "Me and Colton can figure something out when it happens … if it happens."

"Wait!" Milos raised his hand. "Director said the guides never see anything … that they miss the souls vanishing. That it's unexpected. Since we're waiting for it, why can't I be taken with them? I could grab onto one of 'em. Couldn't I?"

"Hmm …" Em tapped her chin with her finger. "That would be unexpected. Maybe throw them off. That would leave the six of us to fly into the forbidden quadrant."

"I can fly T.G." Landon raised his hand. "Since they're planning on being kidnapped."

"That works," Em replied. "Aleia, can you help Landon?"

"Sure." Aleia smiled at Landon.

Rosie hovered. "Then I'm left with you?"

Em nodded. "Unless you want to go with Yutu and I'll take Keekee?"

Rosie frowned. "I want to stay with you."

"What's the matter, Rosie?" Yutu snickered. "You don't like me?"

"I like you plenty. But I like riding in Serene better," Rosie replied.

"I know what you mean," Keekee said. "I'm used to LYK and wouldn't want to change. The butterflies picked us for a reason."

"Glad you'll be sticking with me," Em said, nodding. "I mean … riding in Serene."

Rosie nodded.

"So … what do we do once we're sucked into the forbidden territory?" Jenni asked.

"You mean when we arrive at Sheol?" Milos cringed. "Hell?"

Rosie shivered. "I don't like this."

Em pursed her lips before frowning.

"What if the butterflies could merge into one?" Aleia added. "We could all go at the same time!"

"I like that idea," Em said.

"I agree," Landon added.

Em scratched her head.

"What?" Landon asked.

"I'm just wondering," Em replied. "What if someone is feeding information to *His Plan* workers or vice-versa?"

"Like what?" Landon stepped closer and frowned.

"Like knowing about our comings and goings," Em replied. "Like knowing we're tied to *The Prophecy* … and other things."

"Other things?" Rosie asked.

"Like *Pi* …" Em replied.

Ja Crof stared down at her StarWriters.

"Ja?" Michael asked.

"Yes?"

"Now, now," Michael said with a little grin. "I know what you are doing."

"What are you talking about?"

Michael shook his head. "With Em."

Using her fingers to make a point, Ja Crof sighed before replying, "Just helping a little."

"Oh ye of little faith." Michael laughed.

"I have plenty of faith. Just placing a few ideas in her head."

Michael sighed. "Then what happens after she asks you to take them to *Pi*?"

"Haven't figured that one out yet." Ja Crof shook her head. "But that's my point."

"Breaking *His* rules now?"

They stared into the red glow as it deepened in the distance.

Ja Crof squinted and frowned. "It's getting worse." She took a deep breath and rubbed her arms. "Maybe that's what *He* wants. Stir the pot if you get my drift … mind asking *Him* for me?"

Michael vanished.

Ja Crof appeared in front of the StarWriters. "You need to know about *Pi* …" She crossed her arms.

Em's eyes widened.

"First …" – Ja Crof looked at Em – "… tell me your plan."

Em glanced at her partners. "We decided as a team."

"Which is?" Ja Crof held out her hands.

Em hesitated … "Milos, Jenni, and Colton will pretend to be new souls guided by Milos, and they'll be stolen from Eternity Present –"

Ja Crof huffed. "You volunteered?" She squinted at the three.

"Yes," Jenni replied. "We did."

"And?" Ja Crof asked.

"And," Em whispered, "be taken to Sheol."

"Why?" Ja Crof asked.

"So we can go in," Em whispered.

"How?" Ja Crof asked.

"Um …" Em's eyes widened.

Jenni stepped up and sighed. "*I'll* figure something out when they take us, and Milos will grab ahold of one of us. Then we'll land in the *damned* place." She took a deep breath and sighed.

Ja Crof glanced from Jenni to Em.

Em frowned. "We thought we could fly into the forbidden quad together."

"You think that's possible?" Ja Crof asked.

"Um …" Em glanced down, pulling her sandal through the sand.

Ja Crof sighed. "And that's your plan?"

"Yeah …" Rosie huffed. "That's our plan. Right, Em?"

Em pulled her shoulders back and lifted her chin. "After we go to *Pi* first."

"And?" Ja Crof asked.

"And … pretend to be bilocators and snoop."

"How will you accomplish that?" Ja Crof asked.

Rosie hovered with her hands on her hips. "Yeah … how will we accomplish that?"

Ja Crof glanced up and frowned. "Thank you, Rosie. But I believe I can handle this on my own."

Rosie flew behind Aleia and pouted.

"With your permission and help?" Em replied.

It's a go. Michael's words echoed through Ja Crof's ears.

"It's a go," Ja Crof said. "Sounds like a plan."

Em smiled.

Rosie hovered by Em and whispered, "I think she likes it. You passed."

Em's stomach tightened and her mind whirled. *How in God's name can I do this?*

You can do this, Ja Crof's voice replied inside her mind.

CHAPTER 30

"How bad can this place be? There're angels on the door." Isla walked through the large oak entryway and froze. "Ew!" She gagged. "What's that disgusting smell." She pinched her nose.

Beck pushed on Smillie's shoulder. "Keep moving."

"We're moving!" Té snapped. "I'm really getting tired of you ordering us around."

"Just shut up and keep walking," Beck stated, holding up the mysterious vial.

Red and yellow flames waved along the walls as clouds of dark smoke swirled making it difficult to see.

"That smell is sulfur," Smillie said in a low voice. "The stench of pure evil." He coughed.

Té and Shoupi covered their mouths, and the large doors slammed shut behind them. Puffs of dirt and dust floated through the air making it even harder to breathe.

Beck shoved Smillie again. "Deal with it."

Té squinted and glanced around. The dimly lit room appeared somewhat cave-like. Somewhere near the back, arched doors of various sizes didn't look appealing. He glanced up but could only see darkness.

Beck pointed at the gateways. "Over here."

"Which way to my mummy and Messy?" Isla asked.

"How many doors are here?" Té whispered to Shoupi.

"I counted twelve," Shoupi replied, trying not to breathe.

Beck stepped up to the first door and placed his hands on his hips. "Gotta get this right or else …"

"Else what?" Té asked, stepping up next to him.

"Nothing," Beck whispered. "Third from the left. Now move!" Beck pointed at the tall, black entrance. "Isla, you open the door."

Isla slowly reached out her hand. She paused, staring at the soot covered knob. She took a step closer and touched the handle. "Can't turn it." She frowned. "Too slippery."

"That's impossible," Beck stated. "Try it again."

"It's like it won't let me," Isla replied. "I can't even –"

"I was told …" Beck stepped up behind Isla and sighed. "I'll do it!" He twisted the knob, and the door creaked opened. "Isla … you go first. I'll be last."

"Beck …" Isla stood in the entryway and leaned forward. "It's too dark. I can't see a thing."

"Go!" Beck yelled. "Stop complaining. I'm tired of your constant whining."

Isla grabbed Té's hand and took a step into the darkness.

Té's fingers tightened around his robe. "Give me light, please," he whispered, but nothing happened. The air felt uncomfortable as if he had just passed through something most would not consider normal.

The darkness seemed to control his thoughts, his actions, his emotions. It was as if this darkness was more than just a place where light would not shine. It was almost as if the darkness was – alive.

Smillie walked in behind Té holding Shoupi's hand. They watched as the door slammed shut.

"Now it's even darker," Isla said.

Té took a step, bumping into Isla. Someone tripped over Té's foot, and a slight yelp filled his heart with dread.

"Who just fell?" Té asked.

"I'm taking baby steps," Isla replied.

"Who fell?" Té repeated.

"I twisted my ankle," Shoupi replied.

"I think I can help," Smillie said, and a bright light lit Shoupi's feet.

Shoupi laughed. "Smillie your mouth!"

"How are you doing that?" Té helped Shoupi to stand. "Nothing's working for me."

Opening his mouth wider, the light brightened. "I e…olv…"

Té patted Smillie on the shoulder. "Last time it was your eyes." He chuckled. "Can you walk?" Té asked Shoupi.

"I'm okay." Shoupi nodded.

Isla tapped Té's arm. "No one is yelling at us."

Beck felt his soul seep into a void that twirled him into a nothingness. His feet landed hard against a solid surface, and the flames shot up around him. He shivered although he was not cold. A dark, gray ash covered his feet.

"What is this place?"

A growing stench seemed to be invading his very essence. A mountain of scrolls filled his vision. Or was it a memory? As he contemplated the thought, the pile of scrolls morphed into an open field. Bloodied bodies were scattered about. Beck leaned over to take a closer look.

"These are men?"

Iron tunics, spears, axes, and dented helmets decorated the smoldering ground. The air felt odd, as if this was a place no one should ever walk. His stomach churned.

Someone yelled for help.

"Where am I?" Beck asked no one in particular.

He followed the scorched trail through the dead or dying. His memory made him shudder as a recognition hit. These were the militia of the German king.

"Reinhart's battle," Beck whispered. "1650." He shook his head. "How do I know that?"

The ground vibrated, and the pounding of hooves slapping against the dying Earth echoed from the distance. Beck froze as a dozen soldiers galloped closer, the horses' breaths feeling warm against his face. The men dismounted and started searching through the fallen.

"Do not leave this field until you find my brother," one of the men ordered.

The soldiers ignored the dyings' pleas for help, shuffling from body to body.

"Over here, General," a soldier yelled, staring at a bruised and battered man.

The dying man grabbed ahold of the soldier's arm and begged for mercy.

"He's alive," the soldier stated.

The other man walked over and knelt. "Brother, I am grateful to have found you. Our father be praised."

"Help me," the bleeding man pleaded.

"I shall help you, brother. I shall help you enter the gates of Hell!" He pulled out his sword, locking his eyes into his sibling's fear. "Our father lie dying."

He pushed the sword slowly into his brother's neck. "You shall never be king. I shall be crowned. You will, however, be honored for your heroics … leading our troops into battle." He chuckled, glancing around. "Though you failed. What you could not accomplish in combat, I shall as king."

Beck shivered and stared at the now dead man. "That was me." He glared at his younger brother and laughed. "I always knew you could not be trusted, Wolfgang."

Beck reached out to grab Wolfgang's neck. His mind spun as he faded into the smoldering flames. He opened his eyes and stared at the growing mountain of burnt scrolls.

"I *was* to be king."

"You can ssstill be …" a hissing voice slithered through his ears.

Beck's eyes widened. "How?"

"Open a ssscroll," the voice hissed. "Read it … aloud."

Beck glanced down, and a scroll rolled, stopping only inches from his feet. He picked it up and pulled off the golden string. As the slender cord floated through the air, it burst into flames before hitting the ground.

Beck stared at the now open scroll. His mind wandered as he contemplated the possibilities that etched around him. He dropped the parchment and opened another – and another – and another –

"Read them to usss," the voice hissed.

Slowly, Beck looked into the swirling clouds. "There are no words!" he yelled. "I hear only the sound of an ocean breeze."

"Hsss …" It was as if the sound was taunting him – challenging him. "Bring usss the girl. The one you call Isla. She is the prophesied one. Only *she* can read what is written. Hsss …"

"Prophesied?"

"She is the key to your new found kingdom, your highnesss …"

"I don't know where she is," Beck yelled.

Smillie's light guided them down the dark and smokey corridor. Isla was leading the way.

"How's your ankle?" Té asked Shoupi.

"It's okay," she replied. "I just want outta here."

Té nodded. "Smillie are your jaws tired yet?"

"Uh, huh," Smillie replied straining to keep his mouth open.

"Take a rest," Té added.

Smillie closed his mouth.

"What happened to the light?" Isla yelled.

"Smillie needs a break," Shoupi replied.

"Wish you would've told me. I thought I saw something. There's someone out there. I want to ask them about Mummy and Messy."

"Maybe we can find a way out without Beck seeing us," Té suggested.

Smillie opened his mouth, and again, a bright light lit the path.

A man wearing a black tattered jacket turned. His long, white hair was pulled into a loose ponytail. The old man's eyes were wrinkled with an inner countenance that Té didn't understand or appreciate. His eyes were large, perhaps too large and looked to be bulging from his face. The front of his jacket was covered with soot.

"If you hurry," the old man stated, "you can catch up with your family."

"Mummy and Messy?"

Té stepped closer. "We're looking for a woman named …"

"Mirium," Isla stated. "She'd be with a little girl named Messy."

"Everyone was herded that way." The old man pointed toward the flames. "Beware of falsehoods."

"What's over there?" Isla asked.

"Limbo," the old man replied.

"Do you —" Isla whispered as the smoke engulfed the old man who had just vanished.

Té glanced in the direction beyond the smoldering flames. The old man's warning echoed through his mind, *'beware of falsehoods.'*

Returned to where he had first vanished, Beck jumped as the door slammed behind him. *Damn if I can see a thing.* "Isla! Isla, are you here?"

Beck reached out and waved his hands through the darkness. He took a step and when he touched the jagged edges of the rough stone wall, he chuckled. The wall was now his guide. Flames dancing in the distance gave him a moment to pause.

"A moving shadow," he whispered. "How convenient."

The shadow morphed into the figure of a man who seemed to be hunched over. A white pony tail swung through the air as the figure came into view. The front of the man's jacket was dirty. Beck stepped closer and the old man started.

"There's more of you still here?"

"Which way did they go?"

"Into the next dome." The old man grinned and pointed.

"Why are you still here?"

The old man vanished.

Now where'd he go? Beck shook his head, taking the path the old man had suggested. However, only smokey shadows and endless flames greeted him.

"That old geezer snookered me!"

Beck glanced around and sighed. Various flaming paths now surrounded him. Beck was lost.

"Over there," Isla said. "I see something."

Té coughed from the dense smoke. Flames shot out, giving them a little light. But the flames never seemed to last very long, which made it difficult to walk.

"Smillie, your light please?" Té asked.

Smillie's light barely hit the back of Isla. She turned and shook her head. "It's too dark up here. I need more."

"She's right, that's not enough," Té said. "Go up front, so Isla can see where she's going."

"Okay," Smillie took several steps and the light dimmed even more. "That's weird. What's happening to my light?"

"It was brighter back there," Isla said.

"What's wrong?" Té asked.

"Something's wrong with Smillie's mouth," Isla stated.

"Oh, no," Shoupi said, running up to Smillie.

The light brightened.

"Hey," Smillie said. "False alarm. It's back."

Shoupi stopped and sighed. "Don't scare us like that." She walked back to Té.

"Hey," Smillie yelled. "Lights gone again."

Té ran up to Smillie. "Quit playing around."

"I'm not, look!" Smillie opened his mouth and only a dim beam hit the back of Isla.

"What's up?" Shoupi asked, stepping closer.

The light brightened.

"It's you!" Té stated.

"It's me what?" Shoupi asked.

"Smillie's light only works if you're next to him," Té replied.

"Nah!" Shoupi shook her head. "That makes no sense."

"Smillie open your mouth," Té ordered.

Smillie opened his mouth and a bright light almost lit the entire hallway.

"Shoupi, go back to where we were standing," Té instructed.

Shoupi backed up and the farther she stepped, the dimmer the light. "Wow!"

Té laughed. "See, it's you. We need to investigate."

"No!" Isla yelled. "We need to go! I see something. It might be my mum."

Té sighed. "Fine, but we need to figure out what's going on between Shoupi and Smillie."

Shoupi pulled her hair into a knot as a larger flame lit the hallway. "Is anyone else feeling this heat?"

"It does seem to be getting hotter." Isla also pulled her hair into a knot. "But keep moving. I saw others and they're close."

Té frowned. "Then let's stay together so we don't lose Smillie's light."

Shoupi took Smillie's hand. "Is this close enough?"

"Did you hear that?" Isla asked.

"Hear what?" Shoupi shrugged.

"Listen," Isla whispered.

Té, Shoupi, and Smillie stared at each other.

"Come on," Isla said. "I can hear coughing."

Té laughed. "Are you sure it's not me?"

"Augh!" Isla hurried her pace and was soon folded into the darkness.

The three inched forward, and a large flame flashed announcing a door. Isla ran back and pointed.

"There, you see!" she yelled. "People!"

"Close your mouth, Smillie," Té said. "Let's not announce ourselves."

Standing by the large, open door, a group of what looked like older women and men had gathered. The hallway seemed wider here as if designed to accommodate more than just a few. Té pulled Smillie and Shoupi back. For some reason, his comfort level felt off.

"I don't like this," Té stated. "Why are all these people here?"

"They look old," Smillie said. "They all have white hair."

"Why don't we just ask?" Shoupi sighed. "Instead of standing here gawking!"

"Fine, you ask," Smillie replied.

Shoupi puffed out her chest and nodded. She boldly walked up to a woman. "Where is everybody going?"

Isla stamped her foot and sighed. "This is too much and they're wasting time. Excuse me! She asked you, where are you going?"

"You deaf or something, lass?" The old woman huffed and crossed her arms that were covered in ash. "You didn't hear when they ordered us to proceed to the second pass?" She turned around and stared at the small and startled group. "You look fresh, you just get here or something?"

"Something," Té replied, smirking.

"By any chance have you seen a woman with a young child?" Isla asked.

"No I ain't." The old woman smirked before turning back around.

Isla grabbed the woman's arm. "Please. It's very important that I find them."

The old woman jerked free. "I'd keep my trap shut if I was you. If yah know what's good fer yah. We ain't allowed to speak around here."

"We're sorry," Shoupi stated. "We didn't mean to offend you. My friend is just looking for her mother and sister."

"Who you be?" the old woman asked.

"I'm Shoupi, and we're on a mission to help our friend."

The old woman scratched her chin. "A little girl, you say?"

"Yes. My mum has brown hair," Isla added.

"Can't see much down here." The old woman stumbled and Shoupi grabbed her arm. "Yah a nice lass … maybe they'd be up front. They take the youngins' first, yah know. We follow cuz we slow."

"Thank you." Isla sighed. "The crowd should break up when we pass through. Then we can push our way up front. Follow me."

Shoupi pointed to the old woman's worn shoes. "Smillie, shine a little at her feet. I think they'll move faster if they can see better."

Smillie opened his mouth just a little. The ground lit and the older group walked easily through the door and into the second dome.

Té took a deeper breath as a large shadow approached from behind. "Isla, I think Beck's back."

Isla grunted and pushed through the crowd. She disappeared into the darkness with a sea of gray heads swallowing her.

"Stay close," Té whispered to Shoupi and Smillie. "And, shut off your light."

"Where'd the light go?" the old woman asked.

"What light?" Beck replied.

"Where'd those kids go?" she asked.

"What kids?"

"They was just here." The old woman pointed. "They askin' 'bout a mother and child."

Beck pushed the old woman to the side. The ash covering her arms sprinkled around her feet.

CHAPTER 31

Jenni walked along the shimmery, blue water as the waves gently tapped against her sandals. She glanced up at the swirling white clouds, allowing her thoughts to wander.

Horizon's going nowhere. Just like us. How are we supposed to be taken? "Eternity Present has to materialize," she whispered.

"You say sum'in?" Milos scooped up a handful of purple sand and tossed it into the water.

I should be in charge. I need to show Director I'm good at it … better than Em. Jenni stomped the water, allowing the drops to tickle her legs. "Director said to get into a pace … a rhythm. Then Eternity Present'll show itself."

Colton whistled.

"When do you think we'll be taken?" Milos scooped up a little more sand.

"I'm tired of walking," Colton stated. "We've walked up and down this shoreline twenty times already." Colton shook his head. "What's taking so long?"

"This *is* boring." Milos sighed.

"Not from here." Jenni frowned. The thought of them acting as if she was in charge sent a wave of motivation all through her.

"What does that even mean?" Milos asked.

Jenni scoffed. "O ye of little faith." She jogged a few paces and laughed. "Let's turn it up a little."

Milos and Colton sighed.

"This is nuts," Milos stated.

"Wait up, Jenni!" Colton yelled. "We're supposed to be taken at the same time. Remember?"

Jenni stopped and faced them. "You two are getting lazy." She splashed water at them with her foot.

Milos splashed back. "I'm the guide, not you."

"Fine, then you take the lead," Jenni stated. "Cover your head with your robe."

"Director never said anything about covering our heads," Milos added.

"Camouflage," Jenni replied.

Milos ran his fingers through his hair. "Our robes don't have hoods."

"Then request it." Jenni laughed.

"Robe, make a hood," Milos stated and nothing happened.

"Maybe it has to be more specific like … robe headcover," Jenni replied.

"Robe, headcover," Milos repeated … nothing happened.

"Try again," Jenni said. She imagined Milos' robe covering his head, and the robe slowly extended up and over his curly hair.

"I did it." Milos' eyes widened.

"See, you did it." Jenni grinned.

"Walk behind me and let's pretend I'm leading you somewhere," Milos stated.

Jenni closed her eyes. *Show us Eternity Present.*

Graying clouds gathered above as their robes flapped in the sudden gust of wind. The water gurgled and swayed into taller waves.

"Get back," Jenni yelled.

The water parted and dark walls grew tall on each side. A purple path wound between the tumbling water, and a bright light flickered in the distance.

"It's our invitation into Eternity Present," Jenni said.

Milos raised his arm. "Let's go."

"This is so cool. "Colton stared at the tall walls of water held back with nothing more than a thought.

"Remember," Jenni yelled, "we're supposed to be newbie souls. So keep your head down."

As the purple path vanished behind them, the water slowly filled in the void, sealing the running group's fate into Eternity Present.

"Did you have anything to do with that?" Ja Crof asked.

Michael watched as the three disappeared behind the darkened waters. "No, I thought it was you."

Ja Crof sighed. "I was going to make a path after they showed a little more patience. But obviously –"

"Obviously our little girl is evolving. A gift perhaps? What guidance did you give them for after they're taken?"

"I felt it best if they learned for themselves. Better not to give us away."

Michael chuckled. "And … it begins."

Ja Crof sighed.

"Maybe Jenni will rise to the occasion," Michael stated.

"She might," Ja Crof replied. "I guess we'll find out soon enough."

A bright light flickered and swirled, pulling the three StarWriters closer. Milos paused and Jenni gasped. Colton laughed as the wind whipped and whistled, sending an eerie feeling down their backs. Jenni glanced over her shoulder, and the darkened waters swarmed as if fighting to break free. Ahead was the twirling light.

"Don't turn around," Jenni whispered, taking the boys' hands. She took several steps. "Keep your head down and walk slowly."

Colton whistled and Milos held his breath as the three stepped cautiously into the circling whirlwind of liquid light. The air thickened and their world melted. No floor, no walls, no ceilings, just an ever-evolving whiteness.

Colton stated, "Wish we'd get taken soon."

"Me too," Jenni replied. "I hate uncertainty."

Milos yanked Jenni's hand. "Shh, someone's coming."

Jenni peeked around Milos. "Looks like two guys. Stay vigilant. Milos, you talk to 'em."

Milos pulled his hand from Jenni's and closed his eyes. He took in a deeper breath, letting it out slowly. He stared at the two boys. The choppy blonde smiled. The purple-haired one frowned.

Jenni and Colton kept their heads down.

"Can we follow you?" the choppy blonde asked.

"Uh, to where?" Milos replied.

"Aren't you the guide?" the blonde asked. "We're going to the same place as you. Promised paradise?"

Milos frowned and sighed. "What happened to your guide? How can you travel without one?"

"There were three of us and one guide," the boy with the purple hair replied. "Something grabbed 'em. We're now alone."

"Don't know what to do," the blonde added. "Can't we follow you?"

Milos pointed at Jenni. "Get behind her."

Jenni followed behind Milos. With each step, her sandals sunk deeper into the clouds. Or at least what she considered were clouds. She crossed her arms, allowing the whirling light to comfort her. Every so often, she glanced over her shoulder only to feel light-headed and somewhat enchanted. She allowed her mind to wander and took a step, running directly into Milos.

"Hey," she whispered. "Why'd you stop?"

"We have to choose," Milos stated.

"Choose what?" she asked.

"Choose right or left." Milos held out his hands.

"Stop," the blonde boy stated. "You're no guide. Guides don't talk, they think."

Jenni clapped and laughed. "Okay, you two. Cough it up. We happen to know that they don't take guides … just souls." She tilted her head. "Hmmm?"

The two boys stared at her.

"You were to grab us and take us to Sheol, right?" Jenni asked.

The purple-haired boy frowned. "What are you talking about?"

"You believed us to be scabs," Milos said. "You wanted to take us to Sheol."

"Where'd you hear we'd bring you to Sheol?" the blonde asked.

"The guy on *Pi* told us," Jenni replied.

"You mean Beck?" the blonde asked.

"Yeah, Beck," Colton replied, glancing at Jenni. "Beck said you're the best. And you're gonna need help taking the new souls to Sheol."

"Are you gonna tell Beck we passed?" the purple-haired boy asked.

"You bet," Jenni replied.

"We just drop the souls off at the first dome," the blonde stated. "We never go in."

"Same here," Milos replied. "Beck never told us what to do after you drop us off. So, which way do we go?"

The blonde smiled. "About time we get some help. Been doing this alone for a while now."

"Glad we aired it out." Milos pointed from right to left. "Which way?"

"Straight." The blonde shook his head.

Milos frowned. "Not left? You, sure? There's nothing straight ahead."

"Precisely," the purple-haired boy said. The boy walked past Milos and stepped onto nothing.

Milos took a step and the ground crunched. "What is this?"

Jenni took a step and her feet suddenly felt wobbly as she stepped onto – "Oh, no!"

"What is this?" Colton asked. "Bones?"

"That's exactly what it is," Jenni whispered.

The three now stood on a road made from broken and cracked human bones.

"Voila …" the blonde boy stated.

"This is how you bring souls here?" Jenni asked.

"Yeah," the blonde replied. "But first we flash."

"Flash?" Jenni scrunched up her nose.

"Beck gives us an elixir, and we vanish from *Pi*. Then we take a secret entrance and grab souls before anyone sees. If we can touch the soul it vanishes with us. We come here and reappear."

"We better get going," the boy with purple hair said, taking the lead.

With each step, the path behind dissolved into the swirling mist. The air felt cool and hot at the same time.

"How come you didn't flash us?" Jenni asked. "And why are there not more souls on this Eternity Present path?"

"Every soul's journey is different," the blonde replied.

"Then you pick souls … randomly?" Jenni asked.

"Sorta," the purple-haired boy replied. "The elixir acts like a magnet and draws us to the new energy."

"You didn't answer my question about how come you didn't flash us?" Jenni added.

The blonde laughed. "We ran outta elixir and couldn't find Beck. Have you seen him?"

"Uh, yeah," Jenni replied. "Earlier, are you gonna teach us the ropes?"

"Just did," the blonde stated. "Sheol just appears out of nowhere."

The strong aroma of sulfur filled their senses and Jenni coughed.

"We're almost there," Colton stated.

"We're used to it," the purple-haired boy replied.

Jenni's eyes followed the crushed-bone path that ended at rusted gates. Along the horizon sat three smoldering, red domes. Each one higher than the other.

"Why three domes?" Jenni asked.

The blonde shook his head. "Didn't Beck teach you anything?"

"Not really." Jenni shrugged. "Said you would."

The blonde pointed. "The first dome is where we drop 'em off. Some kind of a welcoming center."

Jenni's eyes widened.

"Where's Hell?" Milos asked.

"It's just beyond the third dome," the purple-hair boy replied.

"Yup," the blonde stated. "And you gotta want to go there."

Jenni frowned. "Does Beck tell you what to do or does someone else tell him what to do?"

The blonde glared at her. "He's guided by someone else. Why all the questions?"

Jenni shrugged. "Just curious."

The blonde snickered. "If we do good, Beck will take us with him."

"Oh, where?" Jenni asked.

The purple-haired boy pointed. "Just go through those doors. You'll see for yourselves."

"How many souls did you drop off earlier?" Jenni asked.

"About twelve," the purple-haired boy answered.

"This is as far as we go," the blonde said. "Tell Beck we did good."

"With flying colors," Milos replied.

"See you at *Pi*," the purple-haired boy said and vanished.

Serene coasted past a snowy mountain range and landed inside a grassy field. A long shadow ran across the transporter's floor as the tall reeds brushed against the viewing windows.

Em released the control stick. "We're in *Pi*."

"Remove band." Rosie flew out of her seat and pressed her hands to the viewing window. "You sure we're in *Pi*? There's nothing out there."

"Hmm …" Em joined her. "Serene knows where to land. Anyway, it's probably camouflaged. Like hiding in a corn field."

"A what?" Rosie frowned.

A deep rumble made Em start. When the ground shook, she yelled, "Hold onto something!"

Rosie shrugged, continuing to hover. "Wow!"

Em and Rosie stared out the window, searching for the source of the roaring blast. Serene shook more violently, jerking Em off her feet. Rosie reached out and helped her up.

"What's happening?" Em asked.

"Look!" Rosie pointed.

Buildings made from what looked like concrete were rising high into the sky, darkening the transporter and the two passengers. The light no longer reaching the ground.

"What is that?" Em asked.

"Looks like a building to me. But there are no windows."

"It's so big!" Em shouted above the noise.

Rosie covered her ears and closed her eyes.

"*Pi* has tall buildings," Em yelled. "Director Crof did say that the buildings would just appear."

"What?" Rosie yelled. "I can't hear you."

The buildings continued to grow, seeming as if it would take forever before finally stopping. She tried to see the top but the puffy clouds blocked her view.

"What else did she say?" Rosie asked.

"Not much. Just that Serene would bring us here … that *Pi* would appear."

Rosie sighed. "Well, it's appeared. Is that all she said?"

Em nodded. "Oh … and Godspeed."

Rosie tapped her foot in the air.

"Cross my heart and hope to –" Em glanced away.

"You were gonna say die but you're already dead!"

Em shook her head. "Michael said we're very much alive. Now, let's get moving. We can wait for the others outside."

"What're we supposed to do here?"

"Pretend we're bilocating. Mingle and wait. I'm hoping someone will say something about Sheol or *The Prophecy*."

"Long shot," Rosie said, following Em down the stairs.

"At least we can hide in this grass 'til the others get here."

"I can't see a thing," Rosie whined. "I need to get higher."

"I don't think that's a good idea." Em waved her hand through the air, concentrating on the transporter.

Serene's wings fluttered. As the craft raised, it morphed into an emerald butterfly. Its dotted wings shimmered as it flew away.

"Where's it going?" Rosie asked.

"Don't know, don't care." Em pointed at a darker area near several large rocks. "We'll wait for the others over there. Maybe you should fly lower so no one can see you." Em glanced around and sighed. The green blades of grass reached several feet over her head. She pushed an armful away only to have more fill in behind.

"I can't see a thing." Rosie flew up a few feet. "Hey, there are two guys walking out of a cave over there."

"A cave?"

"Yeah, there's a mountain over there …" – Rosie pointed – "… and a cave and …"

"Guys?"

The grass rustled and Em grabbed Rosie's foot and yanked. "Encase us in ground cover." Em stated and her robe changed color blending the two into the tall grass.

"That was awesome man," a young male voice said. "We passed with flying colors."

"We need to find Beck," the other male voice replied. "I want to gloat a little. And we're gonna need more elixir if he wants us to go back to Sheol."

The voices trailed off, and Em made her robe turn back to normal. She glanced up and sighed. "Rosie!" she whispered, loudly. "They'll see you."

"I'm gonna follow 'em."

"No. *I'm* your guardian."

"Just want to see what building they're going to. I'll be right back."

"You're all pink!" Em placed her hands on her hips.

"I'll fly high." Rosie giggled and flew away.

A fluttering sound grabbed Em's attention. She took a deep breath and frowned. "LYK and T.G. are here and now Rosie's gone." She frowned. "Ugh, a dog would've been easier."

No it wouldn't, Rosie's voice echoed through Em's mind.

Milos, Jenni, and Colton walked passed the decaying iron gates. Wind swirled through their legs. Dust and debris circled around, creating a malevolent atmosphere of dread.

"I just hate the sound of crunching bones," Milos stated. "Whatever that smell is, it stinks!" He pinched his nose.

"Ignore it." Jenni pointed at the huge, red domes. "Looks like they're opening for us."

The small group inched closer to the tall, carved doors.

"This thing has angels on it!" Jenni entered, leading the small group into the smoke-filled lobby.

"Creepin' me out," Colton stated. "Promise we'll stick together?"

"Look for the doors those guys talked about," Jenni whispered. "They said to take the third from the left."

Milos strained to see better. "Too smoky in here."

"I think the smoke is dissipating," Jenni stated. "I can see something –"

"Six, nine … ten … eleven … twelve." Milos' voice rose higher with each appearing black door.

"Purple dude said there were twelve." Jenni pointed, and the three stood silently in front of the tall, black third door from the left. Jenni reached for the knob.

"Wait!" Colton said, holding onto her hand. "Are we ready to just walk into Hell?"

"Not going into Hell," Jenni replied.

"How do you know?" Colton asked.

Jenni shook her head. "They said that the third dome enters Hell and that you have to *want* to go there."

Milos nodded.

Jenni grabbed onto the knob and smiled. "You guys ready?"

No one replied.

"Then, let's go," Jenni said. "We'll deal with whatever is on the other side together."

The door creaked as the three peered in.

"It's too dark," Milos whispered.

"Wish we had some light." Jenni giggled. "Hey check it out. My sandals are glowing."

"We should try that too," Colton added.

"More light, more attention," she replied.

"Yeah, you're right," Colton said. "We'll follow you."

Jenni walked into the darkness looking at her feet. She squealed when she bumped into a white ponytail.

"There are more of you?" the man asked.

"Sorry," Jenni whispered. "Can't see much in here."

The man nodded. "You'll need to hurry if you want to catch up with the others. They just passed into the second dome."

"They?" Milos asked. "Did you see two guys with a girl?"

"I saw two girls. Is it Isla you askin' about, and a fellow with long, black hair?"

"Which way did they go?" Jenni asked.

He pointed in both directions at the same time.

Jenni sighed. "Then which way should we go?"

The man pointed again in both directions before vanishing. "No feet light," his words faded as did her sandals.

Milos raised his 'brows. "You think they were brought here against their will?"

Jenni squinted and frowned. "Not sure. That man said *they* were helping *her*."

"What about the guy with the black hair?" Milos asked.

Jenni took in a deeper breath and let it out slowly. "I know who Isla is."

"Spill." Milos placed his hands on his hips.

"Well," Jenni replied, leaning in closer to her friends. "You remember when Michael brought us into *His Plan* room?"

The boys nodded.

"A girl was winking at Té."

"A girl?" Milos glanced around. "But we're invisible to others."

"Perhaps everyone but this girl Isla. I remember that she had long, light brown hair. Remember anybody like that?"

Again, the boys shook their heads.

"How are we supposed to remember something like that?" Colton asked. "There are so many workers around here."

"I overheard Té talking to Michael," Jenni added. "Something about souls evolving and such."

"Evolving?" Colton squinted his eyes.

"Maybe she evolved enough to bring 'em here for a reason." Jenni shrugged and looked down at her darkened feet. "I think we should keep going to the right."

Milos sighed. "Hopefully they're not that far ahead of us."

Jenni glanced up at Colton. "Can you see anything?"

"Just smoke and flames," Colton replied.

CHAPTER 32

Té glanced over his shoulder and into the slow-moving crowd. Beck was moving fast. His black hair swayed as he pushed the others aside.

"Move faster," Té whispered to Smillie and Shoupi. "Beck's here. Gotta catch up to Isla." He strained to see over the heads of the souls in front of them. "She can't be that far ahead."

Smillie looked back. "Yup, that's him and he's almost here."

"I don't see her anywhere," Shoupi whispered.

Smillie grabbed Té and Shoupi's arms and pulled them into the shadows. He pointed at Beck who pushed against two old women, rushing past.

"That was too close for comfort," Smillie whispered.

Té frowned at Smillie and Shoupi. "You can wait here, but I'm going after Isla."

Shoupi glanced out of the shadows. "Don't have too. He's already got her, and they're heading back this way."

"Then hide," Té said, pulling them deeper into the darkness.

"Please … pardon us …" Isla smiled at the sea of slow-moving souls. "Really, Beck? You know where Mummy and Messy are?"

"Yeah and they're not up there. They're still in the back of the first dome. If not, then we go through the third door again and into the seventh." Beck stared straight ahead.

"Are you sure? How do you know?" Isla glared at Beck. "An old man said everyone was moving toward the second dome."

"Well ..." Beck stated. "He's wrong. I have my sources."

"Té, Shoupi, and Smillie are here somewhere," Isla said. "Let's find them. They were with me the whole time."

"We'll find 'em *after* we find your family. That's our priority, right?"

"Did you hear what he said?" Shoupi whispered from the shadows.

"He's lying and she's falling for it again," Té replied.

"Are we going back to the first dome?" Shoupi asked.

"Stay behind me," Té whispered. "Hug the shadows. Smillie, keep your mouth shut. And don't believe a word Beck's saying."

The three remained several feet behind Isla and Beck. It was slow moving, but when they reached the door, they peeked in.

"They must have gone through the seventh door already," Té said.

"Do I count from the left or the right?" Smillie asked. "This place is confusing."

"Left," Shoupi replied, pointing at each door.

"One, two, three, four ... seven." Smillie grabbed onto the knob.

A dark, hot wind, creating a denser smoke, hit. The small group coughed.

"We need to get outta here," Shoupi whispered. "I'm covered in ash and it's burning me!"

Smillie turned the knob. "It won't budge. Locked or something."

"Hey, wait for us!" a female voice stated from somewhere inside the darkness.

"Jenni?" Shoupi stared into the shadows.

Milos chuckled. "We were at the back of that crowd. I spotted you."

"How did you know we were brought to Sheol?" Té asked.

Jenni sighed. "Director said you were highjacked. We volunteered to rescue you."

"Well, you made it," Smillie said, coughing. "But how did you know where we were?"

"We tried to get highjacked too," Milos added.

"And you wouldn't believe whose doing the hijacking," Jenni said, rocking back on her heels.

Colton frowned. "It's two weird dudes from *Pi*. And someone they called Beck."

Shoupi glanced at Té and Smillie. "Beck! He promised Isla he would help her find her family. They snuck onto our transport."

"They mentioned something about an elixir that allows them to become invisible," Milos explained. "The other StarWriters are on *Pi* trying to learn anything they can."

Jenni and Shoupi gasped as the seventh door slowly creaked opened.

LYK and T.G. landed in the tall grass. Aleia, Yutu, Keekee, and Landon stepped down the stairs and glanced around. They waved when they spotted Em walking toward them.

"I told my robe to light and it did…" – Landon smiled and glanced around – "… where's our little cherub?"

"You don't want to know." Em sighed.

The small group glanced into the sky.

"She's behind me, right?" Em whispered.

Rosie giggled. "I have info."

"Long story short …" – Em bounced on her heels – "… we saw these guys coming –"

Rosie pointed toward the mountain range. "I saw them come out of that cave –"

"We heard 'em say something about passing with flying colors," Em added. "And that they had to find Beck cuz they need something … I think they said *elixir* …"

"Elixir?" Landon repeated.

Em nodded. "Yeah, that's if they want the stolen souls to go back to Sheol with 'em."

Yutu glanced at the tall mountains. "An easy connection to Sheol could definitely be through that cave."

"Yeah," Em replied. "But that would create a small problem."

"Problem?" Yutu asked.

Em nodded. "First, we'd need an elixir from that Beck guy. And second, the director wanted us to stay with our butterflies for protection."

Rosie giggled. "I saw what building they went into."

"You're a daring little one, aren't you?" Landon shook his head. "Then lead the way."

"They're over there." Rosie pointed. "In that really tall building. I followed them and they walked into a big, black box."

"A box?" Yutu asked.

"Yeah." Rosie nodded.

"Stay close to us." Aleia said, motioning to Rosie.

Em frowned. "I told her *not* to follow 'em."

"I can take care of myself," Rosie stated. "And I'm the only one who knows what they look like."

"That's why I said to stay close," Aleia replied.

Landon positioned himself directly under Rosie. "And don't fly too fast."

The small group stepped into the building and gasped. The floor, walls, and ceiling were made from glass – glazed – but from glass. The vast lobby held a brilliant light with a single metal box in the middle of the room. No furniture. Just an open and empty space.

Rosie flew over to the big, black box and pointed. "See!"

A note beckoned for them to enter and push a button for the 20,000th floor.

"They got into this thing." Rosie placed her hands on her hips and nodded. "Told yah so."

The small group stared at each other and shrugged. One by one, they stepped inside the oblong, tall box. Em's hand shook as she pushed the button. The doors rolled shut and a bell dinged. Before anyone could say anything, the doors opened. A room that seemed to have no beginning or end greeted them with thousands of souls staring into the distant but twinkling stars. Laughter and a rhythm of praise filled the StarWriters' ears. Em grabbed at the hem of Rosie's robe, and together, they inched forward.

Rosie yanked her robe away. "I'm not a dog!"

"Don't want you to get lost," Em whispered.

Yutu stepped closer to Em. "Where do we start looking?"

Em struggled to see above everyone's heads but there were just too many. "We'll let Rosie fly around a little."

"And then what?" Yutu asked.

Em shrugged. "We'll figure out something."

"Let me go!" Rosie tugged, and as her robe snapped free, she toppled over the heads of the crowd.

Aleia gasped. "She won't blend in like we will. She'll be seen!"

Keekee stared into the twinkling sky and sighed. "I wish I was a bilocator."

"Thought you liked being a StarWriter," Yutu said.

"I do." Keekee grinned. "I just want to have some fun like they're having."

"This isn't enough fun for you?" Yutu asked.

Rosie sped toward her friends, huffing and puffing. "They're heading this way. One's a blonde and the other has purple hair."

The crowd parted and the boys walked out. They studied the small group standing in front of them as if searching for answers. The blonde stepped closer and crossed his arms.

Em took a step and said, "Heard you're looking for Beck."

"You know where he is?" the boy asked. His eyes were wide as if he were close to panicking.

"We're looking for him too," Em replied.

The blonde winked at his friend and laughed. "Another test?"

"Uh …" Em took a step back.

"You're not a part of that Jenni group are you?" the blonde boy asked.

Em glanced at her friends before answering. "You met our friends at Sheol?"

"Beck sent 'em. They gave us a test, and we passed with flying colors." The purple-haired boy pointed at his chest, taking a deep breath.

"Beck said you had some elixirs for us?" Em asked.

"Oh?" The blonde boy raised his 'brows. "Then what's it like when yah take it? Huh?"

"Uh … well …" Em studied their expressions. "Beck said to ask *you* how to use it. Said that *you were* professionals."

"Professional? Really?" The blonde boy shook his head. "Wow, that's great! Then welcome to the club."

"Yeah … we're happy to be part of the club." Em glanced at Aleia and winked.

"What happens when we join your club?" Aleia asked.

"You get to take Beck's elixir," the purple-haired boy replied. "Then you're instantly invisible. Can walk through the cave and be on Eternity Present." He snapped his fingers.

"That's where we take the souls and …" Em shuffled her feet.

The blonde laughed. "You tap 'em and they turn invisible. At the fork in the road just go straight. Leads you to Sheol. Take 'em to the door and your job's done."

The purple-hair boy added, "Good to know we're gonna get more help. Tell Beck that we got yah covered." He smiled.

"Yes, absolutely." Em returned the smile.

As the boys walked away, Landon leaned over and whispered, "Who is Beck and where is *he* getting the elixir from?"

"Everything seems to lead to this Beck guy and Hell," Rosie added.

"He can't be making it himself," Yutu added. "He has to be getting it from somewhere." Yutu bent down to tighten the strap on his sandal, and a slight whisper tickled his ear.

You will find Amelia in Sheol. She needs your help. Don't let her down like last time when you allowed her to die.

"What?" Yutu jumped up and glanced around. "Who said that?"

Landon stood by the black box and yelled, "You coming, Yutu?"

After grabbing a scroll from the pile, Beck shoved it into Isla's face. "Keep trying."

"That's the fifth one!" Isla pushed the scroll back at Beck. "I *told* you, I can only hear wind and waves crashing. You said Mummy and Messy were here. So, where are they, huh?"

Beck tossed the scrolls behind him and sighed. The pile was twice his height and probably three-times wider. He walked casually to the other side before picking out several.

Isla followed and her eyes narrowed.

Beck sighed. "There's got to be one you can read around here somewhere. Afterall, you're –"

"I'm what?"

"Nothing," Beck replied, refusing to make eye contact. "Keep opening them until you find one you can read!"

Shoupi snuck out from the shadows and grabbed several of the tossed scrolls. She stuffed them into her pockets. As she reached for another, Té grabbed her arm.

"We have to stay hidden!" Té whispered, guiding Shoupi to where Smillie was hiding inside a sunken alcove. Jenni, Colton, and Milos were farther back in the darkness.

"No one is allowed to read these except for *Him* and the Saints," Shoupi whispered. "We *have* to save them." She stuffed two more into her pocket. One of the scrolls fell and hit the floor. It opened.

Smillie's light shined on the parchment.

Shoupi's eyes widened. "Can't be!" She allowed her eyes to read over the secret message. "Don't look at this." Shoupi's voice cracked.

"I just hear wind and waves." Smillie closed his mouth.

Jenni stepped up and whispered, "But *you* can. Can't you? Should we be calling you Saint Shoupi?"

Té frowned. "You can read that?"

Tears ran down Shoupi's cheeks. "This one is addressed to me."

Té hugged her. "You've evolved. It's okay, Shoupi. Don't cry. I've never met a real Saint before."

"None of us have," Colton said, "Do we congratulate you or what?"

"Cool," Milos said.

"It's okay, Shoupi," Té added. "The prayers are written to you and you must answer with a miracle."

Shoupi's hands shook as she opened another scroll, and Smillie shined his light directly onto it.

"I don't believe that I am a Saint," Shoupi replied. "I mean, I don't *feel* any different. I can just read this scroll. I don't know how to do miracles."

"Maybe you're a Saint-in-waiting." Té smiled.

Colton nodded. "I'm sure someone will teach you how to do miracles."

"Tell us what the scroll says." Jenni placed her hand on Shoupi's shoulder. "Read it to us."

Milos smirked. "C'mon, Jenni. You know she can't do that. You heard Director."

"Nobody can say a word about this," Té said.

A smokey wind swirled and the group shivered.

"What happened to the scrolls I threw away?" Beck yelled.

Té placed his finger to his mouth.

"I don't know," Isla replied. "They were just here."

"Fine!" Beck huffed. "Keep opening them until you can read something."

"I'm getting tired, and why are you doing this?" Isla yelled. "I need to find Mummy and Messy. We need to get outta here."

The ground swelled and a blanket of ash encircled them.

"If you don't read something fast, they won't let us near your mummy and sister."

"What do you mean?"

"Exactly what I said." Beck picked out several scrolls. "We'll be of no use to them."

"Who exactly are you talking about?" Isla slapped her hands on her hips.

Pushing back the tall grass, Landon sang out … "Come out, come out wherever you are … T.G.?"

Em added, "And Serene?"

"And LYK." Keekee squealed.

Rosie giggled. "I see Serene and T.G. and LYK."

"Those two guys gave me the creeps," Aleia stated. "What're we gonna do now?"

Em made eye contact with each StarWriter one at a time. "We're going to Sheol. Director said to tell you once we're on board to say *iridescence*."

"Is that in honor of Irid or something?" Landon asked.

"No," Em replied. "We're going into the forbidden quadrant … invisible."

"Beck!" Isla screamed. "Don't talk to me like that. Tell me the truth. Why am I here? I'm tired of your lies. I should have listened to Té. He was right. You're using me!"

Beck didn't answer.

Isla stared at him for only a few more seconds before walking away. "I'm finding my family and true friends, and then I'm getting the *hell* outta here!"

Beck ran after her and grabbed her arm.

"Let me go!" Isla growled.

"Fine," Beck released his grip. "I'll tell you what's going on."

"The truth."

Beck nodded.

Isla tapped her foot and rolled her eyes. "Go on."

Beck sighed. "I'm a king … and you're my only connection."

Té and the others looked at each other.

Jenni mouthed, "King?"

Placing his finger to his mouth again, Té motioned for them to remain quiet.

"I'm *really* tired of your lies," Isla said, turning her back on him.

Beck took her hands into his. "Hear me out, Isla." His tone softened. "I'm not lying. Just like your intuition about your family … so is mine but what I was supposed to be."

Isla stared at him. "You were supposed to be a king?"

"Yes." Beck frowned. "They showed me my death. I was the eldest and in line for my father's crown. But I was injured in battle, and my younger brother finished me off."

"My family is here," Isla replied. "My guide said so. That I must free them." Isla sighed. "Did your guide show or tell you that?"

Beck remained silent.

"Where are you supposed to be a king now? There's only one kingdom and one king here. We came to find Mum and Messy. And we're going back to –"

"I've been promised to be a king here in Sheol, and you, Isla, shall be my queen."

Isla yanked away her hands and screamed, darting into the darkening shadows. Té grabbed onto her arm, pulling her into the alcove. Isla's eyes widened.

"Isla! Where are you?" Beck stared into the thickening smoke. "I know you're here. Come out … *all* of you!" He held up the dark vial.

The small group stepped out from the shadows.

"Good. More hands," Beck stated. "She's going to need your help in opening these scrolls."

"I told you, I can't read them," Isla whined. "I have to find Mummy and Messy!"

"Sounds fair to me," Té said, scowling at Beck. "Your *royal highness* can stay here in your kingdom."

A howling wind blew through the cavern surrounding Beck. He shook his head. "Really? That many? You can all come out now. Isla needs your help."

Jenni, Milos, and Colton stepped out from the shadows.

"What if we don't want to help?" Milos asked.

"They wouldn't like that," Beck replied with a singing voice.

Jenni stepped forward. "We'll help."

Her friends scowled and frowned.

"The sooner we help," she said, "the sooner we can get outta here."

"No one ever leaves Hell," Té whispered.

"Exactly *what* are we looking for?" Jenni asked.

Beck glared at her. "I like you. You're smart …" – he pointed at Colton – "… you're a giant and you …" – he frowned at Milos – "… what're your names?"

"I'm Jenni. This is Milos and that's Colton."

"Open the scrolls until Isla can read one!" Beck ordered. "*They* want to know."

Isla pouted. "What makes you think I can read these?"

"Because you're the one prophesied." Beck glared at her.

Serene, LYK, and T.G. aimed for the forbidden quadrant.

"It's time ..." Em grabbed tighter onto the control stick. "Iridescence."

The three transporters dissolved into the darkness. Em stared at the pitch blackness and sighed. The control stick remained rigid and stuck in place. Serene was definitely in charge. She let go of the stick and sat back. A strong odor of stench gently caressed her soul as if a morning dew was settling onto an early spring flower.

"Eww ..." Rosie squealed. "What is that smell?"

"Evil," Em whispered.

"How can the butterflies enter evil?" Rosie asked.

"Remember? Director gave them a mission," Em replied.

"Are we gonna storm the place?" Rosie asked, shoving a tiny fist into the air.

"Don't know. Let's just wait and see what happens next. The butterflies are in charge." Em tensed when Rosie's arm touched hers.

"You think the butterflies'll be able to see each other if they're invisible?" Rosie asked.

Em reached over and rubbed Rosie's arm. Her fingers ran down the cherub's skin, and when she touched her plump, baby fingers, Em wrapped her hand around Rosie's. "I'm sure they can somehow sense each other."

"Wish *we* could be invisible," Rosie said.

Em gently patted Rosie's hand. "I'm proud of you, Rosie, and glad you're with me."

The two jumped as something splashed against the viewing window.

"We must be there," Em whispered. "The darkness is gone."

"What's on the windows?"

"Ash," Em replied.

The butterflies exited the darkness and hovered near the iron gates. Em stood and stared out the window. The tall, red domes looked menacing against the starless background. She replayed her conversation with Aleia and Landon before they boarded T.G. Landon believed they needed to resemble the two guys who were kidnapping souls and taking them to Sheol. When Aleia had asked how they could do that, Landon said to hide their face inside their hoods.

Em remembered how they all looked afraid. Keekee had tears in her eyes. Landon was as white as freshly fallen snow. Aleia glowed a slight shade of green. And Yutu couldn't stop his hands from shaking. Em glanced at Rosie who was playing with a pink band. The director's words echoed through her mind, "*He* is with you. You are stronger than you realize."

Serene landed and the stairs extended down.

"It smells even worse now!" Rosie wiped her eyes.

"Everything stinks ..." Em stared out, wishing they were someplace else.

Isla laughed and laughed. She grabbed her stomach and laughed harder. "The prophesied one?" Isla wiped her eyes. "You *obviously* have me confused with some Saint."

Jenni and the others stared at Isla. Shoupi lowered her gaze.

"Then you lied to me?" Beck asked.

Isla stopped laughing and stared at him. "What are you talking about?"

"Your guide's words, remember? *It will be you Isla to free them.* And didn't you say you always had these memories? Something special you couldn't forget."

"Yes, but that doesn't have anything to do with being the prophesied one. I was talking about *my* family."

Beck huffed. "I beg to differ." He pounded on his chest. "Sounds like *you're* the prophesied one to me and to them." Beck pointed into the darkness.

"You mean them?" Isla glanced at the small group.

Té stepped closer to Isla and touched her shoulder. "He's talking about his evil friends. They whisper to him from inside the shadows."

"Evil whispers?" Smillie asked.

Shoupi wiped a tear from her face. "The third dome."

"Third dome?" Isla asked, staring at Beck. "I'm not going into the third dome!" She stomped her foot. "I just want to find Mum and Messy."

"You'll do as I say," Beck stated.

Isla cringed and stepped closer to Té. "Let us go, Beck, and we'll find 'em ourselves. They're probably just in the second dome. You can stay as king if you want, but I'll never be your queen!"

"Queen?" Jenni repeated.

"You can't stop us from leaving, Beck!" Milos added.

Beck chuckled. "Maybe I can't … but *they* can."

A hot wind howled and ruffled through the scrolls.

Jenni picked one up and smiled. "Tell us what we need to do." She glanced at the others. "I think we should listen to Beck."

Beck smiled and nodded. "I like your attitude. Keep opening the scrolls until Isla can read one."

The wind died down.

"Just one?" Shoupi glanced at Té.

Beck clapped his hands. "Get busy! As they open these things, Isla, look at them until you find the one you can read. Now move!"

Isla stepped over and stood by Milos and Colton. She glanced at their scrolls and shook her head. Té and Jenni held up theirs.

"Nothing," Isla frowned.

Smillie unrolled his.

"No." Isla glared at Beck. "This is a complete waste of time."

"Keep opening!" Beck waved the vial through the air. He glared at Shoupi who was collecting the undeciphered scrolls, gently placing them in a small pile. Beck yanked her back and pointed the dark vial at her face. "What in the *hell* are you doing?"

Shoupi pulled away her arm. "These are sacred!"

Beck pushed Shoupi onto the huge pile, and she yelled as hundreds of scrolls fell around her. "Collect all you want … after you find the one I need. Otherwise, you are nothing but a vapor."

"Beck … what prize do I win if I open the one that's readable?" Jenni asked.

Té scowled. "He's not your friend, Jenni."

Beck paced and stared at Té. "Things will go much easier if you cooperate."

As the undeciphered ones fell, Shoupi gathered the scrolls, adding to her pile.

"We're getting nowhere." Isla frowned at Beck. "I'm tired of saying *no*."

Shoupi pulled the scroll from her pocket and nodded at Té. "I have to do something."

Té frowned and shook his head. "No!"

"Do it!" Jenni stated. "I can't take much more of this wind and wave crap."

"Stop talking!" Beck ordered.

Shoupi straightened her back and took a deep breath. "I can read them." She opened a scroll. "But I can only read the ones that are addressed to … me."

"To you?" Beck glanced at the scroll in her hands.

Isla peeked over Shoupi's shoulder and shrugged. "Don't see any words just hear wind and ocean sounds."

Jenni laughed. "Shoupi is a Saint."

Beck chuckled. "Right … and I'm Santa Claus."

"Shoupi," Té said. "Don't do this."

"I have to," Shoupi replied. "I'm here because of this." Shoupi lowered her eyes and read, "*Dear Saint Shoupi. The Christian families in our village are being harassed. Some have disappeared. Others are killed to set an example. We need your help. Please send a miracle.*"

The whispers echoed from the darkness, seeming to be growing louder.

Beck laughed. "Well … well …well … Saint Shoupi is it?"

The dust spun as it rose into the nothingness and several fire tornadoes formed, churning the embers of the lost souls until they floated down remixing with the burnt ash. Three transports cautiously landed in front of the iron gates. Not visible to the naked eye, stairs lowered, creating a slight indentation into the broken and cracked bones.

Aleia nodded at Landon before closing her eyes. She concentrated as the others appeared before her. Their figures waved as if nothing more than a misty vapor. Although they were in their own butterflies, Aleia now had everyone's attention.

"Okay," Aleia said, squinting at her friends. "Remember … me and Landon are Robbers of Souls. We just kidnapped you. So look confused and afraid. Since our butterflies are invisible, it'll look like we're suddenly appearing … as if we just walked through the dimensions."

Landon nodded. "And be quiet. If you talk, you'll give us away. People are not friends with the Robbers of Souls."

Em, Rosie, Keekee, and Yutu nodded.

"Then here we go." Em swallowed. *HE is with us … HE is with us …*

Aleia leaned over and peeked out. The path looked evil with the swirling, burning embers and broken and cracked human bones. *How deep do these bones go?* Aleia took the steps slowly, looking around to see if anyone was watching. As soon as she stepped onto the ground, she would be visible. Taking in a deeper breath, Aleia pulled her hood over her head. Lowering her eyes, she stepped off the bottom stair. The sound of crunching bones intensified with each step. Her foot slipped and she froze. Falling would only give her away. Steadying her stance, she walked as upright as possible. *Concentrate … concentrate … HE is with us.*

Rosie gasped as Em grabbed her hand. "We're next," Em whispered. "Stay quiet. But look afraid."

"Oh, I don't have to *look* anything!"

Keekee stepped down and her knees locked. "I can't do this," she whispered.

Yutu held Keekee's arm. "Too late to turn back now." They stepped onto the broken bones together.

Keekee slapped her hand over her mouth. Tears filled her eyes.

"*He* is with us," Em whispered loudly. "Do not fear."

Aleia pointed at the large doors of the first dome.

"We're going in there?" Em's voice cracked.

Landon nodded, keeping his gaze lowered.

Rosie flew up to the ancient doors and ran her fingers along the carvings. "Baby angels! Just like me."

Landon pulled open the doors and bright flames soared upward, scorching the air. A dark smoke made him cough.

"It's a cave?" Em asked, trying to see inside.

Landon stepped in first. The flames died and the room darkened. It was as if the shadows were somehow alive and breathing or had heartbeats. He took a deeper breath and tried to follow the path but it was just too dark. Landon reached out to use the wall as a guide, but the flames roared back to life. Yanking away his hand, he blew on his fingers. He reached out again, only this time, counted until the flames roared.

Ten seconds …

Landon took a few steps and reached out his hand. The flames shot up as he studied the pathway. Each time the flames died, he waved his hand at the wall. They now had an odd and temporary way to guide them.

Aleia had waited outside as the others followed Landon inside. Keekee was basically pulled in by Yutu. Aleia stepped up and sighed. She turned to grab the door but it was already closing by itself. She shivered.

Keekee pointed at a shadowy figure that seemed to be moving toward them. "Who's that?" she whispered.

Landon motioned for them to keep walking.

Keekee froze.

Em tugged on Keekee's robe. "Not now," she whispered. "There's strength in numbers."

The figure with a long, white ponytail disappeared and then reappeared in front of them. Studying the hooded guides, he whispered, "Keep moving. Use door three, it will take you to the second dome. Everyone is waiting."

Landon looked up and locked eyes with the man.

"Keep right and stay in the shadows."

"Who are you?" Landon whispered.

"You'll arrive at a big door," the old man replied. "It may be closed and locked. If it is, tap three times and the door will open."

"Who's waiting for us?" Landon asked.

The old man nodded. "Why … the Saint!" The man vanished into the ash and soot.

Em took a step and felt something touch her shoulder. She turned around but no one was there.

Té stepped up to Beck. "She read you a scroll. Now, it's time to find Isla's family."

The two locked eyes. Beck frowned. Té frowned.

"You promised," Isla whined.

Voices reached out stroking everyone's ears. As the whispers grew louder, the small group rubbed their arms as if cold.

Milos and Smillie turned, trying to pinpoint the sound.

"Who's there?" Milos yelled.

Colton covered his ears.

"What's going on?" Smillie asked.

Beck looked as if he was straining to hear.

Jenni stepped closer to Té. "Beck's communicating with them."

"Sure ... sure ... yes, of course ..." Beck was talking to someone, but no *one* or *thing* was there. He turned to Isla. "As promised, we're going to the second dome." He pointed and smiled. "Through those doors."

"You lead," Jenni replied, stepping aside. She winked at Té. Té nodded.

Beck glanced around. "Where'd the Saint go? Not leaving without her."

"Shoupi!" Té yelled.

Shoupi stepped out from behind the unread pile of scrolls. She crossed her arms and tapped her foot. "We're not leaving until we have these sacred scrolls."

Jenni frowned. "And how do we do that?"

"Fill your robe's pockets," Shoupi stated.

Milos sighed. "We can't carry all of them."

Shoupi shook her head. "Take as many as you can."

"Té glanced at the others. He picked up several scrolls that fit nicely into his pockets.

The small group gathered as many scrolls as their pockets would carry. Feeling overstuffed and a little heavier, the group wobbled through the large doors.

Beck shook his head and laughed.

Em rested Rosie on her hip.

"It's too hot for my wings," Rosie whined and wiped her eyes.

"I know, you just stay with me. Keep your wings in close." Em stepped up to Landon and whispered. "Who's the Saint?"

"Where'd the old man go?" Keekee asked.

Em tugged on Keekee's robe. "Start humming … loudly. Don't ask just do it."

Keekee hummed and the others stopped walking. Em ran up to the small group and as they huddled together, she whispered, "I think this Saint is *The Prophecy*. That ponytail guy said everyone is locked inside the second dome. That they're waiting for the Saint. I don't know how I know, but it has something to do with getting them into the third dome."

"You mean … into Hell?" Yutu asked.

Em smiled. "Nod if you understand."

They nodded.

"Again, I don't know how I know, but this has something to do with *The Prophecy* and why we're here."

"*The Prophecy*?" Rosie asked.

Em nodded. "That's why our transports are waiting for us. It's why all four had to be here."

"Why?" Yutu asked.

"To rescue these lost souls," Em replied. "Otherwise, they'll be sucked into Hell."

Keekee stopped humming.

"We got this," Em whispered.

Landon waved at the wall and the room lit for a few seconds. He aimed for the second dome, waving his hand to awaken the flames.

A twinkle in the shadows grabbed Em's attention. She stopped walking and strained to see through the darkness. Flames darted up around the old man, and he winked just before disappearing. Then, a whisper tickled her ear. *"The Prophecy … hide inside the shadows. They are coming."*

Em ran up to her slow-moving group. "We have to hide … now!"

"Hide where?" Landon asked.

"In the shadows!" Em replied. "Now."

The small group slipped into a darkened corner that was filled with swirling, black smoke.

A familiar voice echoed, and they watched and listened as their missing StarWriters walked past.

"Hey, that's –" Keekee said as Landon slapped his hand over her mouth.

"Shh." Aleia placed her finger to her lips.

"Té," Jenni spoke first. "How much farther to the second dome? It's so smokey I can't see a thing."

"Quiet everyone!" a tall man with long, dark hair and holding something in his hand ordered. "We're almost there."

Aleia and Landon looked at each other. Landon shrugged.

"Yeah, Beck," Isla stated. "How much farther?"

"Just a little," Beck replied. "Now keep moving or you are all vapor."

As the group walked past, Rosie squirmed on Em's hip and whispered, "Those are probably the bilocators that kidnapped them, and that must be Beck!"

When the path was clear, Aleia motioned for everyone to follow. She stepped closer to the entrance to the second dome. The group huddled in the shadows and listened.

"Isla … knock three times," Beck stated.

"Why me?"

Beck sighed. "Cuz I told you to!"

"Are you sure about this?" Isla asked.

"Positive," Beck replied.

"Mum and Messy are behind this door?"

Beck nodded.

The smoke and flames thickened as Isla knocked three times. The door to the second dome creaked open and half of the StarWriters disappeared into the darkness.

The wayward group inched their way up to the mysterious and ominous door. Landon reached out and knocked three times. A loud click and the door slowly creaked open. Glowing, hot embers filled the room.

Keekee refused to move. "I'm not going in there!"

"You can do this," Em whispered. "We have to save our fellow StarWriters."

"Apparently, all the other souls too," Yutu added.

"I can't do this," Keekee whined.

Yutu grabbed Keekee's hand and whispered, "I won't let anything happen to you."

Landon stepped through and flames, slapping his legs. The remaining few gathered as close as possible and inched their way past the blazing fire. The door slammed shut.

Em pointed. "Shoupi looks frightened."

"Looks like she's crying," Rosie replied.

Beck called out to the lost souls.

"What's he saying?" Em asked. "I can't hear him."

Beck waved his arms. "Everyone … come closer. I have wonderful news to share."

"Why is he pointing at Shoupi?" Rosie asked.

Beck puffed out his chest and bowed to the lost souls. "In your midst is the Saint." He grabbed Shoupi by the arm and pushed her in front of the crowd. "This is Saint Shoupi, and she's gonna lead you to paradise."

Rosie sighed. "Oh, this is gonna be good."

CHAPTER 33

Saint Shoupi? Paradise? A twinge of pain surged through Em's heart as she glared at Shoupi. The other StarWriters stood quietly looking dumbfounded. *Must be in shock like me.*

Beck nudged Shoupi into the murmuring crowd.

Why isn't she fighting back?

"This can't be for real," Landon said, breaking his silence. "Shoupi, a Saint?"

Aleia placed her finger to her lips.

Landon nodded.

As Shoupi stepped toward the murmuring crowd, Beck glanced back at the StarWriters and smiled. His grin didn't look normal — too evil and sinister.

"Maybe she is a Saint." Em said. "I'll bet Director and Michael knew all along when they told us about *The Prophecy.* And there's no paradise here … just Hell."

Rosie frowned. "How would you know what the Director or Michael did or did not know? Are *you* not telling us something?"

Em glanced at Rosie and shook her head. "Of course not. Sometimes, a little voice just tells me things."

"Great, so you're hearing voices now?" Rosie placed her hand on her hip.

"Shh." Aleia pointed at Shoupi.

Té stepped up to Shoupi and held out his hand. Shoupi looked at it for only a moment before shaking her head.

"Saint Shoupi's telling Té, *no*," Rosie whispered. "She's waving him away."

"I wonder why?" Yutu asked. "Doesn't she want our help?"

"Shush," Em whispered. "Listen …"

"Saint Shoupi has something to say," Beck stated and again he nudged Shoupi into the crowd.

"I don't think Saint Shoupi wants any part of this," Rosie whispered.

"It makes no sense," Yutu whispered. "If she's a Saint, then Shoupi can only do good and not evil."

"Good point," Em replied.

Shoupi cleared her throat and said something.

"I can't hear her," Rosie stated.

"Shush!" Em scolded.

"Louder!" Beck ordered. "No one can hear you."

It looked like Shoupi didn't want to make eye contact with any of the lost souls for she kept her gaze focused on the ground.

"What's she doing?" Em asked.

"She's struggling," Rosie replied.

"More like hesitating," Yutu stated.

"Uh … I'm Shoupi …"

"Louder!" Beck stated, clapping his hands.

"I'm Shoupi," she said, louder. "I'm a Saint … I'm here to help you. Beck wants everyone to follow him to the third dome." Shoupi pointed. "I will follow him and you will follow me."

A heavy cloud of silence traveled through the smokey cave.

"Something's not right," Em whispered. "I think Beck's pushing everyone to the third dome and using Saint Shoupi as bait."

"Why?" Rosie asked.

"He probably believes he can pass them into –"

"Hell!" Rosie gasped.

"Yeah, but Shoupi said to follow her to the third dome," Yutu whispered. "Not to go through it."

"Smart girl," Em whispered.

Isla stepped in front of Beck and blocked his path. He grabbed her arm but she jerked it away. "You promised!"

"Now, what's she doing?" Rosie asked.

"I'm looking for my mum," Isla yelled. "She has brown hair and her name's Mirium. My sister's with her. Her name's –"

Beck yanked Isla by the arm. "Shut up! You're done, let's go!"

Isla yelled, "If anyone sees them, tell 'em I'm at the third dome!"

The murmuring grew louder as Beck pulled Shoupi and Isla through the thickening crowd.

"We need to follow them," Em whispered.

"I have an idea," Yutu stated. "Let's split up. We can catch them from both sides."

"I like that idea," Em replied.

"*Yutu …*" a faint whisper tickled Yutu's ear like a feather on a breeze.

"Did you say something, Keekee?" he asked.

Keekee shook her head. "No."

"*Yutu …*"

Yutu tapped Landon on the shoulder. "You want me?"

Landon shook his head and pointed forward.

"*Yutu …*"

Yutu dashed in front of Landon and glanced around. Keekee almost tripped trying to hold onto his hand. Yutu was searching the shadows.

"What's wrong?" Keekee asked. "And stop pulling on me."

"Someone's whispering my name. I think I saw something."

"You look like you just saw a ghost," Keekee said.

"I just remembered something. Something before I arrived here. I killed her."

Keekee smirked. "You wouldn't be a StarWriter if you had killed someone."

"I didn't kill her directly, but she's dead because of me." Yutu released his grip on Keekee. "I've got to go."

Landon shook his head.

"Where're you going?" Keekee asked.

"To find my ghost." Yutu pushed his way into the crowd.

"Excuse me," Yutu said, inching his way through the souls.

"What's your rush, boy?" An elderly woman grabbed his arm.

"Sorry … gotta catch up to that girl. Please let go."

The old woman's grip seemed to be getting stronger.

"Ma'am, please," Yutu pleaded.

The old woman pulled him in close. "I don't see any girl or any girls up there. Just us old folk."

Yutu pointed. "Over there … look … the girl with the dark hair. Her ponytail is swinging. Can't you see her? There she is again … inside that smoke."

"That's just mist, boy," the old woman stated. "Someone is yanking your chain."

"Yeah, you are." Yutu pulled his arm free and pushed his way toward the swaying ponytail. He grabbed onto the girl's shoulder and yelled her name. "Amelia! It's me, Yutu."

An old woman with silver hair turned around and smiled. "What you want, boy?"

"Sorry, I thought you were …"

Another ponytail swayed in the smoke.

"Amelia! Wait up!"

The ponytailed girl turned a corner and disappeared into the clouds.

Yutu pushed ahead. *It has to be her.*

Rosie giggled. "Gotta luv Té's pink hair. It sparkles through the ash." Rosie coughed into Em's ear.

"Cover your mouth. I wish I could give you a mask." Em smiled. "Mask!" Nothing happened. "Just when we really need these uniforms to work, they don't."

"Thanks for trying." Rosie grinned.

Slipping up behind him, Em tapped Té on the shoulder. "Don't turn around. It's me, Rosie, and Aleia. We're right behind you. Aleia's dressed like a kidnapper of souls along with Landon. He, Keekee, and Yutu are trying to flank you guys as well."

"Shoupi's a —" Té started to whisper as he slowly shuffled along with the moving crowd.

"We heard," Em replied. "We've been following you since you emerged from the door."

"The others are just ahead. They're following Saint Shoupi," Té whispered.

"We know," Em replied. "Don't turn around or you'll give us away."

"How did you find us?" Té asked.

"When you didn't return, Director and Michael told us you and Irid were taken. We devised a plan."

Té coughed. "I know. Jenni, Milos, and Colton told me the same thing but they came through Eternity Present."

Em followed Té's lead and coughed. "The rest of us took the transports. Visited *Pi* where we learned a lot from Beck's helpers."

Aleia inched closer and coughed.

"What do those two have on Saint Shoupi?" Em asked.

Té slightly turned, trying to keep pace. "Not Isla. Just Beck. He used Isla, telling her *she* was *The Prophecy*. He convinced her that her mother and sister were here, and he'd help get them out." He coughed louder.

"Then her mother and sister are not here?" Em asked.

"Isla believes they are. She said her guide told her after they were taken. That she had to free 'em."

Em chuckled. "Beck believes Isla is the prophesied one? But it's really Saint Shoupi?"

"Poor Saint Shoupi," Rosie said, lowering her eyes.

"Only in the sense that he wants her to do something against her *saintly* will," Em replied. Now she cleared her throat. "And they brought you here with an invisibility elixir. We learned about the elixirs on *Pi* from Beck's goons."

"Isla used it to get on board Irid and take control," Té said. "I don't believe she knew Beck was there. He placed Irid in a trance with a different elixir."

"How's Beck controlling Shoupi?" Em asked.

"I overheard him talking to her. If she doesn't lead everyone to the third dome, Beck threatened to destroy her home in the Middle East. I think he showed her something that really frightened her cuz she cried."

"But Michael and Director would never allow that to happen," Rosie added. "Would they?"

Té shrugged. "All I know is that when Saint Shoupi read the scrolls, everything changed. Beck decided he didn't need Isla anymore and started using Shoupi."

Em sighed. "We believe he's going to use her to get everyone into the —"

"Third dome," Té stated.

"But … you have to enter on your own free will," Em added.

Aleia nodded.

Té shrugged. "What better way to enter Hell than with a Saint?"

"Poor Saint Shoupi." Rosie shook her head. "I wouldn't want to be her right now."

Em and Aleia stumbled into the back of Té.

"Careful!" Rosie whispered loudly.

"Sorry," Em replied. "Why'd everybody stop?" No one seemed to be moving. "Where's Isla going?"

Té shrugged. "I think we've arrived at the third dome. I'm going to have to go after her. She won't give up until she finds her mom and sister. You follow Saint Shoupi. Beck's gonna make his move any minute now."

Em grabbed Té's robe. "Something important you gotta know. We're bringing everyone back with us on the transports."

Té pulled away without answering.

"Think he heard you?" Rosie asked.

Em shrugged. "Hope so."

Té disappeared into the tangled web of lost souls.

"Look …" – Em said to Aleia and Rosie – "… Beck's pulling Shoupi away from the others."

The StarWriters followed Beck and Shoupi through the thickening crowd.

"Where's Yutu?" Rosie asked. "Don't see him anywhere."

"He's not with the others?" Em glanced around, bouncing Rosie on her hip. "And *you* … don't get any ideas about hovering. I want you with me."

"Okay," Rosie whispered, grabbing tighter onto Em's neck.

"Hold onto my robe," Em said to Aleia. "Wouldn't be good if we got separated."

Em pushed past several older men and slipped in behind Jenni. She tapped her on the shoulder.

Jenni grinned. "You made it. Now, we're all here. We were following Beck and Shoupi. But I think we just lost 'em."

"I guess we're on our way to Hell," Landon whispered.

"Shouldn't you be silent?" Em asked. "Robbers of Souls don't talk."

"Does it really matter anymore?" he frowned.

"I want to leave," Keekee whined.

Em ignored Keekee and said, "Where's Yutu?"

Landon shrugged. "Took off a while back. Said he killed his girlfriend, and she was here whispering for help."

"What?" Em squealed.

A voice suddenly whispered to only Em. *"It's a lie."*

Em glanced around and frowned. She looked at Rosie. "Did you hear anything?"

"Just you guys talking," Rosie replied. "Why?"

"We need to find Yutu," Em stated. "I think some *thing* is lying to him. Maybe the same *thing* that Beck was talking to."

"How would you know?" Rosie asked.

"I just know," Em replied.

Rosie frowned. "You heard a voice in your head again."

Em nodded.

Milos waited for the others to catch up. "We have to get up front. I think that's where Beck is."

Where are you? Té maneuvered through the souls before spotting Isla's light brown hair several feet ahead. He wanted to yell out but was afraid of frightening her. Instead, he sighed and pushed past an elderly couple.

"Take it slow, boy," one of the men said, shoving him back. "What's your rush?"

"Sorry, just trying to catch up to my friend." Té frowned and sighed. *Some friend Isla turned out to be.* She had lied to him, used him, and now he was trying to help her … again.

Té thought about Michael and his words, *'Everyone evolves around here. And for a reason.' Is that why I saw her in the Plan Room? Am I supposed to help her find her mom and sister?* He grabbed the back of Isla's robe and yanked, hard.

"What're you doing here?" Isla started and glared at him. "Did Beck send you?"

"I want to help," Té whispered.

Isla smiled. "I just know they're here somewhere."

"What makes you believe that?"

"Look around. Everybody's old and ailing. Just waiting for something to happen. All the younger ones are up front."

"Good point," Té replied. "I think we'd make more progress if we walk closer to the wall. Not as many people."

Isla nodded. "Thank you, Té."

As they passed an old soul, Isla asked, "Did you see a girl with blonde hair or a woman with dark hair?"

"No …" the man replied.

"Ain't seen any youngins'," a woman said.

Others just shook their heads.

"This doesn't feel promising," Té stated.

Isla sighed and stepped up to another woman, asking her the same question.

"I did," the woman replied. "But some time back. Caught my eye when –"

"Where'd you see 'em?" Isla demanded. "Up ahead?"

"A while back," the woman replied. "Caught my eye. A blonde youngin' hanging onto a sad-looking woman. Covered in soot she was." She blinked a few times. "Can tell you're newbies. Not dirty like the rest of us. We been here awhile."

"Thank you so much." Tears formed in Isla's eyes.

Té hugged her around her shoulders. "Let's go."

They plowed through the crowd as spits of fire flamed around them.

"I think we're close. Not as many old people," Té whispered.

"I think we're in another section of the second dome."

"Then, let's move to the center." He pulled her hand, leading the way.

Isla continued to ask her question as they walked. "Have you seen a little girl with blonde hair ..."

"Yes," a woman pointed. "Many children are up front."

"Té, over there, women with children!" Isla stated.

"I just see smoke," he replied.

They squeezed through the crowd that seemed to be growing thicker.

"Mummy!" Isla squealed, letting go of Té's hand. She ran and disappeared into a wall of smoke.

"Isla! Isla!" Souls pushed into Té, and he braced himself to not fall. More souls gathered when he spotted the back of Isla's head. "Isla, wait up!" Té pushed against the crowd and reached out. He grabbed onto her robe. "Don't do that … stay with me."

Isla hugged Té and cried. "It wasn't them."

Several others pushed and shoved. Isla took a step, and Té grabbed onto her arm. A wall of souls was storming toward them like an ocean wave. Holding onto Isla, Té tried to push back, but the souls were too thick.

"Will I ever find them?" Isla cried. "This crowd is endless."

"We'll just keep looking," Té said, pulling her in closer to him.

Isla screamed, "Messy!"

"Isla?" a distant echo replied.

Isla pointed to her right. "I think it came from over there."

Té pointed to his left. "I'm sure it came from that way."

"Mess –"

Té placed his hand over her mouth. "Shhh, we can't bring attention to ourselves. We'll go to the right like you said."

"It's now or never, Té. I know they're here. Messy!" she whispered loudly.

Té inched them to the side, straining to hear more. "I wish there was less smoke and more light."

A small hand grabbed onto Isla's robe, and two arms wrapped around her shoulders.

"Quiet, my darling. Do not speak," a voice whispered into Isla's ear. "I'm happy to have found you. Is Grayson with you?"

Isla stared into her mother's brown eyes and cried. The woman's face and hair was covered in soot. "Mummy, Grayson's not here. But he's safe."

Mirium sighed. "Thank heavens."

"It's really you? I've missed you so." Isla reached out and hugged her sister. Messy's plump cheeks were blackened by the soot as well as her hair. "Messy, I've missed you the most." She turned back to Mirium. "Té and I are here to rescue you."

Té inched closer.

"How will you do that?" Mirium asked.

"We have transports," Té replied, pushing back the crowd threatening to pull them apart.

"But how will we get out of here?" Mirium asked. "And what about these other souls?"

"All I care about is you and Messy," Isla replied.

"There's something I need to tell you, Isla," Té said.

Isla wiped the soot from Messy's face with her robe. "Now I can see more of the real you."

"You're going to save us?" Messy asked.

"Té and I are going to take you and Mummy to safety that's far, far away."

"Really?"

"Yes, really, cross my heart," Isla replied. "Té's my friend, and he's a StarWriter."

"What's a StarWriter?" Messy asked.

Isla wiped more soot from Messy's face. "He takes our purposes and prayers and sends requests to our stars. We each have one you know."

"Can I see mine?" Messy asked.

"I'll ask Té."

Té tapped Isla's shoulder. "You gotta see this."

Holding on tight to Messy's hand, Isla glanced around. "What's going on? Why is it getting brighter in here?"

The smoke was disappearing as flames shot up around them.

Té pointed to a high cliff that was not far away. "It's Beck … and he's got Shoupi with him."

CHAPTER 34

Trying to avoid the flames, Em held onto to Rosie and pushed through the crowd. "We can't lose sight of Shoupi."

Aleia grabbed onto Em's robe.

"Stay alert and together," Em said.

Rosie tapped Em on the shoulder. "The smoke's clearing."

The small group inched through the crowd, and a clap of thunder shook the cave.

"What was that?" Em asked.

Rosie pointed. "Look!"

"Beck …" Em whispered.

"To all you poor souls who are stuck in Sheol for eternity … I am your new king and ruler …" Beck yelled.

The lost souls stopped moving and stared up at the shouting man.

"Look who's standing behind him." Aleia sighed.

"Shoupi…" Em whispered, shaking her head. "We have to plan so we can rescue her."

Beck raised his hands. "And as your new king and leader … I propose an end to this and a new beginning …"

Em tapped Landon on the shoulder, "Don't turn around, but any sign of Té or Yutu?"

Landon shook his head.

Beck raised his voice and flames shot up closer to him as if obeying his commands. "Listen to *me* and you *will* be rewarded …"

"Maybe Yutu's with Té?" Em asked.

"Don't know," Landon replied. "But Yutu ran off after his girlfriend. So, I doubt it."

"It's a lie," Em whispered. "It's not his real girlfriend."

"But how can you be so sure?" Landon asked.

"A voice is warning me," Em replied.

"Look," Rosie said and pointed to the cliff.

Beck dragged Shoupi by the neck to the edge. He held on firm and shook her head at the crowd. "Behold!" Beck yelled. "Here stands the true Saint Shoupi! What guidance do you have to those standing below?"

Shoupi lowered her head, and Beck whispered into her ear.

"She seems to be a little tongue tied, folks," Beck shouted. "She wants me to speak on her behalf. Saint Shoupi you just nod."

"Looks like he's doing the nodding by pushing her head," Em stated.

"Poor Shoupi," Rosie whined.

Em tapped Keekee's shoulder. "Keekee … Landon … tell the others to follow. We have to get to that cliff." Em pushed through the crowd.

"You know where we're going?" Rosie asked.

"There has to be a way up there," Em said. "Rosie, make sure the others are following."

"Yup, they are," Rosie replied.

"As your new king …" Beck yelled, "… Shoupi assures me you will be led to a new paradise …"

The group stopped in front of a shallow crevasse.

"Stairs!" Jenni whispered. "Could be the way up."

"Wait!" Milos stated. "What are we going to do when we get up there? Do we fight Beck and pull Shoupi away?"

Em nodded. "What if four of us go up, and the others stay here and distract Beck. Then we can grab Shoupi."

Jenni stared at Em. "And do what exactly?"

"Bring her down here, with us," Em replied.

"Like I said … and do what? Maybe four of us could somehow grab Beck, hold him down, and let Shoupi tell these souls the truth," Jenni replied.

Rosie nodded. "I like Jenni's plan."

Aleia nodded.

"Okay, then we go with Jenni's plan," Em replied. "Whose going up?"

"I will," Jenni stated.

Colton took a step. "I'll go."

"Me too." Milos rocked back and forth on his heels.

"I'll go too," Aleia said, sighing. "I'll help Saint Shoupi announce to the crowd when you three hold down Beck."

With Jenni in the lead, the four stepped into the crevasse and were gone.

"What happens after Shoupi makes the announcement?" Landon asked.

Em sighed. "Haven't got a clue."

"We run?" Smillie asked, furrowing his 'brows.

Beck shook Shoupi again and her head nodded. "Saint Shoupi said that the third dome will open any minute and she'll lead you to paradise …"

Jenni disappeared into the darkness. She glanced around and the narrow alley gave her chills. Instead of heat, the area felt cold and foreboding as if the pits of Hell had just slipped into a frozen wasteland. Darting deeper into the shadows, she tripped when her foot hit a bottom step.

"Darn," she said, working to steady herself.

"Jenni …" Milo's voice echoed through the tight passageway behind her. "Wait for us!"

Jenni ran up the stairs, taking two at a time. Flames spiraled on the landing. She glanced behind her for the others, but she was alone. Colton, Milos, and Aleia were nowhere to be seen.

I have this … Jenni grinned. *My time has arrived.*

Beck's voice bounced down around her. "Prepare yourself for paradise!"

Jenni stepped onto the landing, slipping past the flames. Beck was still holding onto Shoupi's neck. "Beck!"

Beck turned and frowned. "What are you doing up here?"

Shoupi struggled against Beck's strong grip. "Jenni! Help me."

Jenni bowed her head. "I'm here to help you, my king."

"Help me?" Beck asked. "How?"

"Come over here, and I'll tell you, my king." Jenni walked to the other side of Beck and crossed her arms. "I need to tell you something in private."

"What? Can't you see I'm busy?" Beck shook his head.

"It's really important, I have to talk to you!"

"No!" Beck yelled. "We're going into the next dome. I need the souls to follow Shoupi."

"My king …" Jenni stepped closer and grabbed his arm. "It's important, please."

Beck stepped away from the cliff, pulling Shoupi with him.

"You're hurting her neck," Jenni stated.

"Is that what you wanted to tell me?"

"No, but you're hurting her neck. Hold her arm instead."

Beck released Shoupi. Jenni grabbed Beck's arm and pulled him to her. She leaned in and whispered. Beck grinned and his eyes widened. After slapping the vial from Beck's hand, Aleia and Milos grabbed for Shoupi, latching onto her arms. They ran back for the stairs. The vial broke and the liquid slowly oozed under Beck's boots. Nothing happened.

"Hey!" Beck cried out. "She's mine!"

Jenni batted her eyes at Beck, holding tightly to his arm. "Trust me, my king. My plan shall work." She glanced down at the dark liquid. "It's obvious that yours is not."

Em, Smillie, Keekee, and Landon huddled together, staring up at the commotion.

"Did you just see that?" Rosie asked.

Em frowned. "That seemed way too easy."

"I agree," Landon replied. "Too easy. Why didn't Beck go after Shoupi? She's the one that's supposed to lead everyone to the third dome. He needs her, doesn't he?"

"Everyone!" Beck yelled.

"Shh," Em whispered. "He's saying something."

Beck stepped back up to the cliff's edge, holding Jenni's hand. "Our Saint Shoupi will guide you to paradise. I will follow with your new queen. Welcome, Queen Jenni!"

Jenni bowed. "Yes, listen to Shoupi. She is our Saint who will fulfill *The Prophecy*."

Em raised her arm and sighed. "What is she doing? Why is she talking about *The Prophecy*?"

Smillie frowned. "I don't like this."

"Maybe it's part of her plan?" Landon asked, shrugging.

"Look!" Keekee whispered.

Milos and Aleia, holding tightly to Shoupi's hands, stepped out of the crevasse.

Aleia coughed. "We have to get outta here."

"What just happened up there?" Em asked.

"We rescued Shoupi when Jenni sweet-talked Beck," Aleia replied. "And his vial broke. Nothing happened. No one turned to vapor."

Shoupi nodded. "They grabbed me, and Milos knocked the vial from Beck's hand."

"Why are we still standing here?" Milos asked. "We need to go."

"That was brave, Milos." Landon chuckled. "Jenni sweet-talked him right into making her his new queen of Sheol, huh?"

Aleia eyes widened. "What're you talking about? Jenni's right behind us. She helped us."

Em adjusted Rosie on her hip. "I guess she changed her mind."

Aleia sighed. "She didn't tell us about this, are you sure?"

Aleia and Shoupi glanced up at the cliff.

"Beck's still there with Jenni," Aleia said. "Maybe she's holding him back for us."

"Don't think so," Rosie replied. "They look way too cozy."

"She's hanging in tight with him." Em shook her head. "Is she his queen now? Did you know about this?"

"No." Aleia's eyes widened. "She ran ahead. We just grabbed Shoupi and left."

"What're we going to do now?" Shoupi asked.

"We leave," Keekee replied.

Shoupi looked behind them. "I have to go back. I'm not leaving without the scrolls."

"We'll see what we can do," Em replied. "We also can't leave until we make every soul follow us."

Rosie squirmed in Em's arms. "We have to do that?"

"Stop moving around," Em said.

"It's not me. Lyon doesn't like it here, and he's pushing on my leg. Stop, Lyon." Rosie slapped her robe.

"Em what did you just say?" Landon asked.

"I told Rosie to stop squirming," Em replied.

Rosie stuck out her tongue. "Let me go. I want to fly."

"You're not flying anywhere," Em stated.

Landon nodded. "Actually … you have the perfect plan."

"What plan?" Rosie asked.

Landon walked over to Colton and pushed down on his shoulders. "Get on your knees."

Colton laughed. "Why?"

Landon motioned to Shoupi. "Sit on his shoulders … better yet … stand on him."

"You have a reason for this?" Em asked.

Smillie helped Shoupi to keep her balance and replied, "Shoupi, stand tall and speak as Saint Shoupi!"

Em nodded and laughed. "And get everyone to follow you to the transports."

"Beck said my village would be destroyed if I didn't follow his orders," Shoupi whispered.

"In my heart …" – Em rubbed Shoupi's arm – "… Director and Michael would never allow that to happen."

"But how can you be sure?" Tears ran down Shoupi's cheeks.

"I have faith," Em replied. "Besides, you're a Saint."

"But I don't know how to be a Saint yet." Shoupi wiped her cheeks. "Can we ask everyone to take a scroll?"

"One step at a time," Em replied. "First, let's see how this works."

Colton stood and Shoupi raised her arms as she was lifted into the hot air.

Landon nodded at Rosie. "Are you ready to fly over her head? With your pink wings, you'll add color and interest. Look more … angel-lee …"

Rosie giggled and flew above the standing Saint.

The small group gazed up at Shoupi.

Smillie nodded and opened his mouth. A bright light lit Shoupi and the flying angel.

Milos cleared his throat. With a deeper voice, he yelled, "Here is your Saint Shoupi! Hear her roar."

Shoupi whispered, "I'm Saint Shoupi —"

"Louder!" Milos stated.

"Every soul in Sheol!" Shoupi yelled. "Listen to me and only me. Follow me to the first dome, and I'll lead you to the true paradise you have longed for."

Smillie grinned.

"Let's hope this works and that Té and Yutu see us leaving," Em said, glancing around.

"Everyone's moving now," Aleia whispered.

"But will they follow?" Em asked.

Queen Jenni stood next to Beck as they stared down at the shuffling crowd.

Beck pointed. "What's going on down there?"

"I told you to trust me," Jenni stated. "The whispers have changed the landscape, and Saint Shoupi is now leading everyone straight to Hell. Look at 'em." Jenni giggled. "The whispers will not disappoint us, my king."

"You better be right on this one." Beck jerked Jenni closer and glared into her eyes. "Shall you betray me … I *will* destroy you."

"My king," Jenni whispered, "I have chosen you over the StarWriters. Though they believe I am trying to confuse you for their benefit, I assure you, I am not."

"Why should I trust you? Why would you want to be with me and not them?"

"I stand beside you," Jenni stated, still watching the small crowd. "I want to be your queen."

"Why would *you* want to be *my* queen?" Beck asked.

"My destiny is with you. It is written in *The Prophecy* and now, everything is evolving."

"What are you talking about?"

"You thought Isla would be your queen –"

"That's what I was told." Beck's eyes widened.

"She has betrayed you. Used you."

"You seem to know how to play both ends." Beck chuckled.

"You have my trust." Jenni stared into his eyes without blinking. "Shoupi is slowly revealing herself. *The Prophecy* is unveiling."

Black smoke ran across the floor, encircling Beck's and Jenni's feet. Beck tilted his head, and from somewhere inside the ever-evolving darkness, the whispering grew louder. Beck lowered his eyes.

"Can you hear what they are saying?" Jenni asked.

Beck laughed. "Those StarWriters are leading those damn fools in circles. Soon, they will be walking straight to Hell, and I will be rewarded."

Jenni grinned.

"And Isla will receive her just rewards," Beck said.

"What do you mean?"

"There is no family here for her to rescue. And ... *she* will *not* be returning."

"I'll be here to assist you," Jenni said.

"Then to the third dome with us!" Beck laughed and the sinister whispers echoed across the cliff, drifting down and into the crowd. "Come my queen, we must go. We should be there to greet the StarWriters and their new followers."

Jenni nodded. "Yes, my king." Jenni wished she could hear those whispers again. The ones she heard the day she died. The whispers that comforted her before she met Michael. A secret she had kept from everyone.

The car plunged over the mountain's barrier and into the deep ravine. Twisted metal caressed Jenni's body as the steam spewed from what remained of the hood. She was sleeping peacefully between the steering wheel and front seat when a low whisper entered her consciousness.

"Sss ... you're gifted ... say nothing ... sss ..."

Her heart thumped one last beat. The blackness that had devoured her now filled her with a longing – a craving that never existed before. Jenni understood she was on a different plane from her mortal reality, and her mind searched as her eyes fought against the growing shadows.

"Sss ..." It were those whispers again.

Are they trying to talk to me? "Who's there?" Jenni yelled. "Help me!"

"You're a gifted one ... sss ... you shall see ... you are an asset ... sss ... say nothing about us to *Him* ... when the opportunity presents, you shall be rewarded ..."

"Who are you?"

"Say nothing … sss … it shall evolve …" The whispering stopped.

In the distance a speck of light filtered through an enlarging hole that expanded and filled her inner soul. The light felt warm and inviting. Standing at the shore of an endless ocean, she allowed the florescent water to run across her sandals.

"Where am I?" Jenni asked.

She reached down and the coolness slipped through her fingers. But her skin remained dry. Jenni stepped into the water and sat. The water reminded her of a velvet chair that she often enjoyed as a young child, so soft and flowing. Laying back, her head touched the sand and the water gently covered her face. She opened her month and took a deep breath.

The sky looked fuzzy and darker from under the water. A smiling man was staring down at her.

Jenni sat up.

"Welcome, Jenni," he said. "I am Michael."

She stood and studied the odd-looking man who was blacker than the evening sky with hair as blonde as the morning sun. She counted the bands entwined in his many braids.

"Who are you?" Jenni asked.

"As I said, I am Michael."

"Nice braids." Jenni glanced around. "Where am I?"

Michael chuckled. "Your soul is in the band that surrounds Heaven."

"Then, I'm dead?" Jenni thought about the whispers … *'You are gifted, say nothing. Let it evolve.'*

"I need you on my team," Michael stated.

"Team?" Jenni asked.

"The StarWriters."

"StarWriters? Doing what?"

"Working *His Plan* for our souls."

Jenni shrugged.

"Walk with me," Michael said, reaching out his hand.

Té had watched the scene play out on the cliff, and wondered about a *Queen Jenni?* What was Jenni trying to do? Té was behind the group of souls following Colton with Shoupi on his shoulders, allowing his mind to wander.

"I don't get it," Té said, glancing at Isla. "What is Jenni doing?"

"I don't know," Isla replied. "But Beck's always about power. He said he was a king and was searching for his kingdom."

"Who's your friend, Isla?" Mirium asked.

Messy stepped out from behind Isla. "Hi, I'm Messy."

"I've heard all about you," Té said, smiling.

"I like your pink hair. It's my favorite color." Messy grinned, showing teeth that were covered in soot.

"This is my friend, Té," Isla replied. "He helped me find you and promised to help get you outta here." She glanced at Té and smiled.

"Thank you, Té," Mirium said. "Pleasure to meet you."

"Thank you, Té." Messy whispered.

"Did you see where Aleia, Milos, and Shoupi went?" Té asked.

"I think –" Isla yelped as the lost souls pushed into them, moving them deeper into the shadows. Té grabbed Isla's arm as Isla grabbed Messy and her mother. "Why is everyone heading the wrong way?"

"Maybe we should follow them," Mirium said, pushing against an old man and woman.

Isla glanced at Messy. "Wish we had Whiskers with us now."

"We don't have whiskers," Messy replied. "What are you talking about?"

Mirium nodded. "Messy … you remember don't you? Whiskers was our –"

"Kitty." Isla frowned. "Did you forget about our kitty?"

"I remember now," Messy replied.

"Of course you do," Mirium said. "We never forget about our creatures of comfort."

"I wish we could be Whiskers and scamper away from these souls." Isla stared at her mother. "She was always your favorite, wasn't she Mummy? Not just a creature of comfort."

"Of course," Mirium replied, glancing down. "My poor feet, they are quite pitiful."

Té smiled. Mirium's feet were filthy.

"Té! Té!" Yutu yelled, holding onto a girl's hand.

"Yutu?" Té smiled. "Glad to see you. Now we can find the others and get out of here."

Yutu nodded at a girl who's dark hair was pulled into a pony tail, decorating an oval face covered in soot. "This is Amelia, my girlfriend. Thought I had killed her. I mean … I *did* kill her … I mean we died together. She reminded me and now I remember. I was sent to the StarWriters, and she was brought here."

Amelia glared at Mirium. "Yutu says they have transports that will bring us to a special place."

"I heard." Mirium nodded. "Most fortunate for us."

"We just spotted Shoupi," Yutu added. "I mean, Saint Shoupi. She's headed this way. She's standing on Colton's shoulders. That's why everyone is confused. She's leading them back to the first dome."

"Isla …" Mirium touched Isla's arm. "We should move in the same direction. Since that's the way out according to *your* Saint Shoupi."

"She's everyone's Saint." Té furrowed his 'brows.

"Of course she is," Mirium grabbed Messy's hand. "We are most grateful."

Isla smiled at Té. "Thank you. We are finally leaving this place. I'm so happy to have found Mummy and Messy. Couldn't have done it without you."

Té smiled. "Our team's heading this way. We can join them and help lead everyone to the first dome and then to our transports."

Mirium glared at Té and frowned.

Milos yelled to the lost souls. "Follow Saint Shoupi …"

Colton walked behind Milos with Shoupi balanced on his shoulders. Rosie flew above Em and Aleia.

"I can see Yutu," Rosie said. "He's pulling a girl with him."

"I hope he hears Saint Shoupi," Em replied. "We need to be together … all of us."

Aleia tried to look around Colton. "I can't see a thing. He's so tall."

"I can see everything from up here," Rosie said. "What do you want to know?"

"Stay above Shoupi," Em replied. "So everyone can see you."

Rosie nodded, flying back to her post above Saint Shoupi.

As the small group walked, the souls parted creating a path for Shoupi and Colton.

"To all!" Milos yelled. "Hear and follow Saint Shoupi."

Shoupi held onto Colton's hands. It was difficult to balance and watch where they were going.

"Shoupi," Em stated. "Say something to your followers."

Shoupi nodded. "Listen! I will lead you to the holy place."

Aleia smiled. "Seems to be working. Everyone's following us."

Em placed her hands over her ears.

"You okay?" Aleia asked.

"My head hurts," Em replied. "Bad."

Smillie stepped over to Em. "Do you need me to help you walk?"

"I think I'll be okay. But what is Jenni doing?" Em asked. "Is she helping us by stopping Beck? Why isn't he behind us pulling Shoupi from Colton's shoulders?"

Smillie sighed. "You think that maybe Jenni sold us out?"

"Queen Jenni was jealous of you, Em," Aleia said. "When Director said you would lead us, Jenni was mad. I could tell."

"Very jealous." Smillie nodded.

Standing on her balcony, Director Crof sighed. The view on the horizon troubled her. Through her window of thoughts, she glanced into *His Plan* room. The clocks often flipped from good to evil and back again on a continuous basis. However, this time, the hands jerked to evil and remained.

Orange flames rose in the distance, turning to a raging red. Her apprentice StarWriters were in trouble. She prayed that her thoughts were being heard by Em.

Had the heavenly Messenger that Michael sent to Sheol made contact with her StarWriters yet? They needed strength and clarity.

"They're going to need our prayers," she said toward the heavens.

"I think I see something," Té said.

"I don't see anything, just smoke," Isla replied.

"I can see Shoupi. She's standing on Colton's shoulders. Rosie's flying in a circle above her." He chuckled. "Rosie's fanning the smoke, making it look like Shoupi has a halo."

"We need to catch up," Isla said.

"Push through the crowd," Té replied. "I'll stay behind so no one gets lost."

"Thanks," Isla said. "I'll never forget you for helping us."

Té thought about the first time he set eyes on Isla. Her tall, wispy body and waist-length hair had caught his attention. It was in *His Plan* room where she had just winked at him. Her beauty had stirred something – perhaps happiness? But the feeling of fear and maybe a little disgust grew when he believed she was using him.

He thought about what Michael had said after he confessed to her wink. What he didn't tell Michael was that he had winked back. He wondered if withholding information was just as bad as lying. That was when he noticed the clocks flipping.

He remembered what Michael had whispered to him in secret. "It is *The Prophecy* … you will be called upon to care for Isla."

"How?" he had asked Michael.

"It shall evolve," Michael had replied.

Everything was starting to make sense. His attraction to her, and her needing him. It was part of *The Prophecy,* and he was a part of it … as were all the StarWriters, even Queen Jenni. He remembered how Jenni had eavesdropped on him and Michael. Had she heard the secret? Was she still part of their team or had she gone over to the dark side? The side within the third dome. He didn't want to think about that evil place and what resided there.

Té sighed as they stepped up behind Milos and his small group. "Right behind you." Té tapped Em's shoulder.

Em glanced over and smiled. "Happy you could join us."

Té laughed. "Me too."

"Now that we're all together again, let's just follow Shoupi. She's leading everyone to the transports," Em said.

'Lies … lies …'

"Did you just say something?" Em asked Té.

"What about Queen Jenni?" Aleia asked.

Em stumbled into Té who reached out and caught her. "You okay?"

Em tried to stand steady. "It's my head. But I think the pain's gone now."

'Beware of trickery … falsehoods,' the voice blared through Em's thoughts.

Em grabbed her head and bent over. She yelled and fell to her knees. "Beware of trickery … falsehoods …"

Té knelt and shook his head. "Beware of what?"

Michael materialized on the balcony and stared out at the dark, red horizon. "If you keep trying to communicate with Em, that poor child may soon lose her mind."

Ja Crof sighed. "I was hoping to provide a little insight."

"Is not Gabe with them? Has he not relayed your messages?"

"But he must keep the secret."

Michael shook his head. "You know why."

"*The Prophecy.*" Ja Crof stepped closer to the railing. "And a child with children shall come forward. One leading the others to free those gripped by the loss of *Him.*"

"Gabe will not reveal himself," Michael replied.

"How much longer until my StarWriters are returned to me?"

"Things often move from bad to worse." Michael sighed.

"And Jenni?" Ja Crof glanced at Michael.

"*His* gifts to her were abundant. But I received word from Gabe that Jenni has chosen to cut ties with *Him.*"

"From the start," Ja Crof whispered.

"Your intuition amazes me." Michael glanced at Ja Crof and frowned. "I have a confession to make."

"Oh?"

"In Eternity Past, I kept a vision from you."

Ja Crof tilted her head.

Michael nodded. "A visitation moments before Jenni's death."

"Why would you do that?" Ja Crof furrowed her 'brows.

"I did not want you to be biased."

"The whispers," Ja Crof stated.

"They promised her power."

Ja Crof frowned. "Power that can never be."

"Temptation," Michael whispered, "and … with someone with gifts such as Jenni's."

"She lied about the visitation?"

"Remained silent," Michael replied. "I afforded her every opportunity."

"Sad."

Yes." Michael sighed. "However, it was written in the stars."

"As it always is." Ja Crof stared into the fiery, red flames that snapped toward the heavens.

"It is time, my friend," Michael whispered, and his spirit faded into the mist.

Ja Crof held her breath and closed her eyes. "It is time."

"Saint Shoupi is here … at the first dome," Milos yelled. "We have arrived!"

Rosie flew in circles above Shoupi's head. "I'm tired."

Aleia reached for Rosie. "I'll carry you the rest of the way."

Rosie settled in Aleia's embrace. "Wings don't want to work anymore." Rosie rested her head on Aleia's shoulder.

Colton stood in front of the giant, arched doors. "You good, Shoupi?"

"I'm good," Shoupi said, smiling down at him.

"Awesome." Colton slowly turned around and faced the souls and StarWriters.

Shoupi waved at Rosie.

Rosie waved back.

"Follow me into the first dome," Shoupi yelled. "We will soon enter the transports that will take us back to *Him*."

The crowd cheered. The soot-covered souls looked weary from their endless journey.

Shoupi cleared her throat. "The StarWriters will now open the doors. I will tell you when to follow." She nodded. "You will soon be in Paradise with *Him.*" Shoupi's voice echoed through the cavern.

Em closed her eyes. Her head was pounding. Director Crof's words blasted through her mind loud and clear this time, *'You must stop them!'*

Colton knelt and Shoupi stepped off.

'Find a way, Em! Find a way.'

Em grabbed her head and bent over.

"Em? Are you okay?" Té asked, holding her arm.

"Stop!" Em yelled. "I must lead them back. Ja Crof told me this when we were under the tree."

The others stood aside when Em stepped up to the smoldering doors. But something was wrong, very wrong.

She touched the panel and a sinister sensation ran up her arm, burning her neck. "What in the world?"

"We can go now," Yutu stated. "We can go back to the band." He squeezed Amelia's hand and smiled.

Té pushed on one of the doors. It easily swung open.

Em peered into the darkness. "No smell?"

Keekee clapped. "Okay … let's get out of here."

Té chuckled. "Ready when you are, Em."

"Wait!" Em glanced at the others. "Let me go in first. Something's wrong."

Mirium stepped up with Messy and Isla in tow. "What are you waiting for? We can all go with you."

"Beware of false trickery," Em whispered.

Miriam shoved her body against Em as if trying to pass. Amelia was behind her, pulling on Yutu. Em glanced at Té and shook her head.

"Stop!" Em tried to block their path.

"Get out of our way!" Miriam ordered. "It's time for the souls to meet their maker."

"False trickery ..." Em whispered loudly.

"False what?" Té asked, helping to block the doors.

"Something's wrong!" Em cried out.

"Just move!" Miriam, pushed harder.

"Listen to Em," Té said. "Something is very wrong."

"Nothing is wrong," Amelia said, shoving from behind.

Miriam pushed again, and the StarWriters screamed as they were sucked into the third dome, a dark smoke filling the void behind them. Em's heart felt heavy with a deepening dread.

"What the hell!" Té yelled.

He reached out, helping to steady Em. A blazing fire erupted, lighting the area, and tortured voices screamed out from the shadows – ominous moaning full of pain and regret.

"What's going on?" Té asked.

"I'll explain it all." Beck stood in the middle of the towering flames. He took a step and the fire lowered. He pulled off his black hood and tilted his head. "Well hello, Em." Beck said, smiling. "It's so nice to see you again."

"Beck?" Té's eyes widened. "What are you wearing?"

Em pushed on the door, trying to keep the other souls from entering. Her heart raced and her mind whirled.

Beck laughed. "Welcome to the entrance to Hell."

CHAPTER 36

Em braced herself against the large door. "Go back!" she yelled. "We were tricked!"

Mirium pushed the StarWriters from behind, shoving them deeper into the darkness. "Get out of my way!"

"Shoupi!" Em yelled, her eyes wide. "You have to go back!"

Shoupi leaned into Mirium, trying to free herself from the woman's tight grip. "Em, help me!"

The hot air thickened and a smokey mist rolled through the StarWriters. A pounding echoed as the lost souls screamed for help from the other side of the door. Mirium shoved Shoupi toward Beck and Jenni. Flames shot out from the cave's walls and the air grew hotter, and again, voices full of agony surrounded them.

"We need to escape!" Em yelled. "This is all wrong!"

Milos sighed. "Not an option anymore."

Jenni stepped out from behind Beck and pulled off her black hood. "I'm a queen!"

Keekee grabbed Landon's hand. "What's going on?"

Landon shook his head.

"Jenni!" Rosie flew out of Aleia's arms and hovered over her. "What do you think you're doing? I'm gonna singe my wings in here. It's too hot!"

"Rosie!" Aleia yelled. "Come back here!"

"No!" Rosie said. "I want to know what's going on."

Té stepped over to Yutu. "This is not good."

"No, you're wrong," Amelia said, caressing Yutu's arm. "You'll see."

"Mummy!" Isla yelled, holding onto Messy's hand. "What are you doing?"

Mirium glanced over her shoulder, and her eyes smiled widely with an unusual, evil-looking grin.

"We have to get outta here!" Aleia grabbed Smillie and Colton by the arms. "Please, we need to go."

"Damn you all!" Beck yelled.

The whispers grew thicker and louder.

"Listen!" Em stated. "StarWriters, please listen to me!"

"I think Em's right," Té said, taking a step toward the door. "Listen to her."

Colton shook his head. "I think we're screwed."

Rosie stuck out her tongue at Jenni and flew back into Aleia's arms. "This place is evil. It burned my wings."

"The only place you're going is with Saint Shoupi and back through that door!" Beck stated. He pointed at the door behind Em. "All of you will lead those souls in here to me!"

Hot, red flames swirled around Beck and Jenni as the whispers grew even louder.

Jenni grabbed Shoupi's arm. "Move!"

"No, I won't," Shoupi cried out. "I'll tell them to run!"

"Then say goodbye to your village," Beck replied. "I'll destroy it with my new found powers!"

A wall of smoke filled the cave with the stench of rotting eggs.

Smillie pinched his nose. "Evil."

"StarWriters!" Té yelled. "Hurry, think tent!"

"Tent?" Colton repeated. "Have you lost your mind? We're being led into Hell and you're thinking about camping?"

Té shook his head. "Our robes will protect us. Now, hurry."

Cries from damned souls echoed eerily from deeper inside the cave, and again the flames shot out from the walls.

"It's not working!" Em yelled.

Té glanced around and sighed. "Darn, our robes won't work in here."

Jenni yanked Shoupi closer to the doors and nodded at Beck who smiled.

Em whispered to Té, "We have to protect Shoupi."

"Form a circle!" Té shouted. "Hurry, StarWriters."

"StarWriters!" Em stated, still holding the doors closed with her back. "Colton … come block the door for me. Don't let anyone through!"

Colton nodded, slamming his back against the doors.

"Stand around Shoupi," Em yelled. "Hold hands and protect her! We must shield our Saint."

Shoupi yanked free from Jenni's grip and darted into the middle of her friends. The StarWriters locked hands, creating a spiritual barrier around Shoupi. Shoupi stood in the middle, gathering her strength and courage. She felt a surge as the power of *Him* filled her.

Mirium pulled Messy aside and Amelia followed.

"I'll help," Isla stated.

Jenni laughed. "Think of your poor, poor village, Shoupi. It will soon burn with fire!"

"I'm not afraid." Shoupi stood inside the protection of the StarWriters and glanced up. "*He* will protect my people."

"Only you can protect them, Saint Shoupi …" Jenni's voice now oozed with sweetness. "Tell those souls beyond these doors to follow you. That's all you have to do."

Shoupi closed her eyes, raised her hands to the heavens, and whispered a prayer.

Jenni's eyes narrowed. "Give me Shoupi!" she ordered, running to the circle.

"You're one of us," Em said, glaring at Jenni. "You're a StarWriter."

"I was *never* one of you," Jenni stated, pulling on Em's arm, trying to break the bond.

Em held tight to Té's hand. They locked their gaze and a power surged through their arms from somewhere deeper inside their souls. As the power grew stronger, Em smiled.

"I was promised glory before I died," Jenni stated, jerking on the unbreakable bond. "I just had to evolve, and Beck and the whispers convinced me. I see a glorious path unlike any I could ever imagined."

"Come back to us," Shoupi stated. "*He* will forgive you. *I* will forgive you."

"Never!" Jenni replied.

"It is time I become who I am to be," Shoupi whispered.

"King!" Jenni yelled. "I have a problem over here."

"There is no problem." Beck raised his hands above his head.

The whispers grew louder, drowning out the tortured pleas for help as he pointed at the StarWriters. Beck rose into the air and hovered several feet above the ground. "Now!" Beck yelled.

Dust and flames swirled.

Em screamed. "*He* will protect us!"

Landon's eyes widened.

A glowing crevice cracked open sizzling across the cave's floor. Heat and flames hit the StarWriters, pushing against their bond.

"No!" Rosie screamed. "Lyon, protect us!"

Saint Shoupi stood firm as a strong wind circled her.

Beck laughed and Jenni nodded.

Creatures as thin as a whisp rose from out of the depth of the bottomless pit. The air filled with an acrid smell that reminded Em of rotten eggs. The demons circled the apprentices and whispered their names.

> *Aleia …*
> *Colton …*
> *Smillie …*
> *Em …*
> *Té …*
> *Landon …*
> *Rosie …*
> *Yutu …*
> *Shoupi …*
> *Keekee …*
> *Milos …*

"Remember our lessons!" Em shouted.

Messy darted away from her mother.

Isla yelled, "Messy, come back!"

Yutu's and Isla's bond weakened, and Yutu released his grip.

"Amelia!" Yutu yelled. "You'll be sucked into the pit." He ran to her.

"No!" Em stated. "Come back, Yutu. That's not really her!"

Isla grabbed Messy and stared at her mother. "I got you."

"Don't break the bond," Em yelled.

"It's too late," Shoupi stated.

Yutu grabbed Amelia.

"Mummy told me to come get you." Messy looked up at Isla and smiled.

"Why would Mummy ask you to …"

"Messy!" Amelia yelled. "Ready?"

Messy waved.

Amelia nodded.

"Messy?" Isla again glanced at her mother for answers.

Messy pulled away and glared at Isla. She backed up before slamming into her. Isla screamed, losing her balance and falling into the pit. Messy stood back and laughed.

"Messy just pushed Isla into the fire!" Yutu yelled.

Amelia giggled. "I know."

Yutu stepped closer to the pit, trying to peer in. "Why?"

"You're going to join her." Amelia's voice filled with an eerie laughter.

Yutu glanced back and frowned. "What?"

Amelia ran at Yutu, hitting him hard. Together, they fell into the pit.

Té's eyes widened. "Isla?"

Messy stood next to Mirium and laughed even louder.

"Beware of false trickery!" Em's eyes opened wide with only the whites showing.

Aleia held onto Rosie. "Em, are you okay?"

"They're not real," Em whispered loudly.

"Who's not real?" Aleia asked.

"Messy, Mirium, and Amelia," Em stated. "They're part of the whispers … false trickery."

"How would you know?" Smillie asked.

"I'm being told … from inside my head," Em replied.

Jenni grabbed Shoupi by the arm. "So much for your *power* efforts."

"Help me, StarWriters," Em yelled. "We can't allow Shoupi to pass through that door!"

Té shook his head. "Where's Isla and Yutu?"

Em sighed. "False trickery, remember?"

Té glared at Em. "What're you saying?"

"Mirium, Messy, and Amelia were sent by the whispers," Em replied.

"Uh, oh," Rosie said, pointing. "They're crumbling."

"Turning back into sand," Landon added.

Mirium and Messy smiled and nodded as they slowly shifted to the floor. The sand swirled, before soaring over Em's head and disappearing against the door.

Em glanced at Té and shook her head. "False trickery."

"What did they do with Isla and Yutu?" Té asked.

Beck laughed. "They're in Hell!"

Michael stood next to Ja Crof on the balcony. He sighed. "Prepare for Eternity Future," he whispered, staring into the flaming horizon.

"*The Prophecy*?" Ja Crof replied.

"We are now a part of that prophecy."

Ja Crof tilted her head. "I see and accept and understand."

"I knew you would when the time came."

Waving her hand from her head to her torso, Ja Crof's hair transformed from short and choppy to a single, long braid. Her petite nose and green eyes morphed into a straight long nose with large brown eyes. Her lips remained pouty. She now resembled a StarWriter and not the motherly figure she had taken for her new StarWriters' arrival to the band surrounding Heaven.

"Welcome back Ja or should I say, Joan of Arc, battle warrior." Michael nodded. "Glad you're on *His* side."

"Where else would I be but on the side *your* working for … the better good of *Him*."

Michael smiled.

Her transformation continued with steel armor that covered her black t-shirt and pants. "I'm ready," she stated. "Been over half a millennium for me though it seems like only yesterday. I did win the war for France … with your help of course." She nodded. "My how eternity flies."

Michael chuckled. "Working on that sense of humor?"

"I'm trying."

"What about your horse?" Michael asked.

"He'll get an upgrade."

"Can't wait for that one." Michael smiled.

She gave him the once over. "What about your transformation?"

"I'll work on it once we're on our way to Eternity Future."

Together, they faded into the mist, but the red horizon remained red.

CHAPTER 37

Té leaned over the edge of the bottomless chasm. "Isla! Yutu!" Not hearing an answer, he walked back and forth like a caged lion, hot flames scorching his face. "Isla!"

Em pulled on Té's arm as the bubbling inferno was about to devour him. "They're part of *that* world now." She couldn't bring herself to say, *Hell*.

"No!" Té yelled. "Isla's not gone. She'd never let that happen. We have to rescue her."

Em lowered her gaze. "I'm sorry."

Aleia shook her head. "Sorry."

"Me too," Rosie added.

Em glanced around. The cave was filling with smoke making it difficult to see, and eerie moans making it difficult to hear. She sighed, knowing that if she didn't pull Té away from the edge, she could lose him next. "We have to help Saint Shoupi!" She yanked Té's arm again. "We need you. Help me stop Jenni." She glanced at Beck. "Looks like Beck's in a trance, now's our chance." Em patted Té on the back. "Beck is probably using his mind to keep this pit open."

"You're right," Aleia replied. "He's mumbling something."

Squirming in Aleia's arms, Rosie whined. "I want to leave."

Té yanked away his arm. "I'm not giving up on Isla or Yutu. I'm staying right here." He crouched on all fours, ignoring the heat and flames and screamed. The smoke thickened as he fanned the air. "Isla … Yutu … if you can hear, answer me!"

Rosie tapped Aleia's shoulder. "He's in love with Isla."

"This isn't the time, Rosie." Aleia glanced at Em and frowned.

"Just saying." Rosie shrugged.

Em pulled on Té's robe. "We'll scream together. Let's hope the others are protecting Shoupi."

Landon lined up Keekee, Smillie, and Milos in front of Colton and the large door. "Arms of steel," he said. "Hold on tight. It's up to us to save Shoupi and the lost souls."

"No one will pass by me!" Colton stated.

Jenni pulled tighter on Shoupi's arms, pushing her through the smoke and growing flames.

"You won't get me past that door!" Shoupi yelled. "And I won't order them to follow me back in here."

"You will cuz your friends will be joining Isla and Yutu in Hell if you don't." Jenni's laugh bellowed off the walls.

"They're not in Hell!" Shoupi squirmed as Jenni pushed her toward the blocked door.

"Yes, they are." Jenni snickered. "Mirium and Amelia helped to put them there."

"They'd never do that." Shoupi locked her knees trying to slow their walk.

"News flash, Saint Shoupi, they're part of *my* team now not yours." Jenni's laugh grew louder.

The StarWriters' line blocked the large door. They clung to each other's arms, holding their breaths. Keekee closed her eyes. Landon and Smillie pushed out their chests. Milos frowned.

"We're not letting you through," Landon yelled. "Jenni, let Shoupi go!"

The ground shook, but the StarWriters held firm, their arms locked together.

"Keep it up, Beck," Jenni yelled. "They're no match for us."

"Hope this works," Keekee whispered. "I'm not that strong."

"We are strong," Smillie stated, "together."

Glancing over the edge, Em, Aleia, and Rosie yelled for Isla and Yutu.

Té hollered again, "Isla … Yutu! If you can hear me, answer."

The ground shook. Em fell back as Aleia held on tighter to Rosie.

"We almost fell in!" Rosie cried out. "Take me back to the Wonderous Tree now!"

Em helped Aleia to her feet.

"Hey," Rosie whispered. "Where's Té?"

Té reached out, grabbing onto nothing as the flames caressed his face, the heat searing his hair. He screamed. Tumbling over and over, he suddenly understood. He was falling into Hell.

"Robe! Parachute."

Té gasped as a large boulder stopped his fall. His mind fell blank, the hot air charring his lungs. He coughed and rubbed his eyes. He was on solid ground.

Did I just stop myself from falling into Hell?

He tried to look at his robe, but all was dark. Shaking his head, he pushed himself onto his knees. A large boulder now blocked his view. He stood and wiped his eyes again.

"Help!" a female voice screamed.

"Isla? Is that you?" Té tried to see but the smoke and darkness was too thick.

"Help me, Té!" the voice yelled back.

"I can't see you!" Té hollered. "Walk toward the sound of my voice. We'll both keep talking."

"Té! Help me. I can't see anything. Where are you?"

"I'm close." As he yelled and inched his way through the darkness, his eyes slowly adjusted. A figure was approaching. "Isla?"

Isla jumped into Té's arms. "I'm so happy to see you! I don't understand," Isla said, wiping her eyes. "Why did Messy push me?"

"That wasn't Messy," he replied, hugging her. "It never was."

"What are you talking about?"

"Mirium, Messy, and Amelia turned into sand."

Isla wiped her eyes again. "If that wasn't –"

Té nodded. "All a part of Beck's –"

"Will I ever find my mum and sister?"

Té used his robe to wipe her face. "We need to get out of here."

Isla nodded. "How did you get down here?"

"I fell. Yutu is here somewhere too," Té whispered. "We need to find him."

Aleia and Em glanced over the edge.

"Té!" Em yelled.

Rosie flew up behind them.

"I see nothing for the future NEXT," Rosie said.

"Aleia, can you see anything?" Em asked.

"Doesn't work that way," Aleia replied. "Rosie must see it first, then a vision will appear to me."

"Rosie," Em whispered. "Concentrate. Can you see anything?"

"I can't." Rosie frowned. "Nothing is happening." Rosie cuddled closer to Aleia, holding up her hand. "Wait!"

Em nodded. "You see something?"

"No," Rosie replied. "I hear …"

Aleia smiled. "Yutu! It's Yutu!"

Rosie sighed. "I hear him too."

"Yutu!" Té yelled. "I wish we could see better."

"Too much smoke," Isla replied.

"Listen." Té tilted his head.

"I'm here!" a voice yelled out from inside the moans.

Té hugged Isla. "Yutu, is that you?"

"It's me."

A wind swirled and the smoke faded. Yutu stood several feet away on the other side of the large crevasse.

"I heard someone screaming for Isla, and I followed the voice." Yutu waved. "Thought it was you."

Té waved back.

"Glad to see you're okay, Isla," Yutu yelled, glancing over the edge. He shook his head. "I saw you fall."

"I know about my mum and sister." Isla grabbed tighter onto Té's arm.

"The real Amelia would never push me like that," Yutu said. "Had to be a setup."

"Messy wasn't herself," Isla replied. "She didn't remember Whispers, our cat. And my mum …" Isla sighed.

"You didn't know," Yutu yelled.

Isla shook her head.

"Now what?" Té hollered.

Yutu shrugged. "How do we get outta here?" Yutu yelled back.

Boulders whizzed down, and Té pulled Isla away from the edge.

Rosie pointed. "Look at Beck!"

"You see Next?" Em asked.

"No and stop yelling." Rosie shook her head. "His lips are moving. He's raising his arms. I think he's trying to chant something."

The ground shook again.

"Lyon!" Em stated.

"He's safe," Rosie replied.

"Take him out," Em ordered.

"Why?" Rosie asked.

"Something's telling me to tell you –"

Rosie frowned. "I need to protect …" Rosie stared into the smoke. "I see …" Rosie pulled Lyon out from under her robe and held him to her chest.

The pink rabbit yawned.

"Lyon," Rosie stated, "grow big with wings."

Several boulders bounced past before falling into the pit.

Aleia screamed. "I can see them. They're not that far down. Yutu's on one side and …" – she closed her eyes – "… Té and Isla are on the other side. They're safe."

Rosie shook her head. "Won't be for long if we don't act!"

Large florescent wings suddenly expanded out from Lyon's back.

"Go, Lyon!" Rosie yelled.

Lyon's wings fluttered. He grew larger as metal armor replaced his fur and he morphed into a flying, mechanical rabbit.

Rosie waved. "Be careful, Lyon."

Lyon disappeared into the pit, flames and smoke replacing him. The ground shook, and Em pulled Aleia away from the edge.

A rumble and the ground rolled. Landon and Keekee fell, pulling Smillie to his knees. Milos yelled as he too dropped to the ground.

"Beck!" Jenni shouted. "Open the door. We're almost there."

The ground shook harder and the small group watched as Jenni pushed Saint Shoupi.

"What's keeping *them* from falling over?" Colton asked, trying to find his balance.

"Beck's chanting something," Landon yelled, grabbing Keekee's hand. "Maybe that's it. If we could stop him."

"Saint Shoupi!" the souls yelled from beyond the door. "Let us in!" They pounded harder.

"We're coming!" Jenni gripped tighter to her captive's arm. "Move, Shoupi!"

"I'm not going through that door!" Shoupi screamed, trying to pull away her arm.

The StarWriters stood only to tumble as another ground-wave passed. Smoke surrounded Em and Aleia.

Rosie flew over to Colton and the others. "Just saw NEXT and Lyon's going to rescue our friends."

"Your rabbit?" Landon yelled. "How?"

Rosie giggled. "Lyon grew big and turned into a robot. He has wings now too!"

"Where are they?" Landon asked.

"They fell into the burning pit," Rosie replied. "Actually, Yutu and Isla were pushed."

"Pushed?" Milos asked.

The ground shook again as another wave rolled. Colton tried to balance but the shaking was just too strong, and he fell to his knees.

"Messy and Mirium dissolved into sand," Rosie said. "They were never real."

"We know." Landon stared at Rosie. "Can you see what's gonna happen next?"

Rosie nodded.

"Then our evolve should be working too," Smillie stated. "Light!" Smillie opened his mouth and a bright light glowed, dissipating the smoke. "Look!" Smillie pointed at Beck.

Beck was mouthing something.

"Stop him!" Landon touched his robe and said, "Lacross balls." As he pulled off a sandal, a dozen balls fell from his pockets. "Grow!" he ordered, and his sandal formed into a stick with a triangular net at the end.

"Finally!" Colton looked at Milos. "It's up to you now."

Milos nodded. "Fly! I want to fly!" Milos rose and hovered over the StarWriters. "Rosie, look! I'm actually flying!"

Rosie laughed. "Guess our powers are evolving?"

"Milos, grab Shoupi," Landon ordered. "I'll handle Beck."

"I'm helping." Keekee handed Landon a ball.

Landon smiled and nodded. "Find more!" Landon swung and the ball hit King Beck in his chest. The ground-shaking stopped. "Got 'im." Landon pumped his fist.

"Aleia," Rosie yelled, "I need to check on Lyon."

Keekee handed Landon another ball. "Looks like Beck's chanting again."

"Not for long." Smillie opened his mouth and his light shined.

"Do you see that?" Té asked Isla. He fanned the smoke thickening around them with his hand.

"The ground-shaking has stopped," she said.

"I saw something …" Té pointed into the deep crevasse. "What's that?"

Isla turned. "I see only smoke."

"I could've sworn I just saw wings."

"Like a bird?" Isla asked.

Té shook his head. "Bigger. Much bigger." He tried to look over the edge. "Huge and … white."

Yutu screamed. "Help! Help me!"

"Yutu?" Té yelled. "What's going on?"

"It's got me!" Yutu screamed. "Help!"

"What's got you?" Isla yelled.

Té hugged Isla as they stepped closer to the edge.

"He's not answering us," Isla whispered.

"Maybe something happened to him?"

"I don't know," Isla replied. "I'm just hoping something evil doesn't drag us into Hell too."

Té nodded and hugged her tighter.

"If some *thing* got Yutu, then it's coming for us next," she whispered.

Em and Aleia peeked over the edge, and Rosie grabbed onto Aleia's robe.

"See anything?" Aleia asked.

"No," she replied. "Wait … what's that?"

"What's what?" Rosie asked. "There's nothing but smoke."

"I just saw a …" Em whispered.

"What?" Rosie asked.

Em stared at Aleia. "A horse's head on a motorcycle …?"

"I can't see anything," Rosie said, grabbing tighter onto Aleia.

"No, honest," Em stated. "It *was* a horse!"

"Wait!" Aleia whispered. "Something's coming."

Yutu struggled to free himself as he rose directly in front of the girls. Lyon's wings flapped, and the smoke scattered.

"Help!" Yutu screamed, struggling to get loose.

"Lyon, drop him." Rosie ordered. "Good job. Now find Té and Isla."

The large rabbit dropped Yutu next to Em before disappearing back into the billowing flames.

"Nice to see you." Yutu stared at Em and Aleia. "Thought I was a goner. What *is* that thing?"

Rosie nodded. "That's Lyon!"

"Rosie's rabbit morphed," Em added.

"That doesn't look like any rabbit I ever saw," Yutu replied.

"It's a bribe," Em said.

"A bribe?" Yutu asked.

"Never mind," Em replied.

The ground rumbled, and Em pulled her fellow StarWriters away from the edge.

Beck's chanting grew louder, and an eerie glow surrounded him.

"We got him good." Keekee giggled. "But the balls are missing him now."

Smillie's light dimmed, and he screamed, "Watch out!"

Large stones dropped around the small group, bouncing and clipping their ankles.

"Some *things* are helping Beck," Landon stated. "Let's collect these smaller stones. I'll use these instead of the balls."

They rushed to gather a small pile as more fell.

"Touch my hand," Landon ordered to Smillie and Keekee.

The three clasped hands and stared at each other.

"Helmets!" Landon stated.

The robes stretched out, covering their heads.

"I just need to be more assertive," Keekee whispered, glancing around as one of the large doors creaked slightly open.

"Help, Colton!" Keekee yelled.

Milos glanced over his shoulder and nodded. He rammed into the door and it slammed shut. Colton sighed as two now held it closed.

"Help me, StarWriters!" Shoupi yelled, reaching out for Milos.

"Little good they'll do." Jenni raised her arm, and Milos and Colton flew toward the pit, landing with a thud next to Em and Aleia.

Colton jumped up and ran back to Jenni, grabbing her arm. Some *thing* pulled him high into the air.

"What's happening?" Colton shouted, kicking his legs.

Jenni again waved, and this time, Colton hit the floor, landing hard next to Milos.

Isla stared into Té's eyes. "I'm *so* sorry. Beck promised me Mum and Messy. I believed him. I was told I would be the one to save them. Now, we're stuck on this stupid ledge, and we'll be sucked into Hell."

Té sighed. "Don't think the worst. Maybe Yutu —"

Isla frowned. "Yutu what? Climbed outta here? Didn't sound like it. He was screaming for help and there was nothing we could do."

Té pulled her in close. "I don't know if I should tell you this. But I think it's important that you know …"

The large door opened, and Jenni's thoughts moved the souls back. She silenced them with a swipe of her hand. "Just as promised." She pushed Shoupi in front of them. "My dear souls, listen to Saint Shoupi. She will guide you."

Shoupi cleared her throat.

"Don't say anything stupid," Jenni whispered. "Just one word from me, and your StarWriters will see the fires up close and personal before they know what hit 'em."

"They're *our* StarWriters, Jenni." Shoupi turned and glared into Jenni's eyes. "Don't do this. Turn everyone around before it's too late."

"Too late already." Jenni laughed. "*The Prophecy*'s being fulfilled."

"What prophecy?"

"*You* are *The Prophecy*, not Isla like Beck thought."

"What is it exactly you think I'm supposed to do?"

"Lead everyone to their final destination. They've been here for millenniums. Held by my new friends since the last time the souls were freed by *Him* … revenge!"

"But that's –"

"Enough!" Jenni yelled. "Start leading!"

Shoupi smiled and nodded. "Souls! I am *The Prophecy* …"

The bike resembled a 1950 Harley Davidson without the sidecar. Except, for the head – a black horse's head with a white diamond between the eyes. The black fenders shined and glittered from the flames, and the polished chrome and side mirror gave her a chance to check her hair after such a long ride.

"You are always with me in battle," Ja Crof stated.

The horse neighed.

"Vittorio!" Ja Crof chuckled. "Are you ready for another, my friend?"

The head nodded and neighed again. Vittorio had been a European quarter horse when alive, and her trusty companion through many a battle. With just a touch of the divine, he was transformed from a sleek and beautiful horse to a sturdy and rugged machine.

Ja Crof reached up and petted the head between the ears. A head that rested just above the front fender with his black mane flowing just inches above the tire.

The two hovered inside the deep, immortal abyss where sinister shadows swelled through gusts of red flares that scorched the air. Whispers and tormented moans hovered just beyond their reality where truth and goodness waited with a veracity that only a true believer could understand.

Ja Crof rubbed the horse's ear and sighed. "Thought so, my friend."

Revving the engine a few times, the horse-cycle lurched forward, taunting the repeating whispers. A mere distraction from the real reason behind her eternal existence. Ja Crof welcomed the oncoming fight as much as leading the French into battle against the British.

"Joan …" the horse-cycle stated. "Joan of Arc. We will be victorious."

Ja Crof laughed and glanced up at the swirling whispers. The honor was hers and hers alone. *He* personally requested her help. To play such a part in *His* Prophecy was indeed a tribute to her mortal life.

Michael flew by her side, his wide, white wings in full contrast to his glorious black body. He was a sight to behold with his long, blonde hair and sea-blue eyes. A true presence of the almighty. When Ja Crof was a mortal and just before combat, Michael would often encourage her through her dreams. Then when she was strapped to a stake and set to burn a fiery death, she shouted out for *His* mercy. But it was Michael who appeared as a friend and partner. Her pain and fears dissolved, and her soul followed Michael to the band around Heaven.

"Am I not worthy of *His* presence?" Ja Crof had asked Michael. "Why did *He* not come for me?"

"You are quite worthy." Michael had chuckled and nodded. "He doesn't send his highest-ranking Archangel to save just anyone."

Ja Crof's tears fell and Michael wiped them away. From that moment on, their bond was sealed and her dedication to her new blissful existence had begun. Michael had chosen her, and she stepped into his role as director of the StarWriters. A decision he had made at the beginning of time.

She admired Michael's towering, white wings and the glowing sword that flashed in his hand. The long, silvery blade with the golden guard and grip always gave her a moment of reflection. His copper plated armor decorated with red rubies gave him an authoritative command. He winked as he hovered ready to take his place as protector of the Heavens.

"Contentious relationship?" Michael asked, nodding.

"You're listening to my thoughts again?" Ja Crof smiled.

His red cape swayed, but his long, white braids remained banded by the thick, black bands. His muscular, dark thighs glistened with sweat from the heated flames. "Always thought we were good together," he said.

"If only my StarWriters could see you now. Full armor and that red … powerful and handsome."

"They almost caught a glimpse when I prevented Isla, Yutu, and Té from falling into the lair."

Ja Crof shook her head. "You disappointed the whispers … they were waiting for those three."

"Té spotted my wings in the smoke."

Ja Crof laughed. "Hard to blend in? Em caught a glimpse of my horse-cycle." She sighed. "I like your transformation."

"Thank you." Michael glanced up and into the darkness. "*He* is relying on you to permanently seal the third dome."

She petted Vittorio again who neighed and nodded. "My StarWriters' courage is starting to show."

"I had faith. It is most unfortunate that we lost such a bright soul."

"Jenni did choose poorly." Ja Crof sighed. "But it's not over yet."

As much as she wanted to join Michael for the final battle, Ja Crof understood that she was needed for something else. Michael was carrying *His* powerful and all-seeing knowledge. She only carried her hopes and prayers. She pointed at his black bands that bound his blinding locks.

"Keeps my hair in place, that is all," Michael stated.

"Perhaps I could use a band or two myself."

Michael laughed and glanced down as a red flame soared up from the depths. "My fallen brethren are down there."

"I understand."

"I must once again settle them down until they attempt to rise again."

"That they always do." Ja Crof shrugged.

"Souls are easily swayed, my friend."

She nodded.

"The whispers offer a solace before mixing with confusion." Michael nodded. "Time for me to stop the mayhem."

"God speed," Ja Crof whispered.

Michael pulled in his wings and dove into the spiraling, red flames. The tip of his sword glittered before disappearing into the dark void.

Ja Crof revved the engine. She and Vittorio were ready to battle. It was her responsibility to ensure that no fallen brother escape the third dome – the true entrance to Hell. The first two domes of Sheol would remain unlocked as a place of anguish for the lost who must repent. Those not worthy to enter Heaven but not yet destined for the underworld. She thought of Michael battling his fallen brothers.

"The last time your whispers shall take revenge and rob young souls during their journey through Eternity Present." Ja Crof glanced around and spotted the large and odd-looking rabbit. "Lyon! Rescue Té and Isla before all hell breaks loose."

"What's important?" Isla asked, staring at Té.

"It was written in the stars," Té replied.

Isla pulled away and gasped. "What do you mean, it's written in the stars? You're StarWriting on me now?"

"Yes and no." Té glanced around, searching for the right words. "Let me explain."

Isla nodded.

"You're supposed to be here … with me … at this juncture. You're as much a part of this prophecy as I am … as any StarWriter. I accept that now."

"How would you know that?" Isla fanned at the thickening smoke.

"I was told to protect you. That tells me that what your guide told you was –"

"Who told you to protect me?"

"Michael. That's how I know you are needed here."

"Needed for what?" Isla frowned. "I'm here to find my mum and sister. I don't want to be a part of a StarWriter prophecy."

"Not a StarWriter prophecy. *His* Prophecy. You are needed to help rescue the souls that are here against their will. You are to free them."

"Then my mum and sister were never here? It was all a lie?"

Té nodded. "Whatever you have to resolve inside the band … well, you've paid your dues and –"

"Not if we're in Hell!" Isla's eyes widened.

Two large, mechanical legs rose out from the dense smoke, aiming straight for them.

Isla screamed.

Colton glanced around the smoldering cave before nudging Milos. "Get up. The shaking stopped."

"Huh?" Milos shook his head. "Gotta help Shoupi."

Colton sighed. "We're too late. Jenni's already pushed her through the door, and it slammed shut."

"Then let's open it." Milos stood and adjusted his robe. He pointed. "Beck's still chanting."

"We need more stones," Landon yelled, positioning his lacrosse-type stick.

"I'll find more," Keekee replied.

Colton and Milos ran up to the door. They grabbed the handle and pulled.

"It won't budge," Colton yelled.

"Smillie!" Milos shouted. "We need help."

"Go!" Landon yelled. "Go help!"

"Maybe the three of us can move this thing," Smillie said, still pulling on the handle.

The three pulled but the door refused to budge.

"Give me strength," Colton ordered. "Colton's arms and legs thickened and grew longer. He now towered above his friends.

"Wow!" Milos looked up at him. "Great evolve."

Smillie's eyes widened. "You're a real giant now."

Colton yanked the door's handle and pulled. The door opened.

Milos smiled. "We need to help Shoupi."

Shoupi was standing next to Jenni with her arms raised.

The three StarWriters stepped through the door and froze.

Shoupi stared into the crowd of souls, gritting her teeth. "I am *The Prophecy* ..."

Jenni poked her in the back. "Tell 'em it's all clear and wonderful through that door!"

Shoupi closed her eyes. "By all that is *Him*. Help us now."

Everything and everyone, except for Shoupi, froze where they stood. It was as if time had suddenly stopped. A bright light blasted, bathing Shoupi in an ethereal presence. An angel descended from the darkness and hovered in front of her. He held out a small black leather book with gold lettering.

Shoupi blinked. "My bible? I was protecting it when I ..."

Michael smiled. "When you died?"

Shoupi took a step back. "You're Saint Michael? The Archangel? Then ... you're the same ... Michael —"

"Who greeted you when you first arrived at the band."

Shoupi's smile widened. "But I had met you once before. I remember now. It was during Mass. You were standing next to me, and I said that it wasn't time for Communion yet."

"And what did I say to you?" Michael asked.

"Do not fear and prepare for wonderment for it is written in the stars."

Michael nodded.

"I turned to assist the Father and you were gone."

Michael held up Shoupi's bible. "Thank you for bringing *His* word home. Very powerful action." Michael studied the small book. "Provides me with strength."

Shoupi bowed, understanding.

"It was at the moment of your death that you became a Saint in *His* eyes," Michael stated.

"I evolved?"

"You evolved the moment you arrived."

"Do I get my bible back?" Shoupi asked.

"*His* words are within you now."

Shoupi nodded. "Thank you. I understand."

"You were the prophesied one," he said. "It is time for you to lead these souls home."

Rosie cheered as Lyon dropped Té and Isla next to her. "Lyon, shrink back to normal," she said.

Em patted Té on the shoulder. "Glad you two are good."

"Thank you," Té replied. "That's some rabbit, Rosie."

"Thanks, Lyon," Isla said.

Lyon yawned as Rosie slid him into her pocket. "You can go back to sleep now."

An explosion echoed from the pit. Em glanced at Beck who was still hovering as if in a trance. He looked slightly slumped forward.

Landon and Keekee ran up and smiled.

"Looks like you finally hit Beck," Em said.

"Don't believe it was us," Landon replied. "He just seemed to poop out of steam."

"Oh, no," Keekee said, staring into the pit.

Red, molten lava was now bubbling up from the depths.

"We better get outta here." Em pushed on Aleia. "Let's run!"

Landon pointed at the opened door. "Jenni just shoved Shoupi back through. They're going to lead everyone into the boiling lava."

Em was the last StarWriter to run past Beck.

"Jenni!" he yelled. "Bring the souls to me. It is *my* time."

Lava bubbled to the surface, spilling over the edge.

"Keep running!" Em hollered to the other StarWriters.

Aleia and Rosie slipped through the doors and back into the second dome.

"I'm right behind you!" Em quickened her pace as the doors inched farther and farther away. Her legs moved and her feet pounded on the ground, but she was still no closer. Her heart raced. Em held out her arms, her fingers grasping through the hot air, praying it would help her to reach the gateway – to reach the other StarWriters.

Beck laughed as dark shadows rose out of the bubbling pit, surrounding him. "Bring them to me!" he yelled louder.

The wisps formed into heads devoid of eyes, housing eerie bodies with short, pointed tails.

Em closed her eyes, still struggling to move. The dark shadows now surrounded her.

"Emika Siobhan Iverson," the whispers chanted. "Join us … join us …" Sharp claws scraped and cut, grabbing at her long, blonde hair.

She slapped to free herself.

"Sss … Emika Siobhan Iverson … join usss …" the whispers hissed.

Help! Em screamed through her mind. It felt as if she was glued to the air. She prayed for a release. Claws grabbed at her ankles, dragging her down. Reaching out, her fingers dug into the jagged-rock floor, holding onto nothing. She screamed and reached and screamed again. The whispers drew her closer to the rise and fall of the flowing, molten lava. Em screamed again as her skin burned.

The StarWriters took a blind step as did the other souls. The whispers grew louder, rising within the smokey cavern.

"Did I miss something?" Milos asked, glancing at Colton. "You're no longer a giant." He pointed. "Shoupi's with Jenni."

Jenni held firmly to Shoupi's arm.

"We have to get outta here," Landon stated. "The lava is starting to flow. We'll be burned alive!"

Smillie tapped Té on the shoulder. "Are we all here now?"

Still holding Rosie in her arms, Aleia panted. "Em's right behind us."

"Good," Landon replied. "Let's grab Shoupi and get outta here." He glanced at the bubbling lava. "We don't have much time."

Shoupi yanked her arm free and pushed Jenni back through the door. Jenni stumbled and fell.

"You have *no* power over me!" Shoupi ran to the lost souls who stared at her. "Listen to me! I *am* Saint Shoupi, and I *will* lead you to your rightful place with *Him*." Shoupi disappeared and a bright light glowed above the souls' heads, dissipating the smoke and darkness.

"Where'd she go?" Rosie asked.

Aleia shrugged.

Colton pointed. "There she is."

"No!" Milos pointed at the ledge. "She's up there!"

"I can see her over there," Smillie replied.

"But I see her over there," Landon added. "I think she's quading."

The souls followed Shoupi's light back toward the first dome.

Jenni stood and ran up to the pit. "Beck! Beck, where are you!"

Aleia smiled at the StarWriters. "We should probably follow Shoupi. But I want to give Jenni another chance."

"Chance for what?" Rosie asked.

"To return to *Him*," Aleia whispered.

"Where's Em?" Té asked.

Aleia and Rosie glanced around.

"She is right ..." Aleia's eyes widened. "She was right behind us."

Rosie pointed at the doors to the third dome. "They're closing and Em's still in there!"

"Let Em go!" Jenni ordered Beck. "She's too good for us. It'll just cause problems."

"Help me, Jenni," Em yelled.

The lava inched closer, and Em screamed as the creatures that floated around Beck whispered louder. Jenni hovered before placing her foot on Em's shoulder forcing her head to scrape against the hard ground.

"Where are my souls!" Beck yelled, soaring over to Jenni. "*You* were to lead *them* to *me* along with *my* Saint."

"You tell me!" Jenni placed her hands on her hips. "I told you to help me! Some *thing* rescued her."

"Some *thing?*" Beck repeated.

"I had no power over her," Jenni yelled back. "I kept asking for help. Where were you? What were *you* doing?"

"I was here." Beck sighed and shook his head.

Jenni laughed. "Some powerful leader you turned out to be. Saint Shoupi is leading those souls of yours back to the transports. I would have been better off –"

"You defied me!" Beck yelled.

"You defied me!" Jenni screamed. "You and your whispers." She glanced down at Em and shook her head. "I don't have to listen to you …" Jenni looked above Beck's head and stated, "I *will* listen to them!"

The shadows swirled and soared over Jenni. She smiled as they whispered into her ear. She nodded. "I understand." She grinned. "Yes … please do."

Em screamed as Jenni's face twisted and bubbled. She no longer looked nor spoke like Jenni. The girl had evolved, but evolved into what? The ground shook and the cave walls trembled. Em closed her eyes and prayed. The shadows grew darker and circled around Beck. He shuddered, and bit by bit, he crumbled into little, black flakes that swirled into the smoldering lava.

Jenni laughed.

Em fought against the shaking ground, trying to stand. "Come with us, Jenni." Em extended her hand. "Please, Jenni, come with us."

"Next time we meet, I won't be so kind," Jenni stated. "I have the promise of a greater glory."

"You're a StarWriter," Em said as boulders tumbled and fell around her.

Jenni opened her arms and willingly leaned back, falling into the lava. The red, fiery liquid seeped around her, pulling her into the flaming red void, collapsing and sucking in the light and the whispers with it.

Em stared at the bubbling ooze as her fellow StarWriter slowly melted into the molten core. She took a step and gasped, her heart pounding and the smoke blurring her vision. The stench made her stomach churn. She ran for the second dome, and with each slap of her sandals, she counted. "One, two three …" The door was so very far away. "Eight, nine, ten …" Her mind whirled and she fought for each burning breath. "Twenty, twenty-one …" The large doors loomed ever so far away. Em panted and wheezed. The air was hot, so very hot. "Please, StarWriters, please be on the other side of *that* door." The handle burned as she yanked it open. Taking a step, she turned for just a little peek. Jenni was gone but a woman with a long, brown braid nodded at her.

The door closed and Em paused. "Was that a motorcycle with a horse's head?"

A bolt of energy sizzled through Em as she raced away from the third dome, and an understanding of things to come flashed through her mind.

But an understanding of what?

Em wasn't sure where that thought came from, but something was developing that would be forevermore. Another eruption and the ground shook, although not as bad as when Beck was hovering over everyone.

Who was that strange woman?

Was a benevolent spirit somehow helping her, sealing evil from re-surfacing? Was fate changing or was it just a fractional shift of the eternal timeclocks? As she ran, her spirit called out to that woman on the horse. Em felt a kinship, a closeness. Something about the woman, her demeanor –

Em thought about the loss of a StarWriter to the underworld. *Had Jenni just saved her?* But she understood that people chose with their free will. She glanced around and spotted Aleia with Rosie.

Taking in a deeper breath, Em yelled, "Oh good! You're all here."

The StarWriters were pointing in different directions. All staring up.

Aleia turned. "There you are! What happened? I thought you were right behind us."

"Why are you all just standing here?" Em glanced up at the bright light. "We need to get out!"

"Jenni's a traitor." Rosie said from Aleia's arms.

Em sighed. "Who cares! We have to go, and we have to go now!"

"Saint Shoupi just evolved," Aleia stated, pointing to the light.

"She's quading." Landon laughed. "There are four of her leading everyone to the transports."

Keekee frowned. "Shoupi doesn't need us anymore."

"She needs us now more than you'll ever know," Em replied, waving for the lost souls to join them. "We need to run!"

"Why?" Landon smirked. "Shoupi has everything under control."

Em pushed Landon and Keekee. "There are a lot of souls here," Em stated. "We need to get moving!"

"Miracles," Rosie said. "Calm down, Em. It's called miracles."

Aleia nodded. "Saint Shoupi is asking everyone to grab a scroll on their way out."

"Grab a scroll or whatever you want!" Em yelled, pushing on the StarWriters. "Just move!"

Rosie flew out of Aleia's arms and hovered near the door.

"Rosie!" Aleia hollered. "Come back, you'll get lost."

"Uh, uh." Rosie shook her head.

"We're to make sure everyone grabs one or two." Té handed out several scrolls. "Help me, Isla."

"Why do I have to give these out?" Isla picked up a scroll and tossed it back onto the pile. "You don't need me. I'll wait on one of the transports."

Té frowned. "I know you wanted to find your mom and sister. But I honestly do not believe they were ever here."

"I'll probably never find out." Isla sighed, handing a scroll to a passing soul.

"By the way, your wrong." Té smiled.

"Wrong about my mum?"

"No, about needing you. I need you."

Isla handed out two scrolls.

"You're a StarWriter in the making. You're one of us now."

"I don't feel like a StarWriter." She handed out three scrolls. "I feel used." Isla smiled. "Fine, I'll help you."

He spotted one of the images of Shoupi looking down at him, smiling.

Aleia and Em stepped back, allowing the souls to pass. Colton stood at the doorway, welcoming them into the first dome.

"I'm gonna fly ahead," Rosie said, "and tell Colton we're behind everyone so he'll know when everyone is out."

Aleia frowned. "Not a good idea, Rosie. Stay with us."

"I'll be just above your heads," Rosie replied. "You can see me. The door's right there!"

"Fine." Em looked at Aleia. "Hate it when she doesn't listen."

"A mind of her own." Aleia grinned. "Are we the last?"

"Pretty sure." Em replied. "Just hate this darkness creeping up behind us. Can't see a thing."

Em placed her hands on her hips. "Any remaining souls?" She looked around. "Somebody there?" She shouted louder.

"You see someone?" Aleia asked.

"Thought I heard something." Em shook her head.

"Trick of the light?" Aleia asked.

"Or dark," Em replied.

"Who'd want to stay back?" She grabbed Em's arm. "I think we're done."

"Colton's about to close the door," Em said.

"We're coming!" Aleia yelled.

"Hurry!" Colton replied. "It's closing on its own. I can't hold it."

Em and Aleia slipped through the door and it slammed shut.

"Where's Rosie?" Em asked, looking into nothing.

"Colton, where's Rosie?" Aleia repeated.

Colton shrugged. "Never saw her."

"Rosie!" Em shouted. "This isn't the time to play hide and seek!"

CHAPTER 39

"Ow, ow …"

Rosie screeched as her wings brushed against the arch of the opened door. She peered down at Colton.

"Everyone keep moving!" Colton yelled. He braced the door with his back as the souls passed into the first dome.

Rosie waved but Colton didn't wave back. *Have to tell him Em and Aleia will be last.* Her shoulders and back ached from her now singed wings. Hovering sent shivers all through her. She craved the comfort of Aleia's arms. Flying a little higher, the upper cave felt cooler.

Pulling in her wings, Rosie pushed harder with her legs. She swayed back and forth trying to sooth her aching wings. She flapped several times and soared higher above Colton. The first dome seemed a little cooler. She sighed and aimed for the opened door.

If I am able to sit in Aleia's arms, maybe I can sit on this door.

Rosie dove for the opened door and gasped. A strong breeze grabbed hold, pulling her back through the entrance and into the second dome. She screamed and reached out for Colton but he was too far away. Her baby arms hugged only smoke. The more she struggled, the stronger the force that tugged on her little body. Rosie flapped her wings and kicked as Em and Aleia passed through the door.

"Help me!" Rosie screamed and the door slammed shut.

The strong wind sucked her up and into the darkness of the second dome. As her body tumbled through the smokey blackness, Rosie closed her eyes. Her wings were pinned to her back, her arms flinging wildly through the air. She tried to scream when her baby-body slammed against a wall, and the air sucked from her lung, and she slid to the floor. A stabbing pain shot through her shoulders and down into her legs. She tried to move but her body refused to obey. Her right wing was torn. Rosie rested on her chubby hands and knees and cried.

"Lyon?" Rosie whispered. "Help me."

"Are you hurt?" a scratchy voice asked.

"Em?" Rosie searched through the darkness for her friend. "Em? Is that you?"

All remained silent.

"Aleia?" Rosie yelled.

"Sss …" snake-like voices hissed all around her.

Rosie crawled and leaned close to the steaming wall.

"Sss … Rosssie … sss …"

"Leave me alone!" Rosie screamed, covering her ears.

"Keep pulling!" Colton shouted.

Aleia and Colton tugged on the door handle.

"Rosie's not with us," Colton stated. "She has to be locked in the second dome. We have to get her out!"

"Why didn't you tell her to stay with you?" Aleia asked.

"I never saw her or I would have!" Colton screamed.

Em rammed her fingers into the seam between the doors. She screamed as her nails broke and her fingers ached.

"Told her to stay with you!" Aleia yelled. "If she was here, she'd have answered by now."

"Help me open this door!" Em screamed.

A small group of women and children stood in the first dome, looking confused.

Yutu pointed at Té and Isla. "Wait over there."

Milos leaned against the angel-carved door that opened to the outside and waved his hand. "Keep moving, keep moving."

"How many scrolls do we take?" a woman asked.

"Please take a couple," Té said, glancing at Isla. "We're finally cutting into the pile."

Isla wiped her eyes with the back of her hands.

"Please take a scroll or two," Té repeated. "I'm sorry Isla —"

"Leave it …" Isla handed a woman with a young child two scrolls. "I can't stand to look at them."

Té reached out but Isla brushed him away. "Shoupi will help you find them. I honestly believe they went to a higher place."

"Take a scroll and go out that door," Isla stated. "Transports are outside." Isla ignored him.

"Mummy," a young child asked, "what do I do with my scroll?"

"Place it in your pocket, my darling," the woman replied. "We are finally leaving this place and heading home." She nudged the child toward the angel doors.

Isla stared at a little girl covered in soot who stepped up next. "Messy?" Isla whispered.

"Isla?" a woman asked. "Is it really you?"

Messy grabbed Isla around the waist and screamed. "Mummy! It's Isla!" She squeezed tighter. "I missed you, sister."

Isla stared at her mother's tattered apron. A speck of blue gingham peeked through a large rip. "Mummy, you wore that the last —"

"Is your brother with you?" her mother asked.

Isla shook her head.

Té smiled. "Family reunion. Just keep going and head to the transports." He nodded, handing out the scrolls.

Shoupi suddenly appeared next to Té, smiling. "Isla, you and your family, please come with me."

Isla nodded, hugging her sister and mother. She glanced back at Té as another Shoupi materialized, handing out scrolls.

"Take one or two," the new Shoupi said to everyone who passed.

"Which number are you?" Té laughed.

"I'm quading," Shoupi replied. "All and the same."

Milos held open the angel-carved door. "Keep moving toward the other StarWriters standing by the iron gates."

"Messy, what's the name of our pet?" Isla asked. She smiled at Milos as they walked past.

"Did you forget about our kitty, Whiskers?" Messy replied.

Milos pointed at Keekee. "Be careful walking on the uneven ground, folks."

"Why?" a woman asked.

"You don't want to know," Milos replied.

Keekee pointed to Smillie standing near the first transport. "Keep moving, that StarWriter will guide you."

Smillie stood in front of the mechanical butterflies, waving his arms. "This way." He nodded to an old man and woman.

"Butterflies?" The old man's eyes widened.

"Reliable," Smillie replied.

Saint Shoupi appeared next to Landon who was standing near the third transport.

"Hold up," Smillie said, holding the old man and woman back.

"Irid's full," Shoupi yelled.

"You're on the next one." Smillie pointed to Landon who was walking toward Serene. "Follow that StarWriter."

The old man nodded.

Saint Shoupi appeared next to Landon and pointed to the next transport.

"Stop popping in and out like that!" Landon stated. "How did you know Irid was full?"

"She rubbed her antennae to get my attention." Shoupi grinned. "And she gave me the *'I'm done'* look."

"I forget she's yours." Landon smirked.

"Right now, she belongs to everyone." Shoupi nodded. "Everything is working as planned."

"And you know this how?"

"Landon …" Shoupi winked. "Everything is written in the stars."

"But how do you know the butterflies can hold all the lost souls?" Landon shook his head. "There are so many … countless souls …"

"The butterflies will adjust," Shoupi replied.

"You're sounding like Director Crof."

"She would be very proud right now."

Miracles, Landon thought as Saint Shoupi vanished again.

"Rosssie …" the slithering voices whispered. "Come with us. We can help you …"

Rosie covered her eyes. She held her breath and counted. The darkness seemed to be growing darker. Her heart pounded and her hands shook. Her back ached and her wings felt almost numb.

"Go away!" Rosie screamed.

An engine revved.

Rosie hugged her legs and cried. "Leave me alone!"

The engine revved again.

"Rosie?" a familiar and strong voice asked. "There you are."

A high-pitched screech echoed through the shadows. Rosie closed her eyes tighter, pushing her body closer to the wall.

"Lyon?" Rosie whispered.

"Back into the pit you go!" the voice stated as a large crack sizzled through the air.

Rosie opened her eyes. A light flashed and a hand appeared from out of the darkness. "Do not be afraid, little one."

Rosie's eyes widened. "Who's there?"

"You have broken your wing."

Rosie cried. "And burned them."

"I will heal."

A warmth tickled into Rosie's toes, running up her legs and into her wings. Rosie giggled as the pain disappeared.

"There …" the voice stated. "Good as new."

Rosie stood and flapped her wings. "They're working. Thank you."

"I found something that I believe belongs to you." A pink rabbit squirmed, appearing next to the hand.

"Lyon!" Rosie's reached for her friend.

"I will take you to your StarWriters."

Rosie sighed. "I can fly."

"You can trust me, Rosie," the voice said.

Rosie stared at the hand and frowned. "No! I don't know who you are!"

The horsecycle lit and Ja Crof smiled.

Rosie's eyes brightened and she smiled.

Colton stood and stepped back. "I'll grow bigger again. Give me strength to pull the door open."

"Then do it already!" Aleia yelled.

Colton took a deep breath.

"Wait!" Em yelled. "The door's opening on its own."

The three StarWriters stared as Rosie flew through the slight opening before it slammed shut behind her.

"I know something you don't know," Rosie sung out.

Em glared at Rosie's silly grin and shook her head. "Don't want to know. Let's get the heck outta here."

Rosie giggled and flew to Aleia's side.

"Your wings!" Aleia stated. "They're not burnt anymore. How did that happen?"

Dense smoke gathered at their ankles, resembling a layer of fog. As the mist swirled, the darkness loomed.

Colton tugged on Em's sleeve. "Gotta go. Everyone's almost gone."

"I'll lead," Rosie stated.

"No way," Em protested. "You're sticking with us."

"Fine." Rosie fluttered her wings. "We'd better hurry. It's getting creepy in here."

The small group ran, staying only slightly ahead of the shadows as they slipped behind the remaining souls. They followed the men and women walking to the opening. Yutu nodded as they passed.

"Eyes on Rosie," Em stated.

"Keep moving," Yutu ordered.

"We're the last," Colton said.

"Just the four of us," Aleia replied.

"I only count three." Yutu frowned.

Aleia sighed. "Not again." She glanced at the second dome's doors as the mist seeped closer. "Em! Em!"

A hand pushed Aleia back. "Right behind you," Em stated. "Nobody but us."

Shoupi handed a woman the last scroll. "Just walk through that door. StarWriters will take you home."

"I'm really going home?" the woman asked.

Shoupi nodded. "We all are."

"Hmm … funny how that works." Té smiled.

"Isn't it?" Shoupi replied. "We saved them all. The scrolls and the souls."

"Talking about the scrolls." Té chuckled.

"That's everyone," Em stated, glancing behind her.

The fog thickened and inched toward the waiting StarWriters, pooling around their ankles.

"And just in time." Aleia looked down and frowned.

"To the transports!" Shoupi stated. "We are done here."

Colton lowered his gaze. "Our butterfly won't have Jenni."

Em patted him on the back. "She made her choice."

"Just wish we could have saved her," Colton replied.

"Sorry," Rosie flew up next to him. "Your transporter can still be named T.G. but only for you and –"

"Me!" Milos said, patting his chest. "There are just the two of us now."

The angel doors creaked shut behind him.

Em stepped up to Té. "How can doors that welcomes a person with angels have so much evil behind it?"

"Don't ever want to see this place again," Té replied. "Just glad it didn't spit us into a million pieces. And I hate this crunching sound."

Em glanced around. "Did Isla board a transport?"

Té nodded. "With her *real* mom and sister."

"You did good." Em smiled.

Té hugged her. "We all did."

Standing in front of the four mechanical butterflies, the StarWriters waved at each other.

"Looks like all the souls have boarded." Landon chuckled. "Don't know how they all fit."

"Where are we going now, Shoupi?" Aleia asked.

"Only the butterflies know," Shoupi replied.

Rosie snickered. "Here we go again."

Ja Crof's motorcycle boots sunk into the billowing clouds as she walked toward the divide separating Eternity Present with the tall mountains separating her from *Pi*. She stared into the heavens, watching as the large and colorful butterflies fluttered through the clouds. She had already shed her armor and parked her horse-cycle. Standing at the junction, she looked a little more like her director-self.

"Left goes to band, right goes to the pearly gates, so …" She pointed straight ahead to Shoel. Taking a step on the wobbly skull fragments, dark clouds swirled. "Not that we didn't know your pathway to Hell was already here. *The Prophecy* still needed to be fulfilled." She checked off the last item on her list. "Close you up for good." She extended her hand and golden rays beamed from her fingertips. "Let me start with erasing this stench of rotten eggs."

The rays crisscrossed until three figures appeared in the distance.

"Right on time." Ja Crof cringed at the sound of crunching bones.

Michael was wearing his white shirt and khaki's.

Ja Crof patted her head. "Michael, your hair. It's sizzling. A new black band just earned?"

"Perhaps." He waved his hand over his hair and the rising mist fizzled into a new strand.

A choppy blonde and a purple-haired boy stood next to him, staring at their feet.

"Look who I ran into," Michael said.

"No doubt from *Pi*." Ja Crof frowned.

"They've been searching for a young man named Beck," Michael said.

"Uh …" The blonde boy huffed. "Have you seen him? We can't find our way back to *Pi*. The entrance through the mountainside disappeared."

Ja Crof shook her head. "For good. I'm sure."

"I have something to show you two." Michael placed his hands on each of the boys' heads, and they instantly fell to their knees.

"I repent," the purple-haired boy cried out.

"Me too!" the blonde yelled. "Whatever it takes! Make it stop, please."

"Please stop." The purple-haired boy covered his eyes. "I can't stand looking at it anymore."

"Rise," Michael replied. "*He* has forgiven you. *He* knows you are good, just fooled by the evil."

The boys stood.

"Beck said he was our friend," the blonde boy stated.

"Ja, what do you think?" Michael asked. "Would they make good guides for Eternity Present?"

"Maybe." Ja Crof studied their eyes. "You have experience with Eternity Present, since Michael has shown you the eminence of losing *Him,* and you –"

"You can teach others the importance of that going forward," Michael said. "Feel blessed you've been saved."

"Won't let you down." The blonde boy nodded.

"Thank you," the purple-haired boy said, "I won't let you down either."

Michael waved his hand and the boys faded into the mist.

"What did you show them?" Ja Crof asked.

"A glimpse of the new purgatory, limbo, and beyond for the unrighteous."

Ja Crof nodded. "I see why they repented."

Michael chuckled. "Improving on your new sense of humor, I see."

"Trying."

"The transports, StarWriters, and rescued souls will arrive shortly," Michael stated. "*The Prophecy* fulfilled."

"I'll be right behind you," Ja Crof replied. "Just need to clean up around here … a little … permanently." She pointed at the crushed skulls. "Eternity Present can return to its intended journey without this."

Michael waved goodbye.

As streams of light flowed from her fingers, Ja Crof vaporized the crushed skulls. She paused as the essence of lavender and wild berries lingered. She took a deep breath.

"Always did love the sweet aroma of freshly bloomed flowers."

She stared at the *welcome* sign and shivered. The thought of what laid beyond made her sigh. The domes would now house the unrighteous but at only two levels, one worse than the other. The unrepentant would still choose the third dome as many have since the beginning of time – and as always with the treasure of promised lies.

Lowering her gaze, Ja Crof felt grateful that she had never actually entered the abyss. Hades held the true tortures that awaited those who chose to remain for eternity. She thought of Michael and *Him* and the battles fought.

Stepping into the junction at Eternity Present, Ja Crof glanced to her left and then to her right. She raised her hands and prayed.

"I ask *You*. Seal this entrance for evermore. May *You* guide the souls through this divide to the gates or band and be refreshed by the lingering scent of lilacs in *Your* name."

Ja Crof took another step back as purifying golden flames torched the air and ground. She smiled, understanding the outcome for her StarWriters as well as for herself.

"For it is written in the stars," she whispered.

Furrowing her 'brows, she thought about Jenni's progression. Change brings consequences, some powerful, others insignificant.

"Now to the village of *LOH*."

Serene had lifted into the smoldering haze followed by the other transports. Em stared out the window, loathing the domes that loomed along the horizon. They looked much smaller from the outside. More gloomy too. She leaned back and sighed as the outside world faded into the billowing clouds.

"First to leave." Rosie applauded. "We're the lead transport."

A bright light flashed. The domes and horizon disappeared. Serene vibrated for only a moment before gliding to a soft landing. Em gasped as she stared out at the grassy field, the sound of escaping steam hissing around them. A light film covered the windows with streaks of water blurring the outside world.

Em stood as their cabin brightened. She glared out the viewing window. "How'd we get here so fast?"

Rosie flew up next to her. "Didn't even get to see the stars!"

"Serene?" Em shook her head. "Where are we?"

The chamber remained quiet.

"Serene!" Em stated again. "Where are we?"

"Maybe we're in Heaven?" Aleia whispered. "Arriving with the souls?" Aleia shrugged. "Maybe it's a secret."

"Some Heaven." Rosie smirked. "Nothing's here!" Rosie pressed her face to the window. "Just grass and … hey! What's that?"

"What's what?" Aleia asked, now staring outside.

"That!" Rosie knocked on the screen. "Serene! Let us out."

A golden light flickered in the distance.

The other butterflies landed as if creating a half-circle in the grass. LYK and Irid to Serene's left and T.G. on her right. The outside door opened and the stairs descended.

"Let's go!" Rosie aimed for the stairs.

"Wait!" Aleia grabbed Rosie's arm. "We don't know what's out there."

"We'll be safe," Em stated. "We can trust Serene."

"You don't know that!" Aleia yelled.

Rosie yanked her arm from Aleia's grip. "Trust! Ja Crof said we could *trust* our transports."

"But Serene won't answer Em!" Aleia said, trying to see down the stairs.

"I'm with Rosie," Em said. "We can trust our transports. Let's go."

The three StarWriters slowly descended the stairs. They stood on the soft grass and sighed as their view filled with many individuals wearing glowing robes.

"Did you see where they came from?" Em asked, pointing.

Rosie flew into Aleia's arms startling her. "Oh, my!" Aleia stated. "We carried this many souls with us?"

The small group watched as the field filled with the departing spirits, each carrying one or two scrolls. Dirt and soot covered their faces and hands. Walking to the others heading their way, wicker baskets appeared and hovered a few feet above the grass. As they filled, the baskets disappeared, replaced by an empty one.

"This way!" the glowing-robed people yelled.

A young man holding a clipboard stood quietly, checking off names.

"Excuse me?" Em said, walking up to him. "I'm a StarWriter. What is this place? Who are all these people?"

"You're in the village of *LOH*." He checked off something on his clipboard "We're from *His Plan* room, volunteering to guide those returning." He glanced at her and smiled. "You're heroes. Did you know that?"

Aleia stepped closer. "Heroes?"

"*LOH?*" Rosie asked.

"Heroes?" Em repeated.

"Love of *Him*." He checked something else off on his clipboard.

"Doesn't look like a village to me," Rosie stated. "There's nothing here except grass and that golden light over there."

"It's not really a village," he replied. "The *presence* moves at *His* discretion." He smiled.

"There are so many souls!" Em tried to count. "I didn't realize there were so many. Where are you taking them?"

"The *presence*?" Rosie whispered to Aleia.

"*He'll* clean them up as they walk," he said as if this were normal, expected. "To meet *Him* and taken home." He glanced at Rosie. "The *presence* is the light you see."

"Can we meet *Him* too?" Rosie asked. "I want to ask about a pink star."

Aleia frowned. "Of course you do, now hush."

"You're not scheduled," the young man said, reading off his clipboard. "I need you and the other StarWriters —"

"Grayson!" Isla yelled, holding on tight to Messy's hand.

Grayson dropped his clipboard and lifted Messy into his arms. "Messy!" He hugged her close. "Where did you come from?"

Isla wrapped her arms around her brother. "Told you I'd find them."

"I shouldn't have doubted you." Grayson smiled. "You usually get what you fight for."

"I missed you the most, brother." Messy wrapped her arms around his neck.

Isla laughed. "That's what she said to me too."

Miriam ran up next. "I thought I'd never see us together again."

The arriving StarWriters stepped closer.

"What's happening?" Landon asked.

"Family reunion," Té stated. "Grayson is Isla's brother. He's from *His Plan* room."

"He called us heroes," Rosie said.

Keekee lowered her gaze, kicking the grass with her sandal.

Landon nudged Keekee on the arm. "You okay?"

"They're lucky." Keekee frowned.

Grayson set Messy down and picked up his clipboard. "Mummy, I must get back to work."

"You're not coming with us?" Miriam asked.

"Grayson loves working in *His Plan* room," Isla stated. "He's up for a promotion."

Em stared at Shoupi. "Where do we go from here?"

Shoupi shrugged. "Thought you'd know."

"Does anybody know anything?" Colton glanced around.

Milos and Smillie shook their heads.

"I don't think so," Yutu replied.

"I do," Grayson stated, staring at his clipboard. "Aleia Vis Jones, Colton James McMighty, and Keekee Nara … please follow me. The other StarWriters should remain here."

"What about me?" Yutu asked.

"Name?" Grayson asked.

"Yutu Woo."

He ran his finger down the page. "Sorry, you're not on my list." A quick flash soared across the clipboard. "Now, where'd this come from?" Grayson's eyes widened as he gazed into the grassy field.

"Father!" Father!" Isla screamed.

Aleia handed Rosie to Em. She sighed as she walked between Keekee and Colton. "Where are you taking us?"

Colton sighed. "Did we do something wrong?"

Grayson chuckled. "Unfinished business, that's all." He stopped in front of a grassy hillside and pointed at Aleia. "Aleia Vis Jones. Please, wait here. When you are satisfied, you may return to your fellow StarWriters." He pointed at Colton and Keekee. "You two, follow me."

Aleia watched as they walked away. She sighed and glanced around. A thin-looking man with dark skin and kind eyes appeared next to her. "Yikes!" She took a step back.

"I'm sorry. Didn't mean to frighten you, Aleia. Heard so much about you."

"You know who I am?"

He nodded. "A scholar with much potential. You gave your life to save your half-brother, therefore you were chosen to be a StarWriter. Helped fulfill *His* Prophecy. I could continue rambling but …"

Aleia shrugged. "Thanks, I guess. Better get back to the others."

"You look just like your mother," he said.

"You know my mother?"

"I did. I still love her very much." He smiled. "I'm your father, Vis Jones."

"My father?" Aleia's mind raced with all the questions she wanted answered but could only speak one. "Why did you leave us?"

He stared into her eyes. "My life was taken from me. My body was never to be found. Your mother thought I had left her. I would never have left my family."

"Dad!" Colton said, wiping his eyes. "I'm so happy to meet you. I'm named after you. My middle name."

The man nodded. "Look how tall you are."

"Guess I got your genes." Colton laughed, pretending to dunk a basketball. "Got all your moves too."

"I'm proud of you Colton," James McMighty stated.

"Okasan, Otosan," Keekee cried, running to a couple holding hands.

Their colorful silk garments flowed, gathering on the grass.

"Why didn't you take me with you when you died?"

"Keekee, as our only daughter, choujo, you were only three," said Okasan, "our lives were written in the stars … not yours, not yet."

"I want to go with you for Eternity. I no longer wish to be a StarWriter!" Tears ran down her face.

Otosan shook his head. "No, my daughter. It is not written in the stars that way."

Keekee grabbed her mother's sleeve. "I want to stay with you!"

"You have things you must do," Okasan replied. "You must remain with your StarWriters."

Em stepped up to Té and pointed. "Looks like Isla's having a wonderful family reunion with her dad too."

"Looks like it," Té replied.

"She'd make a good StarWriter. Replacement for Jenni maybe?" Em nodded. "I'd put in a good word for her. What about you?"

"Isla's not interested," Té replied.

"How would you know?"

"Heard Shoupi mention it to her when we boarded Irid. Said she just wants to be with her family."

"But I thought Isla has to work in *His Plan* room because of an issue," Em stated.

"Maybe her issue was resolved." Té smiled. "Looks like they're leaving. Grayson is returning to join the other workers. I think he's relocating souls."

Em giggled. "Looks like he loves his job."

Isla waved at them from across the field. Em waved back.

"She owes you, Té," Em said. "Least she can do is say *'thank you.'*"

"Already has," Té replied. "Many times over."

Aleia, Colton, and Keekee walked together toward the small group of StarWriters. Keekee wiped her eyes.

"It's time to head back to the Wondrous Tree," Ja Crof stated.

Em gasped. "You scared me! Stop popping in like that."

Swirling her hand, Ja Crof smiled. "You fulfilled *His* Prophecy."

The Wondrous Tree seemed as if it was sleeping amongst the puffy clouds with its branches reaching high into the heavens. Heart-shaped leaves of various colors glittered in the bright light. The roots, spreading out as far as an eye could see, remained firm and unmoving.

Ja Crof leaned against a limb and gazed down from a high branch. "Your fortitude never fails me, old friend." She patted the smooth bark that resembled a rainbow. "You have offered a valuable training ground for my StarWriters."

Taking in a deeper breath, Ja Crof enveloped herself within the strong scent of spruce and eucalyptus. The bantering laughter from her StarWriters grew louder, and she shook her head and smiled. *Soon.* She sighed. *I shall join you one last time.*

Her thoughts floated through the slight breeze mimicking the glittering leaves. *Change brings consequences ... some powerful while others insignificant.* From a distance, she could hear the clocks in *His Plan* room as they ticked toward *Good.* They would remain there now. The red-hazed horizon had faded as the omen of demise retreated. Michael sparkled a little before materializing one limb over. He crossed his arms.

"Yours? Powerful ..." – he glanced down – "theirs ... perhaps, taking on a new significance?"

Ja Crof smiled. "Reading my thoughts again, Michael? I shall miss that."

He winked. "As will I."

Her hopes faltered as the memory of Jenni's downfall nudged at her spirit.

Michael shook his head. "Several still need to discover why they are –"

"Unfinished business?" Ja Crof shrugged.

Michael faded, and Ja Crof closed her eyes as she entered *His* thoughts.

Michael surfaced from the trunk of the large tree and tapped Té, Smillie, and Yutu on their shoulders. They glanced around.

"Please, follow me." He pointed to each.

Té gasped as cool water tickled his feet. He glanced down at the swirling river that wandered through the green valley with the tall mountains decorating the horizon. Té looked up at the slow-moving clouds as a soft melody caressed his ears. "Is this about Isla?"

"No," Michael replied. "Pinky and her friends."

"What about my sister?"

"You saved them when the club burned," Michael replied. "Do you remember?"

Té shook his head. "I remember my song."

Michael reached out and touched Té's arm. Billowing black smoke now surrounded them. People panicking ran excitedly to the only exit. Té pushed his sister and her band members over several fallen victims. They tumbled onto the street and gasped at the fresh air.

"Nicky!" Pinky yelled. "Where's Nicky?"

Té glanced around. "He's probably still in there. I'll find him." Té shook his head and stared up at the clouds again, biting his lip. "I rescued Pinky's manager … and for what? My death?"

Michael rested his hand on Té's shoulder. "There is no greater love than to lay down one's life for another, Matèo."

Té glared at Michael. "What?"

"You didn't think twice about helping others … Isla … Pinky … Nicky. Pinky re-named her band Loving Matèo. It's a huge success. She now sings your songs."

"My songs?"

Michael nodded. "She found your lyrics and wrote the music. You're Pinky's hero. You will remain in her heart until you meet again."

Té focused on the expanding clouds. "I guess." Té shrugged. "This music I keep hearing … I've never heard anything so … incredible."

"Our heavenly choir. They need an assistant director."

"Assistant director?" Té repeated.

"Someone with fresh ideas."

Té smiled.

Cookies and bodies littered the lobby as Smillie and Michael made their way to the front desk.

"My mother's cookies were all over the floor," Smillie whispered.

Michael nodded and chuckled. "Kept a few busy until reinforcements arrived."

"Kept who busy doing what?"

"The terrorists." Michael laughed again. "They ate the cookies you dropped."

Smillie glanced over the counter. He and the manager were huddled together, hiding. Their white shirts stained red.

"Why didn't you stop this?" Smillie asked. "No police arrived."

"The gunmen made their own paths," Michael replied. "Free will, Smillie. We all must choose … virtuous or wicked."

Smillie stared at the now quiet manager. "He didn't make it either?"

Michael placed his hand on Smillie's shoulder. "Listen and learn …"

"Save yourself," the manager said to Smillie.

"But sir … you have three daughters that need you," Smillie whispered.

Michael pointed at the man. "You tended *his* wounds until you died." Michael chuckled again. "You saved him, Smillie. He lived."

"He did?"

"The manager was grateful and gave your mother a store in his hotel."

"He did?"

"Your mother named her store *Smillie's Heavenly Cookies*."

"She did?"

"Your family now owns three others. She bakes and sells breads and muffins and other wonderful treats."

"She does?"

"Your parents will be rich and soon offer scholarships in your name."

"They will?"

"Yes." Michael handed Smillie a cookie. "They will. Here, take a taste. This is called a *Smillie.*

Smillie took a bite and smiled.

"Yutu …" Michael said as they walked along the riverbank, "… you did not cause Amelia's death."

"I saw her die!" Yutu frowned. "The Whispers showed me."

"That is what the Whispers wanted you to believe."

Yutu shook his head. "You mean like they did with the *fake* Amelia?"

"Exactly," Michael replied. "For it is written in the stars, Yutu. *His* Prophecy was there to be fulfilled."

Yutu's eyes widened. "Then the real Amelia's in Heaven?"

"Watch, Yutu, watch and learn." Michael waved his hand.

The air chilled and the sky darkened. A heavy rain pelted across the waves. Yutu watched as a girl clung to the hull of an overturned boat – alone in the darkness.

"Yutu!" she screamed. "Yutu! Where are you!"

Yutu pointed at the water. "There I am! What am I doing?"

"Being a hero," Michael replied.

Something hit against the side of the boat. "Yutu!" Amelia reached out and grabbed the empty life vest. "Where are you?"

"Where am I?" Yutu asked.

"You were with me."

"Then where is Amelia?"

"With her family," Michael replied. "Safe and very much alive."

Keekee cushioned her back against a massive root that extended past the small circle of StarWriters. She closed her eyes not wanting to hear their light-hearted bantering.

"Don't know 'bout you guys," Milos said, "but, I've never felt so energized."

"Feel the same," Colton replied.

Landon nodded. "Can't wait to get back on LYK and deliver more scrolls to the stars. "Right, Keekee? Right, Yutu?"

"Right," Yutu stated.

Keekee ignored him.

"Right … Keekee?"

Keekee nodded. *I'm not one of you. I'm not a StarWriter. I do not wish to be one.* Keekee's heart was broken. She longed to be with her parents. What did Okasan say? *'You have things you must do.'*

What must I do? I have not even evolved. Keekee rested her head on her knees. She envisioned her robe from top to bottom and how she wanted it to look. *Round out the neckline. Puff the sleeves and cuff at the wrist.* She smiled. *Sinch my waist, take away the leather belt. Hmm … she nodded … give me cargo pants cuffed at the ankles. Run rope from the sandals and crisscrossed up my shins.* And wait … *take the leather belt and use it for trim around my neck, wrists, and sides …*

"Keekee?" Em stood in front of her, pointing. "Look at you!"

Keekee blinked several times. "What?" She furrowed her 'brows.

Rosie flew closer. "Keekee, you just evolved."

Shoupi clapped. "You look incredible."

Em reached out and grabbed Keekee's hand, pulling her to the center of their circle.

Aleia stared. "Wow, you do look amazing."

"Nice," Yutu stated.

"Wow," Tè added.

The StarWriters circled Keekee. She looked down at her clothes.

"Can you do that for us too?" Smillie asked. "But I don't want puffy sleeves."

"I do," Em replied.

"Me too." Aleia laughed.

"I think I want to stay the same," Rosie said. "Lyon doesn't want me in pants."

Ja Crof appeared from the mist and slowly walked up to her StarWriters. They were still circling around Keekee, commenting on her new clothes.

"StarWriters," Ja Crof said, "please take a seat. Rosie, you may float." Ja Crof nodded at Keekee. "Nice look."

Keekee's eyes widened. "Thank you."

"She's going to design our clothes too," Landon stated. "Mine without the puffy sleeves."

"And for me." Colton shook his head.

"Perhaps so," Ja Crof replied. "However, that *will* be up to your new director."

The StarWriters stared.

"But …" Em eyes glistened. "Where are you going?"

"Did you get fired?" Colton asked.

Ja Crof laughed. "Not quite."

The StarWriters shrugged.

"That was a joke." Ja Crof chuckled. "All shall be explained."

"Good one," Smillie replied.

Ja Crof furrowed her 'brows and frowned. "Change has come. I am very proud of each and every one of you. You fulfilled my expectations as well as *His*." She took a deep breath. "Té will be moving on as Assistant Heaven Choir Director."

"Té is leaving us?" Em glanced at Té.

Té grinned.

"Keekee will be joining her parents," Ja Crof said.

Keekee clapped.

Ja Crof cleared her throat. "Saint Shoupi will be leaving for Saint-in-Training."

Shoupi nodded.

Ja Crof clasped her hands and sighed. "Since the very beginning, Michael served as director of the StarWriters club. He chose me as the second director, and I shall choose the third. I must return to my saintly duties as Joan of Arc."

"Of course!" Aleia stated. "Ja Crof is an anagram for J of Arc. The J stands for Joan."

A young woman, not much older than the StarWriters, now stood in front of them, plated in armor holding a sword. Her dark braids, a stark contrast to the shiny metal.

Em laughed and pointed. "It was *you* I saw on that motorcycle! The one with a horse's head."

"A horse's head? Cool." Milos chuckled and shook his head.

"Hah, I rode with her on that horse-cycle," Rosie boasted.

Ja Crof nodded. "I choose the third director of the StarWriters club to be Em. Her assistants will be Aleia and Rosie."

Em stood off to one side of the Wondrous Tree and wiped away a tear.

"StarWriter's Club Director, hmm ..." Té said, stepping up to her. "Pretty impressive. I mean, you being the youngest director and all."

"Assistant Heavenly Choir Director, hmm ..." Em replied. "Pretty impressive. I mean you being the youngest director and all." She smiled. "Congrats, but I wish you were staying with us ... I mean as a StarWriter. You were pretty incredible." Her cheeks darkened.

"I'll be back to visit or you can visit me," Té replied.

"I'd like that," Em said, pulling him in closer, kissing Té on the lips.

He wrapped his arms around her as their kiss lingered.

"StarWriters, please gather!" Ja Crof shouted. "Looks like *LOH* is coming to you."

They watched as Michael walked with a bearded man wearing a white robe. The man shined with a halo of golden light that surrounded him. Michael and *He* talked and laughed as if they were long-lost friends reuniting.

"Is Michael *His* wingman?" Yutu asked.

"On the contrary," Ja Crof replied, "*He's* our wingman."

The StarWriters ran to greet the heavenly divinity with the golden glow. Shoupi leading the way ...

for it is written in the stars

A glimpse from the earthly world ...

A young woman gasped as she grabbed onto the railing of the spiral staircase. Using both hands, she pulled herself to the next step. Her long, black hair brushed across her sweaty, round face. The ancient dome was just within her reach. Her heart pounded with each breath. It felt as if the inner walls were closing in around her.

"How … many … to the frescoes?" She wheezed.

"Four hundred sixty-three," the woman behind her said, breathing heavily.

"No," she demanded. "How … many more …?"

"Only sixty-three," someone else replied. "Been counting."

The world's largest church, consecrated in 1436, the Florence Cathedral, formally the Cathedral of Saint Mary of the Flower, or Duomo, was beyond reach for most, but for Peijing it was a challenge to conquer.

She glanced up, resting her legs for just a moment. "Why no elevators?"

The woman behind her chuckled. "For the experience."

"What experience? To die?"

"No, so you can experience this place as it was centuries ago."

A couple of energetic strangers pushed past.

She wished herself dead – well, perhaps not exactly dead but at least in better shape. Peijing felt lifeless, dragging her weight – and for what? A wish?

'You're so dramatic,' her father always said.

Drama or no drama, she wanted an elevator. An elevator crammed with strangers would be better than these stairs. She had waited hours in line just to trek up four-hundred and sixty-three uneven marbled steps.

She'd been coached for days to climb these stairs and make her wish. She had just arrived in Florence, The City of Love. She walked these streets as Master Joroku's new assistant, therefore, it was her role to know this city and its buildings.

'You can wish or pray for anything and it will float effortlessly into the heavens as if on angels' wings to be heard –' a stranger had said.

"Heard by whom?" Peijing never prayed.

She remembered the stranger's finger as it pointed higher and higher until it stopped at the orange dome. "The duomo's ceiling. It's amazing. Painted to look like Heaven and a descent into Hell. A wish and a prayer travels to the heavens and is answered. Transported to your star by a StarWriter."

"Never heard of a StarWriter," she had replied.

"They are the carriers of our destiny," the stranger had said. "We are born with a life plan, and they bring it to our star."

"Our star?" she had asked.

"Yes. Everyone has their own star and destiny. Our wishes and prayers are kept safe on our star."

"And the wish travels just from this place?"

The stranger had laughed. "Actually, from anywhere and everywhere I'm told. Through channels into the heavens."

"All wishes?" *Even nefarious,* she wondered. "This better be worth it."

Peijing finally reached the entrance to the dome. She stepped onto the catwalk that gave the illusion of touching the magical ceiling. Her eyes widened as the worlds above her opened.

"What is this?" she asked.

"Keep moving!" a guide stated, pointed at the ceiling. "It was painted in the 1500's." Her hand waved in a circle. "The largest fresco in the world. It depicts the description of life in the heavens with angels, saints, and the righteous praising our creator." Her voice echoed. "This is the last judgement, the underworld, where misery befalls those who are evil."

Peijing studied the lower fresco and its befallen inhabitants.

"Say your prayers or wishes and keep moving please," the guide said, trying to wave the tourists to the opposite side of the dome. "You can exit to the cathedral or visit the outer cupola."

Peijing held on to the catwalk's railing and closed her eyes. Taking in a deep breath she whispered her wish. "They all shall learn my name … Peijing Wu." *Will my wish travel to the underworld?* She wondered.

A large popping sounded, echoing overhead, followed by a loud crack. Others pointed at the ceiling as four large fractures ran from the round windows, up through the figures that were staring at the creator. The cracks soared to the inner cupola and stopped. Flakes of the beautiful artwork rained down, covering the visitors as if snow was falling. Many reached for their ringing phones, screaming and shouting.

"Stay calm!" the guide yelled. "Move to your right and exit down."

The murmurs grew as the tourists pushed, trying to reach the opposite side of the dome.

"This is happening all over the world!" a visitor shouted, holding up his phone.

Peijing held tightly to the railing and smiled. *Maybe someone is listening after all.*

A glimpse from the ethereal ...

The stars twinkled as hordes of *His Plan* workers gathered at the circular platform. Holding their empty baskets, they stared at the massive hollow chutes that reached high into the evermore.

"What's happening?" Grayson asked, parting the workers as he walked past to stand in front of the platform.

"That's just it," a worker replied, "nothing."

"We've been waiting for scrolls and none are dropping," another added.

Grayson placed his clipboard on the circular platform and kicked the base. "Maybe it's stuck."

"Don't think so," a worker said, pointing at the myriad of clocks that lined the aisles. "All the clocks' handles just flipped from *good* to *evil*."

Serene coasted into a murky region of space filled with pin-hole clusters that appeared to be spilling over with sparkling lights.

"Reached the star destination in our quadrant," Em stated. "This is good a place as any to begin StarWriting. Glad Michael let us keep our jobs."

Aleia nodded. "Yeah, but now we're only eight." She swiveled in her seat and patted her thighs. "Lovin' my new uniform … thanks to Keekee."

"Me too." Em stated. "Easier to work in pants."

"And climb that wondrous tree." Aleia giggled. "What about you Rosie? Why so quiet?"

"Band away," Rosie said, removing the band around her wings. She flew to the viewing window and pressed her nose against it. "Maybe it's out there …"

"What are you looking for?" Em asked.

"*He* said there was a pink star with my name on it." Rosie frowned.

"Then you'll find it. If not out there, then somewhere else." Em nodded. "Let's start StarWriting."

A clear screen materialized.

"I'm ready," Aleia said, sitting up straighter. "You shall sow kindness into the world."

The message appeared on the screen. Serene's antennae touched each other, and the message, along with a scroll, blasted into the darkness toward the intended star.

"Pink hearts," Rosie said, giggling.

Thousands of pink hearts blasted out with their intended scrolls.

"Good job, Rosie," Em replied. "For you, I guess less is more."

Rosie gazed out the window. "Maybe I'll do more."

Em grinned and thought about Ja Crof, and her conversation with Michael. In many ways Em felt lost in her new position. *Why didn't Ja Crof offer to train me?*

"Baptism by fire," Michael had replied.

"I'll never be as good as her."

"Don't want you to be," Michael had said. "Ja wasn't much older than you when I chose her for director."

"Do I really have to perform my duties from that crumbling fortress? It gives me the creeps."

"It's that way for a reason," Michael had stated.

"What reason?"

"It protects Heaven," he replied.

"I thought that was what you did?"

Michael had sighed again. "Everything will come in due time."

Em had shook her head. "Don't know how to materialize yet."

"Everything will come in due time," Michael had stated again. "As well as four new StarWriters for you to train … a set of twins too. Should be fun."

Em shook her head and laughed.

Her first duty as director was to dissolve the three transports, LYK, Irid, and T.G. With the absent StarWriters, the butterflies had to be released. Her heart pounded and she held back a tear, as the large transports shrunk, becoming three separate colors before flying into the clouds. Landon, Yutu, Smillie, Milos, and Colton where given her blessings to bilocate and visit a few of the villages. As the small group fizzled into the mist, a thought occurred. She could assign a whole new transport to Landon, he'd be perfect with newbies, or maybe not.

New essences would be formed with new butterflies once the replacement StarWriters arrived and were trained. Only Serene would remain with her, Aleia, and Rosie.

"Em?" Aleia nudged her friend's arm. "Em?"

"Sorry, lost in thought," Em replied. "My turn?"

"Don't bother." Aleia shook her head. "Something's wrong. Nothing's reaching the stars."

Strong lines of light aimed straight for their butterfly. Serene caught the returning scrolls one at a time.

"Why are the stars sending them back?" Em asked.

"Look!" Rosie pointed at the screen. "Letters and words."

**ALL CHANNELS TO THE
HEAVENS, THE BAND, AND THE
STARS PERMANENTLY SEALED
– THE QUEEN**

"Director?" Aleia stared at Em. "Who's doing this?"

More letters and words took shape, and Rosie continued to point. "A message for you, Em."

EMIKA! NEXT TIME I WILL NOT BE AS KIND

"Jenni!" Em sighed. "That's the last thing she said before choosing Hell."

Rosie frowned. "Here we go again."

for it is written in the stars

MARY K. SAVARESE grew up in Brooklyn, New York, earning a degree in accounting from City University. She worked in insurance and financing, before marrying her husband and moving to New England to raise a family. She spent thirteen years as a religious education teacher, and for the past decade, Mary served as a Eucharistic minister at her local Catholic church. Mary and her husband recently moved to Florida where they now live.

Her debut fiction novel, 'Tigers Love Bubble Baths & Obsession Perfume (who knew!)' is a contemporary spiritual mystery that transcends three genres: Mystery, Spirituality, and Romance.

The award-winning, 'The Girl In The Toile Wallpaper,' is Mary's second novel and the first in the StarWriter Trilogy. A fantasy adventure intertwined with romance.

www.maryksavarese.com

The Girl in the Toile Wallpaper

Book 1 of the StarWriters Trilogy follows twelve-year old Tyler Charles as he works to rescue the love of his life, CallaLyly of the House of Montevelli of Siena. Although Tyler is allowed to call her Lyly.

Tyler lives within the world of today, and Lyly lives inside a world that existed over two centuries ago. When he is pulled through a lantern's portal and slides into the two-dimensional world of the toile wallpaper, Tyler must remember his class physics to reverse the effects of an evil wizard's spell. When he finally cracks the code and reverses the affects, Tyler finds himself two centuries into the past where noblemen and women dwell, and the world is quite different. It is in the past where Tyler finally discovers the true meaning of friendship and learns to work around the daily hardships and emotional traumas of life. Enjoy 'The Girl in the Toile Wallpaper' and the various lives it explores as the characters endure the pain of love lost and enjoy the emotions of love gained.

ISBN 978-1-953278-20-3 Hard Back

ISBN 978-1-953278-21-0 Soft Back

ISBN 978-1-953278-22-7 E-Book

Acknowledgement

I am forever grateful to my Editor extraordinaire, Lynn, and Indignor House for wishes *do* come true.

I couldn't do it without Katherine and all you do to run www.maryksavarese.com and my many other projects.

Special thank you to Brianna. You are my social media wizard and friend.

Thank you to Shannon and all who work behind the scenes – and who have inspired me.

I bless you.

410

412